THE DOORPOSTS

OF YOUR HOUSE

AND ON YOUR GATES

ALSO BY JACOB BACHARACH

The Bend of the World

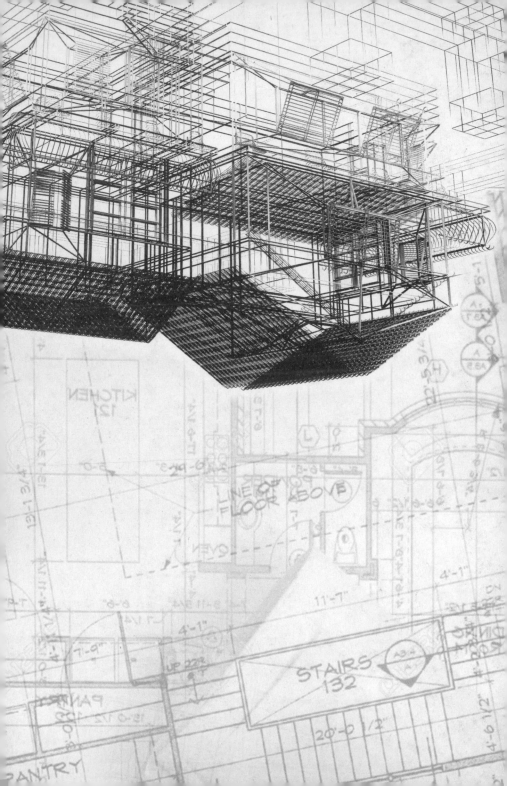

THE DOORPOSTS OF YOUR HOUSE AND ON YOUR GATES

A NOVEL

Jacob Bacharach

LIVERIGHT PUBLISHING CORPORATION

A DIVISION OF W. W. NORTON & COMPANY

INDEPENDENT PUBLISHERS SINCE 1923

NEW YORK □ LONDON

For information about permission to reproduce selections from this book,
write to Permissions, Liveright Publishing Corporation, a division of
W. W. Norton & Company, Inc., 500 Fifth Avenue, New York, NY 10110

For information about special discounts for bulk purchases, please contact
W. W. Norton Special Sales at specialsales@wwnorton.com or 800-233-4830

Manufacturing by Berryville Graphics
Book design by Dana Sloan
Production manager: Lauren Abbate

Library of Congress Cataloging-in-Publication Data

Names: Bacharach, Jacob, author.
Title: The doorposts of your house and on your gates : a novel / Jacob Bacharach.
Description: First edition. | New York : Liveright Publishing Corporation, a
division of W. W. Norton & Company, [2017]
Identifiers: LCCN 2016046981 | ISBN 9781631491740 (softcover)
Subjects: LCSH: Fathers and sons—Fiction. | Single women—Fiction. |
Domestic fiction. | GSAFD: Humorous fiction.
Classification: LCC PS3602.A335 D66 2017 | DDC 813/.6—dc23 LC
record available at https://lccn.loc.gov/2016046981

Liveright Publishing Corporation
500 Fifth Avenue, New York, N.Y. 10110
www.wwnorton.com

W. W. Norton & Company Ltd.
15 Carlisle Street, London W1D 3BS

1 2 3 4 5 6 7 8 9 0

For my parents,
who never once to my knowledge tried to kill me.

You shall love the LORD your God with all your heart and with all your soul and with all your might. Take to heart these instructions with which I charge you this day. Impress them upon your children. Recite them when you stay at home and when you are away, when you lie down and when you get up. Bind them as a sign on your hand and let them serve as a symbol on your forehead; inscribe them on the doorposts of your house and on your gates.

—DEUTERONOMY 6:5–9

I

The vision was like this: he was sitting in the temple and the light was coming through the bad stained glass and he was trying to find a comfortable position on the stupid pews. He'd suggested something better and softer and more ergonomic but they'd said it was a temple, not a movie theater. He couldn't manage it without making noise, although, of course, you could never be sure if the noise that was audible to you was audible to anyone around you; maybe they couldn't hear his shifting and the rustle of the fabric of his pants and the keys rearranging themselves slightly in his pocket and so forth over the sound of the praying and singing and all the other asses reorienting themselves and keys rattling and children whispering and giggling and older people muttering and coughing and Sarah's mother crying and her father clearing his throat—acoustics, after all, were really less science than art; Abbie had dealt with plenty of acoustic consultants and materials specialists in his professional life, and it was pretty goddamn clear that they hadn't the slightest idea what they were talking about. In any event each person's sensitivity to sound, especially in a lively acoustic environment, was deeply personal and idiosyncratic, although Abbie, who liked to imagine that he defied convention in many ways, was in this regard deeply conventional. He was trying to be quiet so as to avoid distracting his wife from the task of dealing with her mother while simultaneously contemplating in a purely hypothetical but deeply personally pleasing way the prospect of a really excellent fire gutting the building that middlebrow bourgeois taste had utterly ruined while also thinking—still vaguely, but with an increasing sense of necessity—of somewhere to suggest for dinner, because after the service concluded and they'd all shuffled around shaking hands and murmuring, "Good Shabbos," he knew he'd find himself on the front steps of the temple with his wife and his in-laws, and his father-in-law would suggest maybe they should all get something to eat. His mother-in-law would neither agree nor disagree even though it would be obvious that she was hungry—she'd say something like, "Oh, whatever you want," or "I just don't want to wait in a long line"—and Sarah would look at him helplessly, and for some reason it would be suddenly his problem. It really was a problem because there was nothing decent in the immediate vicinity, and none of them would want to walk very far or bother with a cab. The congregation was singing *Adon Olam* to a preposterous, lilting melody. The chazan had said that it was Calypso, but it didn't sound Calypso to him; suggestively Caribbean, maybe. Then again, what did he know? The closest he knew to Calypso was that Vonnegut book. You know the one. "*B'et ishan*," they sang. He closed his eyes.

He found himself standing in a field. All around him there were stalks of corn. They were low yet, just at his waist. It must have been early summer. The field fell down a shallow hill to a highway where a few cars passed. Beyond the highway was a tangle of woods, what grows along a highway where land was at one time cleared but over which first weeds and then spindly, haunted trees grew back. Beyond these woods stood another low hill, and on that hill the weedy and unpleasant roadside gave over to a sturdier deciduous forest. Farther away, several miles probably, although it looked closer, a wide blue ridge swelled up a thousand feet. Just to his right, the ridge extruded a lower promontory, a thick knot of land covered in pines. To his left, winding up the face of the ridge, tucked into a sort of notch in its face, was a road; it must have been that same highway he was looking across, which wound around the lower hill and carved its way up the base of the ridge. It was a sunny day, but there were high, white cumuli, and wherever they drifted, they cast shadows on the face of the ridge, ink-dark blots as big as whole towns. It must have been late in the day, as the sun was beginning to go down behind him, which meant that he was facing east toward the westernmost escarpment of the Appalachians, near to Pittsburgh where his sister lived. He squinted. There was a small clearing on top of the mountain, just beyond the knot of land. He felt as if he was being lifted up; he felt as if he was rising toward it, although his feet were still planted in the dirt and the scratchy stalks were still around his hands, which were at his sides, and something in his heart was saying here here here here here here. He felt that he must look away and so he turned his head, wrenched it; it felt as if he'd torn a lung loose; it felt as if something rattled out of his chest. He looked to his right and there, standing in the field, was a deer. It was shockingly close to him. He had never been so close to a wild animal. It didn't look like a dog or a house cat, soft and uniform and sewn like a stuffed toy. Its coat was mangy and matted, not the smoothly speckled brown of a deer glimpsed from the car as you sped down a country road, but a mottled, wild collision of every brown. There were ticks in its hide; his vision was such that he saw them clenched and ravenous against the gray-black skin under the animal's coat. The wind was blowing toward him, and Abbie could smell it, the buck, a wild stink of leaves and digestion. Its small tail flicked a few times. It exhaled, horse-like and sudden and hot. Its shoulders must have been as high as his own shoulders. Its antlers were immense, prehistoric, before the old world shrank to a merely human scale, with eight points on each. They'd just begun to shed their velvet, which was bloody and loose upon them. He could smell the blood, also. The buck's eyes were black and utterly inhuman and they reflected his face. He saw in his reflection, in the eyes of this animal that had no need or will to speak, another self that was his own self before language and beyond language; then, apprehending something without the need for language, he opened his eyes.

"*Va'ira*," sang the congregation.

"Is everything all right?" asked his wife.

. . .

This is how it happened.

Abbot Mayer first spoke with God at a Mostly Musical Shabbat at Temple Beth-El on the Upper West Side. Abbie had been, until then, generally irreligious. He thought of himself rather as a deeply spiritual man in the broadest human tradition. He had flirted in his younger years with Buddhism and then a vague Vedanta that mostly involved an abortive dedication to the rigorous practice of Hatha yoga, a period he now looked back on with some embarrassment, not because there was anything wrong with Buddhism or yoga per se, but because there was something slightly suspect about a hippie kid from a prosperous family of New York Jews engaging in that kind of stoned Orientalism. He'd subsequently settled on a kind of ethnic, ethical Judaism that was not taxing for him and acceptable for his wife, who *did* believe. Her whole family believed, actually, which Abbie accepted even as he found it odd. He'd been raised in a Conservative home, observing many of the forms, even intermittently keeping kosher, depending on his mother's moods and his father's appetites. He remembered their rare trips to synagogue, usually only on High Holy Days, as hazy chains of uninterrupted and unintelligible Hebrew. Sarah's family was Reform, but they went regularly to Friday-night services, sent their children to a Jewish summer camp near Pittsburgh, had traveled as a family to Israel, and believed thoroughly and entirely in Adonai—believed, in fact, with a melodic, tent-revival joyfulness that struck Abbie as oddly evangelical and un-Jewish. But, as he didn't believe in God, he kept these thoughts to himself, and he treated his wife's religious interests with supportive disinterest that, unrecognized by him, bordered on disdain. It had never yet occurred to him that this attitude suggested to Sarah that her faith was some kind of charming feminine hobby. He assumed she was glad he left her to it and didn't offer his opinions, which was, he'd be the first to admit, a habit of his and not, perhaps, his most pleasant.

There were, however, occasions on which it was necessary to accompany her to services. Rosh Hashanah and Yom Kippur, of course, and then, once a year, in the spring, on the Friday night that coincided with her younger brother's Yahrtzeit. Elliot had died at twenty-two, hit by a car in a rain-slicked intersection on 7th Avenue in Park Slope around eleven at night. It had been one of those frustrating accidents in which no real blame can be assigned—perhaps the driver had approached the red light a little too fast; perhaps Elliot had stepped out a few seconds too soon. The driver wasn't drunk. Elliot wasn't drunk or, at least, not very. The preceding week had been dry, the downpour sudden and intense. He'd been at dinner with friends, and when the rain passed, they'd headed for the subway, and then.

They say, whoever they are, that the death of a child is never easy, but it was especially not so for the Liebermans, who were in that genus of family that stays, somehow, almost miraculously untouched by tragedy, each member of each generation, whether family by blood or by marriage, passing peacefully and surrounded by loved ones after nine robust decades on this earth. That, at least, was their self-reinforcing myth. One of Sarah's aunts had in fact died in her sixties of breast cancer, and Sarah's great-grandfather had committed suicide after the crash in '29, a fact that she hadn't learned until she was nearly thirty. Her own mother, drunk and a little maudlin at a cousin's wedding, had revealed it in a lurching conversation overlain with the DJ's exhortations to "the ladies." Like any myth, its historicity was beside the point, and the family believed in it as surely as they believed in God, whether or not Genesis, say, was literally true. Liebermans did not just die.

Like a lot of nonbelievers, Abbie, however much he flattered himself as a materialist and creature of a phenomenal world, secretly held a set of complex and interrelated superstitions, chief among them an abiding belief in a universal principle of synchronicity, a kind of cosmic irony in the inevitable alignment of certain things. If he had, at the time, believed in a god, it would have been less a cruel god or a harsh god or a judgmental god so much as a mordant one. (Later in his life, Abbie would tell people that he came to believe God's evident nonexistence was positive proof that He was, in fact, the God of the Jews, His own nonexistence being the sort of joke that only a Jew would find funny.) One of these synchronicities, also a source of some dismay among the Liebermans, was the fact that Elliot's Yahrtzeit seemed to arrive inexorably on the same weekend as Beth-El's monthly Mostly Musical Shabbat service, a campfire affair transported into the sanctuary and overstocked with young children and guitars. It was also—these were, after all, well-to-do Reform Jews, well populated with academics and public-radio liberals— peppily distressing in its ethnomusicological ambitions; a typical service might involve the chazan's recent discovery of a traditional Ethiopian version of *Ador V'dor*, say, and the temple's core membership of enthusiasts would break out the *qachel*s. Abbie found it both tacky and endearing—certainly the service flitted by more quickly with singing and dancing children, and these people really did seem to enjoy being Jewish, something he could never once recall from his own upbringing, whose religion had mushed in his mind into a lot of dour, unintelligible Ashkenazi mumbling punctuated by the percussive bronchial hacking of his own parents' aging congregation. Nevertheless, all the happy-happy singing lent the whole service a kind of antic, circus atmosphere, and by the time the Mourners Kaddish rolled around at the end, Susan Lieberman would be beside herself with nervous agitation, and Sarah would be just as anxious and upset, ironically, from trying to keep her mother calm.

It was ironic (or not; who could really tell as far as God is concerned?) that Abbie had actually designed the temple or, in any case, had been the head architect for the renovation of its current location; it had been in the commission of this project that he'd first met Sarah, who'd been the token younger woman on the temple board at the time. A crypto-biblical catastrophe involving burst pipes and flooding had ruined the old sanctuary and lobbies and the big dining facility in the basement. The building itself had previously been an Episcopalian church, before, as Elliott had—according to Sarah—put it, they had disappeared up the asshole of their own indecision, and then it was converted haphazardly into a synagogue in the late sixties. By the time of the flood, its combination of obliquely Christian architecture and truly regrettable later-addition fixtures and finishes ("Walden Pond meets the Brady Bunch," Elliott had also called it) had begun to strike some of the congregation as retrograde and embarrassing and Not Very Jewish. Abbie would have told them that the architectural history of Jewish houses of worship was fascinating in its lack of actual historical sources and tradition; the vague hitching of Near Eastern decorative flourishes with stained glass and auditorium seating that seemed, to Beth-El's leadership, as the real and authentic thing was pure invention. But in this case, Abbie was just a junior associate in his firm, and the job offered a nice piece of solo work; every architect's portfolio required a few holy places, he reasoned, and the soggy volume of the ruined temple was an opportunity to put some of his own ideas about salvage and environmentally sound building into practice. Abbie was ahead of the vanguard in thinking about these things; it was what would make him eventually, albeit retrospectively, famous.

"An architect does not design buildings; an architect solves problems." Thomas Arah, who'd become his adviser at Yale, told him so—told a roomful of people, actually, during a convocation in—it must have been 1974 or 1975. It struck him at the time as the sort of self-satisfied banality that was better laughed at than ignored. Arah was nearly seventy and had already lost much of his close vision to macular degeneration. He'd become instead typically drunk—never very, but almost always just a bit—and philosophical. He referred to Frank Lloyd Wright and Mies van der Rohe as Frank and Mies. He was writing some immense book, which he never finished, on the relationships between national character, architectural vernacular, and political economy. During Abbie's junior year, he'd accompanied the old man as some kind of assistant on a trip out West, a tour that was to include several early Spanish missions in California, Pueblo Indian cliff dwellings in Colorado, and a stop in Arizona to visit Taliesan West. He'd done very little assisting and came to believe that he was along just so that Arah would have a body present to prove to waiters and stewardesses that the old man wasn't talking to himself. As the plane had descended into Phoenix—which was not yet the vast sprawl of suburbs and golf courses that it would become but which it was already quite visibly on its way to becoming—Arah told Abbie to look out the window, where the greenish edge of human habitation met the desert. "These people," he told Abbie, "are going to destroy our civilization. Los Angeles is going to break off into the ocean. Florida is going to sink. New York is going to flood. And these poor ignorant idiots, they are going to suck every last drop of water out of the Colorado River, and then they're all going to die." Then he pressed the call button and harangued the stewardess into bringing him another vodka.

Arah's beliefs—that architects were servants and functionaries of the social organism; that architecture was about the practical, if hopefully aesthetically pleasing, solutions to a series of definable and identifiable practical problems; that one must resist the urge to look at the evolution of forms as a teleology of progress and understand it instead as an adaptive response to circumstances; that *Frank and Mies*, et al. were geniuses, yes, but were also reasons to be suspicious of the very category of genius (after all, Lloyd Wright couldn't so much as design a proper gutter and downspout)—eventually converted Abbie, even as he became known among distinctly smaller circles as something very much resembling a genius himself. But he'd resisted them at the time; like plenty of prosperous Jewish kids, Abbie had had no trouble syncretizing the vaguely communal stoner ethic with a derivative version of Objectivism—speaking of vanguards: when you believe all of your friends to be geniuses and revolutionaries, it isn't even a difficult marriage. Reflecting on this period of his life in an interview years later, he said that every young architect imagines himself as Howard Roark at some point in his development, usually before he has to write his first door schedule. "Howard Roark would consider a door schedule unheroic," Abbie had said, "but you can't hang a thirty-inch door in a thirty-six-inch doorway."

No architect ever entirely eradicates that early self-image as some kind of Promethean superman, and none of them ever escapes the occasional desire to just dynamite the hell out of some work of theirs that's been bowdlerized in the process of meeting someone else's budget and taste. That was how Abbie felt about the Temple Beth-El. On the occasions when he was stuck there, if anyone had asked him about the building, which they did from time to time, then he'd have replied with the embarrassed pride that successful writers reserve for their early poetry. Secretly, though, he nursed a pleasing fantasy of sneaking into the place one night and burning it to the ground. His original designs had simplified the already self-effacing, if prosperous, simplicity of the Episcopalians into something of almost Shaker austerity, the only real ornamentation to have been railings and trim and windowpanes that made subtle reference to the Star of David. The congregation had insisted on stained glass; then on carpeting the aisles; then, at last, on replacing his elegant, Japanese wall panels with horrible accordion dividers—this last was a concession to cost, Abbie knew, but still.

So, it was during Mostly Musical Shabbat, during a Calypso version of *Adon Olam*, on the occasion of the observed anniversary of the death of a brother-in-law whom he'd never met, while staring at a stained glass depiction of Moses leading the Israelites out of Egypt that recalled nothing so much as a Saturday-morning, Hanna-Barbera cartoon, that God spoke to Abbie Mayer for the very first time. Of course, God doesn't speak; it's as silly to imagine the Lord uttering actual words as it is to imagine that, because we are made in God's image, He therefore resembles in some actual, physical way, a human being. As we are, body and soul, afterimages of the totality and universality of the divine, frozen, sub-photographic images of a vastness of being that is and moves, so too is our language less even than an echo of the primordial verb of existence. God, Abbie learned, doesn't speak to men at all but rather puts into their minds and hearts the knowledge of and belief in that which He would—if He did, if He even could, speak—have said.

. . .

After the service, they stood on the front steps of the temple in the quick spring twilight until Abbie, feeling oddly ravenous, though not as generally discombobulated as he would have expected if you'd told him earlier in the day that he'd receive a vision from God, asked if anyone was hungry and suggested an Italian place on the next block that he knew they all liked. It was an Italian restaurant as they used to be, unconcerned with faddish authenticity, the sort of place where you could still get lasagna and garlic bread and where the waiters all sounded like a swim in the waves off the shore in Jersey was the closest they'd ever got to Italy. The sun was still higher than the buildings but sinking swiftly, and something about the quality of its light suggested reflection off the water, although you certainly couldn't see the river from there. Abbie disapproved of the neighborhood's sometimes slavishly historic architecture, but he approved of its lowness. He'd never designed a skyscraper. Twelve stories was the maximum decent height for human habitation. It was a question of scale. New York's immensity appealed to him, but not its height. He took Sarah's hand, and she let it hang limply in his for a minute before sliding it out of his grip and shaking it as if she'd touched something wet and unpleasant before shoving it into the pocket of her coat. Abbie gave her an inquiring look, but she stared at the ground. But she was always upset after this service, so he turned back to his in-laws and said, "So, what do you think?"

As was her habit, Susan Lieberman said, "Oh, I don't know. I don't know if I'm really in the mood to sit in a restaurant," and her husband said, "Well, come on, Sue. We should eat something." Susan shrugged helplessly and said as long as there wasn't a wait. There was never a wait. Herman talked about real estate. He'd been retired for almost five years by then but still spoke about it as if he were always in the middle of the next big deal.

"The gays," he told Abbie. "That's how I know."

"The gays?" Abbie repeated. He'd been trying to get Sarah to look at him to no avail; she was embroiled in a quiet sidebar with her mother. That wasn't necessarily unusual, but he could tell that she was upset with him, and, as was *his* habit, he found himself echoing his father-in-law's phrases as a proxy for actually conversing, which fortunately suited Herman just fine. He let his mind file through the inventory of recent sins that Sarah may or may not have discovered—there is, after all, no one so paranoid as a man who makes a habit of lying, if only by omission, to his wife; those normal moments of distance or distraction in a marriage, which a policy of general honesty would render as innocuous as they are inevitable, become, each of them, immensely significant, indicative of some tear in the veil of secrets.

"The gays," Herman was saying, "That's right. I always say, it's a good thing I'm not a prejudiced man. Well, you know, my grandfather was in the theater, not an actor of course, but in the business, so we always knew all kinds in my family and said, live and let live. And for a man in real estate, the gays are the bellwether. If they're moving in, you can be sure that prices are going up, up, and up. That's how I knew to buy downtown, and as you know, it worked out well for me."

"Yes," Abbie said. "That's a good policy."

"You ought to buy downtown, Abbie. A man of your interests? One of these lofts. Can you believe it?" He chewed his scampi. "Lofts," he repeated.

"Sarah likes it here," Abbie replied. He found that invoking Sarah's tastes was a prophylactic against his father-in-law's advice. He sent a pleading look in her direction, but she was still embroiled with her mother.

"And tell me, Abbie, what are you working on these days?"

"Oh," Abbie wrenched himself away from the side of Sarah's head. "Oh, lighting mostly."

"Lighting? Do you do that as well? Don't your electricians or what have you do that sort of thing? After you design the, the building and so forth."

"Well, an architect doesn't so much design buildings as he solves problems," Abbie said. "Anyway, very interesting new technologies in lighting. Fluorescents, actually."

"Fluorescents! No thank you. Like prisons and cafeterias."

"Well—" Abbie started to say.

"Not for me," said Herman, and that was clearly the end of it.

Herman and Susan walked home after dinner, and Abbie and Sarah shared a silent cab to their apartment several blocks farther north. "A nice doorman building on West End Avenue." He could still hear the voice of their broker, who'd hustled them through a series of catastrophes that she must have staged as a sales tactic before ushering them past a uniformed Russian man with huge shoulders and a mismatched, delicate face to the brass elevators and into their new home. "Well," she'd said, whatever her name was. Abbie remembered her voice, but not her name. No, Myrna, that was her name. She was in her sixties and sounded distantly like the Bronx, although she'd polished the rough edges into something more generically New-York career-woman. She wore all black and had large, but tasteful, jewelry. "Well," she said again, and she stood there nodding. They couldn't say no. It was too big and much too traditional. It had wainscoting and radiators. None of their furniture would match. He said as much to Sarah after they'd already said yes. "You'll rise to the challenge, I'm sure," she told him.

Sarah disappeared into their bedroom as soon as they were inside, and Abbie poured himself a scotch and went out onto the balcony to smoke a cigarette. The balcony, that detail he liked. He'd quit smoking years ago, but kept a pack in the freezer and still indulged from time to time in the evening, or when he'd had quite a lot to drink. He took a drag of the cigarette and traced a dollar sign in the dark air and laughed at himself. "That's a little architect's joke," he said. If you looked between the buildings, you could catch sight of the dark expanse of the Park: that carefully constructed fantasy of how the island had been before there was a city there.

He reflected on his experience—well, that was the wrong word, but it would have to do until he could come up with a better euphemism—in the temple. Rationally, of course, it would have been a confabulation, a daydream, albeit a startlingly visceral one. It comported, after all, very closely with a train of thought he'd lately been toying with without permitting himself seriously to commit to considering it: leaving New York. His sister, Veronica, had suggested it; he'd called her to ask her advice about Cathy, the woman he'd been seeing, but when Veronica had asked him if he was calling to talk to her about "that woman," he'd become angry—not so much because she called her "that woman" but more because she'd intuited his purpose before he could reveal it, and it made him feel like the lesser intellect. That pained him acutely, because if his sister was, by the crudest economic measures, more successful than him, he comforted himself with the fact that he was smarter.

As children, they'd been very close; she'd protected her dreamy, artistic sibling by carrying the weight of their parents' absurd expectations on the strength of her intelligence and limitless talents—a musician, a dancer, an artist, an athlete—and then, later, he'd returned the favor a thousandfold when their father had discovered Veronica's first real girlfriend and reacted very badly. Saul Mayer lacked Herman Lieberman's essential libertinism. Herman had had mistresses over the years, which Susan had always tolerated, later confessing to her college-age daughter that, after Elliot was born, their marriage had cooled, passion settling into a deeper, if less physical, sort of friendship. "But it sounds terrible!" Sarah said. "He was exploiting you!"

"On the contrary, honey. I've had my fun too!"

Saul Mayer did not cheat on his wife, nor had they settled into an amicable intellectual companionship. He'd persisted in a state of faithful matrimonial anxiety until his wife, only sixty-two at the time, had passed away. To discover that his daughter was a lesbian was too much for him. But even as a stoned college kid, Abbie had viewed the world with an inconsistent but utterly unbending moralism, and the study of architecture had given him a Masonic presumptuousness about his own mental superiority over most other people, his father certainly included. This would later harden into a less redeemable condescension, but only later—and he'd been a rock against which their father's anger and opprobrium crashed but which it couldn't erode. "It seems to me," Veronica could still hear him saying, languid and probably high, "that the question of whom a person loves is very much secondary to the simple fact that a person loves." Her father had screamed back that it wasn't natural. Abbie had shrugged: "A townhouse in a city of ten million people is natural? Coal-fired electricity is natural? Glass windows are natural? Cars and subways are natural? What's natural? Besides love, what is there but artifice?" This argument hadn't worked on their father, who passed the rest of his life very rarely speaking to his daughter, and if he did, whenever possible, only through the intermediary of his son, but it had worked on Veronica, cementing permanently her sororal loyalty. In the two decades since, Abbie had frequently tested that permanence, but she did what she could, when he let her.

He'd called, as always, at the most inopportune time, and

she'd just hoped he wasn't calling—again—to talk about his stupid affair. She'd always found men to be fatuously moralistic about their own immorality, forever haranguing their friends and wives and children into self-serving arrangements that they then picked at with the childish, masochistic pleasure of little boys picking at their scabs. Her brother and Sarah had never had a traditional marriage—at least not a wholly monogamous one. (Even thinking it, Veronica could hear Abbie correcting her, reminding her not to equate monogamy, a latecomer when you consider the breadth of history, with tradition. "An aberration!" she imagined him bellowing with the particular glee he reserved for when he won an argument that he was having only with himself. "Something new under the sun!")

They'd married in the early eighties. Reagan was the silly president. New York had retained a louche permissiveness that the rest of the country, in rediscovering some celluloid, high desert vision of itself, was supposedly leaving behind. Even in Manhattan, though, you could sense a change in the tolerated transgressions. Everyone wore suits all of a sudden, even the women, who looked terrible in them—the men only looked ridiculous—and did coke and aspired to steal money from retirees. Men had fewer love affairs, but there were more hookers. Veronica was sure that all these ethnographic impressions were completely wrong; if she'd ever mentioned them to her brother he'd have marshaled a statistical counterargument—delivered in that voice of utmost patience that signaled his utter disdain—to tell her very certainly that she was most assuredly wrong about all this. "The plural of anecdote," he'd say with a smile. Abbie loved clichés the way some men love Beatles albums; they recalled the exaggeratedly pleasant memories that are so frequently scattered around recollections of an unpleasant youth. You couldn't argue with him; what would be the point?

The trouble with their marriage wasn't that Abbie fucked other women, but that he fell in love with them. He could never accept this, and he privately accused Sarah of a more general female jealousy. "Female jealousy," Veronica would repeat, and he'd sigh and say, "You know what I mean." The problem was that he didn't even realize that he fell in love with them; like all egotists, he failed to recognize his own reflection, thinking himself somehow larger than the strangely diminished man in the glass. And Veronica knew, to be fair, that he never loved any of them as *much* as he loved his wife, or at least, he never loved her any less than he loved any of them. Sarah, for her part, rarely slept with other men—when she did it, she did it instrumentally, usually because Abbie's attention had wandered, and after all, as Abbie would have said, "We've all got needs." He always tried to hide these other women, despite the fact that they'd agreed to their inevitable presence early on. In his mind, this had to do with her "jealousy issues," whereas it was really the guilt that sprung from his unacknowledged infatuation with them. Veronica always knew when he was seeing someone because he became at once furtive and solicitous. He never knew when Sarah slept with other men. Likely he imagined she didn't.

"Hello, Abbie." When she'd reached across her desk to answer the phone, she'd knocked a sheaf of relief maps onto the floor, and when she heard her brother's voice and greeted him a second time, she leaned on the desk and looked at them forlornly, feeling that stooping to pick them up would represent a kind of defeat. "Fuck," she muttered. It was nearly four, and Phil Harrow, her business partner in the venture whose plans now lay scattered on the carpet, would arrive any moment for the last meeting of the day. She had nothing but bad news for him.

"Fuck you, too," Abbie said. His voice sounded suspiciously jocular. Anytime he was anything other than lugubrious and condescending, she knew he was going to ask a favor. She hoped it would only be money. He'd hinted about it recently, though he never had the balls to come out and ask directly. Probably he was so twisted around about having a sister who made so much more than him that he'd never get over the embarrassment of asking.

"Not fuck you," she said. "I dropped something."

"Ahhh," said Abbie.

No, fuck *you*, thought Veronica. If he was going to be intolerable—when was he not, though?—then she was going to hang up. But he hadn't really said anything, and she was acting like her mother. Or she told herself that she was acting like her mother, which always calmed her whenever she felt herself drifting into sentiment or annoyance, whether or not this was anything like her mother at all.

"How are you?" she asked him.

"In debt."

"Ah." She hadn't expected him to come out with it so easily.

"It's not your problem, of course."

"No," she said, but how could she not have been thinking: then why did you bring it up to me?

"It's a curious thing," Abbie told her. "I'm sought, but not compensated."

"I'm sure you're compensated."

"Undercompensated."

"Mm," she said. Her brother was famous in the minor way that people can become famous within their own professions without ever being known to anyone outside, and he lived grandly, flying from conference to museum to university to give talks about saving the world from impending catastrophe through new paradigms of design. In arguments, he'd even accused her—"you and your housing divisions," he'd spat—of conspiring to drown the world. She knew that his firm was more concept than practice, and although the colleges paid for his flights and hotels and surely compensated him well for his worn-out and frankly hectoring prophesies, she couldn't remember the last time he'd actually built something. She suspected that his and Sarah's tastes in wines and restaurants and the frequent redecoration and renovation of their overlarge apartment were a little more than he could reasonably afford. Having reached a point in her own financial life where there was effectively nothing that she couldn't reasonably afford, Veronica took a slightly pornographic pleasure in speculating on the budgets of the more cruelly leveraged middle class, especially those to whom she was related.

"Also," he said, "I have a problem with a woman."

"Does Sarah know?"

"About the money? Or the woman?"

"Either, I suppose."

"No. The latter, certainly not."

"You should try monogamy, Abbie. It's easier to keep your story straight."

"Lesbians," he said.

"Well," Veronica replied. "Be that as it may."

"What am I going to do, though?"

"About the woman or the money?"

"Both."

Veronica sighed audibly. "Forget the former, concentrate on the latter."

"I might need a loan."

"A loan, Abbie. That entails repayment. With interest, as a general rule."

"Usurer."

"That's Christian, Abbie. I think. And I have no such compunctions. The last time you asked me for money, we didn't speak for a year."

"Why was that?"

"Let's not get into it."

"I didn't pay you back."

"No. It was for the apartment. You told me you needed a larger one for a family."

"Yes, that didn't work out. Not yet."

Veronica's assistant tapped lightly on the office door and poked in her head. "Mr. Harrow is here. Should I send him back?"

"You'd better tell him to wait," she said.

"Wait for what?" said Abbie.

"Not you," Veronica told him. "I was talking to my secretary." Her secretary frowned as she closed the door. "Damn," Veronica muttered. Jill hated being called a secretary, and who could blame her? She had some sort of absurd degree in studio art from some preposterously expensive private college that no one had ever heard of, and Veronica had hired her as an assistant in a rare moment of solidarity—with what, or whom, she wasn't sure. She reminded herself to try to remember to offer the girl some kind of praise for professional acumen when just enough time had passed that it would not seem like a premeditated apology, knowing that she'd forget. Veronica was a feminist, obviously, but she occasionally—all right, more than occasionally—longed for a thick-ankled and omnicompetent older woman with a bad perm and worse attitude to keep her working life in order. Alas, they were like real craftsmen in the construction trades: dead, retired, ever harder to find, frightfully expensive when you did.

She realized she'd let the call lapse into silence. "I have an appointment," she said vaguely.

"You're trying to get off the phone with me."

"Yes," she said. One lesson she *had* learned was that it was pointless to be less than direct about these things.

"Well, a loan, then."

"What's it for, Abbie? Specifically?"

"The firm. We're having cash flow issues."

"I'll think about it. And I'd want to look at the books first."

"Yes, I imagined."

She'd wandered around the desk while they talked, and now she leaned against the other side of her desk. She pinched the bridge of her nose and closed her eyes. Her office overlooked the silver dome of the Civic Arena. She looked out the windows. There was a hockey game that evening, and the lots were already filling up. She looked at the floor, the curled plans flapping in the breeze from the vent.

"Abbie?" she said. "What do you know about hydrology?"

• • •

He thought back on the rest of that conversation and watched the smoke from his indulgent cigarette drift away from the light of the French doors. A vision. Well, he wouldn't be the first, and did it matter, really, the quantity or quality of his particular faith? He finished smoking and went back inside, where he poured himself another drink. Then Sarah appeared. She hadn't changed, and she was holding a paper in her hand. "What's this, Abbie?" she asked. Her face was set in a look of frozen determination that Abbie found especially ridiculous, and he smiled without meaning to.

"I don't know. What is it?"

She slapped it on the counter in front of him. He glanced. "It's an American Express bill," he said.

"And?"

"And what? I've told you, I'm taking care of it."

"Taking care of what, Abbie?"

It occurred to him that he wasn't sure what she was talking about, but he pressed on. "I've spoken to my sister. She's not averse to the idea of a loan. Although, she mentioned, possibly, a project that I might, oh, come out and work on."

"What the fuck are you talking about? I'm talking about this." Her thin finger landed on a line item on the page, and he let himself look and realized his error. He'd always been careless with money. It was a mistake to charge it.

But he'd never known how to back down gracefully from a lost position, so he said, "What's that?"

"That," Sarah said, "is a doctor's bill for a doctor's office I don't go to, and you don't go to, and when I called, I found out that it's an Ob/Gyn."

"Ah."

"Abbie," Sarah said, "Goddamnit, how could you?"

"How could I what, Sarah? These things will happen. It meant nothing. It means nothing. Goddamnit, and I'm having it taken care of, too."

What is it about some men, Sarah wondered, that makes them imagine morality as a matter of accountancy, a balancing of columns, the good against the bad? "You're *having it taken care of*? What are you, the mafia? You make it sound like you're putting out a hit!"

"You're being ridiculous."

That was when she broke the vase. She didn't want to, but it had to be done. You were damned either way, a victim or a punisher, too weak or too angry, too emotional or too indifferent; well, better to do something than nothing; better to be disdained than pitied. Later, she knew, Abbie would comfort himself by recalling this demonstration of her irrationality. And, in fact, he put on his calmest face and asked if she'd been drinking.

She told him no.

Then she didn't speak to him for almost a week, and although she should have hated him, it also reminded her, in an odd way, of why she loved him, because he let her not speak to him, let her glide through the house in a noisy silence—the silent treatment exacerbated by her loud stacking of dishes, phone calls with her parents, television turned deliberately too high. He let her be angry, which, hard as she tried to remain so, exhausted her; it deprived her combustible fury of oxygen, and toward the end of the week, she sat across the dining room table from him and said, "So, what are we going to do?"

"I talked with Veronica, again," he said. "What would you think . . . I know I did a wrong thing. And then there's the money. What would you think about a fresh start?"

"A fresh start?" she said.

"Well, now you sound sarcastic."

Get a fresh start, she thought, as if they were just closing the books at the end of the month and carrying forward the gains or losses to the next period. What a fantasy, that life ever began anew, that it consisted of a series of neat movements, like a classical sonata. Sarah could've killed him for suggesting it, except that Abbie's notoriety had never really translated into regular returns; she knew that. They increasingly faced, frankly, the punishing inevitability of an unmanageable proportion of debt, and here they were in an endless apartment with no real hope of ever filling it.

"What would it entail?" she asked him.

"Well," he said. "How do you feel about Pennsylvania?"

2

saac liked to tell people that they'd met at a dance party, and
Isabel never corrected him, because she didn't want him to
think she noticed that sort of thing. The truth was that they'd
met almost six months before at a dinner thrown by the executive director of her new employer, on the occasion of her decision to accept his offer of a job and move to Pennsylvania. Isabel
had been living in New York for the last ten years, eight of them
with Ben, her ex-boyfriend, an architect who was a couple of years
older. They'd started dating when she was still in grad school, and
the affair flowed swiftly into a narrow channel of inevitability
that looked, only in retrospect, only after they'd gone over and
around the rocks, like something closer to doom. He was from a
rich—but not too rich—New England family, his mother fond of
Tiffany, his father a birdwatcher and dabbler in electronic trading.
They hadn't always been wealthy; both of them had grown up in
working-class Albany before decamping, in the eighties, to woodland Connecticut. Ben's father had made something resembling a
small fortune in electronics when Texas Instruments bought out
the small firm where he worked developing displays for graph-
ing calculators. Their aesthetic of anesthetized Woodbury gentry,
all antiquing and waxy chocolate and civilized alcoholism, was a

little too perfect, and you could tell that it was a deliberate affectation that had matured into habit and then into character.

It was at a party for the opening of a new hotel downtown whose name was the alphanumerical abbreviation of a Manhattan address that might have been someone's password to something, rendered on all the glass doors in a frostily translucent Helvetica. Had you asked her, Isabel would have said, "Lord only knows why I was there." She'd been asked by a friend who sometimes modeled (many of her friends at the time sometimes did this, sometimes that; few seemed to have a particular occupation), who had referred to the party as *this thing*, as in, "I'm going to *this thing*, you ought to come." Isabel had acquired a carapace of blasé sophistication in college, which had further hardened since she'd moved to the city, but she still wasn't the sort of person who casually showed up at *things*. But Jairan, her friend, had said, "Come on, come on, there will be an open bar." So she went. In the earlier part of the evening, she was surprised to feel less completely out of place than she'd expected—there were a lot of finance dudes in those weird, square-toed Herman Munster shoes that no amount of money seems ever to eradicate from a certain portion of the population of men, and there were a lot of girls who, like Jairan, sometimes modeled, who were avoiding the men as well as they could and helping themselves to the bar. Several hours into it, though, they were all drunk, and the banker bros were suggesting restaurants and clubs and other parties, and Isabel was working out how to tell her friend, and her friend's friends, who were by then giddily her new friends too, that she had to go. One of the things that she'd learned about those girls was that even as they prepared to ditch her for a guy with a big car and a little coke, they'd have viewed her own premature departure as a personal affront unless it was with a guy. Even knowing they'd forget it in the morning—most of them would forget her entirely—she decided against slipping out, imagining Jairan's frantic, bitchy voicemails, and she set herself to wait them out by nursing a drink at the bar for another hour. It wasn't yet eleven. This was where she found Ben, in a good suit and expensive brown leather shoes that tapered to a slim, but not too slim, point, which made her assume he was gay. This allowed her to talk to him, which revealed to her that he wasn't. He had a slightly dazed and abstracted attitude that no single gay guy would have permitted himself in that kind of crowd. She ordered a neat scotch, and he, back to the bar, elbows on it, gave her a complimentary sidelong look with a raised eyebrow, so she tilted her glass to him, took a sip, and said, "Never mix, never worry," a phrase she'd picked up from her mother, who had in turn acquired it from a man she'd dated who'd been fond of ironic clichés. Ben told her that he was a wine guy. "Red or white?" she asked him, and he looked disappointed. He asked her what she thought of the hotel. Isabel thought he was changing the subject to spare her any more of her embarrassing philistinism, and she felt obliged to be casually derogatory to make up for the mistake, so she said, "It's like Mies meets IKEA." She thought it was funny.

"Hi," he said, "I'm Ben. I'm the architect."

After it all ended, it seemed impossible that she didn't suspect the effortlessness of it right from the start, the speed with which they progressed from going to dinner together to hosting dinners together at the Lower East Side ballroom dancing studio that he'd converted into a loft apartment, soon thereafter to living and hosting yet more dinners together in the unfashionably fashionable third floor in Greenpoint that he bought and gutted and redesigned himself and transformed into the sort of home that you see in magazines—that you did, in fact, see in certain magazines. Isabel still thought of those as their documentary or cinematic days, a film montage set by some awful quirky director to some sort of idiosyncratic music, Corelli *concerti grossi* or Nick Lowe or something equally unsuspected until it's already played in the background, people moving against the backdrop of a white brick wall and rarely spilling their wine. Ben's firm specialized in hotels, glimmering, trendy places that were designed to last through three seasons of actors and art people and expense accounts before falling out of style and moving out to pasture as a really cool place your Mom and Dad found on Expedia. Honey, you won't *believe* the price.

Ben made a lot of money. Of course, it didn't feel like a lot of money to them. They were surrounded by people with even more money, and they fell into the obscene habit of thinking of themselves as middle class. In looking back, Isabel found it incredible that she'd once had so much, incredible and a little sad. Ben would say, "I'm going to be out of town next week. We're opening the new place in Copenhagen." She'd say, "I'm going to take my mom to Sedona for a long weekend in May." They believed this was ordinary rather than extraordinary; worse, when they considered it—rarely for her, even more rarely for Ben—they considered it, in some way, their due.

Then she came home one day after performing her approximation of administrating graduate studies at Pratt all afternoon and an early dinner with some girlfriends, and there was Ben in the steel kitchen with a glass of wine and an open bottle that revealed he'd polished off one glass already. He had that elided look he'd had the first night she'd seen him, a sort of glazed wonderment that he had in some way caused everything around him to exist. "What's wrong?" she asked him. And he looked at her, and she knew. She'd already known, if she were honest with herself, which was why, months before, she'd accepted first a phone interview and then an interview-interview in Manhattan and then a brief trip to Pittsburgh for a third go-round with Barry Fitzgerald, the Executive Director of the Future Cities Institute at Carnegie Mellon University.

Ben had accepted it all too easily; Isabel knew that, too, even if she was above admitting it to herself. He had clients—they had friends, even—whose married lives were carried out in serendipitous crossings at 30,000 feet, she on her way back from Aspen, he on his way to an investors' meeting in California, neither of them ever in New York for very long, and even then usually without the other. Such an arrangement seemed to Ben and Isabel to be the surest sign of having made it. That, anyway, was what they told themselves. But neither really wanted it; what held them together was a ritual of bourgeois domesticity, the regularity of cooking for other people and buying flowers and making an interesting pairing of an obscure Madiran with the braised duck. "What's wrong?" she asked him, and he looked at her, and she thought that she'd never forget what he said, although she would later exaggerate it and come to believe the exaggeration: a kind of forgetting. He said, "I just feel that our relationship is lacking a core of intimacy. We don't talk." Which was not true, she thought, not literally. They talked constantly; their life together was a skein of prattle about towels and the best kind of coffee and a new lamp for the office.

"Hmm," she said, and then, because that seemed inadequate, added, "I don't know what to say"—as if that wasn't obvious enough.

Then Ben put his glass very carefully and deliberately on the counter, and he said, "I just can't imagine us ever getting married."

By then, they'd lived together for eight years, but she couldn't argue with him. She couldn't imagine it either. Before he'd said it, she'd never tried to imagine it. Perhaps that was the problem. Ben wasn't a bad man, just not an especially adept one. He was charming, handsome, and smart, and yet just as superficial and nonspecific as each of those adjectives that everyone reached for to describe him. He'd hated his parents—despised them, he said; they'd been cruelly indifferent to his brother, who was actually gay, and blandly indifferent to him. They preferred their friends to their children. Et cetera. Isabel never especially sympathized. Although she found them a little loopy, his mom especially emitting a certain gin and oil-soap odor of preservation, they'd never been anything other than lovely to her, and she found them, well, charming. It was one of the few things they'd ever openly argued about. And yet, Ben had ended up, despite the modernist apartment and the disapproval for most liquor and the busy job, very much, and inescapably, their boy. He was forever unsatisfied with affection—its absence tormented him, but when it was offered, it was never enough. It was a trait Isabel came to ascribe to creative people. Isaac, for instance; Isaac reminded her in many ways of Ben.

Four weeks after this last fight, which was hardly a fight, it was settled. He gave her the car, a six-year-old BMW coupe with 80,000 miles. "I need a new one anyway," he said. She'd officially accepted the Pittsburgh job. She left at six on a Sunday morning. It was November, and the broad valleys and ridges in central PA were lightly covered with the year's first snow. She stopped in

Carlisle and ate eggs and biscuits at the Iron Skillet surrounded by truckers and retirees. Pennsylvania, once you get into the mountains, has a subtle beauty, low ridges rising and falling around the highway like the deep swells on an ocean of trees; you could imagine that it was an ocean, swollen and swallowing the whole earth like one of God's punishments. It was early afternoon when she arrived in Pittsburgh at the little carriage house apartment—furnished in the fussy but uncluttered style of a very reasonable grandmother—where Barry Fitzgerald had arranged for her to stay until she found a place of her own.

Barry had a tradition of Sunday dinners, and this one had been hastily re-christened a welcome in her honor. He lived in Point Breeze, a neighborhood in the East End of the city, mostly broad streets lined by sycamores in the manner of French *allées*, the houses a mix of the original, broad-porch-and-dormer Queen Annes set stolidly back from the street and many smaller colonials and faux English cottages where the original acre plots had been carved into smaller lots in the twentieth century. There were also a few mid-century modern places, and Barry lived in one of them, a sort of hash of a Frank Lloyd Wright and a Philip Johnson on an oddly shaped lot on a cul-de-sac lane that bordered the old Henry Clay Frick estate, now a museum. He'd filled the house with a curatorial and boringly correct collection of mid-century furniture. The place had the feel of an expensive catalog, so expressly imitative of life as to appear not so much natively alive as resurrected, but Isabel couldn't fault the correctness of his taste. Over the long dining room table was a small prototype of the Lobmeyer chandeliers that hang in the Metropolitan Opera House. The back of Barry's house was glass, and although he recognized it as a kind of hypocrisy, given his profession, Barry only used incandescent bulbs—his excuse was that these, likewise, were historically accurate. The backyard held a small patio, a fastidious lawn, and a rectangular pool, covered now with a tarp that sagged under pooled rainwater and a few leaves, forlornly pretty in the warm light from the house. Barry was in his mid-sixties, but he was one of those men who was bald by twenty-five and spent the rest of his life passing for a robust forty-eight. He was a small man who gave the impression of being bigger because he had long arms and broad shoulders—he'd been a competitive swimmer in his youth and still religiously swam laps, though not, of course, in his own mostly decorative pool. He gestured expansively no matter what he was saying. Isaac would later compare him to a gorilla. ("Or an orangutan," Isaac would say, hunching in a half-simian impression. "A primate, in general. Non-human, of course. Dr. Zaius!" And he'd giggle.) Barry was single, and there was an air of sexual indeterminacy about him. Isaac would tell her that Barry was post-gay.

("It's surprisingly common, you know," he'd say. "A lot of us decide at some point that it just isn't worth the trouble."

"It doesn't seem to be any trouble for you," Isabel told him.

"Well, no," he said. He giggled. "Not for *me*.")

Like his home, Barry's parties tended toward the *tableaux*; they had the quality of being displayed in a vitrine, which wasn't diminished by the fact that he lived in a glass house. He had invited a few members of his advisory board—*our* advisory board, Isabel reminded herself—who were a serially uninteresting gang of university faculty, non-profit administrators, the rich, the bored. They talked to her, and to each other, as if they were leading a class of morose and sleep-deprived undergraduates. "And of course," one of them said to her, "when you have a high municipal parking tax . . ." and he trailed off and gave her a quizzical look that simultaneously suggested he expected her to answer and hoped that she would not, ". . . you have high parking rates," he said at last, and then, after a beat, added, "which is the problem."

Their conversation ultimately regressed to the conversation that any similar gathering has when it thinks no one who could possibly disagree is listening: the general inability of popular democracy to arrive at the fair and obvious technocratic solutions necessary to the smooth running of a society; it's practically an article of faith among such people. They were inoffensive but banal, and the dinner was only saved by two guests. The first, introduced to Isabel as a "supporter of the institute" was Arthur B. Imlak. She recognized his name, vaguely, but couldn't place it. He was, he told her, one of the richest men in the Commonwealth, using exactly that phrase.

"Oh?" she said.

"Marcellus shale." He smirked, but there was something self-deprecating about the look, something practiced, as if he'd just revealed a mild fetish.

"Aha," she replied.

"Barry," he told her, "despises my business on general principle, but he feels that the FCI is a wastewater treatment plant for the endless river of slurry that is my money." Then, abruptly: "Do you sail?"

She grinned at him—it was such a preposterous question. "I can't say that I do," she told him.

"Never?" he asked, and he pulled a comical pout.

"Well—"

"I have a boat," he interrupted. "Down in Clearwater, a sixty-foot trimaran. I call her, *The Shale Boat*."

"That's very clever," she told him.

"Well, Ms. Giordan," he told her, "you just let me know when you're interested in putting on those sailing shoes."

Now he grinned at her, and she was about to reply, but Barry interjected from the far end of the table: "Is Art telling you about his boat? He loves that goddamn boat."

"Barry came down one time," Imlak said, performing for everyone now. "He fell off the dock." Imlak was handsome, though he was growing into a recently acquired middle-aged belly. He had silver hair and the slightly shabby jacket of a man with a very large fortune. Isabel noticed a preposterous watch glancing from under his cuff. When he looked at her, his eyes winked with a cursory flirtatiousness that she felt sure was an obligatory nod to an expected role. There was interest in there somewhere, but it wasn't sexual; it was for something else, something more obscure and therefore more unsettling. His voice was patrician, but with an edge of the coal patch to it. "My father dug coal," he told her another time after he'd got a few drinks in him. "Then the mines closed, and it ruined most people down in Fayette County, but Dad had been smart and bought up some old houses in Uniontown and turned them into apartments. And that was where I got my start. Buying up shitbag properties and leasing them to shitbag tenants. Then I got into land. A man is not a man until a man owns land." He'd also made this latter statement on the night of Barry's dinner, apropos nothing, and everyone tittered nervously. Later that night, he followed Isabel into the bathroom and offered her a blast.

"A what?" she said.

"A blast," he said, and he mimed it.

"Oh," she said. "A *blast*." She had a weakness for cocaine, and she declined, knowing that if she accepted, she'd want more within the half hour.

"Pretend I was harassing you in here," he said. "I have a reputation."

"Will do," she assured him.

"What on earth are you doing in Pittsburgh?" he asked her.

She said that it was too soon to tell.

"Well, we're very pleased to welcome you to our little kingdom. I hope we can keep you."

Isaac had arrived late. Barry didn't appreciate lateness and made a cursory introduction, although Isaac, younger than Isabel by at least ten years and younger than everyone else by at least thirty, carried with him, even more than Imlak did, a sense of imperturbable importance. Even Barry responded with deference. In fact, Isaac almost resembled Imlak, a more gauntly drawn version of the older man; they might have been distant relatives, and they greeted each other with the casual familiarity of old friends who don't feel the need to spend any more of the evening talking to each other. Isaac spent most of the meal chatting with the wife of one of the advisers, a woman who ran the *Alliance Française de Pittsburgh*. They spoke in a rapid Parisian French that Isabel couldn't understand, despite having studied in France for a year as an undergrad. Isaac was wearing a completely preposterous outfit, a blousy white chemise and a pair of brown jodhpurs. He was very thin and so pale that, when lit from behind, he appeared almost translucent at the edges. He had fine features that you would call effeminate if you didn't look closely—closely considered, he was rather wolfish, or like one of those feral dogs that rides the Moscow subway, emaciated and yet obviously built to survive. His hair flopped all over, effortlessly stylish. He had a hint of stubble, barely a shadow, that must have taken him a week to grow. When Isabel came back from the bathroom, he was describing a building to the table. "We call it The Gamelands," he said, "although technically it's just *outside* of the state gamelands. Anyway, you come to the end of the drive, and you can barely see it. From that side, it's half dug into the hillside. It sort of looks like a lot of rocks. You know, it's all very *green*. But if you walk to the end of the field on the other side and look back at it, it looks like a bunch of fucking glass and concrete teepees. It's supposed to be his masterwork, but I am pretty sure he was stoned when he did it. If it's still around a thousand years from now, someone's going to think the aliens built it."

"What's the building?" Isabel asked as she sat down.

"The Gamelands," he said. He laughed. "My family estate, uh, compound."

"It's not in Pittsburgh, I take it?"

"It's in Uniontown," he said. "Or, outside. Anyway, I have an apartment in the city. The Gamelands is the family house. Mom and Dad . . . and me when I'm there." He smirked. "And of course," he said, "there's the monster who lives in the woods."

"Haha," she said. "The monster, huh?"

"According to Abbie," Isaac answered. He laughed again, and Barry asked who wanted coffee or dessert.

After everyone else left—Barry had Isabel stay for a nightcap and to chat about her schedule for the first week, starting on Tuesday—she asked him, "Who was the kid?"

"The kid?" he said. He probably hadn't needed that last scotch. "Oh, Isaac? He's Abbie's son."

"Abbie?"

"Abbie Mayer," Barry said. "You know."

"Oh, shit," Isabel said. "Oh. *Oh.*"

"Oh," Barry said. "You *know* him."

"No, no. I know of him. I know his . . . work. I didn't know he lives in Pittsburgh."

"Lived. He lives on top of a mountain now doing God knows what. You ought to see the house, though. Isaac doesn't do it justice."

How much should she say? "I love his, well, work. He disappeared."

"He came out here in the late eighties. Early nineties? He was a prick back then, too, although I, like you, 'admired his work.'"

"Admired. Yes. Anyway, the son does seem interesting."

"Honey," Barry said, "that kid is fucked up."

3

"What am I looking at?"

Veronica had driven Abbie up to Fernwald Road below Beechwood and pulled over with her wheels edging onto someone's front yard. It was what people did in Pittsburgh. It carried with it a fifty-fifty chance of a screaming match, and yet it still seemed to be an accepted—if not acceptable—practice: a man who'd threaten to bash your head in for parking on his sidewalk or his grass wouldn't hesitate to do it himself if he had trouble finding parking. Still, this new city was neither as small nor as backward as Abbie had feared it might be. He'd only ever visited once, years before his sister had moved there; he'd delivered a lecture at Carnegie Mellon, and he'd found his hosts a little furtive, whisking him from his grand, worn-out downtown hotel to campus to dinner to the airport. It had been winter, and it had been raining. A cold fog refused to lift from the city, and he remembered it as a perpetual evening. Only on the drive from downtown to the Oakland neighborhood where the universities were did he glimpse something like a city. The car—driven by a pretty graduate student, he remembered that much—rose on some kind of highway clinging to a bluff on the southeast side of the downtown; below, there was a brown river, and on the far side many houses on a steep hill. But although he'd found the city, if not cosmopolitan, at least charming in a rundown sort of way and friendly in a suspicious one, it nevertheless held, in the odd hillside streets and strange gullies carved out of its rugged geography, a certain remnant rural tendency. Small houses had driveways clogged with too many cars and pickups, and sometimes when you came around a particular bend you found yourself deep in the trees wondering if you were in a city at all.

They'd parked, and Veronica had led him over a low metal guardrail on the far side of the street through one of the ubiquitous stands of woods. They were standing on the edge of a steep drop, nearly a cliff, that fell off like a rough staircase toward a twisted little trickle of a stream. The other bank rose almost as steeply. To the right, through the treetops, they could see the muddy river and the Homestead High Level Bridge, like the skeleton of a half-mile-long dinosaur, and the smokestacks of the old Homestead Works, which had collapsed and rusted and poisoned three miles along the river for the last decade, ever since the often-rumored, never-arriving demise of the steel industry at last, and swiftly, arrived.

"Greenview-on-Frick," Veronica told him.

"Who came up with that?"

"Phil. Me. We both did."

"It's terrible. It sounds like some sort of moldering collection of half-timber huts in Buggerallfordshire."

"Phil thinks it sounds classy."

Abbie gave her a sidelong look, and she caught his eye and started to laugh. "Classy," Abbie repeated. He laughed as well.

"I missed you, Ronnie."

"God, don't call me that. Anyway, you'll meet him tonight."

"Bated breath."

"Phil knows classy," Veronica said.

"Oy."

"He's not so bad, and he does know construction. We've done well together."

"Well," Abbie said, and he grabbed a nearby branch and let himself lean a bit farther over the edge of the precipice to get a clearer view. "I suppose the first thing I'd say about it, or ask about it, is where the hell do you plan to put the houses?"

"You're looking at it."

"That's a lot of earth moving."

"That's the problem for you to solve."

"Not my area of expertise. Doesn't your construction king have someone to do this sort of thing? I can do a site plan, certainly, but I'm not certain if I'm quite up to leveling and laying out your whole little Broadacre City here."

"No. This is what we talked about. You're going to be our expert witness against the FNMR."

"What is that, some state agency or something?"

"That's the Friends of Nine Mile Run."

"And Nine Mile Run is—"

"That's right. Right down there."

"It's a fucking drainage ditch. I can see that from here."

"It is now. People call it Shit Creek, actually. Or crick, in the local vernacular. It *used* to be a stream that drained the park and the neighborhoods and municipalities on the other side of the hill. It's mostly culverted and buried now, but the FNMR wants to restore it and create a wetland for the park. What we need to do is convince the zoning board that we're not going to further ruin this grotesque little swamp in the name of filthy lucre."

"Are we?"

"Oh, Abbie. I like that it's already a we for you."

"Don't get too attached, my dear. I am many things: visionary, iconoclast, pathbreaker. Genius, even. But I am not—and I feel that I already emphasized this to you—a hydrological engineer. I'd hardly be convincing. Besides which, I *am* a conservationist. Although, well, I suppose it's already been ruined, hasn't it?"

"You see. I don't even have to prompt you to rationalize. You're going to say yes."

"Possibly. There remains the issue of my credentials."

"The zoning board doesn't care about your credentials. They want to say yes, but they don't want to be the ones who say no to a very nice group of very nice citizens. They need an excuse, or an alibi, as the case may be. Trust me on this. This is my wheelhouse."

"I remember when your calling was the law."

"Yes. Well, that's what got me into all this. Although, did you ever imagine that I'd get into real estate?"

"Actually, yes. I recall as a child, gazing out of my creche at your curly head and thinking, in that particular form of consciousness that precedes language: one day, that girl is going to make a killing building shitty subdivisions."

Veronica smiled at him and kissed his cheek and began walking back toward the car. "And now it can be a family business."

In the car, she asked after Sarah. He thought immediately of his wife that day in the temple, leaning away from him in order to comfort her mother. Sarah was a quiet iconoclast in her family, although Abbie never learned to appreciate it. She found their collective demeanor of blessed, raucous bonhomie weird and tiring; she had an austere and mathematical mind back then. It wasn't that she disliked all the camaraderie, exactly, but that it wore her out, and for his flaws, what Abbie had given her, what her marriage had given her, was a home ruled by work, the turning of pages, the sound of a needle reaching a record's end and susurrating onto the label. Abbie was, in the first decade anyway, reserved compared to her own relations, however grandiose and occasionally irascible he could be regarding his craft and profession. Sarah had loved her late brother Elliot, a sloppy, stoned, ingenious writer, his deceptively shambling style a disguise for a slow but powerful ambition, a tectonic drive toward some kind of brilliant life. He'd already published a translation of Mandelstam's early works. His death had been terrible for her, but she viewed it as less uniquely tragic than her parents did, in part because a sibling is simply different from a child, but also, and in larger part, because she more readily admitted that these things do, finally, just happen—more often than we'd like and to us all.

Regardless, she felt obligated to observe the forms of her family's never-ending mourning, which involved a whole year of circumlocutions—they could hardly say her brother's name aloud—interrupted on his birthday and the anniversary of his death. On these occasions, they gave themselves over almost entirely to his remembrance, and Sarah, who thought they'd all be better off, and Elliot's memory better attended to, if they'd spread these gluts of remembering more evenly across the calendar, participated because she figured it was still better than nothing. Abbie, who'd never known Elliot, was politely consoling on these occasions, and in this case, Sarah rather appreciated his reserve. "Oh, Abbie," her mother would say, "you'd have just loved him. I wish you two boys could have met."

Her Elliot was suspended in a perpetual boyhood. That he'd been in his twenties, living on his own in his own apartment in a borough she never visited, making his first intimations of something resembling very much what people call success—none of these things could dislocate her memory of him as a teenager, volcanically moody, a self-taught Czech and Russian speaker, a pretty good violinist, but still, to her, a precociously intellectual little boy. In the subjunctive reality, therefore, where he and Abbie might have met, Abbie, also, would have had to still be a child. Abbie was older than Sarah and more than a decade older than Elliot was, or had been, or would have been. But he'd just smile ruefully at his mother-in-law and say, "Yes, Susan, yes, I'm sure I would."

To Veronica, he said, "Things have been better, but also, worse. She's taken with surprising alacrity to the apartment." Abbie and Sarah's first place in Pittsburgh was a three-bedroom apartment on the second floor of the D'Arlington on Bayard and Neville in Oakland, a gracious, four-story, yellow-brick, turn-of-the-century building that the real estate agent had called a "slice of old Manhattan" (Abbie didn't correct her), and which Abbie secretly derided as the inhabited equivalent of a box of potpourri. It reminded Sarah of their place in New York. Abbie privately disagreed, but he saw no reason to disabuse her of the notion if it contributed to her happiness. That it did not contribute to her happiness, that it made her sad rather than wistful and mostly suggested, however imprecisely, something that she'd lost, might have occurred to him if he'd thought about it, but it—and he—didn't and hadn't.

"It's a great apartment," Veronica said.

"It feels like a hunting lodge or an exquisite jewelry box. I despise it, but I'm in no position to let sincerity get in the way of a good apology."

"Pittsburgh," Veronica said. "Some apology."

"You seem to have prospered," Abbie told her. They were on

Beechwood Boulevard gliding past handsome twenties-era houses with steep front yards and old trees.

"Yes, true, but I arrived here by chance and it just happened to work out for me."

"Oh, *mein shvester*, you don't give yourself enough credit for your personal vision."

"My vision? You sound like Phil after he's picked up a Drucker book in an airport. Please. It's the people who pursue fixed visions who end up bankrupt."

"Phil reads management texts? Do I really have to meet this person? And I've not found visions to be especially fixed."

"You do. And by the way that sounds very spiritual, Abbie." They'd come down the hill on lower Beechwood past the old mansions on their vast, improbable yards, and she hung a left onto Fifth Avenue. On the corner, a huge storybook Tudor stood in a tangle of unkempt landscaping. "Now that," Abbie said, "is a house. It's like Queen Elizabeth met Mad King Ludwig."

"I'd die to get a crack at restoring it," Veronica said. "The family won't sell, but they're old. No kids. So, one of these days."

"Regardless, and to get back to it, yes. I would say spiritual is the proper word."

"Should I be concerned? Remember when you got into yoga?"

"Yes. Dad was not impressed. 'How am I going to tell your mother that you're into some Jap religion?'"

Veronica laughed. "Oh, God, that's right. I can still hear you. 'It's *South* Asian, Dad. If anyone has a reason to be upset with the Japanese.'"

"Yeah," Abbie said, "'But whatever else they did to those people, the Japs didn't do a sneak attack on them, like they did to us!'"

"Stop. I can't breathe, and I'm trying to drive."

"He forgave the Germans for the Holocaust, but those dirty Japs."

"Seriously, Abbie. I'm going to have to pull over."

"Seriously, though, I did have a sort of a vision. I keep telling you."

"A vision, was it?"

"I can hear the worldly skepticism in your voice, but yes. A vision. I know what you're thinking."

She was thinking that in his early professional years, Abbie had styled himself a sort of scientist, rigorous and rational, devoted to a very mathematical sort of beauty—somewhere along the way, he'd discovered that it was better for his interests to be grandiloquent, and he'd adopted a tone of secular mysticism, speaking of his world-saving projects in a quasi-religious and semi-revelatory language, which had landed him all those speaking gigs while frightening off his more traditional clients, who would have been perfectly happy to save on their water utilities or feel that their new thirty-story office tower was in some absurd way actually *good* for the environment, but who couldn't abide some mad prophet of civilizational doom telling them that an extra hundred dollars a square foot would, over the passage of the decades, at very best, if everyone else did it too, marginally slow the inevitable rising of the tides. She blamed that nut job he'd studied with at Yale; not that Abbie had paid him much attention while he was there, but later, after the old man died, his publisher had approached Abbie about writing the introduction to one last posthumous book. The two men had kept in only intermittent touch over the years, and Abbie was shocked to find that Arah had stipulated the request to his editor before he died. The book was called *The Pillar of Salt: The American City in the Age of Declining Resources*, and it told a grim tale of the last air conditioners cycling off in the great, rolling brownout at the end of the easy-energy carbon civilization.

"I'm not thinking anything."

"You're thinking I've gone slightly around the bend. But I'm not about to start babbling on a street corner."

"Going to keep it to the lecture hall, huh?"

"You're feeling awfully wicked for a woman who needs my help with something."

"That's fair enough. I'm sorry. Tell me about your vision."

They'd come, coincidentally, to a red light at the corner of Morewood. Across the street on their right, the green dome of Rodef Shalom rose over the tops of the sycamores. "I was shown a place," Abbie said. "And I think I've dreamed of this place before, but as is the case with dreams, the particulars dissolved when I woke from the dream, leaving me only with the sense that I'd just failed to apprehend something very important. This time, though, I was not asleep. Oddly enough, actually"—he chuckled—"as I was in a synagogue at the time, which is a place I generally find more conducive to sleep than to epiphany."

"You were in a synagogue?"

"Temple, I suppose. Yes. Sarah's brother's thing, you know. It was all very musical, which made it especially ridiculous. I'm not sure what happened to make every goddamn Reform rabbi decide that he's Pete Seeger, but there it is. Sarah was torturing herself with her usual dutiful reticence, her mother was making a particularly ostentatious show of not quite crying, which is worse and more noticeable than crying—that's plainly the point, of course—and her dad constantly clearing his throat. I was daydreaming about committing arson. And that was when God spoke to me. Of course, God doesn't speak; God's speech is a metaphor for His placing a vision in your eyes and in your heart, which is suffused with the certitude that this is what He would have told you if He did, in fact, literally speak. The place He showed me is somewhere in the Appalachians; I'm sure of that. I stood on a low foothill looking eastward. I know I was looking eastward because the sun was setting behind me. Before me, a highway wound up over the first ridge of a mountain. At the crest of the ridge, somewhere off to the south, I saw a small clearing, and I knew that I was meant to find and to possess some portion of that mountain, for some reason that is, as yet, unclear to me. Naturally, I thought of you."

They turned onto Neville. "Abbie," Veronica said, "I think you're full of shit, but under no circumstances are you allowed to tell your wife that you came out here because of some Old Testament daydream. You are on the apology tour. You are here to save your marriage."

"And save your subdivision."

She pulled to the curb across from the D'Arlington. "It's a planned neighborhood. Dinner tonight is at eight. Are you sure you can find it?"

"God is my copilot."

"Christ, Abbie. Good-bye."

He kissed her cheek and made a suicidal dash across the street in front of an oncoming truck. On the far curb, he blew her a kiss and pointed toward heaven like a quarterback after converting on a big third down.

. . .

"Have you ever met her?"

"What's that?" Abbie glanced at Sarah as they drove up the

McArdle Roadway on the side of Mt. Washington. On the right, through the trees, the city appeared intermittently, lending the impression of riding up an escalator. They passed under the tracks of the Monongahela Incline.

"Edith. Your sister's friend."

"Her friend. That's a charmingly provincial circumlocution. You're adapting."

"Oh, shut up, Abbie. You know what I mean. It isn't always a debate, you know."

"Yes, of course, I do."

"That it isn't a debate, or what I mean."

"The latter. Both."

"It seems absurd to say girlfriend. They're in their forties."

"Edith is in her late thirties, I believe, but you're right, honey. Your point is taken. This is a lovely road, don't you think? The views."

"It's a lovely city. I hadn't expected. I'm glad we came."

Abbie reached across the center console and took her hand. "I'm glad," he said.

She permitted him that much for a few moments before they came to the light at the top of the hill, then removed it, although gently now, as she'd begun forcing herself to do. Sarah had yet to decide if love was in greater part forgiveness or forbearance. They weren't the same thing, but you only learned that out of necessity, and the conditions that made it necessary were terrible. She sometimes told herself that she saw in him something that was worth redeeming. Because if not . . .

Whatever else Sarah believed, she did not believe that Abbie was a genius. This made her an outlier among those who knew him, but maybe not so strange if you think about it. Before she got tired of talking to people, Sarah used to say that their exodus out of New York inverted the usual story of people getting rich, and in so doing rediscovered in some way an older or more original form of American good fortune. People used to go west to make their fortunes, striking out from the rigid castes of the Eastern Seaboard in order to find wealth and freedom on the frontier. Later, the frontier closed and it was to escape the stultifying social and economic circumstances of the agrarian heartland that people fled back to the big cities, where a person might reinvent herself as whatever and whomever she wanted to be. Then people were fleeing the biggest cities again, because no one who wasn't already rich could live in them. They were looking for the good lives and relative material comforts that were still available out in the provinces that began somewhere around Wilkes-Barre/Scranton and rolled across the whole beautiful continent until they washed up against the equally unaffordable cities of California. She meant it all half-ironically, since she never once felt *at home* after they left Manhattan, and her son, with whom she made the mistake of sharing some version of these thoughts years after she'd first had them, was an intolerable undergrad at the time. He thought that they revealed her as a rather facile thinker when it came to sociology and economics and history—the whole notion of the blessed heartland could have been cribbed from any political speech of the past century at least; the ruins of Detroit or the Mexican laborers of the Central Valley or, God knew, a few First Peoples here and there, would have something contrary to say about the sentiment. If he'd been older, or less like his father in that way, then he might have asked if it was fair to blame anyone for the lies that sand down the rough edges of her circumstances.

They met Veronica and her business partner, Phillip T. Harrow, at LeMont, a restaurant perched on the high edge of Mt. Washington, a sort of recherché supper club with vast windows that looked across the converging rivers and the fountain at the Point to the commodal concrete bowl of Three Rivers Stadium. Even the valets wore rough approximations of tuxedos, and the interior seemed designed to seat hundreds, but on a weeknight, it was populated sparsely, and a radio broadcast of the Pirates game that was lighting up the stadium far below whispered tinnily into the hushed room from somewhere behind the bar. Barry Bonds had singled.

Harrow was almost precisely what Abbie had expected, a great, grand buffoon in a loud jacket, gone a bit soft in middle age but with the taut strength of a man who'd worked construction much of his life. A pair of spectacles dangled on a cord around his neck, and he looked—it was his usual state—a little flushed. He greeted Abbie with a rushing handshake, kissed Sarah on both cheeks, and then went back to Abbie for one more throttling shake of the hand and a jolting slap on the shoulder. "So this is the guy!" He said it twice.

In fact, Harrow wasn't quite so crude as he put on. Yes, he was from West Virginia, but he was the son of a WVU professor and a Morgantown Hospital finance VP, and he'd gone to Ohio State, where he'd got a degree in accounting and then an MBA. He wasn't a country boy, really, even if he could do a tolerable imitation of the accent when called upon. His beery bearing had less to do with his native state than with the lingering influence of Greek life in the Ohio Union, that avuncular, overacted jocularity that always seems to be compensating for something. He'd always hated West Virginia, actually. And yet he'd made a great deal of money in it. That was something, he supposed. The truth was that there was a lot of money in the poor states; or it rolled around more loosely than it did in richer and more populous ones; it was easier to shake loose. But he kept a condo in Pittsburgh, and he'd surprise you by knowing a thing or two about wine and the theater, and although he'd never let on, he sometimes wept at the opera.

Edith wasn't feeling well—Edith, they'd learn, was often not feeling well—and she didn't join them. Abbie had only the vaguest sense of his sister's companion—and he was aware of the irony of thinking of her in that term while making fun of Sarah's preference for the no-more-euphemistic friend. She worked, or had worked, for Harrow; he knew that much, and in some way this had led to his and Veronica's partnership. There was, Abbie thought, some irony in the fact that everyone else in the restaurant would assume that Phil and Veronica were a couple. Abbie delighted in inequities of information; they struck him as the true genealogical or etymological origin of humor, the primordial language from which all jokes ultimately emerged.

The menu represented, in that era, an extraordinary archaeology of otherwise lost dishes; this was in the eighties, of course, long before America devoted whole television networks to the fussy preparation of complex dishes, before waiters listed the components of dishes in a sort of catechismal fugue state, but still, it was as if someone had rescued the menu from the first-class dining room of a sunken ocean liner and transported it five hundred miles inland. Abbie ordered duck à l'orange, and when he specified to the waitress that he preferred it medium rare, she shook her head and said, "Oh, hon, you don't want it like that. You'll get that trichinosis."

Abbie began to object, but Veronica put her hand on his arm and shook her head.

When they'd all ordered and the waitress was gone, Abbie raised his eyebrows at his sister. "Really?" he said.

"They mean well," she told him. She shrugged. "It's a city of hypochondriacs, and everyone thinks they've got a goddamn MD. Phil can attest."

"Well," Harrow said, "that and the old joke."

"What joke is that?" asked Sarah.

Harrow tilted his head wolfishly in her direction and leaned into the table as if taking her into a confidence. "How do you get a Pittsburgh girl to suck your cock?"

"Oh Christ, Phil," Veronica said. "It's dinner."

"Mrs. Mayer here looks like she can take it. Can you take it, Sarah?" His grin widened. Veronica looked worryingly at her brother, but he betrayed not the slightest indication of paying attention to the conversation anymore. He was half turned in his seat, examining the room.

"Well, now you have to tell me," Sarah said.

"You dip it in ranch!" He rocked back and slapped the table. Veronica rolled her eyes, and Sarah smiled thinly. "You get it?" Harrow tried again. "Like, ranch dressing?" He narrowed his eyes. "You get it," he said. "Well, anyway, it's a Pittsburgh thing. And here's the wine!" Harrow had ordered a bottle listed at two hundred dollars, and as the waiter—a different one this time, young and male and too thin for his collar—opened and poured his ceremonial taste, he gave it a grand swirl and sniffed and sipped. He nodded brusquely at the boy, then told the table: "A good California cab. Robust! Not like that French shit."

"Yes," Sarah said, "I've read that American wine is really coming into its own."

"Where have you read that?" Abbie's attention had returned.

"I don't know, Abbie. *Bon Appétit.*"

He made a face.

Harrow said, "It's true, it's true. Ever since the seventies, really. Well, a toast, then." He raised his glass. "To new endeavors."

They touched glasses. Veronica watched her brother and sister-in-law carefully. She could still remember when they'd met, when Abbie was slathering his genius all over that poor unsuspecting temple, bullying the leadership into believing that they were courageous to let him use their sanctuary as an experiment, then furious when they managed, late in the process, to work up the courage to question a few of his most objectionable choices. Architects, in her experience, were second only to economists in their preference for models of human behavior rather than humans themselves, an abiding conviction that people were automata who only responded to stimuli, or, if they were not so, then that they ought to be, that through proper design and incentives, they could be made to behave as if they were. And Abbie, likewise, harbored the streak of misanthropy that colored so many of the ecologically minded, an unspoken but obviously present sentiment, a ghost haunting the edges of his mixed-up ideology: that the world would be better off without us. In the strictest sense, of course, that might have been true; but it was one of those immense truths that faded into irrelevance when confronted with the banal details of reality. Abbie had harangued and intimidated the Beth-El board, and Sarah, who was still young enough to consider them all ancient and hidebound, fell in love with him. She'd hitched herself to some idea of his greatness, and even after she'd stopped fully believing in it herself, a kind of invincible bond remained.

Just a few nights earlier, Veronica and Edith had been lying on the couch watching TV, some sitcom about a bickering couple, and Veronica had made a vague comment about the unreality of the setup, so common in TV and movies and the theater, of the eternally miserable couple forever at each other's throats. Edith had laughed at her and told her that that was the way *most* people lived together; that love and hatred were the same sort of unmooring of sentiment from moderation, and it was no wonder that the one would so frequently cohabit with the other. "You're so smart," Veronica told her and kissed her head, then, thinking the gesture might have been condescending, she added, "I mean, really." Edith had been an all-but-dissertation grad student at Pitt before her parents' careless finances and untimely deaths in a car accident, which Edith mordantly called a double-suicide by inattention, had forced her to look for work. Like so many women, she found herself in real estate, and through it, with Phil Harrow, who was just expanding his business into Pennsylvania at the time.

While they spooned through a lobster bisque that had the consistency of pudding, the color of freshly dug clay, and the taste, principally, of black pepper—all of them but Sarah, who pushed a salad around her plate and poured herself a second glass of the leggy wine—Veronica and Phil explained how they'd first met and found themselves in business together. Sarah had asked, because whenever she'd asked Abbie, he'd waved it off with an "Oh, you know how these things are" and gone back to whatever he was doing; the suggestion that he knew but found the whole thing too boring to share was his habitual reply when he didn't know something.

They'd met in West Virginia. "Some motherfucker had told these rednecks that their land was worth two million bucks, and it was going to fuck up a deal." Harrow flapped his hands and smiled. "Two million dollars! It was worth a hundred thousand, *maybe*, on the market. But two million was the max my buyers were willing to pay." Harrow had the makings of a deal to erect a plaza anchored by a Wal-Mart and a Fairfield Inn near Beckley. It was a promising and simple deal, in which the owners of about a hundred acres of mostly woodland would sell to a New York–based developer, who represented Walton interests in the Northeast, of which West Virginia found itself a distant, dangling appendage. They'd already gobbled most of the acreage up, and cheaply.

But thirty odd acres and a gaggle of recalcitrant yokel owners led by some kind of redneck mafia queen named Sherri Larimer and her pair of apparently terrifying sons stood in the way of its completion. Someone had told her to ask for millions of dollars, ten times the price they ought to get, the sort of money that, Harrow knew, would come out of his construction contract on the other end. Harrow could not abide doing business when everyone had the same information. Profit, especially in land deals, was built on information arbitrage; it was hard to dispossess people who knew what they possessed, especially when they were ignorant fucks from deep in the hollers who believed these sorts of transactions to have a kind of moral dimension. He'd tried to approach several of the landholders individually; one defection usually brought down an ad-hoc association of neighbors, but they only stared at him through their screen doors and said, "You gotta talk to Sherri." Senator Byrd was building another goddamn highway through the wildest part of Wild and Wonderful West

Virginia, and Harrow was trying to get these New York fucks to buy beside a future interchange of I-64 and I-77, not far from the New River Gorge—he'd got them to imagine that a seasonal influx of whitewater rafters and granola-eaters was going to support the Wal-Mart and an outlet mall and at least one hotel and a lot of other such nonsense.

Veronica Mayer was sitting quietly in the back of a gang of attorneys who'd flown out from New York (and from Morgantown down to Beckley in a goddamn helicopter, if you could believe it) to represent the General Properties Group, which in turn represented—everyone knew—the Walton family. She was the youngest of them; she didn't even look thirty yet; and although Harrow thought she looked pretty cute, he was in no position to flirt with cute lady lawyers while a deal collapsed around him. They'd been sequestered in a room for a couple of hours now. He was ranting, he knew, but these wingtipped, French-cuffed assholes were going to eat him for lunch if he didn't play it right. Jesus goddamn Christ, he hoped one of the Larimers did something crazy. The lawyers already knew, of course, that the Larimers had upped the ask. Their evident calm on the phone the day before—"That price," said Jerry Meegan, Esquire, "is obviously higher than we'd like, but not wholly outside of the realm of consideration"—had sent him into a panic; no one casually throwing around that kind of money for a few parcels of undeveloped property could be trusted not to fuck you over. No one who used the phrase "not wholly outside the realm of consideration" could possibly be telling the truth.

The first time he'd met the Larimers, he'd spent five hours in a car—not counting the drive down—just trying to find the place. He kept ending up back in Beckley. Finally, when he felt certain he was getting close, he pulled over at an unbelievable gas station whose sign read FUEL, BAIT, VENISON, JERKY and asked the clerk if he knew where they lived and the clerk removed his hat *very slowly* and rubbed his head *very slowly* and drawled *very slowly*, "Well sure, son. You just wanna go about four looks down Sullivan Road that way and then you'll see a sign for Split Lake Hollow Road. Now don't take that. You'll wanna go a little farther along. They're up Ward Road, on your left."

"I'm sorry," Harrow said. "A few what?"

"Well, just a few looks."

"A few looks."

"Yessir. Just a few."

Harrow had a personal philosophy that business success was principally the ability to tolerate the intolerable. Like most things he termed philosophy, it had little or no practical application for him. "What the hell is a look?"

"Well shit," the clerk said. "No reason to get nasty about it, young man. A look. You know. You look down the road"—he gestured back toward it—"and as far as you can look, that's one look. And them Larimers, they're a few more looks down the road."

The Larimers, Harrow discovered, weren't even West Virginian. They were from Fayette County, Pennsylvania, twenty minutes over the state line from his own home in Morgantown. "Right up the road from me," Harrow said genially. Their property, just a trailer, really, with a big wooden deck and an astonishing proliferation of surprisingly expensive vehicles, was, they told him, just their camp.

"Like four goddamn hours up the road!" Raymond, the older of the two sons said.

"Shut your goddamn mouth, Raymond. The adults are talking." Sherri Larimer blew smoke toward him. He would have been in his early twenties at the time. "He's talking about from Morgantown." She eyed Harrow. "This here's just our *camp*. Like I *told* you."

"I have to ask," Harrow said. "Are you folks Larimers like Chet Larimer? Like the Hole-in-Gun?"

"Finest shooting ranges, go-karts, and putt-putts in the Tri-state. That's my husband. He don't come down the camp much, on account of he's on disability." She lit a fresh cigarette and winked broadly. "Plus he don't drink no more, cause of his diabetes. Not much point in camping if you can't drink."

She offered Harrow a beer, which he accepted, and proceeded to listen credulously, he believed, as he told her that he could make her a few hundred thousand bucks, with which she could have her pick of camps.

"What's wrong with this one?"

"Nothing, it's a fine camp. But once they build that highway and interchange, it won't be much good for hunting, will it?"

"Hunting?" Sherri hooted. She pointed at the boys. "Ray don't hunt, and Billy over there's got stigmatism. He couldn't hit the side of a barn. He ain't bagged a deer in ten years."

"Well, it'll ruin the scenery. And think about the noise."

"I'll think about it. To be honest, I don't much care for the drive down here, and we got another camp up near Fairchance anyhow."

"And you'll talk to the other owners?"

"Sure," Larrimer said. She puffed a thin ring of smoke. "I'll talk to them."

Sherri Larimer and her sons showed up at the Holiday Inn conference room—none of the law firms in Beckley had an available or big enough room—in formal clothes, the boys, as Sherri called Billy and Ray, stuffed into smooth-worn coats that pinched under their armpits and Sherri in a lacy white dress that looked like a relic from some evil wedding conducted before the opening credits of a horror film. She'd been in sweats and a Mountaineers shirt when Harrow had met her up at their property. Harrow, who had never been an accurate close observer of human self-presentation, though he believed otherwise, wrote it off as country-folk idiosyncrasy; it was all just coal miners and rural welfare. The idea that she might be putting them all on would have struck him as improbable at best. She took a pack of slender cigarettes out of her pocketbook. Billy lit one for her. "Let's cut to the chase," she said. The lawyers regarded her impassively, except for Veronica, who sat a foot back from the table, as if in deference to her older male counterparts, and regarded the family across from her with a tilted head and look of polite curiosity. Sherri gestured at her with her smoke. "Nice to see yinz brought a lady." Ray chuckled darkly. She narrowed her eyes. "Shut up, Raymond."

"Yes, Ma'am," he said.

"I hate to be the only gal in the room."

"I love your dress, by the way," Veronica said.

Harrow stared at her darkly and allowed his mind to explode with a little fireworks display of select sentiments about women in business. She was going to fuck everything up if she talked down to these people, and yet everything about her expression and her bearing suggested genuine pleasure in Sherri's getup. Sherri just said, "Thank you, young lady. It belonged to my mother."

"I think that lace must be handmade," Veronica said.

"Of course it is," Larimer said, "and I thank you for noticing." She puffed at the rest of them.

"Well, now that that's out of the way," mumbled one of the attorneys.

Ray chuckled again.

"Shut up, Raymond."

Jerry Meegan, the lead negotiator for the property group, said a hundred thousand and Sherri countered with two million. He looked at her with a mix of disdain and admiration. "I can see we're a ways apart," he said.

She mirrored his look with a precision that took him slightly aback, then glanced at Harrow and gave a theatrical wink designed for the whole room to see. "Thing is," she said, "I spoke to my fellow homeowners. Some of them were eager to sell. But I said to them, I said that yinz are holding out on us."

Meegan smoothed a hand across the remnants of his hair and said a hundred and fifty thousand, and Sherri countered with two million. They progressed in this fashion, with the bald, vampire-pale, elegantly reptilian attorney moving incrementally toward the figure that Sherri Larimer repeated fixedly like a magical incantation, never once without a lit cigarette. At seven hundred and fifty thousand, he said he'd need to caucus with his colleagues.

"Yinz need to what?" said Raymond.

"Shut your goddamn mouth, Ray," she snapped, slapping her hand on the table. "I'll bust your eggs, boy." She sighed and lit a smoke. "I'm sorry," she told Meegan. "Yinz want to step out, or should we?"

In the hall, Meegan turned his impenetrable black eyes on Harrow and said, "Phillip, it seems to me that you have under-represented the recalcitrance of this particular party."

"Well shit, Jerry, you said, and I quote, that two mil was 'not wholly outside the realm of consideration.'"

"Not wholly," said Meegan. "Still, we rather expected that as an initial bargaining position, not some *idée fixe*."

"For fuck's sake," said Harrow.

"Perhaps if we approach another owner," said one of the interchangeable male lawyers.

"Phillip?" Meegan looked down his nose.

Harrow considered lying, then thought better of it. "She'd probably drown anyone who talked to you in the lake."

"Really?" said the lawyer.

"It's an expression," said Harrow without knowing precisely what he meant. There was, at least, no lake.

"I'm going to make a call to Arkansas," said Meegan. He adjusted a cuff. "Please excuse me."

"Mr. Harrow," said Veronica—almost, he thought, shyly. "You wouldn't happen to have spotted a ladies room?"

"Sure," Harrow answered. "Sure. It's back by the reception."

"Would you show me? I'm sorry. Who designs these places, right? I'm all turned around."

So Harrow walked her back toward the lobby, wondering how you could get all turned around in a hallway with one left turn, thinking *women,* until in the lobby she turned and faced Harrow with the same look of gentle interest that she'd shown for Sherri Larimer's dress and said, "Mr. Harrow, you seem like a man who likes to make money."

"Sure I like to make money. Who doesn't like money?"

"Not everyone cares about money *qua* money. Jerry Meegan, for example, cares about fucking people over. That he's made money doing it is incidental and not really a major part of his enjoyment of it. In any event, I have a proposition for you."

"*You* do?"

"I do."

"That's why we're out here."

"Yes and no. I really do have to piss." (This, Harrow would later reflect, was the moment when he felt the first throb of sexual attraction for her, the way she said it so nonchalantly: *piss*.) "But you know, two birds."

"Okay." Harrow crossed his arms over his broad belly. He was wearing a polo shirt; he felt that polos and khakis occupied just the right position on the spectrum between big city lawyers and these redneck lunatics. "Shoot," he said.

"This deal," Veronica told him, "is fucked seven ways to next Tuesday."

"I don't know that it's fucked," Harrow protested, although his gut fled toward his always-troublesome bowels at the thought of it. This was not a make-or-break deal for him; part of success was charting a smooth upward trend through a mess of ups and downs, but still, it might represent several million in revenue, with a good margin, too, as these new box stores were little more than piles of cinder block and fluorescent lighting. In a state with few environmental regulations, the earthworks needed for site prep were fast, dirty, and cheap. He could easily be looking at a million in profit. He ran a slim operation, subcontracted almost everything, maintained only one small office in Morgantown and had only a few full-time employees: an engineer, a draftsman, an old, laid-off mine foreman who served as his liaison with tradespeople, and a grim and librarianish real estate agent named Edith—a young woman stuck with an old woman's name, a failed academic of some kind who'd tried to sell houses but hated the platitudinous interactions and came to him for the promise of uninterrupted office work and a steady salary. A million dollars in profit. It was 1985. He could afford the lost opportunity, but still he felt the loss palpably looming in front of him, unavoidable as a sudden deer on a dark, narrow road in the middle of the night.

"You know it is," Veronica replied simply.

"Jerry said he'd contemplate two mil."

"Jerry would contemplate killing his own mother. Quote: 'all outcomes are reasonable in the abstract.' But he's not going to go to two, and even if he does, Sherri is going to decide that she needs three."

Harrow laughed at her; he laughed in such a way as to make sure that she knew he was laughing *at* her. "Young lady," he said, "you seem very smart, and I'm sure you're a very good lawyer back in New York." (He sucked his cheeks for a second. He was very pleased with the way he pronounced New York: with the familiar derision of a person who can afford to disdain the grimy atavism of that city which, because it's populated with so many refugees of the provinces, is quite often the most provincial place in America.) "But," he said, "I know these people. These people are my people. Well, more or less. And they're not going to walk away from that kind of money."

She was disconcertingly unperturbed. She smiled at him revealing rows of capped, Wall-Street teeth. She said, "No, obviously not. But I mean, I think we both know who told them it was worth that much to begin with? Anyway, they can make a lot more leasing it."

"First of all, that's total bullshit. Leasing it? The whole goddamn project is a boondoggle!" He shouldn't have said that to this woman, so he barreled ahead, hoping she wouldn't notice. "The tenants are going to last a year if they ever move in. And the rest of the property is already sold. She *can't* just lease it. And by the way, if you're implying that I—"

She waved her hand. "No, Mr. Harrow. I told them."

"You?"

"You're surprised."

"Yes. Goddamnit! First of all, why would you do any such thing? And second of all, how the hell would you even know . . . I mean, how would you, without me, even get in contact . . ."

"Well," she said. "It's funny. I actually first came out to open our Pittsburgh office. And I was having a drink one night at this little bar called Partners, and I met this very nice woman, about my age, who was up from Morgantown for the weekend. She worked in real estate, it turned out."

Harrow's arms fell. He felt his pits go damp and his small intestines, or something down there, jerk agonizingly. "Edith?" he said. "But she wouldn't—"

"We've been seeing each other, actually, for almost six months now."

"*Seeing* each other. Jesus fucking—"

"Mr. Harrow," Veronica said. "Phil. They're going to wonder where we are. What do you say?"

"What do I say," Phil said, neither quite a question nor quite not a question.

"It's not a boondoggle, Phil. This company, I'm telling you. In twenty years, Sears will be out of business, but there will be one of these fuckers at every crossroads in America. Which is exactly what I told Sherri Larimer."

And the one thing you could say about Phillip Harrow, the Construction King of Morgantown, West Virginia, whatever else bad you might say about him, whatever aspersions you might cast on his character, was that he never let something as small as his own prejudice get in the way of a good deal. So what? This lawyer was a dyke who'd seduced his apparently dyke secretary and screwed his multimillion-dollar deal as part of some longer con whose overall contours he could just barely sense as he stood there stupidly in the plasticine-colored lobby of that godawful hillbilly Holiday Inn. She was playing him, playing her own employers, playing the Larimers possibly, even though he thought—and surely she must have noticed too— that they carried with them the appalling possibility of violence, who did not, he thought, seem like the sort of people you ought to fuck with. But then again, as someone had once told him—he forgot who, where, when, or what it had been in regard to—life was not a dress rehearsal. "All right," he said. "What do you want me to do?"

"Phil," Veronica said. How could someone so sexy be queer? "I just need you to be yourself."

That had been five years ago. Jerry Meegan *had* gone to two million in the end. Harrow's stomach had bucked, and he thought that he was really going to crap in his pants, but then Sherri Larimer had pressed her bitter yellow mouth into a tight little sphincter and said, sourly, "I'm thinking maybe two point five."

Meegan betrayed not one blink of emotion or disbelief and suggested mildly that it suddenly felt as if they were negotiating in something less than good faith. Then Raymond pulled a hunting knife from somewhere inside his ill-fitting jacket and pounded the point right into the table between them and asked if Jerry was accusing them of lying. The New York boys, previously imperturbable, lurched back in terror, Meegan so abruptly that he fell right out of his chair, sprawling onto the polyester carpet in his many-thousand-dollar suit. Sherri Larimer laughed. With a look of fear mingled with despair and disbelief, they all fled the room. Larimer laughed again. "Like cock-a-roaches," she sneered. Harrow stood there. He thought, *I should say something.* He didn't say anything.

Veronica rose from her chair, perfectly, beatifically calm, smiled at Sherri, and said, "Well, I'm so sorry they left so abruptly. Thank you so much for your time."

A little later, a pair of state police arrived. Larimer offered them smokes, which they declined. "Well, I know," she said. "They are *ladies'* cigarettes. But they got the same damn tobacco."

"Was you really gonna cut him?" One of the staties asked Ray. He looked like a teenager and seemed to find the situation amusing.

"Cut him?" Larimer shook her head. She cackled. "Son, Ray-Ray don't even hunt! He faints at the sight of blood."

"Do not!"

Sherri Larimer snatched the knife, pricked the end of her index finger, and squeezed a couple of drops onto the table.

He turned the color of her dress, covered his mouth, and he too fled the room.

. . .

Abbie had giggled through the whole story. "Whatever happened to these Larimers? What happened to the deal?"

Veronica shrugged. "We worked out a lease deal, and Phil and I financed and built the whole thing on spec, and today it is West Virginia's most successful outlet mall. No Wal-Mart, though. They ended up building it up the road. Even Sherri Larimer made a bundle."

"She's got the magic touch," Harrow said, putting a hand on the back of Veronica's chair.

"Market research," Veronica shrugged.

Sarah said, "I don't understand why you were trying to cheat, what's her name, that Sherri Larimer."

"Oh, I wasn't!" Veronica put her hand on her heart and made an approximation of the Boy Scout salute.

Harrow said, "Veronica here figured—and this is what she told Sherri L.—that at minimum, they'd get eminent domained and walk away from the whole thing with a couple hundred thou, which they'd have made in the first place. At maximum, those GP dummies would've given in and paid her a zillion bucks." Phil shrugged. "I'd've gotten screwed, probably, in that deal, but"—he leaned over and planted a brotherly kiss on Veronica's cheek—"Veronica and I didn't know each other yet, so no foul there. Anything in between, well, still good for the Larimers. And Sherri didn't have to kill anybody. As it was, it all worked out."

"And you found yourself in service of this colorful group because?" At some point during the story, Sarah's wine glass had disappeared and been replaced by a tumbler full of something amber. The waitress appeared and asked if anyone wanted dessert.

Harrow told her to bring another bottle of wine, "and some of those macaroons," he added. "Those famous macaroons."

"That's the Duquesne Club, hon," the waitress told him.

"You don't have any macaroons?" Harrow winked at Sarah when he said it.

"Sorry, hon."

"The booze'll do, then."

They were the only people left in the dining room. Far below, on the water, a dark train of barges swam from the Monongahela into the Ohio River. Harrow lit a cigarette and asked if anyone else smoked.

"Surely," Abbie said, and he accepted a Marlboro.

"You don't smoke," said Sarah.

"I do occasionally. When the moment presents itself."

"To answer your question," Veronica told Sarah, "I'd been working on some deals in Fayette County, and their name kept coming up. And I was already thinking of, shall we say, striking out on my own. You know how much I hated that firm. And this was an opportunity, not to put too fine a point on it, to ingratiate myself with the local landowning class."

"Always an angle," Phil said. He made a silent toast.

"To be fair, the Larimers are a nasty bunch. Everyone down there seems to be afraid of them. But Sherri's never been anything but a sweetheart to me."

"Well, look," Harrow said. "To the matter at hand, which we've been putting off with this storytelling."

"Yes," Abbie said. "Well, like I told Veronica, I'm not exactly certain I'm qualified to do what you ask. And *yes*"—he raised a hand to his sister to stop her from interrupting—"I know that you only need some kind of ersatz, quote-unquote expert to assuage the gratuitous concerns of some committee of know-nothing appointees on a zoning board, but still."

"Oh, come on, Rabbi," said Harrow. "Don't tell me, I cannot tell a lie. You've got the bona fides."

"It's pronounced *bona fides*, and, I'm sorry."

Phil smirked, "Veronica told me that you were on a mission from God."

Sarah leered across the table at him. "Jesus Christ, Abbie. You told your sister, too?"

Abbie flapped a hand at her and glared at Veronica, who put up her own hands and said, "What? He's my business partner."

"Aw, shit," said Phil. "I didn't mean anything. I figure, you know, a man's religion is his own business, although I'm not what you'd call spiritual myself. Anyway, hell, your whole thing is that you're some kind of environmental guy, right? Solar power and whatnot. If it walks like a duck, am I right?"

"Not exactly."

Sarah rattled ice in her husband's direction. She was drunk, she knew, but it was an odd thing: she found, when she'd had a few drinks, it became suddenly right to do and say those things that her sober self would never permit out of sobriety's crippling politeness. "Abbie is *very* moral," she said. "Honesty is his policy."

"Well," Veronica said and made a gesture of pushing back from the table.

"Abbie is particularly fond of the third and seventh commandments. Ten a distant third."

Abbie had crossed his arms and let his face relax into a state of practiced impassivity. He'd long ago decided that the most infuriating response to a furious woman was to respond with the inverse of her anger. Sarah glared at him. "Sarah," Veronica said, "I'm going to run to the ladies' room before we go. Would you care to join?" She knew it was the cheap way out, and she felt a twinge of disappointment and frustration, knowing, of course, that her idiot business partner and her dumb brother would interpret it in precisely the same way, affirming whatever it was they already thought about women, those prejudices they knew better than to vocalize, but held and believed with self-congratulation for having the courage of conviction not to turn away from unacceptable, unfashionable, but ineradicable truths.

When the women had gone, Phil stretched in his chair. "You sure pissed her off," he said.

"Like complaining about the weather," Abbie replied.

Harrow laughed. "Good point. She's a great-looking lady, though. Your sister, too, by the way."

"You'd have a better chance with my wife." Abbie permitted himself a smirk.

"Wait, what—" Harrow began, but he noticed the waiter approaching and caught himself short. The waiter deposited the check with a deferential nod. It sat on the table halfway between them for a moment longer than was comfortable, then Harrow grabbed it. "Just kidding, Rabbi," he said. "This one's on me."

"Are you sure?" Abbie asked. Magnanimity was easier once you knew the other guy was going to pay.

"Sure am." He extracted a credit card from a fantastically bulbous wallet. "Consider it a down payment. Now we'll see about the returns."

4

Late that night, Abbie told Sarah that he'd back out if she preferred it, and she said, "Oh, no you won't."

"I will," he said. "If you prefer it."

"But I don't prefer it. A fresh start, remember, Abbie. We need money."

"There's always money."

"Yes, there's always money, but *we* don't always have it. The world is going to end anyway, don't you always say? Sooner or later? Some rancid little stream isn't going to make it or break it."

She went to sleep as far from him as their bed allowed, but when he woke a bit after three—he could never sleep well after drinking, unlike Sarah, who could, after a few, pass right into a deep eight hours and wake in the morning without ever remembering that she'd laid down—he found her arm across his chest. She snored quietly. He touched her hair.

Several days afterward, he met Phil and Veronica for the hearing. Harrow greeted him in precisely the same way as the last time they'd met, an aggressive handshake and a rough smack on the arm. "No cold feet, Rabbi?"

Abbie shrugged. He actually found Harrow pleasant in an appalling way; the man's awfulness was genuine to a degree that most people's politesse was not. "I suppose I'm not averse to a little creative dissembling," he said. "For the benefit of all and the good of the order."

"Good," said Harrow. "Great! The good of the order! Ha! This guy. Anyway, it's because financing depends on approval here. Lord only knows, no offense, we don't want to build this crap with our own money."

"No," said Abbie.

"How's that little wife of yours?" asked Harrow, who was the sort of man untroubled by a phrase like that little wife of yours.

"Champing at the bit," Abbie said.

"Hmm," said Harrow, but Abbie didn't catch it.

The Zoning Board met in a WPA-era office building on Ross Street in Downtown Pittsburgh between the stained exterior of a judge-and-lawyer dive called the Common Plea and the groaning rusted steel trestles supporting the on-ramp to the Liberty Bridge. The hearing room on the first floor was a hazy combination of faculty lounge and prison cafeteria. There were maps of city neighborhoods on the walls, all of them hanging that one degree off level that might as well be upside down. Witnesses and attendees sat in rows of plastic chairs. The committee sat at a long wooden conference table oddly placed in a corner of the room rather than front and center. A window unit air conditioner blew warm air that smelled of something like power steering fluid. The board members were mic'd, but the microphones didn't work. They were largely unintelligible to the audience, with the exception of Joe Termini, the chairman, who sounded as if his muffler had rusted off. A framed photograph of Mayor Caliguiri hung offhandedly on a pillar that occupied, for no particular reason, the exact middle of the room.

The board refused to release the order of testimony and comment for its hearings based on an obscure principle—Joe Termini had inherited this principle from his predecessor, who'd inherited it from his, and so on back into the hazy prehistory of the modern city. Termini, a former officer of the United Steelworkers local who'd campaigned for the mayor and been rewarded with this sinecure, had no interest in the origin of the principle, only in the practical application of it. He viewed the discharge of his duties as something between fatherhood and the attendance of midnight mass on Christmas: better done than not, but best not to dig too deeply into the particulars. Harrow and Abbie arrived early, discovered they were the eighteenth out of nineteen applicants for adjustment, and retired to the back of the room to share a newspaper and, in Harrow's case, to smoke.

Interestingly, Joe Termini's younger son, Eddie, would become, not quite a dozen years later, the youngest mayor in the history of the city. Popularly known by his initials due to a series of unusual weather events that were popularly, if briefly, interpreted as UFOs, Eddie was primaried out of a third term after it was revealed that he and his chief of staff, Jonah Kantsky, a man nearly fifteen years his senior, had been having an affair. Both of them were married to women at the time, Kantsky ostensibly happily, Eddie Termini rather less so. The young mayor was supposedly involved in the diversion of federal funds to his own ends and enrichment as well, but the grand jury disbanded without bringing charges. Pittsburgh, by then, was no less than a model of urban redevelopment, no longer a city of browns and gray concrete, but of green and glass. People like Isabel's new boss, Barry Fitzgerald, flew all over the country, extolling its virtues—high tech, politically progressive, increasingly diverse. This was the city that Isabel moved to when she left New York, a promised land if you didn't happen to be a New Yorker fleeing a far grander Babylon and your far worse mistakes. But although the city had had a woman mayor by then and would surely have tolerated an actually and openly gay mayor, it could not, even in the early twenty-tens, abide the idea of a *secretly* gay mayor who was also the *younger* man, with all that that—correctly or incorrectly—implied. As for the UFOs, they turned out to be ball lightning, just another bit of wild weather in a world where the whole climate was going mad due to human stupidity and avarice. But Veronica Mayer was right: it was, and remained, a city of hypochondriacs, and what is a conspiracy theory if not a form of hypochondria?

Abbie quickly lost interest in the newspaper. He tried to pay attention to the applicants who preceded them, but these applicants and the various witnesses for and against their petitions had to approach and sit at the table with the committee, and with the exception of Termini's occasional booming pronouncements—*You sher about that? Is this gonna be frame or mason-airy? You been up the Permits desk yet?*—the proceedings were muted and incomprehensible. He stared through the windowpane above the air conditioner on the far wall at a riveted girder supporting the ramp and overpass. It was covered with graffiti tags that he tried unsuccessfully to decipher. It was hot and he'd been convinced to wear a suit. He felt the unsettling beginnings of dampness around his collar. He was much thinner then, but still prone to sweat. He wore, as ever, his collar open.

Since coming to Pittsburgh, the vision from the temple had repeated itself twice—or, it would be more accurate to say, he'd had similar, related, but distinct visions. In the first, he found himself back in the field. This time the corn was high, taller even than he was. He walked between the rows. The stalks and leaves had an unpleasant, waxy quality, like the wet skin of an apple. The sky was no longer clear, but overcast, and there was a sense that it has just rained, let up, and was preparing to rain again. After a few hundred yards, he emerged from the corn onto a long, rocky embankment that led down to the edge of the familiar highway. The highway, which appeared abandoned in his first intimation of it, was now busy. Cars and tractor-trailers flew in both directions, and the air was full of the confused dopplering of engine sounds. He looked to his left and saw the deer again. It wasn't alone. It had a fawn beside it. The fawn saw Abbie and froze. The buck stepped forward, as if to interpose its body deliberately between Abbie and the child. Abbie raised his palms in a gesture meant to indicate harmlessness and openness, but the movement, though deliberate and slow, alarmed the buck. The buck made a sound between a cough and a grunt and exhaled loudly. Abbie felt surprise; he didn't know deer could vocalize. The sound was a warning call. The fawn sprang away down the embankment. It reached the highway. A fuel tanker's horn blasted across the field. When the tanker hit the fawn, it seemed nearly to explode in blood and viscera. Abbie mouthed, Oh no! He turned. The buck was gone. This was when he woke.

In the second version, which was briefer and more terrible, he was the buck. He was standing between the field and the highway. There was a fawn beside him. The fawn belonged to him, but his consciousness had no language and therefore no sense of possession, only a yearning that was like a hunger with no possibility of ending. He saw an animal step out of the corn. The animal was strange; it walked on two legs, like a bird, and had two other legs that hung at its sides. It seemed impossible that something so upright could move without falling over like a dying tree. The animal was strangely furred on its head and covered almost everywhere else with something that was not fur. The wind carried its scent to him; the scent was horrible, sweet and strange. The weird animal lifted its upper arms. It was terrifying; it was a thing outside of all other things that he had ever seen. He called to the fawn. The call had no meaning, but it contained within it an urge that he had to give from his own body to the fawn's body. The fawn received the urge and acted. Then he saw it was an error, although he had no sense of error except a vast, dark disquiet like the presentiment of a drop in pressure that he might have felt before a storm. There were other immense and strange animals on the hard strip of land below them, stampeding in every direction, herdless and wild. The fawn ran into them. He would have gone down there, but he couldn't think; he could only flee; the yearning hunger of possession broke open inside of him and impelled him to leap faster and faster. The razor stalks tore at him. This was when he woke.

When at last their turn came, Harrow slapped his shoulder and said, "Go team." A secretary lazily distributed folders full of MH Partners LLP proposals for their development tentatively to be called Greenview-on-Frick.

("We really ought to consider changing that name?" Abbie had suggested.

"It's a great name!" Harrow protested. "What's wrong with it? It's classy!"

"It sounds like some sort of moldering collection of half-timber huts. It sounds like it's inhabited by a gaggle of catamite hobbits."

"Abbie," Veronica said, "we discussed this."

"I don't know about Carmelite hobbits," said Harrow. "But I know classy.")

Abbie had acceded to the name largely because he had no better suggestion. And in fact, he was surprised to find that it wasn't even an altogether terrible plan. The land was scrubby and overgrown, but it was ideally perched on a high outlook with the six hundred wooded acres of Frick Park behind it and the river below; it afforded a nice view of the Homestead High Level Bridge, and from certain spots on a clear day you could see down the river in the other direction as far as the top of the Thunderbolt at Kennywood Park. The old Homestead Works on the other side of the river was a ruin, a rotting monument to a lost economy, but there were already rumors that the city might annex the whole thing with Superfund monies, tear it down, and build a shopping complex. When Veronica had first described the project (*in broad strokes*, in Harrow's words, *a view from 30,000 feet*), Abbie had imagined a lazy subdivision full of sidewalkless streets curling back on themselves and stuffed with cul-de-sacs as if a den of Ouroboroses had been infected by a plague of commas, but the layout she'd finally shown him wasn't actually terrible; it obeyed, more or less, a logic of blocks, with a central avenue and a small, albeit inevitably weedy and sure-to-be unused park in the center. Its flaw was straightforward. If it were to be built, it could not be built on forty-degree inclines. The whole hilly plot would have to be leveled. And there was nowhere for all that land to go but over the last hillside and down the steep slope into the gully of Nine Mile Run.

It wasn't, strictly speaking, a matter for the Zoning Board, and the hearing, officially, was to approve the new street layout and the request to reclassify the newly divided lots as residential (a mix, specifically, of R1 RSD-2 single family detached low density and

RST RSA-3 single family attached multi-unit medium density), but the planning commission, at that time headed by a shambolic attorney by the name of Lou DiPresta, known colloquially as Tee-Time Lou, would approve anything as long as the City Traffic Engineer signed off (and the City Traffic Engineer always signed off, lest he find himself having to read what he was signing off on). And the planning commission, at the time, permitted no public comment. Meanwhile, the Pennsylvania DEP and DCNR had no jurisdiction within the city limits under the Home Rule Charter unless a project presented a "grossly negligent and demonstrable danger to surrounding communities or a manifestly intentional violation of the Commonwealth's laws of Environmental Protection and/or the Conservation of Natural Resources"—a standard so impossibly high as to have never once been applied successfully since the revision of the Home Rule Charter laws in 1972.

The Zoning Board, by contrast, and much to the dismay of Joe Termini, had been obliged to conduct all of its hearings publicly subsequent to various minor apocalypses of urban planning in the fifties and sixties, most especially the razing of the Lower Hill District to make room for the Civic Arena. There had also been the destruction of the East Liberty commercial corridor; the old neighborhood center had been imprisoned in a peripheral boulevard that might as well have been a moat. The city had built a gaggle of obscene public housing high-rises along that same periphery, only to add to the impression that the neighborhood had been redesigned as a Bastille in which to imprison Dangerous Black People. Termini was of the general opinion that if only the preceding generation had wised up and given the Blacks some meaningless and superficial gestures of respect for their historic quarters of the city, then they'd be making a lot less fuss and trouble now. Instead, everyone went in with bulldozers and a barely concealed language of sanitation, and as a result Joe Termini—who didn't, he was quite certain, have a racist bone in his body—was forced to endure a weekly pilgrimage of half-informed ministers and community leaders (he pronounced this phrase, every time, as if it were encased in flashing quotation marks) peddling a furious and often befuddling form of civic discontent.

But it wasn't just the city's dispossessed African-American population, who, even Termini would admit, "had some pretty goddamn legitimate gripes." Since the Zoning Board began working in public, it had become the main forum for any aggrieved citizens who couldn't get a letter to the editor in the paper and couldn't get their dumb state rep to return their frustrated calls. Most of their grievances had exactly fuck-all to do with zoning. They complained about police and they complained about their neighbors putting the trash out on the wrong day and they complained that the storm drains backed up into their basements. They complained about the mayor and the city council and the small claims court judges and the magistrate who upheld their sons' DWIs when he'd only had a couple and he just forgot to turn on his headlights is all. They believed that the government had closed the steel mills and the coke plants. They took these same complaints to City Council meetings, too, but council didn't have to conduct its business in public; their meetings were bread and circuses; their decisions were already made before they trundled out of their chambers. Joe Termini had two black women and one red-diaper Jew on his board, all political appointees like him, and they wouldn't hear of working behind closed doors. (In his opinion, they weren't much for working, period, but then, neither was he if he was honest about it. Twenty years in a mill and then ten years as Business Agent of the Local listening to mill workers bitch that the mills were closing was all the work he intended to do in a lifetime.) So here he was, conducting group therapy for people with nothing else to do in the middle of a weekday but express their vague discontent. "Don't you fucking people have jobs?" he wanted to shout; sometimes he did shout it—never in meetings. "Oh Joe," his wife said. "Put a sock in it. Have a beer."

"Phil," said Joe. Harrow and Abbie took seats at the table.

Behind them, a group of well-meaning citizens led by a thin man with wire glasses angled for chairs, but Termini held up a thick hand and said, "Gentlemen, ladies, please. Grab some seats in the front row over there. We'll get to you when we get to you."

The thin man made an indignant sound between a laugh and a gurgle and led his troupe to the spot Termini had indicated. Termini rolled his eyes in a gesture of friendly conspiracy at Harrow and Abbie.

"Hey, Joe," said Harrow, "nice to bump into you."

"Yeah, we gotta stop meeting in these disreputable type of joints." He winked at the nearest board member on his left, Tonya Weston, who made a point of treating Joseph Termini with the same benign indifference that an old cat shows the big dumb dog with whom she's shared a house for most of her life. "Who's your friend?" Termini asked.

"Joe Termini, Abbie Mayer."

Termini threw a half wave across the table. "Mayer? So you're related to this guy's boss." He grinned at Harrow.

"Partner," said Harrow.

"I'm just giving you a hard time, Phil. Christ." This time Termini offered the wink to Abbie. He grinned. "We all know who's got who by the balls, though, don't we?" He laughed: a bark.

"She's my sister," Abbie said.

"I can see the resemblance," Termini replied. Abbie seemed to wince, and Termini wondered if he'd taken the comment as some kind of Jew thing. "I don't mean like a Jewish thing," he said.

"No," said Abbie.

"Gentlemen," said Zeb Rosen. Rosen was a criminal defense attorney by trade who'd wormed his way onto the board through some mysterious favor to Mayor Flaherty back in the seventies and who'd clung to the seat ever since. Caliguiri could've gotten rid of him but had seemed to find some indefinable use in having "a man of the left" on the board. He was short, fat, and diabetic, which made him temperamental in vague relation to his blood sugar level, and he made a vicious pain-in-the-ass of himself at every hearing, even though he inevitably and invariably cast his vote with whatever majority Termini managed to cobble together. This made him an effective ally, and Joe hated the feeling that he was indebted to the man.

"Yeah, all right," Joe said. "Let's get started." He glanced at the binder in front of him. "Okay, let's see, uh, Madam Secretary, you ready?"

Bernice Brownlee glared at him from the far end of the table. "Mr. Chairman," she said.

Fuck her, he thought. She cast dissenting votes into the record just to fuck with his preference for unanimity and took lousy minutes.

"Ohhhhh-kay," he said. He put a pair of small glasses on the end of his nose. Fuck getting old. He said, "Okay, in the next item, we are, uh, considering the proposal by MH Partners LLP for—uh, is this projected?" He glanced behind him. It was the previously reviewed project, a new circular driveway at a private school in Shadyside. "Can we get the transparency right?" he called toward the back of the room. A skinny young man in a suit that was too big for his chest and too short for his long arms rushed over and futzed around with the projector. The site plan appeared, crooked. Joe drummed the table. The kid straightened it.

"Okay, okay," Joe began again. "The proposal by MH Partners LLP to reclassify as, uh, varying residential a parcel . . . excuse me, parcels, contiguous parcels, which are currently . . ." He trailed off and turned a page over and back again. He looked toward the back of the room again. "Barry, what the hell is this stuff currently?" There was light laughter in the room. The same poor kid shuffled through a stack of papers.

"Uh, sorry, Mr. Termini, Mr. Chairman. Currently mix of Limited Industrial and, uh, some Specialty and some currently un-zoned."

"Yeah, okay," said Joe. "You get that, Madam Secretary?"

"Yes, I *got* that."

"Okey doke. So, all right. Phil?"

"Thanks Joe." Harrow touched the knot of his tie. "So, we request and petition the committee for these re-classifications. I won't list them, as they are enumerated in the submitted packets, which, I believe, you've all had time to review."

"With a magnifying glass," Joe interrupted and laughed.

Harrow laughed. "Right," he said. "Diligently. Ahem. So, you can see we propose a modified block-and-artery street plan with a central avenue corridor. There is, um, also a few spots where we wish to either convert to Specialty or retain current Specialty zones for the purposes of semi-public green space. That's, by the way, the 'Greenview' of our project plan title. In any case, we ultimately propose to build a total of 105 townhouse and 103 separate single-family housing units. That will be in three phases over an approximately four-year period commencing with the, well, the commencement of the project. Uh, we will connect with the current city grid at Old Brown's Hill Road on the southern extension and Forward Avenue above Commercial Street on the northern side. Connect to city sewers, storm drains, utilities, et setra et setra."

"Great," said Termini. "Well, any questions from the board before we approve? That's to say, vote?"

"Mr. Chairman!" It was the thin man with glasses.

"Yes, listen. Public comment comes after."

"How," the gentleman insisted, "Can public comment come *after* the decision?"

"He's right," Brownlee said. "*Mr.* Chairman."

"Christ," Termini muttered.

"Ask them about the leveling!" The man shouted. "The earthworks!"

"What's he talking about?" Termini looked at Harrow.

"Joe?" Zeb Rosen waved his hand weakly. "It's in the proposal. The, uh, the, uh, the, uh, property, uh, currently, uh, is, uh, consists of a series of small hills and gullies on a ridge-like formation above the, uh, Nine-Mile-Run stream. The plan requires significant leveling."

"So what?" Termini turned back to Harrow. "Don't tell me you're gonna dam up the damn crick?" He laughed and stuck out his tongue.

"No, no." Harrow affected a look of shock. "Abbie, here, is, well, here to explain."

"And Abbie's expertise?" Rosen asked, removing his own glasses and rubbing them absently with his tie.

"Abbie," said Harrow, "is one of the foremost environmental

architects in America, a pioneer of Earth-friendly construction and design techniques. His resume is—is supposed—to be in the packets as well."

"Not in mine," said Rosen.

"Not in mine," said Carl Sefchek, a member of the committee who'd strolled into the room and taken a seat only a minute before.

Termini shook his head. "Barry!" he yelled.

"Sorry, Mr. Chairman. That must be an oversight. We'll get that corrected."

"*You'll* get it corrected. Well, look. I'll take Phil on his word. Abbie, you're the foremost whatever you are. *Et setra.* Tell me why this is kosher."

"Well," Abbie said, feeling, as he often felt, an itch of prescient dissatisfaction at what he was about to say, remembering, also, his sister's admonition that he must sound smart but not too smart, expert but not abstracted, forceful but not prideful, competent but not uncomfortably so. "You will actually see that the detailed plans include a very detailed and sophisticated water and runoff remediation plan. It is true that we intend to level much of the property, and some earth will be moved onto the hillside on the left bank, I suppose it would be, of the stream in question. But, I should point out, that this hillside is currently covered with a variety of what we would call invasive species, that is to say, it is mostly weeds, and the streambed itself, though adjacent to maintained woodlands of Frick Park, is, well, frankly pretty blighted. This is not a pristine babbling brook, in other words. If anything, the increased outflow that will result from the natural runoff from our properties will improve the stream's present condition."

"He sounds like a foremost what-have-you to me," said Joe.

"Nine Mile Run deserves to be restored, not turned into a drainage ditch!" the little man shouted.

"It already is a drainage ditch," Harrow snarled back.

"Let's have some order," Joe said. He looked down his nose. "Phil."

"We"—the man indicated his small coterie of citizens, women in loose-fitting clothing and men in jackets that had seen better days; Termini sighed—"demand that this committee table approval of these plans pending a thorough environmental study."

"Uh-huh," Joe said. He glanced at his watch. "That's really a matter for the planning committee, and, uh, Tonya, you're the expert. Would you say that that falls within our purview?"

"Not at five o'clock, Mr. Chairman."

"Good, then. Let's put it to a vote."

"But we object!" the man said. "And you are obligated to address—"

"Gentlemen, ladies." Abbie stood up and turned toward them. He spread his arms in a manner he felt to be vaguely ecumenical. "My name is Abbie Mayer."

"We know who you are," spat a woman with remarkably flat hair. It was unfair, Abbie thought, that the most well-meaning people were so often so plain, as if the development of conviction had, in some manner, sapped the vital energies that would otherwise have gone into their physical selves, leaving them with the half-formed indeterminacy of children. A child's awkwardness was fortunately a passage rather than a destination. Abbie considered that he'd been awkward himself.

Another woman called him a sell-out. He glanced at her. She wasn't unattractive. Well, maybe that invalidated his hypothesis. He realized his glance was turning into a stare. He fixed his gaze just above them, as he'd learned to do when speaking to a crowd. "If you know me—know who I am, in any event—then you know that I, too, am a man who believes that the ecological impact of our society, our species even, is a matter of great import. But . . . let me give you an example, a metaphor. I'm not sure if any of you are religious men or women. One day, I was sitting in temple on Shabbat. I think of myself as spiritual in the broadest human sense. And I was looking at a beautiful stained glass window of Moses leading the Israelites out of Egypt, and you will recall that in that story, too, in Exodus, there was a sort of parable of environmental catastrophe, that is to say, the plagues. And God— Adonai, we call him, as Jews—spoke to me. Don't be nervous. I don't mean I heard voices. I only mean I imagined a particular image, saw it, *envisioned* it, you might say. And I happen to believe that God does not speak, but rather, that He puts into our hearts the knowledge of that which He *would* have said. So, what I saw was a green hill, covered in trees, and a stream flowing down the slope, and a deer, a male deer with antlers. Now, I had been reflecting on this very project at the time, and what else could that have been but a vision of Frick Park and a stream, restored. What I am trying to tell you is, if you know who I am, will you not believe that I believe, fervently, that we might both build this beautiful housing development—no, this *neighborhood*—amidst the trees, and also see the stream restored down there in our urban forest, our jewel of a park that reminds us what this city was before there was a city here?"

Abbie thought it had come out rather well. The bespectacled man regarded him curiously for a moment, a look Abbie recognized from a vacation in Italy, when he'd addressed waiters and hotel clerks in a language he was certain was Italian. Then the man leaned around him and addressed Termini directly: "Mr. Chairman, we *strenuously* object."

"Noted for the record," Termini told him. "We'll even add the strenuously part. It'll be very descriptive. Now sit down. Everyone. All right. We don't need a motion, as this project was already accepted for review. So, aye, for me. Approve."

"Aye," said Rosen.

"Aye," said Sefchek.

"Aye," said Weston.

"Aye," said two more committee members who'd been reading a newspaper.

"Nay," said Brownlee.

"The ayes have it, five to one," said Termini. "God bless America. Meeting is adjourned." There was a noise from the back. Termini glanced up. "What?" Barry signaled with his hand and waved a packet of paperwork. "Oh, shit. One more item?" Termini glanced at his watch. Already, the party was rising in the back. He waved them down. "Well, we'll just table that until our next meeting in"—he looked at his watch for no particular reason—"two weeks' time." He rose and walked out before they could protest.

· · ·

Afterward, in the Ross Building lobby outside of the hearing room, where a layer of dust or grime on the windows gave the late afternoon light the quality of a detective novel, Harrow and Abbie were on their way toward the exit when Barry, the young assistant, called them briefly back. He'd hurried out of the hearing room and was out of breath from the exertion. He carried a cardboard accordion file held closed—possibly held together—

with a thick rubber band. One got the sense that this was his briefcase. His glasses had migrated to the top of his head, where his hair was already thinning. He was in his late twenties. He had, Abbie thought, unusually long arms and unusually short legs, like an orangutan. Harrow had been in the middle of telling Abbie that he may have laid it on a little thick with all that God and religion stuff.

"Mr. Mayer! I'm sorry. Have you got a moment? Just a moment. And Mr. Harrow as well."

"Well—" Abbie began.

"Just a moment."

"Sure, okay. Phil?"

"Sure, okay."

Barry steered them gently out of the main lobby and into a narrower corridor between two banks of elevators, whose old brass doors rattled when they opened and closed, which they did rarely. Like municipal offices everywhere, everything moved placidly. Even the dust in the beam of sunlight from the narrow window above a wilting potted tree seemed lethargic.

"More private over here," Barry said.

"Yeah, okay." Harrow caught Abbie's eye, but Abbie shrugged. They had nowhere to be themselves. It was the end of the day. Harrow had already suggested, before the hearing, that they could duck into the Common Plea after it concluded. "It's a lawyer bar," he'd explained. He winked. "Long on the pour."

"Mr. Mayer, first, let me say that I'm an immense admirer of yours. Really. When I was an undergrad at UB . . . uh, the University of Buffalo, I heard you give a talk at the school of architecture. I was in the studio . . . the fine arts at the time, but my interests were always more in design. It was a fascinating lecture, truly. Very moving and also a little frightening. I wondered if you thought things were really so dire."

Abbie tried to remember what he might have said in Buffalo four or five years ago, but it was fruitless. His talks hadn't changed much in substance from year to year, but he had learned to pitch them with varying degrees of apocalyptic fervor depending on his audience. If Buffalo had been at the university, in front of students, then he'd probably predicted something like the end of the world.

"I think things are likely to become fairly dire," said Abbie, "but one does occasionally exaggerate for effect."

Barry appeared pleased by this answer, laughed, and almost clapped. "I would imagine so. Nevertheless, I was very moved by the talk. The image you describe of seeing Phoenix from the air and having this revelation was quite, uh, powerful. Quite powerful."

"Abbie is a powerful guy," Harrow said with his customary assault on Abbie's shoulder. "But we've really got to be, you know. We've got another appointment."

"Yes, yeah. I'm sorry. Just a moment of your time. Yeah? Okay, thanks. So, first of all, let me formally introduce myself. My name is Barry Fitzgerald. I'm a, well, in addition to working on the staff of the zoning board here, I'm also a graduate student, uh, writing my dissertation currently, about the development and decline of rust belt cities at CMU. I mean, I'm at CMU, the cities, well, you know. And, I'm sorry, this is . . . I don't mean to be awkward. The thing is, I'm setting up a, a sort of institute, a non-profit, sort of, think tank. At CMU. Affiliated with, I should say. I've already filed for 501 status, actually! But what I'm really looking for, from a fundraising and capacity perspective is, frankly, guys like you."

"Like us?" Harrow was amused.

"Well, like Abbie in particular. In an advisory capacity. As a board member, perhaps. And contributor."

"So you're asking for money."

"Well yes, that, too."

"I'm more of a March of Dimes kind of guy," Harrow told him. "And I toss the occasional check at some venerable cultural institution on the knife edge of dying off."

"The thing about the Future Cities Institute, though—that's what it's called—is that we're going to be doing really vital work, I can assure you, and in your field. And I would love to meet, you know, formally, to go over a sort of prospectus."

"A prospectus," Harrow said, "is for investors. There is a promise of return. Nonprofit *institutes* are charities. Now, I like charity. Looking out for your brother man and all. But I only *give* to worthy causes."

"Mr. Mayer," Barry turned to Abbie. "Your work was actually a major inspiration. Your early design principles. For instance—"

"Yes, Barry. Thank you, but I'm familiar with my own principles, design and otherwise. I'm afraid that I have to go with Phil here, on this particular question."

"But." Barry looked at the ground briefly. If he was not then, as he later became, a consummate raiser of monies, he had, even in those early and awkward days, that imperturbable fake earnestness that pursues every no as if it were yes. "What if"—he lifted his head—"what if there were a return."

"Young fella," Harrow said, "distribution of proceeds to shareholders is emphatically not what a non-profit does. I'm not sure what they taught you as an *art student*"—he pronounced it to be certain that it was heard, and understood, as *faggot*—"but in business school, you learn that kind of thing is illegal."

Barry pressed on. "Joe Termini is screwing you."

Harrow perked, and he and Abbie exchanged glances again. "How?"

"Well," Barry said, seeing, even then in his inexperience that he had set the hook, "that would be confidential information of the zoning board. I would be, I'm afraid I am unable to divulge that information at this time."

"Goddamnit." Harrow began to raise his voice. Abbie put a hand on his arm. He went on, measured but angry: "What the fuck are you playing at? I'm a good friend of Joe Termini—"

"I've got no doubt that that's the case. But seeing as he is, despite this great friendship, about to completely screw you . . ."

"Phil," Abbie said. "Let's have a word."

They walked across the lobby leaving Barry alone between the elevators. Harrow seethed. "That little shit. He's full of shit, too."

"Be that as it may," Abbie said.

"Be that as it may nothing. Joe Termini is a friend of mine."

"A friend, really?"

"An acquaintance. Whatever. Are we debating it?"

"In your friendship. Acquaintanceship. Would he, I believe the phrase is, screw you?"

"No. I don't know. Sure! I mean, it is what it is! You gotta spend money to make money. But what the hell, here? What's the angle?"

"Well, sounds like we can find out if we give this kid some money."

"Fuck that little cocksucker. Did you hear his voice? Queer as a three dollar bill. He can suck my cock, how about that?"

"Phil," Abbie said.

"Abbie, do not give me that look. We're partners now, but you're still just a hired hand on this one."

"Listen, how much can it cost? I bet you can throw him a thousand bucks. I'll go on his board. That's probably less than you spent on dinner the other night. If it's bogus, cancel the fucking check! Rat him out to his boss! But listen, Phil. If it's not bogus, maybe it works in our favor. And *plus,* this is more up your alley than mine, but isn't he basically offering to be our paid guy on the inside of the zoning board? That's got to be worth something."

"You're a scheming motherfucker," Harrow said.

"Well," said Abbie.

"No," Harrow said. "That's good. That's a compliment. But you're the one he's wet for. Let's see if you can Jew him down to five hundred. I'm not made of money."

"Jew him down," Abbie said.

"Aw, come on Rabbi. You know what I mean."

Five hundred and a handshake commitment from Abbie Mayer proved more than enough, and it was only two martinis and a half dozen cigarettes later, in the dim back bar of the Common Plea, surrounded by loud judges and attorneys, that Phil could bring himself to talk about it without just muttering, "God *fucking* damnit!"

They'd called Veronica from a pay phone, and she'd joined them about one and a half martinis in. She got a gin and tonic, and Abbie explained to her the broad outlines: that there had been, for more than a decade vague talk of building a new highway connecting Pittsburgh and Uniontown, a shot in the arm to the rusting mill towns of the Monongahela Valley and the declining coal towns that nestled against the Laurel Highlands farther southeast. This project, whose economic and topographic complexities hinted at a price tag in the many billions of dollars, had been, for most of those ten years, hardly even a dream, just a whisper of a fantasy that an occasional businessman or state legislator would murmur to himself after the twisting, poorly lit, stop-lighted haul up Route 51, a bare forty miles from Uniontown to the Liberty Tunnels that took a half an hour longer than it should have. And Pittsburgh, in those days, was hardly booming itself. Its population was old and falling. And what would a highway do? And who would pay for it? But Reagan had recently lost the Senate, and Jack Murtha in the House had talked to Robert Byrd from West Virginia, who said he'd support the thing if they extended it to connect to Morgantown, and all of a sudden there was the prospect of an open spigot of Federal money with all of its attendant benefits.

"What's that got to do with Greenview?" Veronica asked.

"Well, apparently, that's where they intend—assuming this thing happens—to have the interchange with the Parkway." Abbie shrugged. "So we buy the land, we prepare the land, then they eminent domain it out from under us to build an on-ramp. It has a certain poetic simplicity. I'm almost impressed."

"God fucking damnit," said Veronica.

"That's what I said," said Phil.

"The thing is," Abbie said, "I don't think it's all bad."

"How the fuck do you figure that?" Phil clinked his glass against the bar as the bartender passed. "Another, darling."

"Well," Abbie said, "You guys have worked on road projects before."

"Tangentially," Veronica said.

"And don't we know . . . You two still know what's her name down in Fayette County, no?"

Harrow looked up.

"Sherri Larimer," Veronica said.

"Sure. And she's some kind of raja down there, yeah? And how much can land cost in Fayette County? So why don't we get in on this highway business and build some beautiful housing divisions . . . neighborhoods, out in the country." Now Abbie shrugged. "Away from the crime and poverty of the city. I *did* see a highway in my vision, after all. Who are we," he grinned, "to doubt the will of Hashem."

"Abbie, you're out of your fucking mind," Veronica said.

"But still," Harrow said.

"No," said Veronica. "Yeah, I agree. A drive wouldn't hurt."

5

"I don't stand next ta no juice!" Isaac laughed. It was a punch line, but in her spinning and slightly goggle-eyed state, Isabel felt unequal to the task of connecting it with whatever joke preceded it. There were just the three of them left in the apartment, and only the two of them were still awake. It was late—3:30 AM, if the restored brass clock on the white wall could be trusted; and Isabel wasn't certain it could be trusted—but not yet so late that she felt too badly about it. It was Friday night, or Saturday morning; she told herself that she had no particular need to be anywhere in particular anytime soon. The truth was that Isabel was five years past an easy recovery from a night that tipped past two in the morning. Knowing this didn't dissuade her. Quite the contrary.

They'd been drinking, and they'd done some lines. Isaac's speech and grin had that fluttering and effervescent quality that accompanies youth and cocaine, like a face caught permanently in the moment before a hiccup. Isabel had the rictus of approximate fun that occludes the face of people over thirty who are acting as if they're still under it. Isaac's hand rested on the little white ball of a dog beside him. He was telling another story about going to school in Uniontown, in Fayette County. He'd been telling them all night. The vice principal who had, over twenty years, stolen nearly thirty thousand dollars in quarters from the pop machines and pleaded, when he was finally caught, that he'd only ever intended to use the money to pay for his own kids' college tuition. The boy rumored to have a glass eye, the result of tossing a can of aerosol hairspray into a bonfire at a party, whom they'd tormented in dodgeball, thinking they might knock it loose. ("Did he really have a glass eye?" Isabel asked. "Got me," said Isaac.) His junior-high English teacher, Mr. Krupp, who'd taught them about acrostic poetry using the word DIVORCE. The life-sized statue of a mustang—the high-school mascot—commissioned, built, installed, and then unveiled rearing back from a horrified crowd of athletic boosters, its gigantic mustang dick presenting between its fiberglass legs.

Why, Isabel asked, didn't his parents send him to private school in Pittsburgh?

"Sarah," he said. "My mother," he added, as if it weren't clear. "My mother believes in public education. She is, in the immortal words of David Bentley Hart, a fideist who thinks she is a rationalist."

"Who's David Bentley Hart?"

"He's an Eastern Orthodox Anarchist Monarchist. God. Don't you read the internet?"

"Okay, well, I guess not, then. How can an anarchist be a monarchist? No, actually, never mind. And what's the thing about juice?"

"*Jews.*" He over-articulated his pronunciation. "Jews. My peoples. In the local vernacular pronunciation. Your peoples too, from the look of that nose."

"Ouch."

"No, it's a lovely nose. Take this with a grain of salt from a huge fag, but there's something hideous about women with cute little noses. A woman should have a real nose."

"Thanks, I guess. And my father was, I think. Jewish."

"You think?"

"Well, he and my mom weren't married. I mean, I never knew the guy."

"Oh. That's nice."

"Most people say they're sorry."

"Yes, well," he said.

There was a silence. He did a line, throwing his head back theatrically.

"Anyway," he said, "Later on, I told her that I wanted to invite Adam Martens to my bar mitzvah, and she was like, 'The boy who said the thing about Jews?'"

Isaac made his mother sound like a bubbie from some long-lost Borscht-belt comedy act, even though Sarah sounded precisely like the American neutral product of Fieldston and Wellesley that she was.

This was the night that Isaac decided he and Isabel had really met. He may or may not have believed that. He may have forgotten about the dinner at Barry's or just chosen to efface it in favor of a better story. He may have believed both stories. He was untroubled by contradiction. This was how they'd got there:

After a couple of months at her new job, and at Barry's urging, Isabel bought a house, an old Sears catalog bungalow on a steep hill in Edgewood, with a wide porch and big eaves and a vegetable plot at the back end of the backyard that she never got around to planting. When Barry had first suggested that she buy a place (they'd been on their way back from a tour of Fallingwater), she'd laughed at the idea. She could imagine shouldering a mortgage in

Pittsburgh, where houses were old and beautiful and cheap, but with only a paid-off used car and no prior equity and no down payment, how would she ever get a loan? Barry shrugged and said she should at least take a look. The next day he and his own old real estate agent hauled Isabel around from property to property, each of which, the agent assured her in a brittle, Virginia-Slims voice, would be "perfect for a girl like you." None of them was perfect for a girl like her, least of all the Sears & Roebuck bungalow on the steep street in Edgewood; it was perfect for a married couple twice her age, academics or administrators, their children already adults and long-since departed, its walls to be heaped with books and its kitchen to be stuffed with too many sets of stemware; so of course, she fell in love with it. Isabel always loved inappropriate things. "But," she told Barry, "I can't make an offer. It isn't 2006. I'll never get a mortgage."

"Oh, honey," he said, meaning that she didn't know what she was talking about. She permitted him to condescend to her about money out of a vague sense that she might benefit from his unearned paternalism. Like a lot of gay men his age—and how he'd have hated it to learn that Isabel considered him a gay man of his age—he evinced a desire to take a younger girlfriend under his wing. For a month she protested weakly that the whole idea was impossible. By then he'd called Art Imlak, and Imlak had called someone at Dollar Bank, and then a chirpy young woman called Isabel to tell her that she'd been pre-approved and just needed to fill out some paperwork.

"But how?" She'd asked Barry, because it would flatter him to pretend not to answer.

"Oh, honey," he'd said, meaning she didn't have to ask.

Living in Pittsburgh had been—so far—revelatory; it was the

first time since her childhood that she'd had a house in which she wanted to live. The New York apartments with Ben had been designed for photography, not for habitation, and every piece of low, lovely furniture suggested that perhaps you might not want to sit on it. Before that had been smaller apartments, shared houses, dorms. She'd long since lost the habit of just coming home after work, and she'd forgotten how to stay in at night. There were plenty of work dinners with supporters and visiting professors and local developers and politicians, and there was a dingy bar still hanging onto business between new Thai restaurants on Braddock Avenue in Regent Square, just a ten minute walk from her house, where she'd occasionally drink a decent scotch for which they charged only four dollars. But in those early months in Pittsburgh, if she wasn't working or having a drink after a working dinner, then she was mostly at home on the big white slipcover couch she'd bought for the living room, sipping wine or tea, reading and writing emails while some or other movie played on the TV across the room. She'd made a few friends: a married pair of architecture profs who had her to dinner from time to time; a lawyer named Brad who took her to openings and fundraisers and probably wanted to date her more seriously but spared them both the embarrassment of ever bringing it up; Barry, of course; improbably, his—and now her—real estate agent, who'd seemingly sold a house to everyone in the city. But these weren't *friends* friends; they were all nice and charming and wanted her to stay in the city, and she wanted to stay in the city, too, if vaguely and in an unsettled way. The truth was that, six months in, she loved only the house. Everything else was only fine. She still thought about Ben and stalked his Instagram account, which was as professionally architectural as ever, simultaneously hoping for and dreading a photograph of humans that never appeared.

She called her mother a couple of times a week, as much out of boredom as out of love. Of course, she'd told her mother about Abbie right after that first dinner that first night at Barry's, and her mom still asked her if she'd spoken to "that man."

"No, mom."

"Good."

"I've met his son, though."

"His son," Cathy said. "My God."

. . .

Then Jenny and Penny, two graduate students whose unlikely rhyming names had compelled them to become friends, who both interned at the Institute while pursuing nebulous graduate degrees at Carnegie Mellon and texting a lot, invited Isabel out. She'd hardly spoken a dozen words to either of them. She never understood why they'd decided to hang out with her. She assumed that they saw her as a charity case, not yet old enough to be irredeemably adult: de-radicalized and conventional beyond all hope of reform or reprieve, but not yet over the hill, not yet socially irredeemable, maybe a little tragic in her inexplicable flight from a more glamorous life in a bigger city, but still *from* that city, and therefore in some way cool enough to bother with. They were, in their mid-twenties, still able to believe that a city offers up a career rather than the other way around. "We're going to, like, this party," they said. "It's like this dance party. It's pretty gay. Like gay gay, not gay gay. Anyway, you should come, maybe? It's definitely the best party in the city. And The Eastern Front is playing. He's a DJ from like Miami or San Diego, I can't remember which. It's kind of late though, but maybe we'll have drinks and then go over? If you want."

If Isabel never did quite puzzle out why the girls asked her to go out with them, then she was even less sure why she agreed: maybe the same loneliness that she was keeping secret from herself; maybe the boredom; maybe it was that, with the exception of one more dinner—this time at Imlak's downtown apartment— she hadn't managed to find any coke since she'd come to the city, and a gay dance party seemed like a good opportunity.

The Imlak dinner had been quite an absurd event involving many cases of Veuve carelessly wasted on mere drunkenness. He occupied half a floor in a new downtown skyscraper above the Fairmont hotel, an immense glass cube like something out of a science fiction movie, a near but imaginary future. Afterward, after most of the other guests had drifted away, he'd sidled up to her, grinning his rich man's grin, and asked her if she wanted a blast. This time she said yes, and he beckoned her to follow him toward a distant bathroom. He locked the door behind them and removed a small jewelry box from a drawer in the vanity. There was a lot of coke in the box. They did a few blasts. "Good, isn't it?" he said. It was rhetorical. Arthur Imlak wasn't a man who required that you agree with his opinions; he assumed you already did.

"I get it from Miami," he told her. "Same guy who sells to Donatella Versace."

"Oh?" Isabel said.

"I can only do very high quality coke," he told her. "All the shit they put in the rest of it makes my feet swell up."

"Uh-huh," she said. It was good coke, and she really felt it.

"Well, all right," he said. "Back we go." He slapped her ass collegially, as if she'd just made a game-saving tackle.

"Arthur," she warned, although she was also grinning, mostly because she felt obliged to.

"Don't worry," he said. "You're not my type." But he patted her ass again as he unlocked the door, and she wondered if it was true.

Jenny lived only a few streets away from her in Regent Square, so she picked Isabel up, and they headed off to get Penny. Jenny drove a mid-nineties Nissan that sounded as if it had only three working cylinders. It was a 5-speed, which seemed like an affectation, but then, Isabel thought, Jenny was affected. Penny lived between Oakland and the Hill District, on a narrow street above Schenley Farms that cut horizontally across a steep hillside with houses on the uphill side and a near-vertical drop on the other. It was one of the charms of the city: no one in his right mind would have built a city there. The street was so narrow that even Jenny's tiny car could barely pass the cars that were parallel parked on the other side, all of them with two wheels canted onto the sidewalk or sunk in the mud of someone's front yard. The city of Pittsburgh insisted that all such streets must remain two-way. Just before they got to Penny's place, another car came from around the bend, and they sat for a while in a standoff, the other driver and Jenny gesticulating at each other through their respective windshields until the guy in the other car, with one last baleful laying-on of his horn, backed up and pulled into a little driveway to let them by. Jenny cranked down the window to scream a parting "*fuck you!*" as they passed. Isabel later learned that the car belonged to one of Penny's roommates. "He's from Ohio," Penny would say, as if it were something slightly distasteful. "He's a grad student."

"*You're* a grad student," Isabel reminded her.

"Yeah," she said, "but he studies, like, chemistry or some shit."

The dance party was a monthly affair that was called Midnight Mass. First held two years earlier on an actual Christmas Eve, an orphans' event for students and hipsters who didn't or couldn't go home for the holidays, it had started out with a fairly even mix of sexes and genders and sexualities before becoming, as these things did, a largely, though not exclusively, gay event. Isabel generally found the prospect of bouncing into a gay club with a bunch of other women as slightly gross, a bit past its sell-by date, but they'd assured her that this was in no way officially a gay event and there would be plenty of women and possibly even a few straight guys. The party, having spent its first year migrating around the city, was now regularly held in the vast backroom of a bar in Lawrenceville, a recently cool neighborhood of old row houses and steep, parallel streets. The bar had been an Owls or an AmVets or some such in a past incarnation. The front was narrow and fetid; it smelled as if it deserved its own nature documentary in which some giddy Brit would describe the fungal agriculture of an immense colony of ants. The back was big enough to hold two basketball courts, although a low, stained ceiling gave it a perversely claustrophobic feeling. It smelled mostly of the many varieties of human sweat.

It was loud. The girls had been nattering about the event on the way over. "It's always a different theme," they said. "Sometimes there are, like, projections. Once they actually tried to fill the place up with, like, bubbles, but they used the wrong kind or whatever, like, the wrong kind of bubble mix I mean, and they had to cancel that one because it just turned into a bunch of absolutely disgusting water on the floor."

In their defense, by the way, these were two very smart and intellectually competent girls; it's only a sign of the democratization of the era that everyone sounded like exactly the same idiot. But being told how good a party is going to be is like listening to someone explain the punch line of a joke, and Isabel was glad to be momentarily free of it. There was a jukebox playing a punk song that she recognized but couldn't place, and despite the party's supposed sexual provenance, the dudes actually drinking at the bar out front were a collection of thoroughly straight crust punks and bike messengers, the former in that sort of seventies bondage look that punks had adopted for whatever reason, the latter in short, cut-off jeans with elaborate tattoos on their calves. She socked this info away for later. Before Ben, she'd had a bit of a thing for bike boys: their silly hypertrophied thighs and skinny arms and hard asses. If she got sick of the party, then she could find one to take home, even if it meant convincing some half-fluent Uber driver to let them try to jam a fixed gear in his trunk.

The sound emanating from the back was something else altogether, a quirky, repeating cadence of deep, concussive beats. The bartender was a fat man with a red face and tiny ears who wore a Steelers sweatshirt and a Penguins ball cap. He had the bored efficiency of a real bartender. He'd tended that same bar since before the steel mills closed, but he viewed the changing clientele with the utter equanimity that was also the mark of his vocation. He called women sweetheart and men brother, and he drank Bacardi from a plastic cup throughout his shifts.

Isabel bought a round and followed the girls through the narrow hall that led to the party in the back. They were stopped at the doorway at the far end by a familiar boy on a tall stool behind a cocktail table. There was a cover. The boy was taking cash. He was wearing something skintight that, when Isabel got closer, revealed itself as cycling bib with no shirt. She didn't even recognize him as Isaac at first. With his chest exposed, he was even more painfully thin and pale than he'd seemed that night at Barry's, but there was also something about his prematurely

gristly arms and the tight, smooth skin on his chest that inti-
mated strength and elasticity. It was only when he spoke that
she recognized him from Barry's dinner all those months ago.
Isaac had a remarkably specific voice, surprisingly deep, like a
lot of skinny guys, but with a choked, sinusy timbre that made
it seem higher pitched than it was and a habit of overly correct
pronunciation—like, for instance, how he'd say, "*Tyoosday*." If
he recognized Isabel, he didn't give it away, but he was smiling,
and he shouted something that she couldn't hear through the
noise. "What?" she yelled. She leaned closer.

"Nice shoes!" he yelled back.

"Thanks! They're Louboutin."

"I know," he said. "I'm going to give you the good shoe discount!"

Isabel raised an eyebrow and he said, "That means you can go
in for free."

"Thanks!" she screamed.

"But you have to tell me your name for your sign," he said.

"My sign?" she replied. She noticed that beside the cash box
the table was spread with construction paper and markers.

"Yeah!" he yelled. "It's a *dance* competition! You have to get
a sign so we can tell who you are! I'm the judge! Well, one of the
judges. The *preeminent* judge! The Russian who ruins the Americans' chances!"

"That's okay," Isabel told him. "I'm good!"

He just grinned and shouted again, "What's your name?"

"Isabel," she shouted back.

"Isabel," he repeated. He laughed. "That's gay!" he said.
"G-H-EY gay!" Then he scrawled MISS HELL on the paper and
checked a list beside him and added the numeral 76 beneath it.

He pinned these to the back of her dress and sent her and her vodka into the party.

An hour and several drinks later, she found herself on the edge of an undeniable and now surely unavoidable drunkenness. There was another bar in the back room, and that bartender, a guy about her age with a little gut beneath a black tee-shirt and a pair of impossibly large, round glasses clinging to the last inch of his handsome nose, slung under-mixed drinks in her direction and seemed to enjoy her company. He was surely gay, but they were among the few people in the room over thirty, and they shared the quality of being *amused*. He asked her name and told her that his was Ryan. He asked where she'd come from and where she worked and where she lived and who she'd come with.

Isabel said, "These two girls. Penny and Jenny."

He laughed—he laughed at everything, funny or not—and said, "Oh, those two."

"What do you mean?" she asked him.

"Nothing," he said, and he laughed again. Unlike Isaac, whose constant giggling seemed fraught with significance, Ryan-the-bartender's seemed as specifically meaningful as a dog's happy bark. "Just—*those* two." A younger man came to the bar and they exchanged a quick kiss and a whispered conference before the man went back to the party, where he was dancing against a tall boy with the alien beauty of a fashion model. Ryan the bartender said that was his boyfriend, Steven.

"The tall one or the short one?"

"The short one."

"Who's the tall guy?" she asked.

"Oh, I don't know his name," said Ryan. "He's a model or something. I guess that probably means he works in a store." He grinned and laughed some more. "We're gonna fuck him tonight, I guess." He laughed again.

Then Jenny and Penny can over, sweating and loose-eyed, and grabbed Isabel's wrists and pulled her toward the dance floor. "I'll be back!" she shouted over her shoulder.

"Sure thing, Miss Hell," he said.

Isabel danced with those girls for a while in a sea of boys with mustaches, all of them by now in various states of undress. There were no straight guys back there; the straight men were out front drinking shots of whiskey and smoking American Spirits and glancing at the hockey game on the one little TV. It kept occurring to her that she ought to ditch these girls and try to get laid, but Jenny kept saying, "I love this song, I love this song," no matter what the song was, and Penny kept grabbing one boy after another and pulling him over to dance with them and saying, "Oh my god! It's Aaron; I love Aaron!" or, "Oh my God! It's Kwame; I love Kwame!" and these boys did or did not dance with them for long. The dancing was largely bobbing up and down, up and down, because the place was by then too crowded to do much else. Then Isabel was spinning around through a small clearing, and Isaac was standing behind her with a drink. His mouth moved.

"What?" she yelled.

"Vodka tonic!" He was near her ear. "Ryan said you were drinking vodka tonic."

"Thanks!"

He'd slung the suspenders of his bib off. He shook his head and hopped up and down and sweat hit Isabel's face and mouth. "What do you think of my party?" he screamed.

"Your party?"

"Mine!" he said.

She didn't answer because he didn't seem to expect her to answer. They danced together for a while, then he drifted over to Steven and the model and insinuated himself between them. The model was rubbing his jeans-bound dick on Isaac's ass; Steven rubbed his head in an oddly feline gesture on Isaac's chest. Isabel glanced toward the bar, where she caught Ryan the bartender looking in their direction and laughing some more. He was at the end of the bar, standing beside another somewhat older guy, broad-shouldered and severely handsome, dressed unlike anyone else in a crisp and expensive-looking white shirt, the cuffs unbuttoned and loose around his wrists. He was not smiling. He was not laughing. He appeared thoroughly self-contained.

Around one-thirty, the music trailed off and Isaac was up on the stage kissing the DJ on the lips and announcing the winners of the dance competition; he said, "Second place, MISS HELL!" and Penny said, "Oh my God! It's you! Izzy!" as if Isabel had really won something. (In fact, she'd won a bar tab worth twelve bucks, which she used to buy drinks for Jenny and Penny.) After the announcements, the music resumed, quieter and less singularly insistent now that a body move in time to it, and people began drifting out. By last call, Isabel was back at the bar, where Ryan introduced her to Sawyer. He asked if they'd met before. "I feel like we've met before," he said.

Isabel said that they hadn't.

"Sawyer is Isaac's boyfriend," Ryan explained.

"Yes," Sawyer said. "In a manner of speaking."

"A manner of speaking," Ryan repeated, laughing.

"What manner of speaking?" Isabel asked.

"Ours," Sawyer said, "is a very modern relationship."

"What does that mean?"

He didn't answer. "So what do you do?" he asked instead.

"Oh," she said, "I work for a nonprofit."

"What nonprofit?"

"It's called the Future Cities Institute."

"Oh, sure," he said, "Barry Fitzpatrick's outfit."

"Outfit. Ha. You know him?"

"Isaac knows him," Sawyer said.

"Isaac knows everyone," Ryan said as he passed carrying a bag of trash.

"He knows a lot of people," said Sawyer. "This is true." He seemed to roll his eyes no matter what he said.

Isabel asked him what he did.

"What do I do or where do I work?" he replied.

"Either."

"I'm just giving you a hard time," he told her. He glanced once over his shoulder, then he observed with a droll smile that Isabel looked like she could stand to sober up.

"Haha," she said.

"No," he said, and then he repeated himself more deliberately. "You could stand to *sober up*."

"Ohhh," she said. "*Sober* up."

Ryan was returning to the bar, and Sawyer flicked his head toward wherever he'd just returned from. Ryan nodded, and Sawyer led Isabel past the bar and past some restrooms and through a door and down a flight of smooth-worn creaking basement stairs and through the tubular underground tangles of a tap system and past cases of booze to a little office set up in a corner with an old metal desk and some filing cabinets and a couple of computers and a little white dog sleeping placidly on a little plaid doggie bed.

"Cute dog," she said. The dog raised its head and made the sort of contented peep that only a small and immeasurable happy dog is able to make and curled back about himself.

"Whose is he?" Isabel asked.

"She. Isaac's," Sawyer told her. "Nominally."

They did some blow. It was not as good as Imlak's. "So what *do* you do?" Isabel asked him.

"I'm a doctor."

"You're too young to be a doctor."

"Please, I'm thirty-four."

"What kind of doctor?"

He was folding up his packet of cocaine. "Addiction medicine," he said.

"Shut the fuck up."

"My mouth to God's ears. Come on." He gestured toward the stairs. Back in the bar, the lights were up. Isaac was drinking a beer against the bar, while Steven and the model made out. Ryan was capping the liquor.

"Hmm," Isabel said. "I appear to have lost my ride."

"I sent them away," Isaac told me. "I told you were coming with us."

"You what?"

"Come on," Isaac told her. "*Il faut qu'on vive sa vie.* No one died from a little stranger danger. Sawyer, will you get my dog?"

"Where are we going?" she asked.

"Our place," Sawyer replied from behind her. "Come on. We'll give you a ride. We're just up the hill. I've just got to grab the little girl."

Isabel bent herself into the back seat of Sawyer's car. It was a small Mercedes, and she supposed then that he must really be a doctor—what a world, wasn't it, where a car confirmed an occupation? Isaac kneeled on the front seat so that he faced her while Sawyer drove home. The dog was in the back seat with her; it had pirouetted once and settled into a ball, immediately asleep.

"So Isabel," Isaac asked, "do you like to party?"

"I suppose I do," she said.

"Sawyer hates parties. Sawyer is seething right now, just thinking of all these people about to invade our domestic kingdom."

"He doesn't seem to be seething," Isabel said. She could see via the rearview that Sawyer had a crooked grin on his face.

Isaac sniffled. "He just hides it well. So, what do you do?"

"What do I do, or where do I work?" She replied.

"*Oh là.* I can see you two have been talking. Did Sawyer already offer you an amuse-bouche? *Il est tout comme toi,*" he said, laying his head briefly on Sawyer's shoulder. "*Il se comporte comme un adulte, mon copain, mais il aime faire la fête.* Do you speak French?"

"A little, and badly."

"When Sawyer first hit on me, on Grindr, he tried to show off by acting all bilingual, all because he lived in France for like four months when he was in college a hundred years ago."

"This is true," Sawyer said, his voice at once sardonic and affectionate. It was a question frequently posed by their friends: why, exactly, did Sawyer put up with him? There was the obvious: Isaac's age and strange beauty, but there was nothing especially sexual about their relationship; it lacked any sharp edge of carnality, suggesting far more immediately the habits and tolerances of a long-married couple. They reminded Isabel of her and Ben, two people locked into the inevitable aesthetic of their own shared life, characters who discover their story is not their own.

They lived in a big apartment in a new building near the intersection of Penn Avenue and Butler Street across from the bronze statue of a World War I doughboy that gazed forever forlornly toward downtown. It was a dull piece of corporate architecture— "Yuppie dormitories," Barry called them—the sort that got thrown up in six months in gentrifying neighborhoods and then leased off to a lot of Young Urban Professional types. Like Sawyer, Isabel thought. It surprised her to think that Isaac could live there; it seemed a little too drywall-and-mid-range-fixtures for someone of his background and apparent tastes. It turned out that Isaac did not live there, not technically, although he spent most of his time there, since Sawyer, as an adult, managed to keep food in his refrigerator and extra toilet paper under the sink. It was very much Sawyer's place, decorated very much as you'd expect from a mid-thirties gay yuppie making low six figures who, Isaac would tell you, had patterned his taste on the occasional design magazine tossed in with the yogurt and juices.in the checkout line at Whole Foods. Isaac often made fun of Sawyer's style behind his back. "His parents live in a four-bedroom colonial in a *subdivision*." He was a snob, but he was right about the genealogy of his boyfriend's tastes in art and housewares. Isaac had his own apartment in the city, a loft (owned by his aunt) that was almost uninhabitable due to his insatiable addiction to the acquisition of things: furniture, art, taxidermy, bolts of fabric, exotic houseplants (both living and dead), mannequins, costumes, and boxes and boxes of paperback books, which he never seemed to unpack or shelve. All of these collections were in equal parts wondrous finds and utter junk. Ironically, for all the furniture, he didn't even have a proper bed, just a mattress roll and pad that he'd lay out on the floor when he needed it, which was usually to say, when he was fucking someone other than Sawyer and wasn't able to do it in Sawyer's place.

The first time Isabel visited that loft, it was the middle of the day, and Isaac wanted to get stoned. "It's the middle of the day," she said.

"Yeah," he told her, "but it's Saturday!"

She did a lap. It was like walking into an insane Victorian curio. "I can't believe your aunt lets you wreck her place like this."

"Veronica's been crazy since all that shit with her girlfriend," he said. "She doesn't give a fuck."

"What shit with her girlfriend?"

"You don't know?" Isaac had a way of being astonished that people didn't already know things that they'd have no way of already knowing. "Oh man, wait till you hear *this*."

In Sawyer's apartment, on the contrary, everything was in its place, and the white rug aligned perfectly with the edge of the gray couch. They arrived and Sawyer made Isabel a cocktail. The dog trundled around her legs. She crouched and scratched its ears. "What's his name?"

"Hers. Moth," Sawyer said.

"Moth," Isabel repeated, rubbing his head. He gazed up at her.

"It was originally Behemoth," Sawyer said. "It was shortened out of either necessity or laziness."

"Nonsense," Isaac objected. "It's *still* Behemoth." He bent and took the animal's tiny, beautiful face in his hands. "He lieth under the lotus trees, in the covert of reeds and fens, doesn't he now, doesn't he? Yes he does. Yes he does."

The dog promptly lifted its little back leg and pissed on the floor.

"Moth!" Isaac exclaimed.

"Christ," Sawyer said. "I'll go get some paper towels."

"Aw," said Isaac. "Shall any take him by the eyes or pierce through his nose with a snare?"

The bartender and his boyfriend and their model showed up. A few girls arrived and eyed Isabel suspiciously before settling prettily onto a chaise. The bar boys drank beer. Isaac had a laptop open and kept starting songs and then changing his mind about them. "Honey," he told Sawyer, "give everyone a little of the stuff, yeah?" They all did a little of the stuff, and Isaac settled on some music with a hint of North Africa or the Eastern Mediterranean. They all sat around looking at each other. The boys and girls from the bar were posing and biding their time, hoping for more free drugs. Isaac and the model made faces at each other. After a short while, the boys and girls realized that they weren't going to get any more coke out of Sawyer and departed when their drinks were dry. Isabel made a move to go with them, but Isaac, who was perched on the arm of the couch beside her, put his hand on hers and said, "*Ne pars pas, toi.*" He raised an eyebrow, and she nodded as imperceptibly as she could.

Incidentally, this was one reason to suspect that Isaac *did* remember Isabel from their previous meeting. They'd shared a few words in French at Barry's house those several months before. It was true that Isaac spoke French indiscriminately, maybe most often to those who had the least idea what he was saying—this was all part of his own affectation. But he seemed to know that Isabel would understand him. This, in any case, was her theory.

Sawyer came back from shuffling their other guests out the door. He yawned. "I'm going to bed," he said.

Isabel was surprised he could be tired after doing coke.

"Drugs make Sawyer sleepy," Isaac said. "Everything makes Sawyer sleepy."

This seemed to be a subtle dig, but Sawyer laughed and touched his hair and said, "It's true." And then he smiled and said, "Even you, honey," at which Isaac frowned. He offered Isabel his hand as if they'd just concluded a very productive business meeting and told her that it was very nice to meet her. Then he went to bed. Isaac got beers and then pulled out more drugs, which he'd given no prior indication of possessing. There was nothing, Isabel thought, as squirrely as a cokehead.

"You and Sawyer are cute," she said. What was it that compelled her to say such a thing? (She could hear Penny or Jenny shrieking, "Omigod you guys are so kyoot!" over the pulse of imaginary bass.)

"I'm cute-ish," Isaac said. "Although I am also very weird-looking. Sawyer is handsome. He's my silver fox."

"He's not that old! He's younger than me. And also, he doesn't have gray hair, which I think is a prerequisite."

"Oh, he does. You just have to get up in there. It's hidden."

"It's well hidden. You guys remind me of me and my ex. My ex and I? Me and my ex. Ben. He was older than me as well."

"What did he do?"

"Architect."

Isaac raised his eyebrows. "Oh dear, how dire."

"Well," Isabel said, missing his point, "Sawyer's a doctor!"

"I like a man who brings home the bacon." He sprawled across the couch, his legs dangling over the armrests. "It suits me."

They did a little more blow and sipped at their drinks, and Isaac played absently with his phone, a habit that Isabel was old enough to find rude and a bit off-putting, although at three-thirty in the morning, what did social graces matter, really, besides which, she knew that her sentiment was hopelessly out of date. They yammered at each other about trivia. He asked her about her work again. That was the night that he described Barry as post-gay, in fact. Isabel asked him about Arthur Imlak. "My father hates him," Isaac said, "which endears him to me."

"Who, Arthur or your father?"

"Oh, either. It depends."

"Why does your father hate him? By the way, I'd really, really love to meet your dad someday. I'm sure you're sick of hearing it, but he's really . . . well someone I'd like to meet. God, sorry, that sounds so creepy to hear myself say. I admire him, is better. He, I mean, he practically invented my field."

Isaac had produced a cigarette from somewhere and lit it. He rolled his eyes. "My father is bonkers, but I guess I'm glad you find his bullshit convincing. I guess it beats the alternatives. We've all got to believe in something. He hates Imlak because Imlak fucked him over in a property deal or something. Don't ask me the details. I'm a spoiled rich kid, so I have no idea how money works. If Dad hasn't stolen everything out of my trust yet, I intend to fritter it all away on utter frivolity and die penniless and young. I'm thinking thirty-eight." He exhaled.

"I'm thirty-eight," Isabel said. "I guess that means you just gave me a compliment."

"I do the strangest things when I'm not paying attention."

"What was this deal?"

"Fuck if I know. I *do* know that my dad actually made a bunch of money in it, which is the irony, I guess. I suppose Arthur made a lot more subsequently, and I suspect that this pissed Abbie off, because he believes himself to be uniquely entitled to the best fortune available in any given situation. Do you know that he originally was going to name me Dieudonné. Thank God, my mother objected—bless her heart, she remains just subtly racist enough to tell him that it sounded Haitian. Personally, I love Arthur. He helps me out, money-wise, from time to time, whenever Abbie's gotten shady about my accounts. He takes me sailing down in Florida sometimes."

"The Shale Boat," Isabel said.

Isaac laughed. "Yes," he said. "How did you know? I call it the S.S. Minnow, on account of the fact that Arthur sounds like Thurston Howell, III. He has a house right on Tampa Bay. Sawyer and I were down last fall. Arthur knows all the Navy generals down there and got one of them to bring over an actual working cannon from some battleship from the War of 1812, which he fired out of his front yard into the bay during a party."

"Does the Navy have generals?" she asked.

"Whatever they are. I told Sawyer we ought to try to get one of them to fuck me and get it on tape. He's such a prude, though. Anyway, it was *à cause d'Arthur* that we moved to fucking Uniontown in the first place, I guess. See, he owned the land where we built The Gamelands, which Abbie was desperate to get his hands on, and there was some kind of complicated switcheroo. I sort of imagine them like the contract scene in *A Night at the Opera*. Of course, in the deal, Mom and I also get hauled down to Fayette County. Fayette Nam. The *not-what-we-were-promised* land. Well, I mean, I wasn't born yet, but you get the idea. Everyone else at the Uniontown Country Club had a father who was either a lawyer or owned a car dealership, and they'd all been playing golf together since they were white-wine-pickled zygotes riding along in their mothers' foursomes. Abbie, in one of his vain attempts to buy me off, got me golf clubs when I was like twelve. Well,

I managed to talk Marco Larimer into letting me blow him in the woods behind the seventh green, but then he told his mom, who was—is—a fucking county commissioner. She took it well enough, because she's a criminal and criminals, even the prejudiced ones, have a higher tolerance for perversion than ordinary decent folks, thank God. And she didn't tell my parents either. But you know, word got around, and no one wanted to talk to some little homo."

"Sorry."

"Eh." He shrugged. He told her his stories about going to school in that old coal town. "So, like, it's the first day of school at Laurel Highlands Jr. High School, and I've made it through half the day without getting noticed by anyone, really, or so I think, which is a minor miracle for me. Then I'm back at my locker right before lunch and this kid—Adam Martens, locker right next to mine for the next six fucking years—looks at me and says, 'Mayer. I heard yinz were *joosh*.' I mean, I don't understand what the fuck he's talking about. I just look at him. I'm probably not even five feet tall at the time, and he's this big rangy redneck from North Union Township with fuzz on his lip and a bad buzz cut that makes him look like he's got a bold future going on a shooting spree on an army base after a bad tour in Afghanistan. He's scowling at me and I don't know how to respond, so I say, 'I'm sorry?' About as dorky polite as I could possibly be. I mean, what am I, Maggie Smith? And he says it again. 'I heard yinz were joosh.' Oh, fuck; I realize he's saying *Jewish*. He's like a legit Fayette County boy. It's another dialect, I swear. And this is like the worst nightmare, because I really just have no experience with actual anti-Semitism. I mean, it doesn't really come up in elementary school, except the one time I had to explain to the class what a menorah was. I was all prepared to be called a fag, not a Jew! So I just sort of nod and mumble, 'Yeah, I'm Jewish.' 'Huh,' he says. I realize he's come to his locker to get a can of Skoal. He puts in a dip, then spits in this disgusting cup that he's got in his locker. 'Well,' he says, 'I don't stand next ta no juice.'"

"God," Isabel said.

"He wasn't so bad in the end. He came to my bar mitzvah, believe it or not. Anyway, he's in jail, now."

"What for?"

But he was bent over the table again, and when he looked up, he said, "So, you really want to meet my dad, huh?"

"I mean, yeah. Yes."

He nodded and handed her a rolled ten dollar bill, which Isabel waved away. Then she thought better and accepted. It was late. They talked for a while longer. She left, despite his offer of a couch, drove home, foolishly and recklessly. The next morning, when she came out onto her porch to get the paper, because she was the sort of person who still got a paper, believing, probably incorrectly, that it represented some kind of defiance of history's dumb momentum, she saw that she'd parked with two wheels in the grass and a headlight, still lit, now dying, nudging into the hedge below the porch.

6

While Isabel wanted to become friends with Isaac, she expected to become friends with Sawyer. They were closer in age for one thing, both professional, neither prone to Isaac's preferences for excess, or in any case slower to recover from excess, more prone to regret it, and therefore less assiduous in its pursuit. And that's what seemed to happen at first. They fell into an easy rapport with each other. Of course, to become friends with a couple is necessarily to imagine where your loyalties will lie when they split up. Isabel was especially prone to ideating the inevitable dissolution of any human unit with more than one member. It presented an obstacle, because what she really needed was to contrive a way to meet Abbie Mayer, and Isaac was the obvious path.

Sawyer and Isaac were perpetually on the rocks, and both of them exquisitely calculated their behavior to embarrass and frustrate the other. Isaac was transparently unfaithful, although his infidelity was often more a matter of style than action, while Sawyer, though he wasn't shy about betraying a degree of annoyance, typically reacted to Isaac's deliberate provocations with a blithe unconcern that infuriated the younger man. "I've never understood jealousy," Sawyer told Isabel. It was just the two of them at dinner two months after they'd met. "It seems," he said, "to reveal a lack of self-confidence."

Isabel protested that you could be confident but could still experience jealousy.

"Maybe." He put on a face as if mulling it over, but he was just composing his next sentiment. "But I still think that in a relationship, a romantic one, I mean, jealousy is really just anxiety about sexual performance, which is, I don't know, sort of related to that social anxiety that some people have where they're always worried that someone, somewhere, might be having more fun than they are at any given time." This observation about someone, somewhere was a mantra of his. It often showed up in a talk he gave on addiction.

He was close to being right. Sawyer was very convincing in person. It was only when you got away from him that his insights started to smell like exquisite rationalizations. Isabel believed him when he told her he felt no anxiety about his boyfriend, but later, when she'd known them a bit longer and thought about it a little more, she saw that he was *very* jealous of Isaac, and that his ostensible indifference was a form of hard-willed self-possession that was nearly imprisonment. Sawyer deserved better, she thought, and she later regretted that circumstances didn't permit them a real and durable friendship. They did remain friends online for a few years, until she discovered that she'd been unceremoniously blocked and dropped and defriended. He'd moved to California to work for a medical technology start-up whose name was a common noun, phonetically misspelled and randomly capitalized. He ended up making a lot of money. Sawyer was smart in a mechanical way, but he preferred to avoid thinking too deeply, and these were the people who tended to get rich.

Isabel did ask him that night at dinner what it was that he really saw in Isaac. "Besides the obvious," she said.

"What's the obvious?"

She sipped her wine. "Looks and all that," she said. "To be honest."

"I think you'll find that if you really look at Isaac, he's not that especially good looking."

"He's striking."

"No, that's true. But it's not the same thing. Anyway, he's very good at sort of tricking you into thinking that he's cute. Maybe he's beautiful, but in an ugly sort of way. I've always found him ever so slightly grotesque when I really look at him."

She said that seemed like a terrible way to talk about your boyfriend, although once more, she thought he was very nearly right.

"Is it?"

"To say that he's ugly? Yes. I mean, whatever else we might tell ourselves, physical attraction is still a big part of love, isn't it? In the beginning especially."

"I didn't say he was ugly. And you're right. In the beginning. But our relationship has never really been about all that. It's always lacked a core of physical intimacy, actually. For someone who likes to fuck around as much as Isaac, he's actually pretty prudish when it comes to sex and requires a great deal of chemical courage to really get into it."

Isabel frowned. "So what do you see in him, then?"

"Need," he said, and he didn't elaborate.

. . .

Several weeks after their dinner, she complained to Sawyer that Isaac still wouldn't commit to introducing her to Abbie. Sawyer laughed and told her she was mildly obsessed. "I just want to meet the guy," she said too sharply. "He practically invented my field."

They were having lunch in Oakland. Sawyer's office was in a small research annex of the UPMC Hospital complex, and Isabel's was in a ghastly new Koolhaas-inspired complex on a rotten hillside at the edge of Carnegie Mellon, just across the ravine from the museums. Over curry noodles, he'd mentioned that Isaac had in turn mentioned that he did indeed want Isabel to see his father's last realized building, since she was, in his words, "such a precious *devotée*."

"Isaac hates it," Sawyer said, "but it's really pretty extraordinary. I mean, I'm a philistine where architecture is concerned, but it's very impressive. The kitchen, for instance, is built around this enormous rock that's been flattened off into an island. It's really something else, and the view is amazing. On a clear day, you can actually see the top of the Steel Tower."

"Right," Isabel said. "But he isn't following through."

"The thing about Isaac," Sawyer told her, "is that he only pursues projects that are authentic expressions of his own personal genius. He's like his Dad. If you just shut up about it, he'll eventually decide it was his idea in the first place, and then he'll insist. How do you think we ended up together?"

And so she shut up about it, and not long after he cornered her and insisted. They ended up driving to The Gamelands to spend a weekend in August. Sawyer was out of town, visiting family. Isabel left the office early on Friday. This was something she was still getting used to. People in New York, even in her own abstract and largely academic field, came in after ten but stayed late, often going straight from the office to their evenings out, whereas in Pittsburgh, the whole city seemed to rise early and then leave work at three in the afternoon. She'd never lost the habit of coming in late, but she discovered that she was still able to knock off whenever she wanted. Barry was usually traveling anyway, or else off begging some or other corporation for money and sponsorship. Isabel reported to him directly, and there was no one to mark her comings and goings, not that Barry, or anyone, would have cared when she came and went. She went home and packed a weekend bag: a dress, a pair of jeans, a black bra and a white bra and a sports bra and some running clothes just in case, a bathing suit because Isaac had texted that there was a pool. She bought iced coffee for the drive and then picked him up in front of Sawyer's place.

"You don't have a bag?" she asked.

"Nah, I've got plenty of stuff down there."

Almost immediately he asked if he could smoke in her car. She said no. He clarified that he meant weed. She said maybe once they were out of the city.

"No," he said. "You've got it backwards. City cops don't make traffic stops. Not for white people. They don't care. It's staties who'll get you."

"Oh really?"

"*Je te jure.* I'm a country boy."

Isabel shrugged her assent, and he took a little spring-loaded wooden case with a compartment for weed and a compartment for a one-hitter from his pocket and got stoned without offering any to her.

He directed her out of the city by following Carson Street along the Monongahela below a wooded hillside before cutting off on a series of steep roads that ran up through the gullies of Hays, a now-decrepit neighborhood of shadows and knotweed and foreboding hills choked with sickly sumac trees. Then they rolled up though the calcified remains of a prior round of sub-urban development. The Dairy Queens and car dealerships and shopping malls that once beckoned and drew people out of the city's core as it fell into disrepair had begun their own inevitable afterlife of decomposition, as lately people wanted downtown condos and sidewalk dining again. They passed the back end of Century Three Mall, so-named, Isaac said, because it once housed three hundred stores, but now held, "one Piercing Pagoda, a decorative sword shop, a vape joint, and a Penney's."

"I'm sure there's more than that," Isabel said.

"There used to be an Orange Julius," he replied. "Alas, the creative destruction of capitalism."

They turned onto Route 51, a lumpy highway Isabel did recognize vaguely, but just a few more miles down the road, he instructed her to merge onto 43, a toll road she'd never noticed.

"We're in Large, PA," he told her. "I love Large. There's a big local construction firm called the Dick Corporation that used to have its headquarters out here. The Large Dick Corporation!"

Isaac called 43 the road his father almost built.

"How do you mean?"

"Back in the eighties, early nineties, my dad and my aunt and this guy named Phil Harrow were in business together, and they were all planning to get rich off this highway, which was the biggest boondoggle in the history of the state of Pennsylvania. You know they spent more than ten billion on it? Mostly federal money." They were doing eighty and were the only car on the road. "Empty!" he exclaimed. "It was supposed to revitalize the Mon Valley and Fayette County, or anyway that was the excuse. Really, it was just a lot of greedheads siphoning money out of the government. Anyway, you'd have to ask Abbie the whole story. He still hasn't told me. All I know is that he fucked over his sister and her partner, her business partner somehow, and they don't speak to this day. Anytime she wants anything, my aunt I mean, she has to relay it through me, and vice versa."

"Family," Isabel said.

"There's family, and then there's my family. Anyway, this primordial act of betrayal made my dad rich, supposedly, and it also introduced his crazy ass to Uniontown, which is how he found the mystical magical location of our humble family compound. I will say it's good cycling terrain."

"You bike?" she said. She hadn't noticed bicycles or bike gear in either of his apartments. She'd assumed his dance-party outfit was just a sex thing.

"I used to. I loved it, but I find it difficult to sustain affections for very long."

"That seems unfortunate."

"Yes, well."

The road took them through several dozen miles of round hills and valleys full of dairy farms and little brick houses on long driveways. Every few miles, the hills grew a bit higher, the houses smaller, the American flags larger, until, upon being dumped off on the Uniontown Bypass, they were in the real foothills of the Laurel Mountains. Ahead of them, Laurel Ridge rose as a deep indigo wall, and Isabel thought, as she'd thought when she drove across the state in the opposite direction months earlier, of a wave on the ocean, although this time it felt as if she were on the shore, and the wide, undulating mountain was rushing in to sweep everything away.

"Home sweet home," Isaac said. "God. This place is so evil. It's amazing I survived."

"I think everyone feels that way about where they're from," Isabel said. "I mean, I grew up in New York and lived there all my life, basically, and all the young women I work with can't imagine ever wanting to live anywhere else, and even though I've only been here—in Pittsburgh, I mean—for a little while and still sort of feel like it's not really *my* place yet, the truth is that I also feel like I escaped from something."

"Yes," said Isaac a little impatiently. "But, I mean, really. It's amazing I *survived*. When we were still in school, me and my friend Jake sort of had this idea that there was a sort of evil presence under the whole town, you know, vaguely Lovecraftian, kind of a slumbering and insatiable and unnameable elder god. Well, not really unnameable. Jake decided that its name was Daroba, maybe because it sounded Egyptian to him? Honestly, I don't know. Anyway, we used to blame all the local weird happenings on his evil influence. Like when White Adam Martens went to jail for killing the old woman. 'Oh, Daroba did it.'"

"White Adam Martens?"

Isaac laughed. "God, sorry," he said. "I've told these stories so many times. I forget you're new. You should use that to your advantage, somehow. Something about you suggests that you've been here all along."

"I'm not sure how to take that."

"It's a compliment, more or less," Isaac replied. "So, there were two kids named Adam Martens in high school. One of them was black, so everyone called him Black Adam Martens. And the other one was White Adam Martens, who killed an old lady."

"That's awful," Isabel said.

"What? The black and white thing or the murder? He was this giant redneck, really, and if I remember right, he ended up going to the Vo-Tech for high school. That's where they dumped all the patch kids and trailer trash with disciplinary problems. We were actually friends, almost, in junior high. He picked on me for being Jewish, although I think he had a crush on me." He shrugged. Isaac thought everyone had a crush on him. "Didn't I tell you this?"

"Not the part about killing anyone."

"Well, I was pretty tore up, if you'll recall, on the night in question. Anyway, meanwhile, Black Adam Martens was this huge bully. The worst. They left all the black kids with disciplinary problems alone, on the theory, I think, that there weren't very many black people in the district to begin with. The whole county was only like six percent minority. So you can just imagine. Then poor Adam Martens—White Adam Martens, that is to say—ended up with a big Oxycontin problem, which is normal enough around here, and he and this older dude, whose name I forgot—something Polish-y that ended in -ski—they tried to break into some old lady's trailer to steal a bunch of Walmart gift cards. This is like right in the middle of the day, because they're idiots and also probably high. The old lady is watching TV, and how about that! Today is the one day she actually remembered to put in her hearing aid. I remember that particular fact was widely reported. She hears them, and *of course*, this being the *scenic* rural hamlet of Lemont Furnace, she keeps a loaded .30-06 under the kitchen counter for just such an occasion. She gets off a shot, which hits the older guy in the shoulder. He goes down. Adam Martens panics, grabs the nearest thing, which is a cast-iron frying pan, and knocks her fucking brains out. Got tried as an adult, too, poor guy. The worst part is that we all knew that Dumbasski or whoever was the ringleader, such as it was, and it was just bad luck.

Or it was Daroba, take your pick. A blood sacrifice to the ancient gods. So, now, ironically, Black Adam Martens would pick on you relentlessly, but if you ever tried to talk back to him, like, 'Come on, Adam, leave me alone,' he'd just shrug his shoulders and say, 'Hey, at least Black Adam Martens never killed nobody!'"

"That's terrible," Isabel said.

"That's Uniontown."

"Who's the other guy you mentioned?"

"Who? Oh, Jake? Oh, he's a friend is all. You'll meet him, probably. He still lives in Uniontown."

"And this Daroba is the monster in the woods?" she asked, smiling, forgetting that she'd decided not to indicate or intimate that they'd met that night at Barry Fitzgerald's.

"What?" said Isaac. "Oh, no. Daroba isn't *real*." And this seemed to Isabel to both answer and not answer the question.

They merged onto Route 40, the old Braddock Road. The young George Washington and General Braddock had followed the same road in reverse from the headwaters of the Potomac up over the Appalachians toward the French at Fort Duquesne, where they got their asses handed to them. Later Washington, the president, made it the National Road, one of the first great national works in that rough-hewn new Rome. After the Eisenhower era, parts of it had been widened into a four-lane highway, but it was never fit to become an interstate. It retained in its rake and bends the precipitous feeling of a real mountain pass, the kind of road you'd expect in the younger mountains of an older civilization. There were other even steeper and still narrower roads that also made that climb up Laurel Ridge—Hopwood-Fairchance Road, Stone Quarry Road, Jumonville-Coolspring Road, Mud Pike Road. Isaac used to climb them on his fleet, light little bike when he was a teenager with the unlikely dream of competing in a Grand Tour one day. He used to imagine that he was in the Pyrenees or the Dolomites even as pickups rattled past, too close, herding him toward the dangerous shoulders while the laughing girlfriends of the howling drivers yelled "fag!" at the skinny kid dressed in shiny Lycra.

Isabel's car protested even on the grade of the wider and more regular highway. She was a city-trained and casual driver, and she had only a hazy notion of what to do with the gears on an ascent. Isaac was telling her about the Cumberland Classic, a spring race that started nearby in Connellsville and rolled over a hundred miles of these roads into Maryland. The thought of hauling herself up such a road on a bicycle seemed absurd; the thought of doing it over and over for six or seven hours fantastical. But Isaac was almost rapturous in describing it, one of the few really unguarded moments in their whole friendship. "The closest a man can get," he told her, "to a female orgasm comes when you summit a really big hill." She laughed and asked him how he knew what a female orgasm felt like. "It feels," he told her, "like spinning a high cadence up a nine percent grade with the sun going in and out of the trees that are shading the road—first pleasant, just rolling along, then a kind of exertion that gets your heart up and your breathing a little faster like good exercise, then a period of tiredness that you have to think through or else you'll back off the pace and effort and finish without really finishing, then the last five hundred meters when you feel cold and hot all at once and think for the love of God, you're not actually going to make it, then, when you do make it, the Kundalini uncurls out of its resting place in the hollow of your pelvis and goes up your spine and out into all your limbs down to your fingers and toes and it breaks out through the third eye on your forehead and all your cells shudder all at once like all the strings bowed in one chord on a cello and then you're over it with sweat on your chest recovering on the descent on the other side."

She told him that he was off on the details, but it wasn't a bad description as far as these things go. In fact, she found it slightly uncanny, but she wasn't going to tell him that. He was already smug enough. But he caught her smiling.

The road passed a scenic lookout two-thirds of the way up the climb: a pull-off on the right side of the road revealed the narrow, beautiful valley between the Pine Knob promontory and the ridge. Isaac informed her that the area below was called Lick Hollow. He found this funnier than it was. At the top of the ridge was the old Summit Inn, a pile of white clapboard and dormers that called back to an earlier era of American travel. Its letterboard sign advertised STEAK, LOBSTER, and GOLF. They turned right just past the Summit below a billboard for Laurel Caverns, "Western Pennsylvania's Largest Natural Cavern Formations." Isaac, giggling, explained that the caves were owned by the family of a prominent local evangelical, Melvin Chislett, himself a former CPA who had, one April 15, experienced his Road-to-Damascus moment and converted from the sort of tepid, non-denominational, public Christianity that characterizes so much American public life to a full-bore, young-Earth, *sola scripta* apostle of the Good News. He took an online course, got ordained, and founded the Seed of Faith Full Gospel Church. Isaac described this congregation as the sort of Christians who are ambivalent about Jews but over-the-moon for Israel. He used that phrase, actually: "over the moon." It was another habit of his, an occasional anachronism in his speech. It had begun intentionally; then it became his nature and he stopped noticing. Chislett's brother-in-law owned the caverns. His brother, meanwhile, was the chief of police.

"Christ," Isabel said. "Who isn't related?"

"Only us. The interlopers. The immigrants."

They passed another sign for the caverns.

"They're really laying it on thick," Isabel said.

"When I was in seventh grade," Isaac told her, "we went on a field trip there in our natural science class. Our teacher was new to the district; I mean he was probably about my age now. And he didn't know any better. They explained to us how the Flood caused the caves."

"The *Flood* flood?"

"The one and only."

"What an education."

"We used to say it was one of the regular haunts of Daroba. You could really imagine an elder god getting a good laugh slinking around in the slimy, dripping dark, surrounded by cartoon plaques of Adam riding a friendly dinosaur in the Garden."

The Gamelands property was on the western side of the ridge, off a rolling road that traced the ridge's crest between Caverns Park Road and Mud Pike Road. It was marked only by POSTED signs on the trees and a small stone pillar that held the mailbox at the end of a long gravel driveway. The driveway descended into a small hollow full of ferns before rising again through the woods until it met the broad clearing where the house, or collection of houses, was at first barely visible, a suggestion of rocks or peaks rising nearly imperceptibly from the highest point of land ahead, where the meadow finished its rise and rolled down the sunset escarpment for a thousand feet to where the trees closed in again. The Mayers had two dogs, great, dumb, friendly, half-wild black beasts that could just as easily have been bears, and at the sound of wheels on the gravel, they came bounding out of the woods barking with the pure joy of creatures whose lives and senses are unencumbered by the rent-taking middleman of human intellect.

"Holy shit, they're like bears!" Isabel said, braking to avoid them and sliding in the gravel.

"They're my father's familiars," Isaac replied. It was, Isabel thought, the first time that she'd heard him refer to Abbie as "my father." (It was not, in fact, but Isabel had already begun to read the connection between Abbie and Isaac as both more and less fraught than it really was. Like most educated, literate people, she had a crude but persistent belief in a simple kind of psychology. She tended to underestimate the capacity of people to be actually cruel to each other while overestimating minor cruelty's effect.)

The driveway wound around the front of the house. It was a building that defied easy summary. It looked like a movie whose title you can't quite recall, an old teacher whose name you can't quite remember. The complex gave off the overwhelming sense of having been there since the beginning of time, and yet something equally suggested that a person could, with sufficient effort and knowledge, fold the whole thing into the bed of a pick-up and drive away. It was otherworldly in the way that this world's more extraordinary places often are. It had a Hyperborean quality to it, as if ancient astronauts had built it at the height of their hubris before cataclysm swept them away.

The drive spiraled to a dugout carport on the far side of the complex. The carport didn't appear to be connected to the rest of the buildings; they were integrated via a series of semi-buried, skylit corridors through the hillside. The parking, Isaac said, was his father's bitter concession to the necessity of driving up there in the first place. It seemed to Isabel that if that were entirely true, there would have been room for some number fewer than eight cars. They parked and followed a canopied path hidden by vines and a low wall to the entrance of what Isaac called The Children's House. "Ironic," he said, "since I'm the only child. You'll be an honorary child. Hopefully my mother hasn't sold the guest bed. She discovered eBay a while back, and honest to God, anything that isn't bolted down."

Below the drive, a series of terraces that traced the relief of the hill like the lines of an elevation map stepped a hundred feet into the meadow, cut through with gravel and brick walkways and patios and a long, chilly-looking pool surrounded by flagstones. None of it was in particularly good repair. The dogs wagged around their legs and sniffed their elbows. Isabel asked their names. "Leto and Lady Jessica," Isaac said. Isabel raised her eyebrows. "What?" he said. "Abbie named them. What can I say? He's a fucking environmentalist. He loved *Dune*."

Isabel shrugged. "The patios could use a little TLC," she said.

"Oh please," said Isaac. "Abbie should have named this place Deferred Maintenance."

She'd expected—unrealistically, she knew—that the Mayer parents would come out to greet them, but Isaac just let them into the kids' house, a self-contained residence: one large common area with a fieldstone floor covered in cowhides and a hodgepodge collection of not-quite-modern furniture, pieces reminiscent of a prewar Hollywood apartment or a preposterous lounge in a ratty interwar ocean liner. There was an open kitchen with white cabinets and bar pulls, very eighties. A beautiful stairway of granite and beechwood led to two lofted bedrooms overlooking the space below and, through the big front windows, the sweep of property and slope and town and hills beyond. The bathroom was set deep into the rear of the house, lit through clerestory windows on its front-facing wall. It contained a vast tub that was carved out of a rock formation. Isaac showed Isabel to her room. It had a bed—a rather spindly camp bed with a pilled, its-a-boy!-blue blanket.

"Well, I guess she sold the bed," Isaac said.

"This isn't original?" Isabel smiled.

"Kween," he said. He sighed. "You'd better take mine. It's built in, so I presume it's intact."

It was. It had a rootlike quality and appeared to grow out of the wall. "Isaac," Isabel said, "this house really is extraordinary. I don't know what to say."

"Girl, please. It looks like it was designed by a drunken elf. It looks like *Legend*."

Isabel decided it was best not to argue. People were generally forgiving of criticisms of their families, less so of praise. She walked to the railing at the room's edge and looked out. "That's Uniontown?" She pointed down the mountain.

"God's own creation. The U-T." He seemed, very briefly, as if he was going to cry. Then he laughed. "Okay," he said. "We'd better have a drink before I introduce you to the fam. Again, assuming *ma mère n'a pas déjà bu tout* le booze *avant de le remplacer avec de l'eau.*"

"Really?" Isabel said.

"You know the cliché about role reversal as parents and children age? In our case, the inflection point came early. Of course, they were already old when they had me. Abbie is seventy, you know."

"I wondered about that."

"Mom was on the verge of her 'change of life' as she puts it. I suspect fertility treatments, but then again, if that had been the case, you'd expect I'd have had a twin. Boy, that would've done wonders for my porn career." He saw her face. "I'm kidding," he said. "I haven't got the dick for it."

They went downstairs, and they found plenty of un-watered liquor in the kitchen. Isaac poured her a vodka soda, a scotch for himself. They sat in the weird speakeasy set of his living room while the sun settled somewhere below the house, and the surrounding woods threw long shadows over the terraces and lawns.

"When I was a kid," Isaac said, "all my friends thought this place was great, because, you know, I basically had my own house, and Abbie and Sarah never gave a shit about what we did, so my friends could come up here and drink and get stoned and whatever, although of course, Abbie was always weird about the monster in the woods."

"I feel I'm missing the metaphor," Isabel said. She had a vague sense, which she would have been embarrassed to articulate, that some or other of our comforting superstitions must be true. Nothing so absurd as a singular god, of course, but a hazy half conviction that we went on in some form after we died, that nature as people understood it was an insufficient explanation for all things. But on the rare occasions that she gave it any thought, she convinced herself that none of it was literally true; these things only stood in, in the end, for everything that we did not, as yet, understand.

"No metaphor," Isaac told her. "Like, really. There's really a monster in the woods."

"Like what?" she said. "Like a Cyclops? Like Bigfoot?"

"God, no. Lol." He pronounced it *lawl*. "I mean, you weren't here a couple of years ago, but there was this amazing drug bust up north of Pittsburgh, this sort of notorious local meth dealer-slash-scifi author. Anyway, the cops roughed him up pretty good, and even though he got convicted, he filed a civil suit claiming police brutality blah blah blah. Never went anywhere, but it got some press because the cops said, basically, that he had attacked them when they tried to apprehend him, and he said, no, it wasn't me. It was Bigfoot! Anyway, yeah. Neither here nor there. No, there is a monster in the woods. Hang on." He took his phone out and composed a text.

She frowned. That fucking phone. "What are you doing?"

"Texting Jake to come over after dinner. He'll attest to it. Also, I need more pot. So, yeah, there's a monster in the woods. It's different for everyone. Jake swears it's like a giant, like a capybara or something, with yellow eyes. My mother considers it vaporous. But my mother is pretty vaporous. Monsters are like dogs. They come to resemble us after we spend enough time together. I don't know about Abbie. I mean, I do, but he doesn't actually call it a *monster*. He has a more religious—excuse me, spiritual—interpretation. He says that it's in the form of a giant deer, but I'm like, 'Abbie, that's just, you know, a deer.'" He paused and smiled winsomely.

"And you?"

"I don't believe in monsters." He smirked. "You think we're nuts."

"I'm not especially superstitious."

He shrugged. "It's Fayette County," he said. "It's weird."

"Even so, that seems preternaturally weird."

"Yes," he said. "Preternaturally."

They sipped their drinks, and he immersed himself in his phone. Isabel could hear the pings and assorted percussion sounds of his hook-up apps. You didn't live in New York in a milieu of architects and designers and other specimens who described themselves, quite un-ironically, as "creatives" without becoming familiar with these tools. She herself had even briefly, just after moving to Pittsburgh, downloaded one of the pale hetero versions, attempting to feel liberated as she tapped her approval (acquiescence?) in the app store, but feeling actually rather prim. Before Ben, she'd been able to meet men easily at bars and restaurants and parties and produce aisles; now she was downloading a purpose-driven computer program. It wasn't that she was a Luddite; she loved her laptops (work and personal), her tablet, her Kindle, her frequently upgraded phone. Rather, it was the specificity of the thing, the way it took what should have been freewheeling and anarchic and made it into something practical, almost vocational. Wasn't that a reflection on America, or on the West, or on the dull conclusion of Capitalism, or something? That as our education had become a mere factory for producing employees, so too now our sentimental education became a matter of ruthless efficacy: task-specific, goal-oriented? Anyway, the experience was a bust. Isabel didn't even manage to attract any interesting grotesques, no lurid cock shots (she got a few, but they were the opposite of lurid; they were clinical and detached; one of them included a dollar bill held beside a boner for comparison, making the transactional nature of the whole exchange even more appallingly obvious: truth in advertising! get what you paid for!). There were very few perverted demands, nothing much but the metronomically regular interest of regular dudes, more or less her age, income, and level of educational attainment, who, because they were so busy killing it at the office/at the gym/with their boys/etc. were in search of someone dully ordinary and of that variety of athletically unerotic sex that is best performed within eye-shot of a mirror. Of course, she knew the experience would be different for a young gay guy, or assumed it would, anyway. Her friends in New York had complained about it even as they shoved their faces into it. She let Isaac do his thing and even took her own phone out to nose through emails for a while.

Eventually he got bored. The drinks turned clammy and sweated onto the glass table, and he sighed and said, "Once more into the breach," and hopped out of the chair. He led her through one of the odd hallways—half cave dwelling and half space station—that connected one annex of the compound to another, and they emerged into the main house in a sort of atrium-cum-foyer, which held at one end the crystal-palace front doors of The Gamelands. Hung in the vaulted, jagged cathedral above them, there were a number of mobiles that resembled a mad cross-breeding of Calder and middling Judaica, and finally, at its center, right out of some myth about the creation of the world by a wild clan of festive gods, an enormous, slightly yellowing banyan tree. ("It's the third largest banyan tree in Pennsylvania," Isaac claimed. Isabel hummed a sound that she hoped sounded like interested acknowledgment.)

From there they went through a discreet doorway into the grandest room of the house, a multilevel hangar of glass and stone whose lower expanse held several distinctly furnished sitting areas and an out-of-place grand piano. The upper portion included both a large dining area with a comically vast table of curvilinear wood surrounded by a goofy assortment of thrift-store chairs and a kitchen centered around that big boulder island that Sawyer had mentioned, which really was more impressive in the seeing than in the telling, a leveled-off Gibraltar heaved up out of the floor. Isabel had almost expected to find Abbie seated in some kind of seigniorial splendor, throned and waiting to receive them like the ruler of a minor duchy. Instead, the first person they met was a young man—younger than Isabel, older than Isaac—perched precariously on a wooden A-frame ladder beside the windows.

"*Hola*, Eli," said Isaac. He left Isabel in the doorway and headed immediately to the kitchen, where he opened the wide refrigerator and stood, like every son everywhere at every visit home, with the door open, surveying the contents before deciding there was nothing he wanted and walking over to the bannister that separated the upper and lower sections of the room. He pronounced the name Eh-lee.

"Hello, Isaac," said Eli. "Give me just a moment. If I talk while I'm up here, I'm sure to fall off." He had the slightly British accent that many continental Europeans acquire in their studies of English over the barest hint of his native Spanish. He pressed a gooey white substance out of a squeeze bottle onto the joint of a windowpane and its frame. He had an ugly but not unappealing face, a squished nose (terribly broken in his childhood), and cleft chin that looked like an angry fist. He had too-deep eyes that shone like those of a threatened and threatening animal coming out of a cave. He had very wide shoulders, narrow hips, and short legs. The whole effect was vaguely troglodytic. But his voice betrayed a hint of aristocracy, or at least the modern, bourgeois equivalent thereof. He swung off the ladder with a fluid and simian maneuver, laid the squeeze bottle on a nearby bench, wiped his hands on his jeans, and walked toward them.

"Isabel," Isaac said, "this is Eli. Eli, Isabel."

He shook her hand with an American matter-of-factness that indicated he'd been living in the country for a while, a surer sign than any accent. "Isabel," he said. "My pleasure to meet you. Are you a friend of Izzy's?" He held her eyes for a moment too long, and she looked away, pretending to be interested in the architecture.

"Don't call me that," said Isaac.

Eli grinned. "Your father's windows are leaking again. It rained last night and dripped all over the place. I'm trying a new silicone caulk." (He pronounced it *cock*. Isabel grinned inadvertently. Isaac caught her and made a face.) "I doubt it will work. We will have to tear the whole place down."

"Haven't I been saying it?" said Isaac. He turned to her. "Eli," he said, "is my father's factotum."

"I'd hoped to be his amanuensis," said Eli, confirming what Isabel had already decided: that he was not just a handyman, or that, if he were, then it was a reinvention from some other, former life.

"Abbie is his own amanuensis," Isaac told us. "Both king and scribe, like David but less beautiful, like Solomon but less wise. Where is my paterfamilias, by the way? Isabel is a genuine groupie. She has several of his books. I saw them at her house one time after dinner. She'd moved them from her main bookshelf, but I snooped. I want to be there when he signs her tits."

Had she known him better, or known him less, she thought, she'd have smacked him, but she could only stand there and blush.

Eli elected to appear not to notice, although Isabel might have noted a sympathetic softening of his eyes if she'd looked at him. "Your father," he said, "is in Uniontown. He said he'd be back later."

"What car did he take?"

"I don't know. The Land Rover?"

"Typical. We were supposed to have dinner. Where's Mom?"

"He said he was going to bring back fried chicken. Sarah told me she was going to take a nap."

"Yeah?" Isaac smirked meanly. "How many hours ago would you say she said that?"

"Are you two thirsty?" asked Eli. "I thought I'd have a beer on the patio."

Over beers, Isaac went back to talking about his weird upbringing. He wanted to tell the story of the subterranean network of tunnels underneath the Uniontown Mall. He and Jake had been getting high at a small lake—really, a rain-filled and abandoned quarry—on the far side of the Mount Saint Macrina property, a Catholic retreat for nuns built on what had once been the estate of J.V. Thompson, whose coal and coke fortune had been, before bankruptcy, before Frick and Carnegie, one of the greatest of the great American fortunes. Now the Oak Hill mansion had been divided into dark warrens of sleeping cubicles for the nuns and the granite balustrades on the wide patios were chipped. The property held newer buildings, too, dormitories and chapels and a small cemetery, but on far side of the land, there was a ten-acre stand of old woods, and in the woods was the old quarry. In order to get there, the boys had to move quietly across a field of low grass in the dark. "We were afraid," Isaac explained, "because there was a rumor that one of the Fathers had a shotgun loaded with rock salt, and he'd shoot you in the ass if he caught you trespassing." In the summer, the dense trees around the pool retained humidity; the earth threw up ferns; the fallen logs were covered in lichens and hairlike moss. "The pool didn't have a bottom," Isaac said. "It went down, down, down forever until you passed through to the other side of the world."

"To China." Isabel laughed.

"Not the physical world," he said. "That pool was where Daroba came from."

They liked to get high in those woods, and then afterward they'd sneak back across the estate grounds and climb back over the fieldstone wall that separated it from Main Street below the mall. They'd run across four lanes of traffic—except there was rarely any traffic—to the expanses of fast-food restaurants, where they'd giggle as they ordered more food than they were likely to eat. Behind the restaurants there was a rocky gully full of twisted trees and stands of knotweed. Why it was that on this one particular night Jake decided to walk into the trees to take a piss rather than using the bathroom at the McDonald's was never clear. There's something about a teenage boy that impels him to piss outside when possible, a sort of hormonal exhibitionism, the desire to display the dick that's so central to his existence to the whole of the world, even if he's doing so while concealed behind a tree where no one else can actually see him. Jake returned, out of breath. "Isaac," he whispered, although there was no reason to whisper. "Come on, you've got to see this."

Beyond the trees, the gully reared back up in a hillside of broken stone to the mall's parking lots, thirty or forty feet above, but sticking out of the side, like the obscene tailpipe of some immense earthworks spaceship, was an un-barred storm drain pipe a little over four feet in diameter.

"So?" said Isaac.

"*Soooo*," said Jake. "We should go in."

"Fuck no," said Isaac. "Jesus, it's a sewer. That's fucking gross."

"It's a storm drain," said Jake.

"I'm not going in there," said Isaac, but then he shrugged, and he added, "Besides. You'd need a flashlight."

That would have been the end of it, but a month or so later, on the edge of fall, that far end of August just before the start of school when the temperature dropped from eighty degrees during the day to near fifty at night and the long evening light took on that dusk glow that suggests the quick fading of an incandescent filament just after the light switch is flipped off, they were back at the quarry smoking weed, and Jake opened up his over-patched backpack—he defied the local expectations for a black kid by being particularly fond of Anti-Flag and the Dead Kennedys—and said, "Looooook what Iiiii have." He'd brought a pair of long Maglites. Isaac couldn't think of any reason to protest that didn't suggest cowardice and fear of the dark and the wet, so after smoking a little more out of the little purple-and-green glass bowl that Isaac had stolen from Abbie, they dashed back across the half-a-highway and through the parking lot between McDonald's and Long John Silver's and through the ratty trees past the dumpsters and then they scrambled over the sharp stones to the lip of the pipe. Jake lifted Isaac by the legs until he could grab the rim and pull himself up. Then Isaac hoisted Jake up behind him. They turned on the lights and went down the tunnel.

A narrow trickle of water ran in a channel down the bottom center of the passage. The entrance had been matted with slimy, decomposing leaves, but five feet in, it turned surprisingly clean, maintained by the frequent passage of water after it rained. They walked in a crouch with the flashlights making odd concentric ovals down the tunnel ahead of them. A breeze came toward them out of the depths. It carried the faint odor of motor oil and grease. Although the tunnels were concrete and laid perfectly straight, they felt organic, as if the boys had smuggled themselves into the circulatory system of a giant creature from an antediluvian world that had, innumerable eons ago, crawled wearily to this spot and laid down in its final lethargy to die. It was at once haunting and thrilling to be there. It appealed to them in all its weirdness. Who but a couple of pretty weird kids would crawl into a concrete tunnel under a mall at night? After a few hundred yards, they came to a square junction. Some light filtered from above. Looking up, they could see a grate over an opening to the parking lot above. They had a quick debate about which way to go out of the junction, before deciding that they'd come far enough for one night. "Of course," Isaac said, "we were actually terrified, but no one was going to admit it. We smoked some cigarettes. Jake insisted that we turn off the flashlights to conserve batteries, which was hysterical, because we'd been in there for what, fifteen minutes? If that. Anyway, we're sitting there, and it's not quite pitch black, because there's the light coming down from the drain above, and then Jake says, 'Did you feel that?' 'Feel what?' I said. 'The direction of the wind changed.' 'No it didn't.' 'Yes, it did.' 'Did it?' Then we sat there, and of course, we felt the direction of the wind changing, which was it? I don't know. Probably not. Then Jake says, 'Something's fucking *breathing. Motherfucker*! There's something *in here.*' And we both went *motherfucker* and scurried the fuck out. Then we swore that we were going to go back in and find whatever it was that lived in there."

"Did you?" Isabel asked.

"What?"

"Go back and find out."

Isaac swirled the last inch of his beer. "God, no," he said. "We pretended to forget about it, because we were too fucking scared to go back. Anyway, we were fourteen. We were getting into some other shit."

"But seriously," Isabel asked, "why the fuck would you crawl around in a storm drain?"

Isaac shrugged. "It's Uniontown," he answered. He giggled. "What else was there to do?"

This was when Sarah arrived, jangling uncertainly through the doors onto the patio. She was very thin, almost malnourished, although her face gave the impression of slight bloating. Her big eyes were pale green and quivered and seemed ever on the verge of tears, like one of those delicate girls in Japanese anime. Her hair was a nebular mane of gray frizz that blew out from her head in every direction and fell more than halfway down her back. She was nearly seventy herself and gave off the confusing impression of being both older and younger: the slight swelling of her face stretched that skin taught and made her cheeks round to an almost pubescent effect, whereas skin hung loosely on her tiny arms. She moved with the hesitancy of the elderly when they reached that stage of life in which each movement is the potential prelude to a terrible fall. She wore a billowing, sleeveless caftan and flowing pants whose volume emphasized rather than concealed the spindly legs beneath. She wore a great deal of jewelry—bracelets especially—some of it clearly very fine (one diamond tennis bracelet, in particular, shone as if it were reflecting a bonfire made of all the paper money in the world), much of it the kind of hammered copper junk that Isabel would have bought for her mother at one of those white-tented art fairs that spring up in shopping districts during the long days of summer or at stands along the road on the drive from Santa Fe to Taos. Sarah smelled too strongly of perfume, an overwhelming scent of sandalwood and not-quite-lavender: old-lady perfume. And yet she carried an unmistakable whiff of immortality, a freshness underneath the slightly boozy stink of the scent. She was as pale as a vampire, and that, if only because of all the silly talk about monsters, was Isabel's first impression of her: one either risen, or preserved, from the grave.

"I thought I heard your father." Her voice had a gentle tremor. She stood several feet away from the three of them as if she were afraid to approach.

"Nope," said Isaac, who rolled his eyes theatrically at Isabel. He was always trying to draw her into his conspiracies of disdain, and she'd have been ashamed to realize how frequently she obliged. "Just us, as the saying goes."

"I could have sworn."

"He isn't back from town, yet, Sarah," said Eli, who lifted himself out of the seat, hovering for a moment like a gymnast between the parallel bars before dismounting over the arm and giving a broad stretch. Isabel watched him. She wouldn't have expected someone so odd looking to move with such self-accustomed grace. Though why not?

"He went to town?"

"There was a meeting," Eli said. "About the new wellheads."

"Oh, yes. Yes. Goodness, what time is it?"

"Eight," Eli told her without bothering to look at a watch or a phone. "He should be back soon. He is bringing Roose's."

"Your father and that potato salad," Sarah said, now gazing toward her son. "I don't think it's any better than any other potato salad."

Isaac rolled his eyes again. "Roose's is great, Mom," he said. (Though he shared her opinion, and he was only being contrary.) Then he too jumped out of his seat and announced, "I've got to piss." He swept past his mother, barely pausing to plant a cursory kiss on her cheek. Eli followed him into the house. No one had introduced Isabel. She started to get up.

"Oh, you don't need to get up for me," Sarah said. Her tone suggested that they already knew each other. It occurred to Isabel suddenly that Sarah wasn't just old, nor only sleep-fogged, but also quite certainly drunk. "Do you mind if I sit?"

"No, of course not."

Sitting was an effort for her. The chairs were low, and she made a series of quiet, agonized noises as she lowered herself tenderly into the one where Isaac had been.

"These knees," she said.

Isabel murmured general assent.

"Tell me your name again, dear. I'm sorry, I'm terrible with names."

"Isabel."

"How lovely," she said. "It suits you."

"Well," Isabel said. "I can't take any credit."

"For your name?" She sighed. "No, I suppose not. Although don't you think that one comes to resemble one's name, or one's name comes to resemble oneself. I'm not sure in which order. Like pets, you know."

Isabel laughed obligingly, even though she wasn't sure Sarah meant it to be funny, even though it resembled so closely a thought she'd just had herself. She told Sarah that she didn't resemble those two monster dogs very much.

"Oh, no," Sarah said. "But they're Abbie's. Have you seen Abbie?"

"I think he's still in town."

"Oh, yes. Roose's. *How* could I forget?" She laughed, either at

Isabel or at some idea of her husband lugging home tubs of fried chicken and potato salad. She could be as cruel as Isaac, or he as cruel as her. It was hard to say in which direction the genealogy of nastiness ran. Like her son, Sarah took an unnecessary degree of pleasure in chuckling at other people's expense. She'd go on, a few days after this visit, to tell Isaac what she'd thought of Isabel. She said she found that Isabel was uncannily like Abbie. Isaac thought this was funny. "How do you mean?" he'd asked.

"She wants to be believed," Sarah said, "but she'd prefer to be liked." Isaac didn't see it, of course, but that had more to do with his character than with any peculiarity of Isabel's. Who wants to see in his own friends a propensity for sycophancy? What would that say about his friendships?

Sarah played idly with several bracelets, twisting them around her pale forearm. It was a habit born of a kind of insatiable boredom, like a dog that chews the baseboards. In New York, she'd been a busy woman; in Pittsburgh, she'd participated nominally in Abbie's early business ventures, but in the years since they'd come to Uniontown, she'd entered a semi-retirement that had turned the obsessive part of her mind that had once made her almost erudite and, in a conventional sense, successful, in on itself, which left her with nervous tics and a propensity for white wine before noon.

"So," she said. "Isabel. Tell me, what do you do? You'll have to excuse the question. I used to know how to make conversation without asking it, but I've lost my touch."

"Oh, I don't mind. I work for a non-profit."

"That's suitably vague."

"I'm sorry." Isabel smiled a placatory smile. "It's just that not many people have heard of it. We're really more of a think tank, I guess. It's called the Future Cities Institute. We used to be a part of CMU. We're still affiliated, actually, but we're an independent 501, now."

"Oh, yes. Barry Fitzgerald's outfit," Sarah said in an acute echo of her son's lover.

"You know Barry?"

"He was impossible to avoid. I'm sorry. That sounds mean. I used to be a better conversationalist. You see, Barry was just a professor. This would have been in the late eighties, I'd say. Early nineties. He occupied some sort of intermediary stage between being part-time and being tenured—the politics of that sort of thing escape me. Well, you know, those kinds of people are expected to live the lives of the bourgeoisie on the wages of bus-boys, and Barry was always scamming around property develop-ers, as Abbie would say, pitching himself as a sort of consultant. Well, he was attached to an associate, who was at the time a very dear friend of ours, Arthur Imlak, who eventually went into busi-ness with Abbie."

"I've met him," Isabel said.

"Did he try to get you onto his boat? He has wandering hands, I sometimes think, but he's the product of a different moral universe. God, did he make one of his jokes about *sailing*? He's very fond of Isaac. I sometimes think he pays more attention than Abbie. What was I saying? Yes, Barry. Arthur is richer than decency ought to permit now, but even then, he had quite a lot of cash, and he always had some useless minions around. It made him feel important. It's not the worst quality in a man. My hus-band, whom you'll meet, doesn't have this weakness, and I think that may be worse. In any case, I do remember Barry. Does he still live in that house?"

"In Point Breeze," Isabel said. "Yes, he does."

"I used to think he had eyes for Isaac, and you know, Isaac does have a thing for older men, unfortunately. That upsets Abbie more than anything." She shook her head. "Men. He never actually cared that his son was gay, you know. But feminine? Well, thank God Sawyer came along. He's a good influence. Is he with you?"

"No. He couldn't make it."

"A doctor! I'm still enough of a Jewish mother that it pleases me to no end. 'And so good looking.'" She giggled at her unconvincing attempt at imitating a Yiddish matron, which came off like her son's imitation of her. "How did you and Isaac meet?"

"At a party," Isabel said, but she didn't specify which.

"My son and his parties."

"Mm," Isabel said.

"And you, Isabel," Sarah said after a moment, "What do you do?"

. . .

Abbie's arrival at dinner took the form of a minor automobile accident. Sarah had opened a bottle of lousy Malbec, the sort of wine whose label suggested a bad tourism brochure, and they were all drinking and picking at olives in the kitchen. It was after nine. The sun had gone down. Isaac rarely looked up from his phone. Sarah was telling Isabel about an antique store that "you must visit" in Blawnox, just up the Allegheny River from Pittsburgh. "I bought the most wonderful set of milk glass dishes, there," she said. "Do you like milk glass?" She gazed at Isabel with quivering eyes.

Isabel didn't especially care for milk glass. She said, "Oh, I do."

"You must go. I keep meaning to drive out again, one of these days, but you know."

Isabel didn't know, nor, she thought, did Sarah. Then they heard the sound of a car skidding on gravel and the unmistakable dull bang of a car crumpling against a tree.

Abbie had taken the curve of the driveway around the house too fast, fishtailed on the loose stones, and swung his rear passenger side into the trunk of the big tulip tree that he'd planted there the same week they'd broken ground on the main house. Everyone went outside, though you would not say *rushed*, and found him standing in the semi-dark with his door open, the dome light on, the headlights flashing out into the evening. He was in jeans and a sport coat whose purchase had preceded his latest round of weight gain. He glared at the car with the aggressive, proprietary disbelief of all men betrayed by their cars, from which they expect absolute fidelity. His silly white hair was brushed like a mane away from his fleshy, once-handsome face. He appeared unharmed, as did the tree. The Land Rover had acquired a strange concavity where it now leaned against the trunk, almost as if something had taken a bite out of it. "I told you," Isaac whispered to Isabel. "A monster."

She raised an eyebrow, Spock-like, a talent or a curse of her too-expressive face, and whispered back, "He was probably just driving too fast."

"Ah," said Isaac, "but *why* was he driving too fast?"

Sarah had gone gingerly to her husband's side as if she were the one who'd just been in an accident. "Oh, Abbie," she said, "I think we're in trouble."

"What trouble?" His voice exploded like a rifle shot through the woods. "Look at the Goddamn car!" The dogs, reacting to his raised voice, let loose an extended cadence of excited barking.

"Oh, Abbie," she said, this time admonishing.

"Oh, Goddamn it, Sarah! God!" He reeled back and spread his arms and addressed the sky. "You lousy Son of a Bitch!" It occurred to Isabel that he, too, might be slightly drunk. "Not one minute's peace! Not a moment's Goddamn rest!" He shook his head violently and stalked over to the truck, clambering back into the driver's seat in order to peer into the back. Then he was screaming again. "And You ruined the fucking chicken! Smashed!" He slammed the door shut and began to stride toward the house, thought the better of it, went back to the car, opened the door, yanked out the keys, slammed the door once more, and headed back. He paused where Isabel stood with Isaac and Eli. "We'll get it in the morning," he fumed to Eli. He turned to Isaac and said, "It came close to the drive, Isaac."

"It's as afraid of us as we are of it," Isaac replied. It had the quality of a set piece, a scene they'd acted before. Abbie hugged him, drew his slim child against his hugeness and cupped his head briefly with a soft hand. "I'm glad you came," he said.

"All right, Abbie. Christ."

Abbie turned to Isabel briefly. "You're the girlfriend," he said.

"I—"

"Oh, don't look so pinched. I know he's gay. Girlfriends. Friends who are girls. My wife has girlfriends. My son has girl-friends. I have only colleagues and a set of bizarre and probably meaningless visions placed into my head by the Divine. You tell me, who got the better deal? Did you ever try to be a prophet in the twenty-first century? It's like being a cardiologist in the ancient world. Your knowledge is fundamentally inconsistent with the available tools of the time and therefore useless. In any case, Isaac says you're working for Barry Fitzgerald. How's his house? Still look like a bad catalog?"

"Actually, yes."

"Well, welcome to The Gamelands, which does not." He leaned forward and kissed Isabel on both cheeks, placing his hands on her shoulders and swiftly sizing her up. He nodded as if he approved. She frowned. His manner made her feel like livestock. He ran his hands through his hair. "Well," he said. "I suppose I'll go make pasta instead."

At that moment, the headlights mercifully and automatically blinked off.

Isabel had imagined that making pasta would consist of a pack of dried—though probably expensive—spaghetti and a hasty red sauce, but when Abbie said that he would make pasta, he meant it. He'd bounced into the kitchen, tossed his coat over a chair, replaced it with a well-stained apron, and began mixing flour and eggs for the noodles. "Someone turn on *Rigoletto*," he commanded.

"Which one?" asked Eli.

"The RCA Victor, the Solti, with Moffo and Ezio Flagello." He swirled the flour into the eggs with a fork, already operatic. He smiled broadly at Isabel, who was still frowning. "If one is going to make pasta, one should listen to music with an Ezio Flagello." He pronounced it again with an exaggerated Italian accent. "Ayyyy-tseeoh!"

Isabel looked at Isaac.

"Yes," Isaac said. "It's always like this."

"I went into the woods to live deliberately," Abbie proclaimed, sing-song.

"I'm not sure this is what Henry had in mind, Dad."

Somewhere, everywhere, the music came on, those ominous fanfares.

Abbie had magically acquired a glass of wine. He took a moment away from kneading to sip it. "Ach. Terrible! Sarah, why do you buy this swill?"

"It's fine," she protested.

Abbie was looking at Isabel when he answered, already drawing her in as a helpless accomplice. That was the nature of the Mayer men. She saw where Isaac had got it from. "A fine wine is fine, but a wine that's only fine?" Still, he took another sip. Then, improvising to match the melodic line of the overture, he sang, "*Baruch ata Adonai Eloheinu, melech haOlam, borei pri haGafen.*"

"You're laying it on a little thick, Dad," said Isaac, who'd nosed back into his phone.

"Seriously," said Sarah.

"Your friend forgives me," he said. "Don't you, my dear? What's your name?"

"Isabel."

"Eees-ah-bayyylaah! *E' un bellissimo nome così*! Presumably not a Jewess?"

"No," she said. She added carefully, "Catholic, nominally. We weren't especially religious."

"Neither were we," said Abbie. "Which of course makes the predicament of my life the more absurd. Sarah's family were great believers, but when I told her I'd had a chit-chat with Hashem, she looked stricken."

"It," she paused and then said something other than what she was going to say, "was a difficult period."

"Excuse me," Isaac said. He pocketed his phone and headed toward the other room.

"These phones," said Sarah.

"Were we really so different? Remember the opening scene of *Bye Bye Birdie*?" Abbie had wrapped the pale yellow oblong of dough in plastic and was chopping onions into a fine dice.

"I remember that Isaac was *in Bye Bye Birdie* in high school, but I've blocked out the particulars."

"He played the Paul Lynde role. We ought to have known, I suppose. Anyway, my point is that we spent plenty of time on the phone when we were teens, even if they were all landlines."

"He's not a teenager."

"Be that as it may." Abbie waved the knife loosely and moved on to garlic. "I think it's healthy, the constant contact. Imagine if we were still living in tribal groups, close kinship networks. We'd be picking each others' nits and stumbling into each others' tents all the time."

"He hardly speaks to us!"

Abbie momentarily lost his air of playful bonhomie, his Falstaffian clownishness, so committedly performed. A pained look passed over his face, and this time he made no effort to look at Isabel. He looked at his wife. "Let's not," he said.

Eli had never returned from the record player. He was sitting near it, drinking the bad wine, showing every indication of listening to the music.

Sarah looked at Isabel slyly, as if somehow the other woman wouldn't notice, though they weren't ten feet apart. "All right," she said. She twisted a bracelet and took a deep gulp of wine, which she held in her cheeks like a chipmunk, like a college girl who's taken a shot without quite knowing how to swallow it, before swallowing with a convulsive, canine shake of the head and a small sneeze. "How was the meeting?"

"Awful. Sherri didn't show, and Don spent the whole time

unsubtly suggesting that that poor boy accountant who took Jack Schaffer's seat sucks cock for a living. The Lion of Lemonwood, that one."

"The Lion of Lemonwood?" Isabel said.

"Don is a county commissioner," Sarah told her.

"She knows that," said Abbie, although of course, at the time, she didn't. "Don Cavignac, during a prior campaign for his primogenitured portion of this glorious barony we call Fayette County, had a campaign aide, in a press conference, float the nickname. It wouldn't have stuck, except the publisher of the *Herald-Standard*, or, as I like to call it, the *Herald*-Substandard, the *Herald*-No-Standards, is Cavignac's brother-in-law's father-in-law. In the more civilized portions of the world, wherever those may be, that would mean bupkiss, but here, such connections are a veritable staff of life. Now"—he paused for a moment to look around for a can of tomatoes that was sitting right in front of him—"Lemonwood Acres is a housing project, Section 8, of ill repute, which is ironically located just across the parking lot from Isaac's high-school alma mater. Don likes to claim that he grew up there, as if that confers upon him some sort of plebeian authenticity. Well, he did grow up there, in a manner of speaking: *before* it became a project. His father, who was a county commissioner before him—it's a venerable tradition in their family—owned half the property, and the other half was a landfill. So when they went to build the new high school, they covered the landfill. The school district bought up a small piece of the Cavignac property in order to extend the parking lots, and the Cavignacs worked a classic real estate scheme to sell their land at inflated prices to a housing authority controlled by their own cronies, who then threw up a lot of crap frame-and-drywall townhouses, into which they herded the town's most restive blacks."

"Abbie," said Sarah.

"I don't endorse the racial attitudes; I merely describe them, my dear. You can imagine, there's something poetically correct about building a high school and prison on top of a garbage dump. It speaks to the underlying nature of our swiftly dying civilization. Anyway, Cavignac gave that poor kid a public wedgie for about half an hour during regular business. Then some minion of Art's made a glossy presentation about the locations of new wells and the environmental remediation and effect mitigation plans. So many Latinate words. Everyone was nodding off, which was the point, surely. Until someone started yelling about his well water catching on fire because of all the fracking. Needless to say, when we got right down to it, it wasn't *his* well water. *He* has city water. It was a friend of a neighbor of a cousin, who probably just saw it in that documentary, you know the one. He proceeded to demand 'One ah them BP-style paydays for ahr eekanawmic inj-ree.'"

"I read about the flammable tap water," Isabel said.

"It's true, actually," Abbie told her, looking pained at having his story interrupted. "How's that for your End Times? Our water literally catching on fire. But these people are all confabulators; they don't understand the distinction between fact, fable, and myth, and they have no concept of the difference between a thing happening to them directly and a thing happening to a friend who actually just heard about it from someone who saw it on *Inside Edition* the other night. And where, pray tell, is the broccoli *rape*?" He pronounced rape with relish, and his eyes dared the women in the room to take foolish, inexcusable, feminine offense.

"I threw it out," Sarah told him. "It was wilted."

"You threw it out? Lord, forgive us for our waste. The water is on fire, our towns are sinking into piles of garbage, and you'd waste food? Eli!"

"Yo!" Eli called back from across the room.

"Is there any *rape* left in the garden?"

Eli (bless him, Isabel thought) didn't rise to it. "There are mustard greens."

"*Si. Pronto!*"

Eli left through a patio door. The temperature had dropped after sunset, and the cool night came quickly through the open door. "Well," said Abbie, unwrapping the pasta dough and throwing it onto the counter with a thwack, then wiggling his chubby, floury fingers at Isabel: "Isabellissima. Have you got *strong hands?*"

. . .

You'd wonder—Isabel wondered—how she could possibly have remained enamored after actually meeting the miserable, fat old fuck. Well, she had an ulterior motive. But beyond a desire to discover if what her mother said about him was true, she was also independently fascinated by him. They were alone after dinner. Isaac had returned just before they'd all eaten with his friend Jake in tow. Jake was a striking, young, light-skinned black man; Isabel had imagined that he'd look just like Isaac, even though Isaac had already described him, and she chastised herself for it. He wore his hair in a modest Afro that had a bit of the seventies to it. He wore thick, plastic-framed glasses like men wore in the control room when Neil Armstrong walked on the moon, but they were merely fashionable, not necessary. He joined them at the table. Strozzapreti with tomato and mustard greens and flecks of red pepper. "And cacio de Roma," Abbie yelled at them. "*Not* Parmigiano!" Abbie ate voraciously. Like a lot of good cooks, he hardly paused to taste his own food. Eli and Isaac both ate like Europeans, fork in left hand and knife in right. Jake was left-handed and ate without the knife. Sarah didn't eat much but occasionally moved the pile of noodles weakly around the plate. Isaac and Jake told Isabel how they'd met.

"We had English together. And then gym. And health class. With that racist pedo Eddie Milano."

"Isaac," said Sarah.

For someone who claimed to have hated his childhood, to have, as he said, "barely escaped alive," Isaac inhabited a state of perpetual nostalgia for the country of his youth. Maybe it had really been terrible, and the passage of time alone had whittled it down to a skein of grotesque but funny anecdotes, or maybe it had never been so bad and he only claimed it to excuse some of his worse habits. Or maybe a bit of both. Contra the truism, we don't look backward with perfect vision. We drive relentlessly forward into the dark, and when we glance occasionally into the rearview mirror, the objects are never so clearly positioned, and they are closer than they appear.

After they ate, Sarah did the dishes, or anyway made a pantomime of doing the dishes. She'd eaten practically nothing and drank a good deal more, and she stood at the sink, staring off absently and rubbing a sponge weakly around one dish, over and over. Eli disappeared; he'd learned to vanish as quickly and quietly as a cat, slipping off to one of his private retreats around the house to be left alone. Isaac and Jake went back to Isaac's outpost to get stoned; they announced this at the table, but no one else seemed to care. Isabel imagined that she was supposed to join them, but Isaac waved her off. "Catch up with us later," he said. "I brought you to meet Abbie." He gestured to his father like a man presenting a new product on television. "Meet Abbie."

"Perhaps Abbie wishes to retire to his study with a cigar," Abbie said.

"Isabel likes cigars," Isaac said.

"Not especially."

"Take a digestif with me on the patio," Abbie said.

On the patio, Abbie asked if she was cold. She said she wasn't, although she was. He appeared to contemplate putting his arm around her but to think the better of it. Isabel shouldn't have felt grateful for this minor decency, but she'd spent her life awkwardly shrugging off the hands of men who thought they were doing her a favor, and if minor decency was insufficient, then at least it salved for just a moment the general indecency of living in a world with so many men.

"So Barry Fitzgerald," Abbie said.

"Barry Fitzgerald."

"The Future Cities Institute. It has a science-fictional quality that I wouldn't expect in him. It conjures up flying cars and endless rain, George Jetson amongst the Bladerunners."

"No flying cars," Isabel said. "We're much more mundane. Our biggest project is the Race to 2050. I didn't come up with the name." She smiled ruefully. "We get all the big property owners in town, the universities and the big corporate landlords downtown and the hospitals and such to pledge to reduce energy use in their buildings by fifty percent by twenty-fifty." She laughed. "It's a, quote, voluntary, non-binding pledge. So you can imagine."

"Oh, I know all about your employer. He stole the idea from me." Abbie sounded proud rather than aggrieved. "Whole cloth."

He rattled the ice in his glass and smiled. "Not the name, though. What a thoroughly queer name. Yes, I used to give a talk in which I pointed out that while the general focus of energy-savings programs was vehicular efficiency, in fact the largest consumers of energy were commercial and industrial buildings, followed by homes. The amount of carbon you burn to keep the lights on in a typical American house significantly exceeds the output of an automobile. And you can imagine"—he gestured behind him— "how much this thing takes. I designed it to be geothermal and solar powered, of course. When the world's wells run dry and the oil is gone and the vast human herds get moving once again, I intended to be right here burning the eternal flame. I actually got sued by the utility, the fucks. Yes, it is illegal to be a net contributor to the grid. I could've gone entirely off, of course, but Sarah worried, and I acquiesced. The key to a good marriage is acquiescence, in large quantities."

"I would have thought honesty."

"Lord, no."

Now Isabel smiled, and she allowed a needle in her voice. "Would you say yours was a good marriage?"

"Ahhh," Abbie sucked more whiskey. "She's sharper than she looks. I thought that must be the case. I took one look at you, and I thought, *video et taceo.*"

"I don't know that one."

"Elizabeth I. 'I see, and I am silent.' You even share the name."

"That's a flattering comparison."

"The answer to your question is yes, actually. Sarah tolerates my outrageousness, and I tolerate her purposeful decline. We both aspire to the dutiful eccentricities of our respective sexes. I will be a grandiose old kook, and she will be a dotty old lady with a fondness for gin. You young folks think that sounds like an awful settlement, but great dynasties have been built on less."

"I probably shouldn't argue that latter point."

"Regarding your employer, to get back to it: it's a noble effort, actually. I'm a fatalist, but that doesn't mean I don't appreciate a good try, however destined to fail. Look down there." Isabel looked where he was pointing, out over the dark, descending forest to Uniontown, twelve hundred feet below and miles away, glowing against the dark ground like the luminescent creatures sparkling in the wash of the waves of a nighttime ocean. "One day," Abbie said, "the lights are going to go out. This is a popular topic in fiction, these days. The scuttling about of humans in the immediate post-apocalypse. The dull horror stories of surviving in the wreck of civilization. But they make the same error that we make in anticipating our own end, whether that leads us to welcome it or to try to forestall it. That is the failure to look at the *longue durée*."

"Lucien Febvre," Isabel said. She was proud of herself for remembering.

"Marc Bloch, really. I've always thought. But they never went far enough. They still thought in terms of history and economy. But history and economy are nothing in the long run. Let me tell you about the long run. In the long run, the story of the survivors of the carbon age is even briefer and less significant than the age itself. Whether we make it another hundred years or a hundred thousand. The lights *will* go off, and the tall grasses and vines will grow over it all, and the continents will move into unfamiliar arrangements, and should God ever see fit to curse another animal with our terrible, pandemic self-consciousness, all they'll ever find of all of this will be a thin layer in the geologic strata that suggests sometime, millions of years before, a befuddling environmental catastrophe occurred, a strange outpouring of carbon into the atmosphere, a swift extinction of a strange number of species. They'll argue whether it was an asteroid or a volcano."

"That's a despairing vision."

"Is it? I think not."

"I still like to think we could be better stewards of the natural world."

He laughed and placed a hand on her shoulder, almost familial. She shivered, and she did not feel compelled to shrug it away. "Stewards? You see, that's our arrogance, as a species. Even in meaning well, we claim dominion. We are imperialists to the core."

"Well," Isabel said, thinking she could tweak him a little, "didn't God grant us dominion?"

"Even God errs," Abbie said.

"Does she?"

He spread his arms like a conductor before an orchestra. "Are we not incontestable evidence of *His* immense folly?" Then, humming Rigoletto's *lalala*s from "Povero Rigoletto," he left her and walked back into the house. A few seconds later, he leaned back out of the door and said, "And do stay close to the house, my dear. There is a monster in the woods."

· · ·

That night she watched Isaac lounge on a couch and get terrifically stoned and lay his head and legs suggestively or invitingly on Jake's lap, who seemed disinclined to return the affection in kind in front of her, although he was certainly not uncomfortable receiving it. They listened to a scratchy vinyl recording of Sawyer Brown, playing "All I Can Do Is Cry" again and again on a beautiful old Marantz that must once have been Abbie's. Isabel begged off to bed, thinking she'd read, since the bedroom opened right onto the room below, and there'd be no dulling the music or Isaac's never-ending giggling, but the beer and wine and scotch had gone to her head, and she woke up at sunrise the next morning with a thin, three-ring binder butterflied across her chest. She'd wandered through Abbie's library before returning to Isaac's side of the compound, and found, right there on a shelf with the books he'd authored himself, this transcript of a long-ago arbitration, in which Abbie and his sister and their lawyers argued about who had the rights to the proceeds from the sale of a vast tract of land. She found Jake and Isaac still asleep on the couch, clothed mostly, though they seemed to have lost their shirts at some point. She stepped softly past and walked to the main house, which felt empty. She quietly returned the binder to its shelf and then padded to the kitchen. There was a kettle on the stove, and after a little poking around, she found both tea and an old metal traveler's mug. She made herself a cup of Lady Grey—it seemed an odd variety to have lying around—and then walked outside.

It was a cold morning. There was a gray hoodie slung haphazardly across the arm of a deck chair. Isabel assumed it must belong to Eli and pulled it on. Having nothing else to do, the house sleeping, she decided to walk around the property. She set off across the broken terraces and the meadow toward the tree line below. Uniontown looked less lovely in daylight, a grayish-brown bloom like lichen on a rock, but it disappeared from view as she approached the tree line. The woods were attractive, the trees spaced evenly with little undergrowth other than an astonishment of ferns sprouting from the dead leaves. She saw a hint of a trail and followed it. Isabel had grown up in the city, and her experience with woodland in her youth was mostly limited to the imagination of Frederick Law Olmstead, although there had been one fall in which Isabel's mother convinced herself that the two of them would take a road trip to New England for the leaves. Isabel was fourteen then. Their brittle camaraderie had broken down on the second day in the sort of mutual recrimination and acrimony that only mothers and daughters who really love each other are capable of, and they returned home, garnering a speeding ticket in Connecticut that only made things worse. What Isabel remembered most about that trip was that it was the first time her mother had mentioned the fact that her father had been married to another woman. It was during an argument brought on when Cathy had playfully asked Isabel if she had a boyfriend, and Isabel had replied, with all the seriousness she could manage, that she had "plenty of them."

She went to college closer to nature but continued to avoid it. Madison wasn't without woods, but while her friends would go tromping off on hikes, either because they didn't feel like drinking that weekend or else to spend a weekend drinking someplace cool, she rarely joined. But since moving to Pittsburgh, she'd made an effort; she'd visited Raccoon Creek and Moraine State Parks and gone with Barry one weekend to a cabin owned by an adviser of the Institute. The cabin was in Allegheny National Forest, but it turned out to be just a hundred yards from a gas well access road, and the weekend was ruined by the uninterrupted rumbling of tankers going to and from the site. But it was Frick Park that had really convinced her that she could like nature, or its approximation. A heavily wooded six hundred acres in the middle of the city's East End, it was all shale cliffs and gullies and dogs and deer and the uncanny sense, even on the wide, crushed gravel trails, that this was what that city had been before it was a city, and this was what it would be after the city was gone.

She'd started running. She was closer to forty than she cared to think about, and she could no longer be effortlessly thin. She'd been a runner in high school and college, then dropped it for years. She didn't like it, but she liked that she did it anyway. She would run from her house down through the pretty blocks of 1940s' houses in Regent Square, cross Braddock Avenue and follow Hamilton past all the four-bedrooms and the occasional English-style cottage to the edge of the park, then half-stumble down the steep path to the Lower Frick parking lot. She'd run along the restored Nine Mile Run, through wetlands full of crickets and frogs, beneath a housing development on land that someone other than Veronica Mayer and Phil Harrow had eventually developed instead of them, until the end of the trail where the stream emptied into the Monongahela River.

But a park, however canopied and wild it's been permitted to remain, is still a park, and a forest is a forest; the one resembles the other as a man does the god in whose image he was made— an image that's also and only a remnant of the thing itself. What she'd thought was a trail had died out. An experienced hiker could have oriented herself by the slope of the land, but Isabel was almost immediately lost. She'd been walking for ten minutes. She knew this made her comical, a city girl who gets lost before she's gone a quarter mile, but laughing at herself didn't diminish her sudden unease. She found herself in a denser thicket, surrounded by high clumps of waxy, impenetrable mountain laurel, the air still, without even the sound of birds—also dark, because it was early yet, and the steeply angled post-dawn light cast only a vestigial glow, like the last embers of a bonfire. Looking around, forcing herself to remain calm, she only saw more trees and more mountain laurels. The slope was now subtle and harder to discern. She heard a sound—she thought from behind her, but she couldn't tell—and all of her good sense and self-possession fled. She thought of Abbie winking at her and telling her that there was a monster in the woods. A monster! As if anything could be so absurd.

There are so many things we won't admit to ourselves, desires and fears mostly. Isabel, for instance, was mildly afraid of the dark; at home, she didn't mind, but even in a hotel room, she'd keep a light burning in the bathroom all night. She was an easily panicked driver. When she didn't know the way, she'd turn down the radio, as if that would help to navigate. She was afraid of revolving doors and had to put down her panic every time she accompanied Barry to the offices of the Carnegie Endowment downtown. And now she was—to her chagrin—afraid of some spectral presence in a forest, the silliest fear of all.

She stood as still as she could. That's what people did. They didn't pound off into the forest or grab the baseball bat and descend the stairs to investigate the sound in the night. They pulled the covers closer and convinced themselves it was nothing. They turned their heads imperceptibly to see what was behind them and hoped that they'd find nothing there but their own mind imposing pattern and presence on nothing at all. Isabel held her body rigid, and she turned her head imperceptibly, toggling her eyes as far as they would go to get a glimpse behind her, canting them so hard that it hurt. She didn't see anything. Slowly, very slowly, she rotated the other way and did the same. She didn't see anything. She sighed, a long slow exhalation. She'd been holding her shoulders stiffly in place, and she let them slump. She closed her eyes, and she opened them. She nearly screamed and choked it into a rough cough. There was big buck stepping out of the laurels. We consider ourselves observant until forced to realize the basic weakness of the human sense of sight. How had she missed that clot of brown in the sprawl of green? She hadn't been looking for it, and so she hadn't seen it. The animal was fifteen feet from her, no farther than the far side of a big living room. She hoped that it would bound away when it saw her, right back into the bushes, but of course, it had seen her—smelled her, heard her—long before she'd seen it, and it had walked out anyway. It regarded her placidly with one black eye. There was something disconcerting about the gaze of an animal that lacked the binocular arrangement of human eyes. What did its other eye see, and how did it reconcile those two different visions into a single image in its brain? Its new antlers were wide and covered in velvet. It looked at her for a while, and Isabel looked at it. Then a slight breeze kicked from behind her, and the deer's nostrils flared. It made a sound like a bark or a cough of its own, and it bounded back the way it had come.

She'd been holding her breath. She collected herself for a moment. She was still lost. But then she heard the sounds of engines and of men behaving foolishly somewhere off to her left. She followed them, tripping through the low branches, and she was embarrassed when she emerged into the field not two minutes later. She'd been just a couple of hundred yards beyond the edge of the trees the whole time. Up by the house, Eli and Isaac and Abbie and Jake had hitched a pickup to the back of Abbie's wrecked Land Rover and were attempting to drag it away from the tree against which it leaned. They weren't having any success, but they all seemed to be having great fun, even

Isaac, who was the last person anyone would have expected to enjoy that sort of emphatically male entertainment. "Where were you?" asked Isaac.

"Taking a walk," Isabel said. She felt as if she must be covered in leaves and patted her hair. "Everyone was asleep."

"Asleep," Isaac giggled.

Abbie was wearing hiking boots and a huge terrycloth bathrobe with the Marriott logo sewn into the breast. "I hope you didn't venture too far into our little forest," he said.

"No. I did see a deer, though."

"Did you hear that, Abbie?" Isaac turned on his father with a complicated expression.

"I did."

"Abbie's spirit animal is the deer," Isaac told her in that tone of his that implied she'd be over-literal to interpret it merely as a sneer.

Eli leaned out of the window of the truck and said, "Isaac, come help me," even though there was nothing for Isaac to do.

Isabel pretended not to notice the swift tension between Isaac and his father. She smiled at Abbie and said, "I did not, I'm pleased to report, run into anything monstrous, though."

"Oh no?" said Isaac.

Abbie ignored him and told Isabel to come in for coffee. She did, and that was when he told her, without prompting and in great detail, about the vision he'd been granted in the temple many years before.

When she was safely back in Pittsburgh, safely back at work, she went to lunch with Barry. They sat in the little amber dining room of the teahouse on Atwood, where she'd had lunch with Sawyer not a month before, eating the same oily curry noodles, and she told him about the trip. She told him that she found them all very weird. "I thought I liked weird people," she said, "but those are some *weird* people."

Barry told her she wasn't wrong, but, he said, it would be a good idea for her to keep up this friendship with Isaac.

"Why?" She laughed. "I mean, they don't give us any money, do they?"

Barry looked around as if there might be spies, which was his funny affectation before he spilled an especially good piece of gossip. "Iz, come on? You didn't notice?"

"What?"

"Imlak is that kid's dad. *Everybody* knows."

"Jesus, really?"

"Compare the noses. Why do you think I keep him around? For Abbie Mayer? What's *he* done lately?"

"Oh," she said. "*Oh.*"

7

The basic error in every conspiracy theory is that the conspiracy theorist believes, *a priori,* that the conspirators know what the conspiracy is, but plans carried out in secret are no more immune to dumb momentum, inattention, and decay than those acted out in the open. Maybe less so. It would be giving Abbie and Veronica and Phillip Harrow too much credit to assign devilish intentionality to every detail of their crass land grab. In the month or so since the young Barry Fitzgerald had tipped Abbie and Phil off in the dusty hallway outside of the zoning board, Phil and Veronica had quietly pestered their couple of contacts in the Charleston and Harrisburg statehouses respectively, harried midlevel legislative staffers who'd passed their middle thirties without moving on to Washington, who'd hitched their careers to the wrong sorts of idiots and madmen. They'd tell you anything for the price of a costly steak and some booze. There was indeed a plan, or actually, a set of three or four competing plans, to build a new highway route along and through the half-ruined towns of the Monongahela Valley, a decaying industrial artery of the Steel City, and onward through the collapsed coal economy of Fayette County and down to Morgantown, West Virginia, which was already connected to

Pittsburgh via interstate but stood to gain a bunch of construction jobs and federal highway dollars. This was all predicated on a vague theory that the road would somehow revitalize the economies of Donora and Monessen and Charleroi and Brownsville, the actual mechanics of which no one could quite diagram or explain.

The Mayer-Harrow triumvirate had an incidental, or exigent, interest in the highway. Though Harrow had built plenty of roads and interchanges over the years, the truth was that big infrastructure was a jobs program; highways were constituent bribes, high cost but low margin; the loose millions and billions that flowed into them went mostly to payroll, and state and federal contracts made contractors responsible for cost overruns. Since the jobs were bid out and awarded to the lowest responsible bidder, even the opportunities to pad out an estimate and build profit into the budget were constrained.

Housing, on the other hand, was profitable, especially if the land was cheap. There was a great deal of underdeveloped and rural land between Pittsburgh and Uniontown, rolling acres that would be just a half an hour from the city with a proper highway connection, ideal for the development of bedroom communities, a phrase that Harrow had begun repeating with talismanic intensity, as if it might abracadabra the idea into existence. And so they decided to get involved in the bid process on the dream highway, to get in early on the decision about the road's final route, to figure out as best they could the location of future exits, and in so doing, to give themselves an early opportunity to buy up the best parcels for future development, cheaply and quietly, before any other speculators or developers got to it.

Whichever route it took in the end, the longest stretch of the highway would pass through Fayette County. "It's time to call Sherri Larimer," Harrow said.

Phil and Veronica had arranged the meeting, and they'd all loaded into Phil's big car and floated on its glossy suspension over the potholes on Route 51. They crossed 70 and went past the Knotty Pine and the Cedarbrook Golf Course and up the long slow hill that crested right around Blue Top Road and then down the steeper side, past the car dealerships, into Perryopolis, a tiny borough noted principally for its auto auction and its speed trap.

In fact, there was a pretty little village, frame houses and a patriotic town square, a half mile east of the highway. If you could call 51 a highway. Years later, a woman named Beth Yuell who'd once cooked with Alice Waters out in California moved there and bought one of those old houses on a half-acre lot and turned it into a bed-and-breakfast-cum-restaurant. She bought quail from local hunters, and in the spring, she went up into the mountains with her golden Lab and brought back muddy paper bags full of morels, which she served with the white asparagus that she grew herself on another plot of land she'd bought on the other side of the river. She told Abbie that she'd come back— she'd been born in Belle Vernon, twenty miles away on a different river—in order to make less money and get more for it. She'd given Isaac his first, his only, job when he was in high school. He waited tables there for six months to save money for a three-thousand-dollar bike that Abbie refused to buy for him and then stopped showing up. Years later, when he was in college, he showed up with a half case of Chateau Margaux.

His apology, he said. Beth didn't ask where it had come from, although she had a fair idea.

But that was all yet to happen. That day, the proprietors of MH Partners, LLC and Mayer Design Lab were to meet Sherri Larimer at Marge's, which was on the side of the southbound lane of 51, just before the auto auction. Marge's had a reputation as a titty bar, a reputation that was confirmed or compounded, depending, by the presence of the by-the-hour Perry-O Motel a mile or so farther down 51. The Perry-O was reputedly the nexus of area prostitution, and it was also a popular spot, at the time, for married men who preferred to have sex with each other rather than with their wives, in part, one supposed, because if ever spotted on the premises, they could reasonably claim to have been screwing hookers, which was better than being queer. Regardless, Marge's specific reputation was undeserved. It was a dive, to be sure, a windowless pile of cinder block with a grease-clogged fry fan sprouting from the rear wall like an oozing pimple on a featureless face, and there were surely women—and men—here and there, who'd exchange hurried sex in a parked car for a little drug money, but the owner-bartender was a ham-armed woman named Bev who lived with her third husband (a genial but quiet former truck driver now on the Social Security of his late first wife) in a single-wide trailer out back. "I don't need a bunch of meth-sick drop-outs shakin their asses to nig-nog music on my bar," she told Abbie, months later, when he'd tried to joke with her about the bar's reputation. He'd raised a skeptical eyebrow—mostly to convince himself that he wasn't a passive recipient of such an overtly racist comment—then quickly changed the subject and asked why the bar was called Marge's if her name was Bev.

She lifted his glass and wiped underneath. "Marge was my old man's first wife."

"Oh. I take it she moved on," Abbie said.

Bev looked sidelong down the bar to Sherri Larimer, and when Abbie followed her glance, Sherri cracked an evil grin and said, "Oh, yeah. She *moved on.*"

This first time Abbie visited Marge's, though, Bev was frying something or other in the back and only came out to introduce herself brusquely to the Pittsburghers and give a deferential nod to Larimer. They were served by a thin man in a tank top that exposed a Styx tattoo on his shoulder. There were a few midday drunks smoking cigarettes and watching soaps on the tiny TV on a shelf above the chips and pretzels. Sherri and Billy, her older son, were at a picnic table in the back. She was smoking her slims.

This was before Sherri became county commissioner, although she was already rumored to be the money behind Ron Cavignac, the then-sitting commissioner whom she'd eventually replace. The Larimers had some real estate holdings—rentals, mostly—in Fayette, Washington, and Greene counties, as well as their land down in West Virginia. Sherri lived in a great gaudy mansion on a hill above the village of Smock. Her husband, an amiable and stupid man from an amiable and stupid Brownsville family, was nominally in charge of the family's most openly profitable business: combination miniature golf courses and shooting ranges, the Hole-in-Gun chain, of which there were three in Fayette County, one in Greene, and one down in West Virginia just outside of Morgantown. There were rumors that the Larimers also funneled most of the meth, heroin, and coke into the tri-county area. Harrow thought these were only rumors, perpetuated by the Larimers themselves as a prop to their reputation as hard-assed local kingmakers. Veronica thought it was entirely possible that they *were* drug dealers and used their properties to launder the ill-gotten cash.

Veronica had told Abbie to keep quiet. "These people are suspicious," she said, "and they require a delicate touch." So, of course, the first thing he did after introductions all around was to gesture grandly at the bar and tell Sherri that he loved her conference room.

Veronica looked at Harrow, and Harrow looked at Veronica, and they both waited for Sherri to explode or instruct Billy to threaten everyone with a pistol or some such Larimeresque stunt, but she laughed and shook Abbie's hand and said, "Shit. I like this one!" She pumped his hand again. "The new guy."

"Well, thanks," said Abbie. "I hope it's the beginning of a fruitful relationship."

"Fruitful," repeated Bill. He giggled, then narrowed his eyes.

"Shut up, boy," said Sherri. "Why are you so goddamn obsessed with homos? It means productive. Profitable." She studied Abbie for a moment. "Nice suit," she said at last.

"You ever read the *Wall Street Journal*?" Abbie asked.

"Abbie," said Phil.

Sherri tapped her finger twice on the table, in a sign that Harrow and Veronica had learned to interpret as something like a threat.

"On occasion," said Sherri. "The truth is that I ain't real big on what you might call the Wall-Street mentality. I prefer to make my money the tangible way, if you know what I mean."

"Surely," said Abbie. "I'm an architect by trade. Perhaps we have that in common. The tangible. I only brought it up, because if you ever read the *Journal*, you'll notice that from time to time, there are these ads for Hong Kong tailors who come to New York, and you can go and pay, oh, five thousand bucks, and he'll make you five suits, ten shirts, and two hard-boiled eggs. Well, I always thought it was a joke, but then one day, my wife said to me, 'Abbie Mayer, you need some new suits,' and pointed out one of these ads. And I said, 'Sarah, that's got to be a scam.' I'm a native of the New York Babylon, so I assume everything is a scam. And she said, 'No. My father used to go to these guys.' And her father, let me tell you, had some very nice suits. So I went downtown to where this little guy from Hong Kong had set up shop, and sure enough, he made me the nicest suits I ever had."

"I like a man in a suit." Sherri eyed Harrow, who was in his typical golf shirt and khakis.

"What?" Harrow said.

"Phil and Veronica here once tried to screw me in a deal, but Ray-Ray pulled a knife on their suit, and he crapped in his pants."

"That's not quite fair," Veronica protested. "You made good money."

"Not quite fair," said Larimer. "Not quite. But yinz originally came down there with some suppositions about my sort of people."

"Well," said Abbie, "that's why I'm here." He gestured to his sister, on his left, and to Harrow, on his right. "I am," he said, "the people person."

"Can we get down to it?" asked Veronica. "I don't mean to be the bitch who always talks business, but I'm going to be that bitch."

"Let's," said Sherri. "What do yinz drink?"

Veronica and Harrow stuck with ginger ale. Abbie asked for a Sambuca. "Really, Abbie?" said Veronica. She indicated with her eyes that this was not that type of bar.

Abbie in turn grinned at Sherri. "I deduce," he said, "from her name and bearing that Sherri here's got some Italian in her, from way back, and I bet there's some Sambuca in this bar."

"Take this one to Vegas," Sherri told Veronica. She gestured toward the back bar. "Now, like the lady said. Let's get down to it. Phil here told me the general outlines on the phone. Okay. I'm game, in theory. But I don't see how the hell anyone here makes money building a damn highway, except Phil, of course. Even Phil. Shit, you'll have to underbid cost to get the low bid anyway."

"We're not going to build the highway," said Veronica.

"Well, not the *whole* highway," Harrow added.

"We're more interested in the idea of the highway," Abbie said. "The concept."

"The concept." Larimer appeared amused. Two shots of clear Sambuca appeared between her and Abbie. She lifted hers, he lifted his, she tossed hers back, he tossed his back. "Did you ever actually build a highway, Phil?"

"Ramps and interchanges."

"Oh, I see," Larimer said. She nodded and tapped another cigarette out of her pack.

"Do you?" Abbie cocked his head.

"Shit, Mr. New York, I wasn't born at night. So what, you got another Wal-Mart up your sleeve?"

"Better," Veronica told her. "Subdivisions."

"Bedroom communities," Harrow added.

Larimer considered it. "I follow. Sure."

"I don't get it," said Billy.

Sherri slapped the table. The drinks rattled. "Do you need to get it, boy? Will you go play darts? Here." She pulled a wallet out of her purse and a few bills from the wallet. "Take the car down the road and get me some of that fudge at the fudge store."

"Aw, ma."

"Get me some goddamn fudge, boy, or I'll bust your eggs. And scramble them."

"Yes ma'am." He skulked out, but not without turning once in the bright doorway and projecting an angry look back into the room.

"That boy." Larimer shook her head and found a cigarette. "Any of yinz got kids?"

"Three boys," said Harrow.

"I know about *your* kids, Phil. I'm talking to these two."

Veronica shook her head. Abbie said, "Not yet."

"You want mine? I got two and another one on the way. Though I ain't showing yet. If there's any eggs I oughta bust, it's my goddamn old man's. Anyway, where were we?"

"In order to build the thing," Veronica said, "you've got to assemble the land. The right-of-way. And then you've got to figure out your exits and on-ramps, where you're going to connect to the local roads. The majority of this thing is going to pass through Fayette County. I mean, we've looked at the topographic maps, and there are only so many routes the thing can take. We figure probably sixty percent of the overall mileage will be down here. So we've got two issues. One issue is we've got to get a better sense of the route, and that's really why we get involved in bidding, but also, that's a big piece of construction, and we need someone with your . . . connections in the local power structure as well. And issue two is we need to quietly *and quickly* acquire the acreage we'll need down the road, so to speak."

"To build the fuckers."

"Yes," Veronica agreed, "to build the fuckers."

Sherri Larimer took a long drag. "That ain't bad," she said. "That ain't bad. Although you ain't the only ones to think of it, that's for sure."

"No," Veronica agreed, "probably not, which is why time is of the essence."

"Well sure," Sherri nodded. "But at the same time, you don't want to rush in. It'd be too obvious to anyone else trying to buy up the same property."

"Who else would be buying the same property?" Harrow asked.

"It's hypothetical," Sherri said. "You familiar with the term?"

Harrow grumbled.

Larimer said, "The other thing—issue three, you might say, Miss Lawyer—is that you can't just go buying all that land around a brand-new, hell, not-built highway if you're also proposing to build it. There's gonna be rules against that."

"Oh, that's where I come in," Abbie said. Veronica noted a change in his manner; she'd assumed he'd view the whole thing with a prissy moral reluctance, although, needing the money, he'd come around. Instead, he was warming up to a role as some kind of brassy, hilarious gangster. He was probably trying to impress Larimer, but she knew how easily Abbie could fall into a good role. He said, "I'm the patsy." He grinned. "The real question," he added, "is whether or not you think you can wrangle the prized information out of one or other of your charming local officials, and whether or not you can assist in convincing the Farmer

Browns and Miner Smiths around here to sell cheap and sell fast and keep their traps shut when they do."

She tapped her finger once, twice on the table. "Surely I can," she said. "Why, I'm a major benefactor, I think you'd say, around these parts."

"This is some good Sambuca, by the way," Abbie said. Another had arrived, and he was sipping it. "The black bottle, if I'm not wrong."

"You're not wrong." She took his glass and sipped from the opposite side of the rim. "I always did have a taste for licorice." She sighed. "Keeps ya regular."

· · ·

They'd ended the meeting with Harrow suggesting that Sherri let it percolate for a few weeks, and then, on a weird, cold day in November when freezing rain and an early snow entombed the trees and their unfallen leaves in grotesque, translucent cocoons, Sherri called Veronica in the morning and said they had better come down to Uniontown to finish their chat. They met Larimer at the old Mt. Vernon Inn, a sagging motor-court lodge whose shrink-wrapped and mostly unoccupied rooms remained open only to justify the existence of the inn's actual and profitable business, which was its large and raucous bar. It was all later torn down to make room for a Walgreens; all the good places, Abbie would tell you, were sacrificed to uniformity. Abbie thought it would be funny to spend the night there, but Sherri Larimer told him it wasn't for people like him, and she ordered him to book rooms at the Holiday Inn out past the mall instead. Harrow, who'd come up separately, said he'd just drive back to Morgantown. "You might be drunk," Veronica told him.

"I'll certainly be drunk. What's that got to do with it?"

Larimer had insisted that they meet at nine on a Friday night. The bar was packed with men on a rough approach to fifty and a few equally rough, if generally younger, women, who were all angled to gaze mournfully at the drunks walking too carefully past the unattended hostess desk and around the round tables between the front door and their sweating drinks. The whole place smelled of an ashtray left out in the rain. There was a band playing on a riser at the far end of the room. They mostly played Little Feat covers. Larimer bought drinks and insisted they listen to a set. Harrow rolled his eyes and spent the next thirty minutes watching a muted baseball game on a tiny TV over the bar and stuffing stale pretzel rods into his mouth. The screen was so fuzzed with static that one of the drunks beside him leaned over and mumbled through his cigarette, "Hey, buddy, is this TV *fucked up*, or am *I fucked up*?"

"TV looks fine to me," Harrow told him.

"Christ," the man muttered.

Abbie grinned and chuckled and sang along with the band and occasionally tapped Larimer with a collegial elbow at some song lyric that they both found funny. "What's their name?" he yelled.

"Who?" Larimer shouted back. She drank Seven and Seven and smoked slims.

"What's the band called?"

"Alimony."

Abbie's smile grew. "Where'd they come up with that?"

Larimer chuckled and tapped ash onto the floor. "Where do you think?" she bellowed.

Veronica spent the half hour wondering why she'd ever given

up the practice of ordinary law if the price of prosperity was this constant mucking about in the poorest places in America. Like all of the Mayers, she was essentially a snob; unlike them, she admitted it. She'd done very well in this business, keeping her partnerships and exposure limited, using other people's money to buy and build things from which she profited, and well. Unlike her former law firm—or any law firm—there weren't any old men in her way. Yes, she still had to conduct a lot of her business through conduits like Phil Harrow, this male-drag-at-a-distance necessitated by the same sexist systems that would have delayed and stymied her rise in the grotesque fraternity of the practice of law, but at least here this self-diminishment was purely instrumental, albeit still unjust in its necessity.

Her partner, Edith, argued this point with her. She thought these male proxies were absurd for someone of Veronica's intelligence and accomplishment. Veronica pointed out that Edith had worked for Harrow, and Edith would just give a thin smile and say, "But I'm not you." Veronica occasionally worried that they'd fallen into an insupportable, gender-normative relationship in which she fulfilled the typically male role in the household with Edith as the supportive wife, but wasn't that inevitable? For all she wanted to be innocent of the wrongheadedness around her, wasn't she ultimately tainted by it no matter what she did? Didn't everyone fulfill, even in their small rebellions, the very inequities that they'd rebelled against?

After the set was over, Larimer led them through a service door and into a storage area stacked with folding tables and chairs. The band had hauled down a couple of tables and turned the place into a makeshift green room, but three of them skedaddled back to the bar when Larimer came in, all but the frontman, a fat guy with a shiny head and a vaguely professorial air derived mainly from the patches on the elbows of his jacket. He was smoking a joint. "Hey Sherri," he said. "I was just hittin' this nag champa. I'll be going."

"No, Bob. You stick around."

Bob flicked the joint nervously and sent an appealing glance toward Veronica, Abbie, and Harrow.

"Don't look at them, Bobby. Look at me."

"Sorry, Sherri. I didn't mean anything."

Veronica noted that unlike Larimer, unlike most of the people she'd encountered in Uniontown, this fat stoner spoke a perfectly uninflected American English.

"I'm sure you didn't think you did, but I seen you looking. Don't worry, you can go on smoking that weed."

"You mind? I mean, this looks serious." He glanced around again, caught himself, and dipped his head to look at the floor.

"I don't mind. I insist."

"Thanks." He hit the joint. "All that smoke out there really gets to me."

Veronica raised and lowered her foot and said, "Not to be the lawyer of the group, but maybe we ought to find somewhere more private." She indicated Bob with a tilt of her head. Like a lot of lawyers, Veronica believed only provisionally in the law, but she had a rigorous, almost religious reverence for the forms of confidentiality. "If you don't mind, of course, Sherri."

"Nah," said Larimer, and she swung her leg over the back of a chair and sat, folding her arms across its back. "Mr. Krupp is my main man. He's got his finger on the pulse."

"What pulse is that?" asked Veronica.

"The pulse of Uniontown."

"Not much of a pulse," said Harrow.

"Phil, shut the fuck up. Bob," Larimer ordered, "tell them what you told me."

"Ah, man, Sherri. Look, I just was a little short on the child support, and I—"

"No, Jerry goddamn Garcia. Not about the loan. We'll talk about that later. Tell them about the road."

"Well." He took a fortifying hit. "Okay. I was drinking the other night over at the Titlow Tavern. We had a gig. And I heard Marv Edison tell Patrick Dell that he heard from Jerry Rittenhauer that Mantini Construction was going to be hiring for a big PennDOT job in the next year or so and was looking for local guys to do general labor."

Veronica rolled her eyes. "Who are these people?" Of all the things she found difficult and distasteful in Fayette County, the endless parade of names from the mouths of people who assumed you already knew who they were was what annoyed her the most. It was impossible to keep them straight. Edith, who'd grown up in tiny Point Marion, told her that she ought to learn to ignore it entirely. But Veronica had an attorney's mind, and it demanded tags and attributions.

"Well, let's see," said Krupp. "Marv and Pat are cousins, I guess. Not actual cousins, but, I believe Marv's mother's sister-in-law is Pat's aunt, so it's a through marriage thing. They're just a couple of strung-out assholes, but when they're not on disability, they pick up construction jobs here and there. And Jerry—excuse me, Officer Rittenhauer—works for Mack Chislett, who's the chief of police. The mayor tells Mack shit, and Mack tells Jerry shit, and Jerry shouldn't drink whiskey, because when he does, he talks. Then he cries, usually, or gets into fights. Which is good for us."

"Don't worry. I got some shit on Jerry Rittenhauer," Larimer told them. She tapped on the back of the chair. "We go back. Here's what I'm getting at. What I'm getting at is that Bill Pattaglia"—she paused to catch Veronica in a nasty stare—"that's the mayor—Bill Pattaglia and that faggot Jerry—that's Jerry Jernicki, by the way, not Jerry Rittenhauer, who's pretty goddamned fruity himself, if you know what I mean—have been talking to Harrisburg, and they're cooking up some kind of in-state vendor requirement to keep our boy Phil here out of the running."

"How do they even know I'm interested?" Phil asked.

Larimer shrugged. "Yinz been asking around, right? And you probably already asked to get on the list for the RFP."

"Sure." Harrow shrugged. "I've got my sources, too."

"Yeah, well, you think the people who blab shit they're not supposed to blab are real discreet otherwise?"

"Do you mind if I bum a hit?" Abbie asked Krupp.

"Go for it, man. I love your jacket, by the way."

"Thank you." Abbie accepted the joint and inhaled deeply. "One hundred percent Egyptian linen."

"Abbie, for fuck's sake." Veronica knew that she was betraying something about herself by standing while the rest them sat or leaned, knew that her brother found her harsh and her partner found her hysterical, which was what you got for being a woman who gave direction. It occurred to her that she wasn't sure when, or if, Sherri Larimer had *stopped* liking her, when her allegiance had shifted toward her business partner and then toward her brother.

"Well, hell, what if I move my offices to Uniontown?" asked Harrow. "That'd be easy enough."

Veronica shook her head. "There'll be some kind of duration

of residency requirement to avoid that sort of thing. A carpetbagger clause, basically. That's the usual form of these things. We need to head it off, if it's true. Once it's done, it's done."

"Then, how do we get around it?" Harrow tipped back in his chair and nearly fell. He caught himself. Larimer smirked. "Shit." He rocked again. "I mean, there's gotta be a way around it, right? I mean, head it off. Whatever. This is a good nut to crack, in terms of the, you know, the larger ambitions."

"*La longue durée*," said Abbie to no one in particular, and he laughed to himself and then took another hit.

"Marc Bloch!" said Krupp.

"Cheers!" Abbie passed the weed.

Larimer shrugged again. "My guess is that someone already prefers Mantini, for whatever reason, but they know they won't come in with a low bid, so they're trying to preempt that possibility by cutting out Harcon. Or they've got the same plans as us clowns."

"Where's Mantini Construction?" asked Abbie.

"Connellsville," Harrow replied. "Why?"

"Is that in Fayette County?"

"Sure is, hon," Larimer said. "You have a thought?"

"I don't know," said Abbie. He looked at her. "Do *you* have a thought?"

"Weh-ellll." Sherri Larimer was especially terrifying when she smiled. "I think I see where you're going with this."

"Was I going somewhere with something?" Abbie chuckled. He'd taken the one hit, then two, then a third before passing the weed back to Krupp, and had forgotten what exactly they were talking about.

"I think *I* see where you're going," said Veronica to Larimer.

She looked to Phil for support, but the coward looked away. "I'd rather . . . it would be better to not discuss this in front of, what's your name? Sorry?"

"Bob."

"Bob's fine," Larimer insisted.

"Sherri," Veronica said.

Larimer regarded the other woman for a moment, and Veronica, though she found this sort of staring contest unseemly and absurd, the sort of dick-measuring posture better left for boys who imagined business as a contest of wills rather than a simple question of position and interest, matched her stare, until finally Larimer permitted herself a smile that Veronica interpreted as the concession that allowed her to look marginally away. Then Sherri said, "Okay. Get out of here, Bob."

"Well, the thing is—" he began, and he slightly lifted the still-lit roach in his hand, but Sherri tapped twice and bit on the inside of her lip, and Bob reversed course and said, "Yep, I'll let you all be." He dropped the joint on the floor and stomped out the embers. "Uh, cheers," he said to none of them in particular, and he executed an awkward half-bow that was mostly a nod of the head and all but backed out of the room.

"I liked him," said Abbie.

Larimer said, "Bob's fine, Mayer."

"Who?" said Abbie.

"I was talking to your sister."

"Right."

"Fine," Veronica said. "But there's a certain precautionary principle at work here."

Harrow said, "I didn't smoke any goddamn ganja, and I don't know what you're all talking about either."

"What I'm saying," said Veronica, who now permitted herself to lean against a stack of chairs, who wished, though she hadn't had a smoke in years, that she had a cigarette right then, or, barring that, a scotch, "what I'm saying is, if I read you correctly, Sherri, is that we might be able to take an opportunity to, oh, lobby against the other participant in the process rather than the process itself."

"Why?"

"Because no one really gives a fuck about who builds a road. Mantini probably promised someone something. And if he didn't, maybe we can suggest that he did."

"Yes," Larimer agreed. "I'm sure we surely can."

"Yeah, but what will that cost us?" asked Harrow.

"Haven't the slightest," said Veronica. "Sherri, *hon*. Would you care to put a figure to it?"

Larimer said, "Shit, you got a thousand bucks?"

"What's that for then?" Abbie asked.

"Seems cheap," Harrow said.

"Just to be clear," said Veronica. "If we do this, we have to, for obvious reasons, leave the details to you, Sherri. If you're comfortable with that."

She laughed loudly and lit one of her slims. "It's not like we're going to kill the guy!" She raised an eyebrow at Harrow.

"Jesus Christ," Harrow replied. "Don't fucking kill anybody."

"No. Obviously. Hell. I figure we'll just plant drugs in his car. Jernicki."

"What?" said Abbie. "Who?"

"Don't worry, sweetie." Sherri patted his knee affectionately. "That's some good weed, huh? You know where he gets it from?" She winked.

"She's kidding!" said Veronica.

"Well, not about the weed." Sherri exhaled. "I'm just saying, we'll spread some rumors. Pass some dispersions, if you know what I mean."

Later that night, Phil was in his Lincoln on a dark road back to Morgantown, and Veronica and Abbie were sitting in the dull Holiday Inn bar drinking nightcaps. Abbie, no longer so stoned, asked Veronica if they'd just agreed to something illegal. "Not strictly," she said, but then she murmured, "I hope," into her glass. "By the way," she said, "What was Sherri talking to you about when we went back out to the bar?"

"Oh, some property."

"What property, Abbie?"

"None. Nothing. I mentioned to her, a few weeks ago, when we met her at that other charming establishment, that I'd had a sort of vision of a property on top of a mountain, which I described to her. She was telling me—tonight I mean—that she knew just the spot."

"Please don't deal with Sherri Larimer without me."

"No, no. I just. I'm just interested in looking. She told me it's along an old gas line access road up on top of the ridge, actually. And cheap."

"I'm serious, Abbie."

"Yes, okay."

"And stop fucking telling people that you've had visions. They'll think you're nuts."

"A vision, repeated. Like a theme and variations. And why the hell do I care if they think I'm nuts? And also, you'd be surprised, really, how perfectly willing people are to accept the basic fact of it, provided you gauge them properly and describe it in terms they can understand. You yuppies accept it if I cast it in terms of artistic creativity; Sherri accepts it because she's a superstitious yokel. But—"

"She's not stupid."

"No. That's not what I said. By the way, do you know someone named Inman? Imnack?"

"No. Why?"

"She said he owned the property. On the mountain. I was, as you may have noted, slightly looped at the time. I don't think that weed was just weed."

"I'm going to pay, Abbie. Let's get out of here early. This whole town is a dive. I find it slightly threatening."

"Do you think? I find it charming."

"You're not gay. Or a woman."

"No. But you're not visibly. Gay, I mean. You're visibly a woman, which mitigates, I suppose, against the other thing."

"Fuck you, Abbie. That's a fucked up thing to say." She placed a twenty on the counter and kissed his cheek. "Seven A.M.," she said. "Or I leave you at the mercy of the local tribes."

. . .

In early December, Jerry Jernicki was pulled over on 119 heading into Uniontown for driving sixty-five miles per hour in a fifty-five zone.

"I'm sorry sir," said Officer Jerry Rittenhauer, "but I detect the smell of alcohol. I'm going to have to administer a field sobriety test."

"Are you fucking kidding me?" asked Jernicki. "Do you know who I am?"

"Step out of the car, sir."

Jernicki asked for a breathalyzer, but, by odd coincidence, Rittenhauer's unit wasn't functioning.

"Please walk nine steps and turn on one foot," the officer ordered. At eight steps, he told Jernicki to stop. "I'm sorry sir, but you appear to be inebriated, and that gives me probable cause to search your vehicle."

"Search away," Jernicki said. The officer then discovered quantities of cocaine and methamphetamine just below the limit for intent to distribute.

"That's not mine!" protested Jernicki.

"Of course it isn't," said the officer.

"I swear to you," Jernicki said. "I don't know how that got there."

"Me neither," said Rittenhauer. "Now please turn around."

Two months after that, Mayor Bill Pattaglia of Uniontown, County Commissioner Cavignac, and Congressman Menta announced that after discovering "irregularities in the bidding process that may have been related to a possible kickback deal between Alan Mantini of Mantini Construction and County Commissioner Jerome Jernicki, whose troubles with narcotics were a cause for sorrow, and our prayers are with him, we are pleased to announce that the bid for the construction of a new interchange between the Uniontown Bypass and the future Route 43 Mon-Fayette Extension of the Pennsylvania Turnpike has nevertheless been awarded to the other lowest bidder, Harcon Construction of Morgantown, West Virginia, who has covenanted to use ninety percent local labor and/or subcontractors in terms of overall payroll and invoicing, thereby bringing a net economic benefit in excess of twenty-one million dollars directly to Fayette County! And now we're going to ask Phillip Harrow, CEO of Harcon, to say a few words."

. . .

"What the fuck, Ronny?"

"What the fuck what?"

He tossed a copy of the Uniontown *Herald-Standard* on her desk. JERNICKI RESIGNS. SPECIAL ELECTION TO BE CALLED.

"Yes?"

"We did this."

"Calm down, Abbie."

"No. This is *fucked*. This is illegal."

Veronica rubbed her temple. That morning, she'd had the same argument with Edith. "What, specifically, is illegal?"

"Fuck you, specifically."

"The only illegality that I can see," Veronica said, "is this alleged kickback scheme between former commissioner Jernicki and his preferred firm."

"Which is bullshit and you know it! And also, the drugs!"

"Yes, he was transporting quite a large—"

"You put them there!"

"No."

"Sherri Larimer did it!"

"At your suggestion."

"At my . . . Don't you dare! I didn't—"

"Abbie, sit down."

"No."

"Sit down." She said it softly. He sat. She recalled when they were barely teenagers, he and two other boys, boys who weren't even his friends, really, had tossed a neighbor's cat from a fire escape; he'd been utterly untroubled by the death of the poor animal until the woman who'd owned it posted signs around the neighborhood and its broken little body was discovered behind some trash cans in the alley and he saw the lady, who lived in a different building, whom none of them had ever met, standing at the end of that alley holding back tears. She was only in her mid-thirties, though that seemed old to them at the time, and Abbie had only happened to be passing the scene, and he heard her sniff and say, "That poor thing." He made it home before he started to cry. Then he was inconsolable, and Veronica had to hide the cause of his grief—if grief was the right word for it—from their parents, concocting a foolishly elaborate teenage story about Abbie having been bullied by the very boys he'd been with when they killed the cat. Mom and Dad didn't believe her, but they didn't press her either. It was in keeping with their universal preference not to know. There was—in society, in literature, in psychology—a belief in change by degrees, that a person moved by increments from good to bad, each tiny tick of the watchwork gears imperceptible until, over time, the hands on the face had visibly moved. And in this metaphor, Abbie's youthful cruelty was at once an aberration and precisely such an increment. But wasn't it truer to say that the good and the evil, or the right and the wrong, or the sin and the righteousness, always coexisted within each person; he was neither one thing nor the other: not the clockwork, but the quartz, vibrating imperceptibly between alternate states, never, to the observer, in one or in the other; molecular; quantum; even the act of looking might alter it. Look at that sad, dead creature. It was only in the light of observation that it became bad to begin with.

"Abbie," she said, "this is the business we're in."

"Speak for yourself. I'm not in any business where this sort of thing goes on."

"Yes you are. And you know you are. But if you want out, please."

"What do you mean by that?"

"I mean exactly what I said. Say the word. This is a business partnership only. We'll still be brother and sister. I won't forsake you. Phil will hate your guts, but what do you care? You don't have much of an equity stake, but if you want out, by all means, I will write you a check. There's no zoning board. There's no environmental impact study. Your input isn't needed. You can go back to being an architect."

"I never stopped being an architect."

"Abbie."

"I didn't."

"When was the last time you designed a building?"

"I still have speaking engagements. I still write."

"What was the last thing you wrote?"

"Yes, all right. Your point is taken. But this is wrong, Ronnie. And don't look at me like that. I'm not naïve. I understand that we are obliged, sometimes, to live among the barbarians, such as it is. I understand that. I understand that this business is full of unsavory characters and that everyone is on the make and that the first truly honest man in the building business will also be the last, but doesn't it fall to us to try to be decent? If not wholly honest, then mostly? If not mostly, then occasionally? When we can? When we could still do all right by it? Is it necessary to debase ourselves just because our peers and our colleagues are debased?"

Veronica wove the bare fingers of her hands together, and she looked at her brother. He wore a plain gold band. Sarah, she knew, wore their grandmother's diamond. "Yes," she said.

"Yes?"

"It was a nice speech, Abbie, but yes. Yes. Yes! We do what we need to do. Will you calm the fuck down? No one died! You make it into this big thing. This is the way it's done. And meanwhile, you tell me you're working on some private deal with the same woman you think—with no evidence, by the way—you *think* set up some asshole rural potentate on some embarrassing but ultimately irrelevant charge that's gonna get him an admonition and a sentence of going to AA or something."

"It's not a private deal. I mean, it is, but it isn't a *business* deal."

"Oh no? What is it?"

"I'm going to build a house there. You don't understand. I drove down to see that property. I walked on it. I'd seen it before." Where he'd been angry, where he'd pontificated, now he looked at her, pained and desperate. "I'd seen it, Ronnie."

That night at home, after she'd had a glass of wine, after Edith, who was an excellent cook, had served her *coq au vin* and poured her another glass and turned on a Louis Armstrong and Ella Fitzgerald album and ate with her without saying a word, because Edith, alone, knew her, knew when Veronica needed to talk, knew when Veronica needed to be quiet, it occurred to Veronica that her brother might be crazy—not that it hadn't occurred to her before, exactly; it had, in one sense, frequently occurred to her; it had occurred to her in the way that you'd casually call anyone whose eccentricities exceed your own crazy. And it would have meant something almost exactly like that, that her brother's eccentricities exceeded her own. But couldn't it be true, equally true, simultaneously true, that his madness tinged into the psychological; that his pomposity was symptomatic of a pathology; that his yammering on about visions wasn't just a self-promoting self-regard about his own genius, but rather something like mental illness—no, not something like it; rather, the thing itself?

"Do you think my brother is crazy?" Veronica asked.

Edith picked up her shallow dinner bowl and kissed her head. "Yes."

"No, I mean, really crazy. Like, ill."

"Yes," Edith said. "I'm going to flip the record."

"What should I do?"

She heard Edith running water in the kitchen. "I thought you were going to flip the album."

"You flip it. I forgot. My hands are wet."

"But what should I do?"

Edith came into the living room, drying her hands on her stained apron. She laughed. "You're such a man, sometimes."

Veronica turned on the B-side and set her face in an expression of mocking shock. "That's a terrible thing to say!"

"Aw, honey. It's true, though. You always think you have to do something. Why do you have to *do* anything?"

"I love you," Veronica said.

"Yes," Edith said. She walked back toward the kitchen. "You're not half bad yourself."

But that afternoon in her office, facing her brother across her paper-crowded desk, the last gray winter sunlight slanting bitterly through the windows behind her, she'd been too angry to consider the particularities of his mental state at all, had only seen a thickening egoist in a tightening jacket that, like all clothing that costs too much money, was too quickly out of style, and she'd ordered him out of her office, although, when he turned at the threshold and asked if they were still meeting tomorrow, she'd sighed loudly and told him yes.

• • •

That same evening, in another dining room in another part of the East End, Sarah and Abbie had nearly the same conversation, although Abbie's manner wasn't to sit silently in his own thoughts, but to recount them volubly as they scampered through his angry head. Sarah turned the ring around her finger and tried not to appear distracted as Abbie called her sister-in-law a criminal, or at least a suborner of crime. "I understand that this business is full of unsavory characters and that everyone is on the make and that the first truly honest man in the building business will also be the last, but doesn't it fall to us to try to be decent?" He shouted. "If not wholly honest, then mostly? If not mostly, then occasionally? When we can? When we could still do all right by it? Is it necessary to debase ourselves just because our peers and our colleagues are debased?"

"No," Sarah said. "It isn't."

"But?"

"But what?"

"But you have a look."

"What look?"

"A look of grim skepticism. A look that says you're humoring me. A look that suggests you disagree but are reserving comment for the sake of my ego."

"I'm frequently reserving comment for the sake of your ego, Abbie."

"My ego can take it."

"Yes, possibly." She poured herself more wine. "Or possibly not."

"You've been acting strange."

"No, Abbie. *You've* been acting strange."

"I mean since I went to Uniontown. The first time."

"Have I?"

"You have."

"Abbie, did you tell Phillip Harrow that he could sleep with me?"

"What the fuck are you talking about?"

"Did you tell Phil Harrow that we are some kind of swingers, that he would, 'Have a better chance with my wife'?"

"A better chance than what?"

"Fuck you, Abbie. You did."

"I may have joked—"

"He came here, you know."

"Who? Phil?"

"Yes, Phil. He came here. He came here that night. He turned around halfway to Morgantown and drove here. Drunk. He propositioned me."

Abbie didn't reply. He felt a high buzzing in his skull, a pressure behind his eyes. He stared at the space above her head.

"This was supposed to be a fresh start, Abbie. In your words. A fresh start. This whole bullshit. This move. This, I don't know. I even thought maybe we'd have a kid. Or try to, again. Try, at least. Fuck you, you tell your business partner to try to sleep with your wife?"

"I. Did you?"

"Did I? Did I what, fuck him? No, Abbie. No. He went and puked in the bathroom. A grown man! And I gave him coffee, and then he left."

"Good."

"You don't get to say good." Then she got up, and she said, "You can do the dishes."

Then Abbie said, "I bought it."

"You bought what?"

"The land. The land I told you about. On the mountain. The land that I saw in the dream."

"Oh, it was just a dream now."

"Not always. Not just. But this is where it was supposed to happen. This land. This is the new start I spoke of. This is it, Sarah. This is what we wanted."

"Oh, Abbie," Sarah said.

"It is," he said. The sound in his head had become a brightness around his field of vision.

"Does your sister know?"

"Not yet," he replied. "Not quite."

"Oh, Abbie," she said again.

8

It's harder to say what Sarah thought about all this. She was opaque, and the gearworks of her inner life turned so silently that even God strained to hear them whir. This would have been true even if she hadn't retreated into an inconsistent silence that her family interpreted as a sort of effective if not actual dementia. To Isabel, as she got to know them, it seemed just as likely a form of conscious protest. If Abbie were your husband, and Isaac your son, wouldn't you start drinking early, too? Wouldn't you do what you could to avoid their joint penchant for withering disdain? When Isaac was still just a kid, he and Sarah had formed an unusually (perhaps unhealthily) close and confidential bond, a conspiracy of semi-normalcy against Abbie's more mercurial manner. Isaac, Isabel thought, *was* still a kid. But the bond slackened, like old elastic, as he approached puberty. Sarah drank less back then. "Frequently drinking but not yet a drunk," Isaac said, which Isabel found fishy. Her own mother, Cathy, was in AA, and no one ever really escapes the faith of her youth.

Isaac always knew, at least suspected, that the real reason they left New York was an affair. For Isaac, it fulfilled a set of imperishable convictions about his father's character. If he did believe that Abbie had had a vision—truthfully, he wasn't sure, one way or the other, but thought not—then that still wouldn't rule out a more mundane proximate cause. Isaac and Sarah both generally told themselves that artistry, temperament, and the inadequacy of secular language to convey the nature and feeling of creative inspiration were the reality underlying the dreamy claims in Abbie's prophetic streak. In any case, who's to say that any event has any singular cause?

Certainly the affair explained more convincingly how Sarah ended up agreeing to come to Pittsburgh. It's a perverse but frequent trait of relationships that boredom wrecks them faster than betrayal; infidelity tightens the grasp more than faithfulness. If Abbie had been in love with someone else, it would have explained Sarah's desire, or at least her willingness, to flee with him. Certainly it was unlikely, having weighed the evidence, to imagine that she really believed Abbie was talking to God, first, because she was a believing Jew who therefore believed that the age of that sort of miraculous dialogue had passed, and second, because even if that were not the case, Abbie was as supremely unlikely a candidate for a prophecy as any that existed on earth—although, there is a counterargument: is it not frequently the case that God chooses (on the infrequent occasions when He does so choose) to speak to the least likely among us?

Isabel talked about all this with Isaac one day in September. It was still summer. It had been terrifically hot for a week. She'd driven down to visit him at The Gamelands, and he'd made Eli take the Land Rover and drive them farther into the mountains to a state park called Ohiopyle. Isabel remarked that Pennsylvania had some utterly extraordinary place names. "Hmm," Isaac said, which was what he often said when he disapproved of sentimentality. The park was in the hills and steep valleys around a series of cataracts and waterfalls on the Youghiogheny River, a north-flowing tributary of the Monongahela, which in turn flowed north to Pittsburgh. They hiked up a trail beside Meadow Run, a smaller stream that fed the river, climbing over boulders beside a natural water slide formed where the stream cut a narrow channel through a rock bed. Dozens of children with burnt shoulders and white bellies were bombing down the slide, banging their tailbones and screaming at the indifferent parents who sat smoking on the sandstone ledges beside the water.

Isaac turned to Isabel and laughed and said, "You know what we call this?"

"You told me," Isabel said. "The natural water slide."

"No." He laughed again. "That's what *it's called*. We *call it* the Redneck Riviera."

"Hush," said Eli.

They climbed a muddy timber staircase to a trail running parallel to the stream, fifty feet above. Isaac insisted that he knew a secret swimming spot to which they could climb down from the trail. Isabel didn't believe him, because they kept losing the trail and finding themselves on deer paths through the choked, dripping mountain laurels. She held a knot of unease in her chest, and she kept expecting that giant deer to burst forth once again from the underbrush. Rather than backtracking, Isaac would clamber up or slide down another muddy embankment through underbrush and stands of ferns until he found the path again. Isabel and Eli could only follow him. Isabel was tentative, trying to push branches aside gently, to step lightly over or duck under fallen logs, feeling a slightly embarrassing nausea at the thought of touching rotten wood or the wrong type of fungus or a bug with more than six legs, while Isaac was totally heedless, smashing through everything like one of the nightmare feral boars that were retaking European forests and occasionally attacking German ramblers. (Nightmare for the ramblers, that is; what funnier, more apt metaphors for the inevitable decline of an exhausted, dirty, nature-ruining civilization were there than an immense wild swine pursuing a frightened white person through the once-tamed woods?)

While they tried to keep up with Isaac, Isabel managed to elicit a modest biography from Eli: how he he'd met the Mayers. Eliécer Guitiérrez Valensi was a Spanish Jew—contra his last name, he was actually from a small town just outside of Seville, though his family was originally from the East—who'd fled his native country during the first European currency crisis. He joked that his family had managed to survive and even prosper through the Caliphate, which had been good for the Jews, and the Catholic empire, which had been rather less congenial, and the twentieth century, which had been the worst for everyone, regardless, only to see all its children—he had two siblings, one in Canada and one in Dubai, of all places—driven out by the endless, repeating financial crises. His parents still lived in Seville but he never visited. "I don't mind it," he said, "but it makes my mother sad. Do you understand? When we come home, it makes her remember that we had to leave." His father had been, ironically, a scholar specializing in the Almohads. He had worked for a small UNESCO office attached to the Seville Alcazar. Eli's mother had written cookbooks. Eli had studied to be an architect. "Of course," he said. That was how he met Abbie, who, after he'd made his money and finished his marvelous home, had gone back to giving the occasional lecture on sustainable architecture, particularly if it could be parlayed into an expenses-paid vacation—like many men, Abbie only discovered thrift when it became irrelevant to his personal finances.

"We intend," Isaac explained to Isabel a few weeks later, "to remain a mystery to our biographers and to pass therefore into the kingdom of myth." He was smoking a bowl when he said this and lying on a pile of vintage fabric in the middle of his Pittsburgh apartment. She'd asked him why he eschewed Facebook and why there were, in general, so few photographs of him online. In this regard, Isabel was very wrong, but she had no way of knowing at the time. She'd been trying to piece together a time line of the Mayers' travels and occupations, and she kept trying to ask clarifying questions of Isaac without giving the whole project away. A sort of documentary inconsistency bedeviled any attempt to account for their lives; they frequently seemed to exist in a set of parallel narratives, subtly different if broadly the same.

So Eli had been at university, studying to be an architect in Spain during that pre-crash period, when it seemed that the whole of the Iberian Peninsula was sprouting white condominiums like bright mushrooms in a meadow after a rain. Underneath there was rot. Eli had imagined himself designing the extraterrestrial subway entrances and crinkled glass pavilions that had become the particular specialty of Spanish architecture, but he found himself, at twenty-two, without a job or any prospects of a job, certainly not a job as an architect, and so he'd written Abbie a plaintive and ingratiating email, reminding him that they'd met briefly at a reception after Abbie's lecture. In fact, Eli had hardly said a word, and he feared he'd laughed too obligingly when Abbie disdained the Metropol Parasol and then the Gehry Guggenheim—Spain, he'd said, was being ruined by foreigners, a sentiment with which Eli more or less agreed, even if it was an awfully ironic pronouncement from a foreign architect. But Abbie also hated Calatrava and every other major contemporary Spanish architect. "Spanish architecture was all downhill after you kicked out the Muslims," Abbie said. Eli mentioned Gaudí and felt foolish for being so obvious. "Well, yes," Abbie had said, seeming to agree. "But there was a man who really believed in God, even if he believed in the wrong one."

Eli's email went unanswered, and he nearly forgot about it. But two weeks before Christmas, Eli tripped over the splayed body of an unconscious young man in the doorway of his apartment building on his way to work. Through his father's connections, he'd managed to find a job as a gardener at the Alcazar. At first, he'd attempted to believe that in this work he'd found an actual vocation and a truer form of labor than the attenuated, intellectualized, bourgeois pursuit of his once-chosen vocation, but the truth was that the work was miserable and dirty. The constant contact with plants afflicted him with a hypochondriac's conviction that he was always suffering from a rash; the physical labor, far from invigorating, was repetitive. He got back spasms. His shoulders ached. It exhausted him and made him want to drink beer. He found himself gaining weight and softening around the middle.

The young man—the boy, really—was Isaac, down on holiday from Paris, where he was doing his semester abroad. He'd come down to Seville to meet up with another man whom he'd met online on GayRomeo. This man's name was Paolo—well, his name was *activo22cm* but he went by Paolo IRL—and "he was thirty-two and he had an amazing cock," Isaac said. "I tried to get him to come to Paris instead, but he didn't have any money to travel, and I was going to be on break anyway. I got some molly from this bartender I knew in the twentieth and got an EasyJet down to Spain. We spent about twenty hours fucking and then he started to come down and got pissed off and started calling me a rich English cocksucker and telling me that he was going to tie me to the heater and get a bunch of African guys to come over and rape my ass. Europeans are so fucking racist. Let me tell you, that sort of thing will sober you up real fast. I don't think he would've gone through with it. I mean, we'd been doing a lot of fucking drugs. He went to the bathroom, and I just grabbed my stuff and got out of there."

He should have gone to find a hotel. Instead, Isaac proceeded to find a bar and get blisteringly drunk with what he described as one Turkish guy and two Lithuanian women who were probably prostitutes. He woke up the following morning in the cold, tiled doorway with no bag, wallet, or phone and a quizzical, ugly Spanish man kneeling over him and asking him if he was all right in alternating Spanish, English, and German. Isaac stayed with Eli for three days. His only good fortune had been to have left his passport in his Paris apartment, and he had to wait for it to arrive in the mail before he could get money from his Citibank account. Isaac liked to grandly hint that he and Eli had had some sort of briefly magnificent sexual affair during that period. Eli was so cheerfully good-humored in not denying the innuendos that Isabel immediately decided that it couldn't be true. At some point on the second day in Eli's apartment, over soup and beer, Isaac offhandedly mentioned who his father was. Eli was incredulous. "But I want to work for him!" he said. He may have been slightly drunk at the time, because it had never previously occurred to him that he wanted to work for Abbie Mayer, even if he did admire the man.

"He's not an architect anymore," Isaac told him, which was largely, if not entirely, true. Eli said he didn't care, and Isaac said he'd see what he could do. There was no faulting Isaac on this account: he kept his most extravagant promises. He and Eli remained in touch online, and then, rather than do anything so uncouth as bring it up directly with his parents, Isaac simply arranged, the summer after he returned to the States, for a visit from his friend from Spain. Eli was not a documented immigrant: he came to visit, and he never left.

Isaac may or may not truly have known of a secret place, but he found something resembling it. After a half an hour of fitful progress up the trail and back again, searching for some geographic or geologic marker that Isaac could not describe but was certain that he'd recognize, he said, confidently (of course, he said everything confidently), "Here it is!" He slid down another steep embankment. Isabel and Eli followed. They came to a high outcropping, below which they could hear the sound of rushing water. Here, finally, Isaac was cautious. They picked their way down a series of tall natural steps around the cliff, clinging to the twisted trees growing out of cracks in the rock. They shimmied along the wet underside of the cliff. They scooted down and over a rockfall. Isabel was too tentative in hopping from one boulder to the next. She windmilled her arms on the edge and tipped backward toward the twenty-foot drop between them. But Eli grabbed her by a flapping wrist and yanked her onto the rock. She fell briefly against him. "You're okay," he told her. She could smell his sweat.

There they were: a wide stretch of the stream narrowed and cut a channel between two huge, canted boulders with flat tops. It tumbled into a clear waterfall that dropped ten feet into a deep and clear hole below before it flowed around a sharp bend and disappeared down the valley. The walls rose a hundred feet on either side, thick with both the common deciduous foliage and a few slender eastern pines, glowing with that arboreal light, a daylight cathedral, bright in the shade and the color of something other than only sunlight. It smelled of the passage of water over stone.

"You see," said Isaac, who'd sensed that they'd begun to doubt him and hammed up his bushwhacking certainty for effect.

"It's really lovely," said Isabel. Then: "How *did* you find this place?"

"I had a vision," he said.

"Really?"

"Ha. Wut? No. I'm just fucking with you. I was on acid with Jake. I actually don't know how we ever found it."

The precise nature of Isaac's relationship with Jake remained unclear to Isabel, who, although she should have known better, imagined that Isaac fucking men other than the one that he lived with must be more complicated than it was. Also, Jake read as straight to her, even if he did follow Isaac around The Gamelands like a young man in something like love. It didn't occur to her that she didn't read him as gay because he was black and plainly athletic and casually masculine; if it had occurred to her, she'd have been ashamed of herself. That it didn't occur to her was ironically even more shameful, yet immaterial to her self-conception.

She was mildly unsettled by all Isaac's lewd hinting around— if even half of it were true, even a third. Isabel imagined him submitting—she knew this was the wrong, at least, the incorrect word, but thought it anyway—to all of those men. She knew that it was absurd, obviously absurd, for her, as a woman, to think of this fact alone as degrading, to hear her own mind using an expression like, *the passive role*. As soon as she thought it, she could hear Isaac clucking about her internalization of gender norms in her presumption that the traditionally female sexual role was a position of inherent inferiority or submission in the power dynamic.

He would have said it just like that, and she would have agreed as if he were enlightening her. But she'd also have told herself that she'd been hanging around gay guys for as long as Isaac had been alive. They were, if anything, even more stubborn in their embrace of these top/bottom, active/passive, boy/girl dichotomies than straight people. Either way, she couldn't help but consider the whole situation as if Isaac were a girl sneaking off to service a bunch of boys, a scenario so girded by exploitation and overlaid by the subtle threat of violence that it made her feel squeamish and motherly and irredeemably conventional. When she did eventually bring it up with Isaac, he rolled his eyes and launched into a lecture: a lot of specious, over-general nonsense about the ugliness of straight pornography (Isabel agreed with him there) versus the fundamental role parity among young men who slept with other men. "Because the patriarchy exists," he sniffed, "all heterosexual relationships are effectively coercive. No woman can ever truly give consent. Only gay sex can be legitimate."

"Thank you, Adrienne Rich," Isabel replied. (Isaac was, for all the modern mess of the rest of his life, the suicidal cultivation of sex, drugs, and rock and roll, a fastidious, almost fussy poet who could recite the lyrics of Donne and Shakespeare and Auden, who read the New Formalists, and who himself preferred to write metrical verse. His mother viewed his art with both sad pride and loving terror, as if in her own son she saw the ghost of her lost brother. Abbie considered it a kind of challenge or usurpation.)

They sat on the rocks for a while watching birds and insects move through the shaded forest and listening to the water tumble over the rocks and into the pool below—a sound that was somehow interrogative, pitched as a low, repeating question in a form of language even older and further from human speech than the calls of animals. Then Isaac said, "I'm going to swim," and took off his clothes. Isabel was already used to his casual nudity, which she interpreted as a shallow but forgivable impulse to *épater la bourgeoisie*. She was wearing a bathing suit under her hiking clothes, but she'd put a bare foot into the water and found it much too cold to even think about getting in. Isaac was shucking his tight underwear, and Isabel was trying not to look at his dick while simultaneously trying not to look like she was trying not to look. He'd undoubtedly notice and make fun of her for being a prude. Eli, who was lounging on the rock on the other side of the stream, caught her eyes briefly, rolled his own, then closed them again and laid his head on his crossed arms.

Isaac's abandoned passion for cycling, like his poetry, belied his embrace of destructive excess. His body showed all the evidence of all those miles in the saddle on the rolling roads of Pennsylvania, a body that could have been a tangle of knotweed, all reeds and knobs. Had he been a swimmer or a runner, he'd have been unspeakably beautiful, shoulders grown wide and hips narrowed, but as he was, he had instead the kind of alluring ugliness that accrues to living things that have adapted and evolved to one particular environment or manner of being: a desert plant, a nocturnal predator, one of the bioluminescent monsters that live in the dayless and nightless depths of the ocean. His chest was nearly concave and his belly, although taut, was slightly protuberant. His face and his forearms and his legs below the knees were the color of darkly stained wood; the rest of his body was so pale that it seemed to glow around the edges where the sun seemingly passed right through him. He fondled himself idly.

"The nice thing about a small dick," he said, "is that you don't have to worry about it shrinking in cold water." Isabel didn't think his dick was especially small—perhaps a bit below her own experienced average, but within a standard deviation of the mean. He took two long strides and launched himself from the ledge into the pool. The water was clear, and she watched him through its weird foreshortening lens as he sank and rose. She thought of that Millay poem. He broke the surface with a squeal. "My God!" he yelped. "It's cold!"

"Is this typical?" She asked Eli, who'd turned toward her and was leaning on one elbow. His tee-shirt drew tight across his chest.

"I couldn't say. I'm not usually invited."

"Not even as a chauffeur?" She smiled.

"I am the handyman." He gestured with his free hand. It was one of those ambiguous Southern European expressions that means everything.

"How did you end up as the handyman anyway?"

"First, I am very handy. Second, Abbie was not well, even then."

"What do you mean not well?"

But Isaac, who had dipped beneath the surface again and frog-kicked away from them, came up again and turned back. He called up: "You should come in!"

"Too cold," Isabel said.

"You get used to it," he replied. "Anyway, it's bracing. You can feel your heart trying to escape your chest."

She told him she liked her heart right where it was.

"Yes," said Eli. "Our hearts will remain here on this cliff."

"Suit yourselves," he replied. "I won't try to convince you." He made some desultory motions of swimming around for a few minutes more, then swam to the shore, waded out, and did an ungainly nude scramble back up to where Isabel lay. He rolled his tee-shirt into a pillow and sprawled out on a sunny part of the rock with his arms behind his head. The cold water had shrunk his dick, and now it did look comically small. He'd affected to close his eyes, but he hadn't, really, and he caught Isabel looking. "I know," he said. He giggled. "But one makes do with what God gives him, no?"

"Or her," Isabel offered.

"Indeed," Eli said. "She has a point."

"Yes," Isaac said, rolling to face her, "but your endowments are just erotic accessories. Accoutrements. Except for babies, I suppose, who don't care about the aesthetics or architecture."

"Dicks are accessories, too," she told him.

"This is very enlightening," said Eli.

"Don't let it go to your head," she said, and then she bit her lip and wondered why she'd said it.

Isaac sighed. "Would that it were so." He rolled onto his back again. "Alas, while being smooth is one of the youth-preserving traits that men find erotic, a small dick is a small dick is a small dick. Even having a smooth ass is a decreasing currency. All the hipsters and fashion boys are a little hairy these days."

"You don't have a small dick," Isabel told him. (And she blushed. Idiot. She was being motherly again. She might as well have assured him that he was pretty, that people would like him just for being himself.)

"Oh, please." He rolled once more onto his side and propped his head on one hand. "One time I was fucking this guy, and he told me that he couldn't go down on me because it made him feel weird. You know, like a child molester. I mean, that didn't stop him from fucking my ass. Anyway, you don't need to reassure me. I'm not the sort of boy who frets about his body. I am what I am and that's all that I am, you know, et cetera. I don't really like getting sucked off anyway. But in general, the point is that I've got bigger problems, no pun intended."

"What problems are those?" Isabel found herself wanting a cigarette, though she hadn't smoked one in years, and she wondered if Isaac had any in the bag. She didn't ask.

"Jesus, I don't know. I'm not in school at the moment. I have no prospects for a job, really. I always sort of assumed I'd just live off my trust, but I get the distinct feeling that my father is better at getting rich than at staying rich—he's been one hand ahead of the house for too long now. I just get the general sense that whatever blessed sign he's been living under is about to enter a retrograde period. Call it a vision, la la la. Besides which, of course, there's my mother."

"What's wrong with your mother?"

"What isn't wrong with my mother?"

"I don't know," Isabel said. "She seems fine to me." This was not strictly true, but she was no more capable of telling him otherwise than she was of agreeing with him about his cock. The two most precious things a boy had, she thought, smiling at her cheap Freud. She looked to Eli, but he had chosen this moment to lie down again and stare through the high branches. He was pretending not to pay attention.

"Oh, please," Isaac repeated, and he rolled over and closed his eyes.

It was true that there was something off about Sarah, and not only in the colloquial, figurative sense. No one ever seemed to encounter her but to stumble upon her; she was always just *somewhere*—sitting in a chair in some nook in the house, standing in a plot of the garden, leaning on a counter in the kitchen—with a serene expression and eyes unfocused and pointed in the direction of nothing in particular. It was as if she were an android or avatar, lolling without power or animal spirits until some distant operator picked up the remote and turned her on. But she did flick on when she noticed someone. Her conversation had a certain cubist quality to it; it was a picture of something familiar rendered in a perspective all its own. But in a family of eccentrics, a family where one man purported to see divine visions, what was any one other eccentric, more or less?

"Really," Isabel said. "She's a bit . . . she's unique, I guess. But in a family of eccentrics, what's one more eccentric, more or less?"

"God, I wish I had some smokes. Or some weed. I can't believe I didn't bring any. Ugh. I'm so bad at preparing. Anyway, she spends half her time having out of body experiences and half her time sleeping and the rest of it in the process of becoming drunk. Do you know that last year she had to have a part of her tongue cut off? It wasn't cancer or anything. It was just, you know, all used up. Cooked. Like when you leave a piece of meat in a marinade for too long." Isabel squinted at him. How does that happen, she wanted to ask. But he was still talking: "That's why she sounds like a homeless person even when she isn't *complètement beurrée*. It's because my dad had an affair back in New York before they moved out here. She made him move in some sort of hysterical attempt to keep him for herself."

"I thought," Isabel said, although it was hard to keep her voice flat, hard not to betray her piqued interest, "that they came here in pursuit off, you know, his dream. To build The Gamelands. To get away."

"Yeah, whatever sells his books and books his speaking gigs. Mom may be nuts, but she likes money, too. If playing along with Abbie the Prophet falls to the bottom line, well, no sense in belaboring it. But no, the affair, I'm pretty sure. No one ever said anything, obvi, but I can just tell. Then I came along. Which is some kind of miracle—like an actual miracle—because they could never have kids before. At least, that's what they told me. But, you know, you can't be a literalist. The stories"—he sighed— "the myths are only meant to instruct."

Abbie might have said the same thing. Despite all their differences, despite Isaac's superficial cultivation of an attitude of weary condescension toward his father (which mirrored Abbie's attitude of weary condescension toward everyone else), there was a very porous border between father and son—they had the quality of certain twins.

"I still don't know," Isabel said. "Your mom must be pretty committed to Abbie's work." She did not add *to live out here*, but Isaac knew it was what she meant.

"What work?" Isaac laughed and stretched from fingers to toes like a cat that's either rising from or about to go to sleep.

"Come on," she said. "Your dad is like one of the most important architects of the last fifty years. I mean, I know he isn't known outside of the profession, really, and I know he's never gonna win a Pritzker or whatever, but, I mean, he basically invented green building. And before you say it, yes, I also know that I'm revealing my own professional prejudices and green is just a buzzword like organic or sustainable anymore, but shit, Isaac, it's still a really big deal—the underlying concepts, I mean, even if in practice it's a little . . . I don't know, corrupted by reality."

"Corrupted by Reality would be the title of his biography," Isaac replied, annoyed. He didn't like to be contradicted, and he hated when anyone defended his parents. Then he sighed again and giggled his disarming giggle and said, "Anyway, my father is hardly an architect. I know he still gives that talk from time to time. LA is going to break off into the ocean. Florida is going to drown. New York is going to drown. Phoenix is going to dry up and blow away. We're all gonna die!" He pressed his hands to his cheeks and made a cartoon expression of matinee shock. Isabel laughed. "We're all gonna die," he repeated. He sat up and hugged his knees. "Abbie's a fucking real estate developer. Please, you think he built The Gamelands with the proceeds of commencement speeches and one coffee table book? You do know how he made all that money, don't you?"

"I assumed . . ." Isabel began, but she realized that she didn't know what she assumed. She remembered Isaac blabbing about a highway back when they'd come down to Fayette County together for the first time. It was a weakness, contagious and endemic to anyone who spent too much time around people with a lot of money: they forget to wonder how or why or from where anyone got it all to begin with.

Isaac smiled—he had this rare, broad, utterly delighted smile where his mouth broke open and he touched the tip of his curled tongue to his top front teeth, which he deployed when he felt like he was winning something. "Assume nothing," he said.

"Well, then," Isabel said, "how *did* he make all that money?"

"Abbie made his money on a fucking highway."

"A highway," she repeated.

"Between you, me, God, PennDOT, and Uncle Sam," Isaac told her. "The crookedest bunch of land deals since we stole America from the Indians. You didn't know? I thought everyone knew."

"No," she said.

"Not strictly a highway," Eli said in a sleepy voice. He didn't move.

"Right. Not strictly a highway. Like I think I told you before, he really got rich shilling for Arthur Imlak. Like *your* boss."

"Barry isn't rich," Isabel told him. And she nearly asked him, right there, if Arthur was really his father, but, of course, she didn't.

"Please. Don't you ever read your own 990s?"

"No. I'm not a finance person."

"No shit you're not. Anyway, to find out how much your bosses make. You know, your key and highest-paid employees."

"No," she said.

"Barry cleared four-fifty in 2013. Out of a three-and-change million dollar operating budget. That ain't bad. That was the most recent year. You weren't on there yet. Although I can guess."

"That isn't rich."

"Oh my God," Isaac screwed up his face. "You are ridiculous if you think that."

"Says a kid with a trust."

He giggled. "You have to learn to recognize your own class. Otherwise, you'll figure out too late that they're coming with the guillotines."

"Well, I don't make that much."

"I put you right around eighty-five, ninety."

"Wrong," she said, but he was right.

"My dad sees signs and portents and thinks the world is going to end any day now in the fire or in the flood, but we're all just as likely to have our heads chopped off by some sans-culottes first. *Et après, le déluge.* The thing is, to get back to the topic at hand, Abbie never really gave a shit about green anything. He could've just as easily become a right-wing radio host. Abbie just sniffed which way the wind was blowing."

Isabel said that she couldn't say.

"He used to be more into pussy than money. Then the Lord appeared to him, or he knocked one of his girlfriends up. Or both. Thus the decision to forsake the middling equestrian orders of the metropolis for a life of provincial riches. Shit, you're about the right age. Maybe we're siblings."

"God," Isabel said.

"God," said Isaac. "God." He laughed. "Literally, God. How fucking ironic is it that a guy who thinks he's on a mission from Yahweh basically makes it his career to journey west and bung a bunch of poor ignorant yokels out of their land. It's so fucking perfect you'd think it was true."

"Well," said Eli, who'd been listening after all, "part of it is true."

"What part?" Isabel asked, wondering what he knew.

"The God part," he replied.

. . .

A few hundred yards upstream, a fisherman had come off the trail—it turned out that they needn't have clambered over all that lousy terrain like a bunch of fools, and Isaac's secret spot wasn't really a secret. The fisherman waded into a broad and shallow part of the water and began casting his fly, whipping his slim, quivering road as if conducting some old, strange music. When Isaac spotted him, he frowned and grumbled and said it was time to leave. So they packed up and hauled themselves the hard way back up to the trail. Isaac had them continue along in the opposite direction from which they came. After a mile, they crossed a field into a parking lot at the far trail head, and Isaac led them out to Dinner Bell Road, which joined up with 381, down whose gravelly berm they hiked back to Ohiopyle village. Every few minutes, a flock of motorcycles roared past. Almost as regularly, a gas tanker would rattle their teeth and nearly yank them into the road in the vacuum trail of its slipstream. Once, Eli had to pull Isabel back from the road as she stumbled and almost fell into the path of a second tanker trailing the first. "That's twice now," he said, "that I have saved your life."

"Hero," she said.

"Get a room," said Isaac.

Then he stopped and held up his hand. They stopped. He pointed, raising his arm deliberately. Ahead of them, perched casually and unlikely on the road's metal guardrail, a red-tailed hawk swiveled its lovely cruel head and regarded them with an almost human curiosity. They stared at it, and it at them, and it opened its beak as if yawning and screamed, once, a high-pitched collision of all the vowels in every human language. They stepped back reflexively. Another truck went past, and the hawk spread its improbable wings and flapped lazily once, twice, and, even more improbably, let itself be lifted by the changing pressure of the air, flapped a few more times, and disappeared over the rustling trees.

9

Abbie's frequent trips to and from Uniontown for the expressway business and the looming start of construction on what would become The Gamelands and the way that Sarah had taken to wandering around their Pittsburgh apartment with a glass in hand and cleaning things that didn't need to be cleaned led him, in the never-ending spirit of new beginnings that drove their marriage ever onward from its old failures, to suggest that they move down to Uniontown a year early. Sarah didn't so much agree as discover that she could come up with no good reason not to, and so, in 1991, they rented a little house on Virginia Avenue just across the border from Uniontown proper in South Union Township, on the fifth fairway of the Uniontown Country Club. Lest you imagine—as Sarah briefly did before she saw the place—that this location signified some sort of luxurious links-side lifestyle: this was not, as was the case on Belmont Circle just up the street, one of the gracious early-century colonials whose French doors and oak-shaded lawns backed up onto that same fairway. Uniontown had, at that time, a population of just over twelve thousand—several thousand more if you counted the North and South townships—and the rental market, insofar as it existed at all, consisted mostly of dumpy apartments, doublewides, and old duplexes in the coal patches that still clung to an emphysemic life on the outskirts of town. Sarah would have been much happier in the slightly run-down third floor of one of the old Victorians in town; she might have at least talked a landlord into letting her paint the walls and floors white, which would have given her a project to occupy her days. But Abbie thought a house was more appropriate, whatever on earth that meant. When he described it to her, he called it a cottage. By the time she discovered its exact nature, he'd already signed a lease.

It did have a certain charm from the exterior, a collection of mismatched roof lines that very nearly suggested something rural and English, but sometime in the seventies, it had been refaced with a sort of glazed brick that, depending on the height and angle of the sun, gave the alternating impression that the house was reflective or that it was smeared in a fine layer of shit. The interior ground floor had faux wood paneling, and the kitchen had a nautical theme, its notched and eyed cabinets with phony wrought iron hardware resembling barrels to be filled with salted meat for a long sea voyage. There were ships on the linoleum floor. The master bedroom was on the ground floor in an addition set at an odd angle to the rest of the house. It had a high cathedral ceiling, but only a single small window at its far end. The window looked into the back of a rhododendron, and even in the middle of the day, the room sat in a queasy twilight. There were two small dormer bedrooms and a bath on the second floor. These rooms and the narrow stairway that led to them were covered, even the ceilings, with flocked, patriotic wallpaper that picked up the kitchen leitmotif: it depicted bald eagles sewn in pale gold grasping anchors in their talons. The eagles' beaks were open, and in each open mouth there was a tiny golden tongue.

Most of their furniture had to go into storage—what hadn't

barely fit, either too big for the tiny rooms, or too fine for the thick carpets. "Abbie," Sarah asked, "is it your intention to take me to smaller and shittier places forever until we're like the last two people left on earth?"

"Wouldn't that be interesting, to be the last two people on earth?"

"No, honey. It would not."

"You and me, against the world."

"We'd starve in a week."

Abbie did insist that they join the country club. "It's what people *do* in towns like these."

"It's not like we golf."

"We'll start!"

"I don't want to golf."

"You'll meet people. It's important."

Actually, Abbie had a very particular, though unvoiced, reason to want to join the club, and that was in order to meet one Arthur Imlak. Imlak, whom he'd never seen or even spoken to on the phone, had owned the land that Abbie bought on the hilltop. His name kept cropping up in his business dealings around the county. The closing on The Gamelands had been attended only by Imlak's attorney, a Pittsburgh lawyer named David Ben David, who said he mostly did trial work but did handle Mr. Imlak's realty transactions from time to time. Ben David had treated the signing of closing documents with an unconcealed amusement, and when Abbie asked him what he found so funny, the lawyer had replied that he didn't find anything funny, per se, but rather, that he hadn't recently seen Mr. Imlak sell off any of his holdings. "He's acquiring right now. And also, at this price? He must expect a favor from you down the road."

"I've never even met the guy."

"Yes. I understand it was our mutual friend, Ms. Sherri Larimer, who brokered the deal. For being functionally illiterate, she certainly does get around."

"I don't think she's illiterate, functionally or otherwise."

"No, just an expression."

"Is it?"

"What is the expression? It is what it is."

"Where are you from? You have, I notice, a bit of an accent."

"Ah, I'm from here. But I lived for a long time in Israel. It makes me unplaceable."

"Members of the tribe," said Abbie.

"Yes," the lawyer said. And he shrugged and repeated: "It is what it is."

Meeting Imlak proved easy enough. They found him, as anyone could find him in those days, holding court at the far end of the dining room bar at the club, a tumbler of vodka in one hand, the other free to gesticulate in an odd, Clintonian gesture, the four fingers clutched into a fist, the thumb laying straight out past the index, waving and pointing to punctuate each point that he thought he was making. His hair was still mostly black back then, and he wasn't quite as grand as he would soon become. He had a boat, but it was at the Fox Chapel Yacht Club, and he had a place in Florida, but it was just a condo in St. Pete.

The club was an immensely silly institution. Formerly a fin-de-siècle playpen for the county's erstwhile coal and coke millionaires, built as a mad crossbreeding of Tara and a Loire chateau, immense, white, and imposingly scaled, it had burned down in the mid-eighties. That the fire had occurred at almost precisely the moment when the club's membership had reached its historic nadir, and that the insurance payout covered much of the construction of a less imposing new clubhouse as well as the stashing away of a fair chunk of cash to defray operating costs for the next few years, was one of those serendipitous coincidences treated by everyone who'd been around or involved in the institution at the time as a combination wives' tale and knowing joke, like the winking old belief that first pregnancies after a marriage sometimes lasted a wee bit less than nine months. When commenting to the *Herald-Standard* Darryl Pattaglia, the mayor's cousin and the fire chief, was quoted as saying that the cause of the fire was "either a neon light on the second floor, an incandescent light on the first floor, or an Israelite in the basement."

He refused to elaborate on that, and the cause of the electrical fire, or it might be better to say, the cause of the cause, was one of the many reputedly criminal acts whose lack of a clear perpetrator led them to accrue, by reputation, to the Larimer clan. Sherri never said one thing or other about it, but she'd occasionally, apropos nothing at all, make some aside about ball and tube wiring as something like a metaphor for the unreliability and unpredictability of anything really, and people took this as oblique confirmation of what they would have believed anyway. As for the chief's comments, people assumed Larimer had made him say it.

The new, smaller clubhouse looked like the offspring of a Mexican restaurant and a mid-market chain hotel. Ironically, Abbie would discover that it was built using a prefabrication technique that he had, once upon a time, pioneered, if not quite invented. The invention belonged to a group of materials scientists and structural engineers at Columbia, but Abbie had loaned his name and reputation to the project, and he now received, from time to time, a minor royalty for its use.

An aside: Imlak's early fortune was based in large part on precisely those poor rental properties that Abbie had felt inappropriate for his wife. Arthur's father, as he never failed to mention, had been a miner, then a foreman, and then he'd cashed out his whole pension to buy a few properties, which grew into a modest local empire of trailer parks and converted mansions. The younger Imlak's entry into the energy business came later and by blessed accident. He'd acquired a diesel station and truck depot near Grindstone as part of a larger property transaction. He never intended to operate it for more than a year or so, but in that year, he noticed a very slight but nevertheless appreciable increase in gas and oil company traffic through that part of the state. Imlak was unrefined by the standards of people like Barry Fitzgerald, a vulgar businessman, but it was this almost prophetic eye for detail that set him apart from the vast herds of ruminant MBAs in America; it was a few extra trucks a month way back in the eighties that led him to a two-decade project of land and mineral rights acquisitions, a quietly scrupulous long position that made his at-the-time much richer friends think him slightly more eccentric than his minor millions gave him a natural right to be. Only later, in the new millennium, did his foresight result in a series of grand, glorious transactions, when it was discovered that something like fifteen percent of the rights to the extractable carbon in the Marcellus Shale in West Virginia and Pennsylvania were held by the blandly named ABM Corporation.

If great books are frequently predicted by their opening sentences—"All happy families" and that sort of thing—then so too are certain relationships marked out by the first words that one person speaks to another, and so it was with Arthur

Imlak and the Mayers—to which of them, Abbie or Sarah, he was speaking exactly no one later remembered or admitted to remembering. "Order the gimlet," he told them.

"That's the specialty?" Sarah said.

Imlak leaned on the bar and indicated the bartenders with a brief movement of his eyes. "They don't know that it's supposed to be gin, so they use vodka, and they don't know what else is supposed to be in it, so they use twice as much vodka." He swirled his glass. "If you want an especially fun night, ask for it neat. They don't understand displacement either, so instead of measuring by volume, they pour by height."

"That sounds dangerous."

"Arthur Imlak," he said. He shook their hands. "You're new."

"Yes," said Abbie. "We just joined. Abbie Mayer. This is my wife, Sarah."

"Ah," said Imlak. "Members of the tribe."

Abbie regarded him strangely, and Sarah was taken aback. "I'm sorry?" she said.

"Oh, no," said Imlak. "I'm sorry. I am as well, oddly enough. My mother died when I was a little boy, and my father remarried. He'd never previously had much use for religion, but Beth, my stepmother, thought it would be a good idea to give my brother and me a faith, and she was Jewish. Now, my father was from a family of Lutherans who became some form of non-denominational Protestant. Vaguely Baptist, perhaps? I get it all confused. In any event, he didn't believe in anything, but he agreed to a Jewish wedding and occasionally accompanied us to High Holy days and so forth. He appreciated Judaism, in part because so much of it was conducted in a language he couldn't understand. Here, let me buy your first round."

"Thank you," Sarah said.

"No, thank you. Now tell me, Mayer, why is that name familiar to me?"

"It's a fairly common name," Sarah said.

"Yes, young lady, it certainly is. But it seems to have skittered across my desk recently. What business are you in? Oh, Jack, we'll have two. No, three more gimlets, please. I'm running low myself."

"I'm an architect," Abbie said.

"Ah, indeed," said Imlak.

"Abbie is involved in property development," Sarah said.

"A noble calling. A man is not a man until a man owns land, as my father used to say. And that must be where I've heard the name. Are you by any chance related to one Veronica Mayer?"

"My sister, yes. And my business partner."

"We've met, once or twice. Well, cheers." He raised his newly arrived glass. "To new acquaintances."

They touched glasses. Imlak tapped his again on the bar before drinking. "A Western Pennsylvania thing, I think," he told them. "And like a lot of atheists, I make up for it with a surfeit of compensatory superstitions."

"Yes." Abbie sipped. The drink tasted like pure alcohol, like cleaning solution. He took a long gulp.

"And you?" Imlak asked Sarah. "What do you do?"

"Not much anymore. I was an interior designer."

"Do you golf?"

She laughed. "As you noted, we're Jewish. Do you know many Jews who golf?"

"Oh, yes. Certainly. I own a place down in Florida. St. Pete, which is on the Gulf and therefore the more Protestant side of the state. The Atlantic Seaboard is all Jews and Hispanic Catho-lics, but even in the once-restricted environs of Tampa Bay, one finds many of our people whacking away hopelessly at little balls. I chalk the penchant up to our propensity for wandering aimlessly across huge tracts of land for very long periods of time."

Sarah smiled and said, "Perhaps I'll take it up, then."

"You should. You can join my foursome." He winked. "One of us just died. Fiorello Pattaglia. He was eighty-six and smelled like cheap bar soap, but he was a judge, and his son is the mayor. We're a wonderful group. I mostly drink, and Dick and Harry—yes, it's true; it can't be helped—use the occasion to sneak cigarettes where their wives can't catch them. We consider score-keeping to be irrelevant, and sometimes we even forget to golf."

"That sounds like my kind of game."

"Yes. Now, my other advice is no matter what you do, don't join the women's groups. One is called the 9-holers, the other the 18-holers." He laid a hand very briefly on her knee. "Pornographic, I know. The ones who play the half rounds are mostly dotty old ladies, and the ones who play the full round are fiercely competitive and mostly bitches, except for Joyce, our ladies champion, whose going-on-ten-year reign has made her kind to a fault. You're better off playing with men. Of course, the club officially discourages ladies from playing except during their own designated times. I suppose they worry that some sort of plaid orgy will break out spontaneously. But I put together the financing package for the new clubhouse after the old one burned down and they're beholden to me, so I get to break the rules. Also, they know I could join Pleasant Valley instead, so they kiss my ass."

"How did the old club burn down?" Abbie asked.

"Do you know the story of Crassus?"

"Yes."

"Well, it was nothing like that," Imlak said, and again, he winked.

. . .

The author will here risk an anticlimax by telling you right now that Sarah sleeps with Arthur Imlak, because when he thinks about how to tell the story, he has to decide against the false tension of a hinted-at development and consider the pall of inevitability that the ultimate realization of a long-foreshadowed eventuality casts retroactively and retrospectively over everything that came before. It is a sort of a disclaimer. What *did* happen *did not have to happen*. It was, in the mathematical sense, improbable, and that the probability eventually collapsed upon the occurrence of the unanticipated event says nothing about the event's likelihood prior to it actually happening.

Arthur, Sarah, and Abbie became friends, or anyway Arthur and Abbie mutually cultivated a friendship in the secure private belief that it was in his best individual interest to do so, each believing the other to have no inkling that this was the case. Only Arthur was correct on that count. Sarah and Arthur, on the other hand, genuinely liked each other. If Imlak's overt behavior toward women was physical familiarity, then there was nevertheless something in his manner and demeanor that suggested a genuine, underlying, non-sexual interest that his superficial actions were carefully calculated to hide. Which was the truth about him? Who knows what's true or not about anyone? It's flattering to believe that, in imagining a man's life, there's a way to intuit the inner workings out of the visible, external component parts, but people are, all of them, at last opaque. Even God views His creations with astonishment. Their existence is an accident of His majesty. They appeared at the uttermost end of His imagining, and when He finally paused, it wasn't for exhaustion, but surprise.

In the early seventies, Arthur's father had bought an old farm on Blackstone Drive, fifty acres that looked across the last broad curve of Route 40 before it turned perpendicular to the ridge and climbed east into the mountains. The old farmhouse still sat at the low point of the property near a sharp bend in the road, and both Imlak *père* and his son continued renting it to the farmer who'd owned the property previously until he died in the early 2000s, after which, as was oddly common in Uniontown, the structure burned to the ground. The senior Imlak had built a mod house on the high point of the property, out of date before it was even begun. Its only attractive feature was a broad window wall that looked out over the cornfields to the mountains. There was an irony in the fact that this made it—makes it still—a mirror image of The Gamelands; the two houses faced each other across the foothills. The flat-roofed structure had that era's odd flavor, a modernity that assumed that all structures would one day look like high schools or prisons, which were, by that time, architecturally interchangeable anyway. Arthur Imlak had added to the building over the years. A series of architects had done their best to draw out its strong horizontal lines and turn it into something more austerely modern, but it retained its innate characteristic: it was ineradicably ugly. Arthur knew this was the case, and he viewed it with an obscure pride. Contrary to the popular sentiment, money often did buy taste, but if anyone with a bit of money could have good taste, then it became the imperative of those with obscenely larger fortunes to affect a sort of grotesque gaudiness that demonstrated their transcendence of that which any ordinary millionaire—who might, after all, be something silly like a doctor or a lawyer—could buy.

They were at Imlak's house for dinner one night in the July after they'd moved to Uniontown. They'd broken ground on The Gamelands, which now looked like a muddy scar on the mountain, visible all the way from town. It was eight-thirty or so, and the long evening sun blasted through the westward windows into the dining room. Abbie told Imlak he ought to glaze the fucking windows. "Among other things," he said, "you're going to ruin your furniture."

"I'll buy new furniture." Imlak forked a piece of steak into his mouth. "I don't give a shit about furniture. You can't get too attached to material things."

"Abbie just likes to give advice," Sarah said.

"Well, you're also killing yourself on utilities. Your cooling costs have got to be through the roof in the summer, and this place must leak heat all winter long."

"Let's open another bottle. We'll try the Stag's Leap."

"Yummy," Sarah said.

"Look." Abbie swiveled in his chair to talk at Imlak as he went into the kitchen to fetch the wine. "I'm telling you, I know you can afford it. But it's a waste. You ought to hire me to fix it. Buildings are the biggest agents of environmental degradation, you know. It's a fact."

Imlak returned with the bottle and said, "Watch your husband, Sarah. He is always angling to get me to hire him. You may be having cash flow problems. Phil Harrow holding out on you, Abbie?"

"I'd do it as a friend," Abbie grumbled. He looked at Sarah. "Anyway, Sarah keeps the books. She has the mathematical mind."

"Says the architect!"

"Architects are all bad at math. Architects who are good at math are engineers."

"Well," Imlak said. "I don't personally see the big deal. Energy is cheap."

"Now you've done it." Sarah tossed back a half a glass and helped herself to another.

"*Chiudi la bocca*, my dear." Abbie swiveled to face Imlak. "Energy is cheap? Arthur, don't you realize that we stand, right now, in this very decade, on the precipice of peak oil. The Hubbert curve puts it right around 2000. Less than a decade away, now! How's that for a millenarian coincidence. Now, you may wish to believe, as do the rest of the poor flock out there"—he gestured at the window and the field and the highway beyond—"but I am telling you, if we don't act, and act fast, we will face the greatest social upheaval, the greatest catastrophe, in the history of our species. Whole civilizations will be upended. All this, this easy-motoring lifestyle, it'll all be over in a decade. Right over the hill there, down in Heritage Hills, they're building houses with three-car garages on spec. On spec!"

"Abbie," Imlak said, "*you're* building houses with three-car garages on spec."

"How do you? Never mind. Listen. The whole physical development of American society is predicated on inexpensive motoring. Carbon is a miracle fuel; it is an unmatched, never-to-be-repeated form of immediate, fungible, scalable energy. There is never going to be a battery-powered car or a miniature nuclear reactor. That's all a grand boondoggle. When we use up the oil, that's it. *Adieu. Ciao.* Now what I would do, if I were the benevolent dictator, what I would do is I would issue a challenge. I would say: by 2050, you must reduce energy usage by half. You do it city by city. You replace lightbulbs with fluorescents or LEDs. You improve building envelopes. You limit auto traffic in the urban center, which drives people to use public transit. You do all that, and maybe, maybe you prolong the useful life of our society."

Sarah told Arthur, "Abbie is on the board of a non-profit that's proposing exactly that."

"Sure," Imlak said. "Barry Fitzgerald's outfit. I contribute."

"Yes," Abbie said. "I've seen your name."

"Being in the energy business myself, I feel it lends an aura of social responsibility to my otherwise rapacious capitalist endeavors."

"I thought you were in the real estate business," Abbie said.

Imlak shrugged. "About as much as you're in the highway business."

"I feel like you're implying something."

"Not a thing. Although, as a man quote-unquote in the property business, I can tell you that you ought to be cautious in your dealings with your partners, if they've got you acting—not that I'm saying they do, or are—as their straw purchaser. You should talk to my lawyer."

Abbie began to formulate a reply, but Imlak jumped in again.

"In any case, to answer your question: I'm only in it for the energy. Property is pointless unless it's improvable or extractable. The thing I've learned is that if it's extractable, then the extractors are willing to pay you a whole lot of money to guarantee future revenues. Even very far future revenues. You see, you think that the energy companies are hidebound, dirty, old-fashioned Texans or weirdo Saudi royals living in the now, but kids, I'm telling you, they are thinking decades in advance. We are, right now, sitting atop a vast shale formation that holds more exploitable carbon than the whole goddamn Middle East. We just don't quite have the tech to yank it out yet. But in another ten, twenty years we will. So between now and then, we build some new roads and open a few Wal-Marts to support the industry when it comes, and then those of us who own the mineral rights, we lease it and sell it and make many hundreds of millions. My business, my friend, is *patience*. And you, buddy. Why, quite by accident, you're doing the Lord's work." He tipped his glass.

Some hours later, they had consumed at least one more bottle of wine, and Imlak had broken out a bottle of an Armagnac that he'd discovered the year before on a trip to Bordeaux. Imlak excused himself to go to the bathroom. Abbie slid across the couch to Sarah and asked her quietly how the fuck it could be that Arthur Imlak knew so much about the particulars of his business with Phil and Veronica. Sarah said she didn't have the foggiest notion but that Arthur seemed like a man who kept a close watch on that sort of thing. "Ooo, *Arthur* seems like a man who keeps a close watch on this sort of thing," Abbie said. Sarah snorted but patted his hand. They were quite drunk. "You ought to let him think he can screw you," Abbie said. "Get him to tell you what he knows."

"Oh, go to hell, Abbie!" Sarah lifted her hand and backed away from him. She glared.

"What?" he said. "Christ, I was only kidding."

"No. You weren't."

"I was."

When Imlak returned, he seemed oddly invigorated for a man

who'd had just as much to drink as they had. Had they looked more closely, they'd have noticed a fine dusting of off-white grains just below his right nostril, but they didn't look so closely. They had another drink. Abbie tripped over a coffee table. Imlak insisted they stay in one of the guest rooms and not drive. "It's fine," Abbie said, although he was laying on his back on a couch with a bag of ice on his shin. "I've got connections."

"Yes, well," Imlak said.

They went to bed, and Imlak, who'd done a few more blasts, went into his study and poured himself a long whiskey and settled into his leather chair and found a West Coast baseball game in boring extra innings on TV. He sipped his whiskey. He was bending over his glass side table with a rolled fifty-dollar bill in his hand when Sarah came in forty minutes later. She put a hand on his arm. "Can I offer you a blast?" he asked. She extended her hand.

She wasn't the most beautiful woman, and she even looked a little older than she probably was, Imlak thought, but that was one of the delights of aging; you came to prefer women of a certain age. (Well, of course, that wasn't wholly true; there was an admittedly common sort of man who believed that a younger woman would assuage his aging rather than bringing it into sharp and pitiable relief. But Imlak didn't consider himself a common sort of man.) Her face and the exposed skin of her arms were tight and papery, and her hair was brown and severe. She was so pale as to appear almost translucent around the edges. Not beautiful, he thought again, but she looked like no other woman he'd ever seen. She took a sip of his drink without asking and sat on the floor beside the chair. They watched the game in silence for a few minutes.

"Are you trying to screw my husband?" she asked.

"What if I were?"

"It's your business. But I'd like some advance warning."

"No. I'm not."

She stood up and extended her hand to him.

"What about Abbie?" he said.

"He's dead to the world."

"That's not what I meant."

"My marriage is very important to me, but it lacks . . . a core of physical intimacy. We're only married. We understand each other."

They went to his bedroom and went through the motions quietly, and when he tried to say something, she laid a cool hand across his mouth and shook her head. Afterward, she said, "That was lovely, thank you," and she kissed his forehead. He'd been pleased, after all the drinks and the lines, to have no trouble getting it up. He'd suggested, at the pre-penultimate moment, that he go to the bathroom for a condom. "Don't be silly," she told him. "I'm pretty much past all that." They took turns in the bathroom. She was unselfconsciously dressing when he returned.

"That's the part they leave out of the movies," she said. "The desperate rush to pee after you've fucked."

"I like it when you say fuck."

"Oh, please," Sarah said. "Let's not."

"Where are you going?"

"I'm not going to fall asleep in your bed, Arthur. Let's keep this realistic. You strike me as that kind of man. I'd do it again, but I don't want Abbie to find out."

"You said you had an understanding."

"I said that, yes."

"Look, I wasn't entirely honest with you before. I'm not trying to screw Abbie. Not intentionally. I *like* Abbie. I like both
of you. Which is," he shrugged, "ironic, I guess. But you should
know that Veronica and Phil, that's a different story. It's nothing
personal, but like I said, in my business, you take the long view."

"What are you talking about?"

"In ten, fifteen years, there's going to be a huge debate about
gas mining in the state, and I'm going to need a lot of people to
owe me. And a couple-billion-dollar highway project is a pretty
good quid pro quo. And I've known Sherri Larimer since way
back. We went to high school together, actually. Red Raiders, the
two of us. Anyway, what I could really use is your help in all this."

"My help."

"Yes. To get Abbie to sell me all that property that those dummies had him buy up on their behalf with their money on the
cheap."

"Why?"

"Why?" He lay back on the bed and put his hands behind his
head. "Little lady, there's gold in them thar hills."

. . .

Abbie had dreamed of the deer again. In the dream, he was a hawk.
He didn't know he was a hawk. A hawk only feels its hawkness and
has no symbol to name it and place itself in a taxonomy of things.
He was high above a field of corn, which was bordered on one side
by a stand of woods separating it from the big holes over which
the bird-legged mammals would build their square wooden nests
and on the other side by the hard gray path over which the mammals rode their strange, hollow mounts. He liked the path and the
animals the mammals rode; they made heat and he ascended eas-

ily on the air's own rising. He could see everything; his eyes were a miracle; no insect on a leaf was too small for him to detect. Some deer moved through the corn and emerged beside the gray path where one of the mammals was standing. Even as a hawk, Abbie knew that the mammal was him also. He tipped his wing slightly and traced a long arc. The Abbie on the ground moved its arms, and the fawn sprang away toward the path. The Abbie called after it, but it leapt wildly down the embankment into the path of one of the vast, rushing beasts, which hit it with such force that the young creature seemed to explode. The other deer, the adult, had fled toward the woods. The Abbie who was the hawk watched it move through the corn. It thought—though it doesn't think, but feels as an intersection of competing desires—that it was a shame the armored animals didn't stop to eat the thing they'd killed, and thought of stooping to take a taste himself, but there was no attraction in a thing already dead, and he curved back toward the mountain. That was when Abbie woke up.

Of all the blessings in his life, Abbie believed that the greatest was his natural, general immunity to the hangover. It was just after sunrise. Sarah was asleep beside him, her pants on the floor, her shirt twisted around her body with the sheet. He got out of the bed and patted his belly. He pulled on his clothes and went to the kitchen where he gargled a little water. He walked to the windows and looked out over the half-grown corn and noticed then what it seemed impossible he hadn't noticed before. He found himself walking out of the house and across its patios and out into the fields, through the parallel rows that rippled across the wide, descending land until the boundary road and the highway and then, beyond the highway, the foothill rise and the protuberance of Pine Knob and Laurel Ridge and Route 40 climbing it toward the white Summit Inn just then reflecting the rising sun like a beacon. He could see his own property to its right. He walked faster; the corn scratched his arms where he'd rolled his sleeves. He came to the edge of the property, a narrow wire-and-post fence that separated it from a grassy berm beside the road. There was a copse of trees to his right, and he stood there for a long time—or for what felt like a long time—waiting for what he expected to see. When he didn't, when all he saw were a few cars passing on the highway, he turned and walked back toward the house. As he approached it, he saw, through the window, Arthur Imlak standing beside Sarah in the kitchen. Nothing about it suggested anything at all, which suggested everything. He permitted himself to turn around once more and look back across the field. He thought he saw something moving by the trees. He took a step toward it. But whatever it was, it was too distant, and it was gone.

10

A year after she'd arrived in Pittsburgh, Isabel learned that Veronica Mayer had been her neighbor all along. That Isaac had failed to mention it—no, that implies an accident, oversight, neglect. That Isaac had chosen not to mention it surely implied something, but she couldn't quite imagine what. For all his pretensions to aloofness from his odd family, he functioned as the fixed point around which the rest of their rarely intersecting bodies ever orbited. Isabel had known, of course, that he lived in—or hoarded and occasionally crashed in—his aunt's putative apartment, but that wasn't the sort of fact that acquired significance.

It was October, sometime after the nights got cold but before the clocks changed, a period of shortening evenings and very long afternoons. Everyone in the city wore black and gold on the most inappropriate occasions. Barry had convinced Isabel to put her house on the Edgewood House Tour, and they were well into their second bottle of Sauvignon blanc. A steady stream of retirees and public radio types in the same sensible waterproof hiking shoes they'd wear on group bus-and-boat tours of second-tier European capitals nosed in and out, complimenting Isabel's restoration of the window bay bench in the dining room and, when they thought she wasn't listening, murmuring critically about her decision to use stainless appliances in the kitchen. She hadn't done either; the previous owner had done all the renovations. Isabel had only furnished the place; her single building project had been the installation of a sliding glass door on the shower in the guest bath. It wasn't on the tour. "I imagine I'd have gotten dinged for being ahistorical," she whispered to Barry.

"Honey," he said, hand to heart. Then he refilled their glasses.

Barry was telling her about his friend Jeff's trouble with the latest boyfriend who'd started going to AA and stopped having sex. Isabel mentioned that her mother was sober—mostly, usually—and she retained a distant and dimmed but still faithful belief in the broad spiritual themes of that form of sobriety. "Let go and let God and all that," she said. Barry thought it was all very silly, and he was in the middle of explaining, as men only ever explain to women, that "scientific studies" had shown that twelve-step programs had no greater or lesser chance of successful outcomes than any other form of therapy, quitting cold turkey, or even just moderating use "like they do in Europe." He was the kind of man for whom that particular phrase had a talismanic quality, and Isabel could be reasonably sure that it would come up in any discussion of urban planning, transportation, healthcare, elections, or social policy—in other words, nearly everything that they talked about. She let him go on. Barry's friends' relationships were as close as he got to romances of his own. It would have been cruel to take away the vicarious pleasure he took in finding their catastrophic flaws. She told Barry that it seemed to her that if these two only ever had sex when they were drunk, then it was probably indicative of other underlying problems. But Barry seemed to believe that it was both more and less complicated than simply losing the regrettably necessary disinhibition of booze; rather, it was some part of a larger program of abstemiousness, a sort of vow of chastity appended like a dangling modifier to the life sentence of teetotaling.

Isabel normally wouldn't have given it much thought. She'd have composed a look of interest and let him rattle on. It struck her, a year into her job at the Institute, that more than anything, Barry had hired her to be his friend. Also, she felt that just as the irreligious filled the magical void in their lives with compensatory superstition, the perennially single filled the void of romantic absence with a complete, pop-psychological interest in the sex lives of others. She'd noted it in herself. Isaac had recently broken up with Sawyer, and she wasn't immune to the gossipy attraction of such speculation.

She'd accidentally witnessed the immediate aftermath of Isaac's break-up. He'd given her a key to his apartment, where he claimed to have an un-upholstered but otherwise intact Edwardian divan that would make a perfect little daybed for her small third bedroom, which she used as an office. Isaac had made offers like this before, and they almost never panned out; his recollections of purchases and acquisitions were hazy at best, and Isabel had discovered that, like his mother, he was a frequent eBay and auction seller—in Isaac's case, whenever he'd blown through whatever money his trust provided for him in a month and needed to raise some quick cash. (The irony there was that he'd spent from that same pot of inherited money in order to acquire the things that he was now selling at a loss. So it may not, Isabel realized when she considered it, have been so different from Sarah's motivation after all.) There had, however, been at least a few cases where he'd come through spectacularly: a 1960s ceramic espresso service from Czechoslovakia glazed in extraordinarily bright primary colors; a genuine (Isabel thought, and Barry agreed) 1880s Laguiole knife with a corkscrew and carved, though badly chipped, ivory handle; a set of 1950s highball glasses from a line commissioned by Nordstrom, which each bore the name of a deadly poison in a fin-de-siècle druggist font.

He told her he'd leave the furniture out for her to look at, and she didn't bother to ask him why he wouldn't just show it to her himself. He professed to believe in whimsy as a guiding life principle, though he practiced something more akin to thoughtless inconsistency. Isabel left work early and drove over to the apartment. She let herself in. She found him deliriously drunk, almost insensate, his nose and mouth so clotted with bubbling snot as to make him appear rabid, trying and failing to pick himself off a floor strewn with the smashed remains of whatever he'd been able to get his hands on. He was crying—hardly even crying anymore; moaning and gasping all at once—with a commitment that Isabel had never observed in him before. He'd cut one of his hands in the process of breaking things, and he'd left a few bloody semi-handprints around. The scene was slightly ridiculous, like a pre-credit piece for a *Law & Order* episode, the first murder suspect who is never the real culprit. Isabel stood fixed in the doorway. Isaac didn't immediately notice her. When he did, he looked at her with red, swollen eyes and moaned once more; it was the sound of an animal without a lot of imperfect words for its pain. He turned his head and looked at the broken chair beside him, wiped his nose, and turned back to her. "I broke your chaise," he said.

"I see that."

"He left me."

"Who?" Isabel asked. She knew, of course. Or she thought she knew. With Isaac, she could never be sure. He might have meant

Jake, with whom, over the last several months, she'd noticed him spending considerably more time than with his boyfriend; Isaac had been going to Uniontown every weekend. Sawyer never joined him. On one of those weekends when Isaac was away, Isabel had met Sawyer for dinner. It had been months. He got unusually drunk, for him, and then uncharacteristically asked her if she wanted to go out drinking with him. She matched him drink for drink until she felt quite unable to put one more drop in her body, and she begged off. He hardly noticed. The next Monday at the office, Jenny and Penny told her that they'd seen him after hours at The Castle in Bloomfield, talking and eventually leaving with someone, or something, they referred to as one of the local glamor drag twinks.

"Sawyer," Isaac said after a long pause, and just saying the name seemed at once to deflate and to sober him. He wiped his nose again with the back of his hand and took a long, gurgling breath.

"I'm sorry," Isabel said.

"He said he couldn't imagine marrying me. Can you believe that? I never even thought about it."

"I'm sorry."

"He said our relationship lacked a core of intimacy. Excuse me. Whose fault is that? He's the one who never wanted to fuck me! He's the one who was always stepping out with fucking nineteen-year-olds."

"Isaac," she said, trying to inject a little humor into it, "*you're* stepping out with a nineteen-year-old."

"He's twenty-three. And fuck that. It never meant anything to me. *He* fell in love with them."

This struck Isabel as completely incorrect. Sawyer might have occasionally exaggerated his self-possession, but he was observably stingy with his affection. Their own friendship, for instance, had never progressed beyond the facts of their superficial similarities, and it had always felt like it was underlain by an off-putting quantity of rational calculation, as if Sawyer were the model man who inhabits the fiction of economics, for whom even desire is at last mere calculation of relative return value. It was Isaac who, though he could be callow and cruel, though he was flighty and inconsistent with his love, loved wholly and loved well; even his self-love was careless. He was an accidental egotist, who fell heedlessly in love with a self he should, by rights, have hated.

Because Isabel had nothing else to say, she said, "I'm sorry," once more.

For a moment, Isaac stared at the ground. For the first time, Isabel thought he looked less than unnaturally alluring, just a puffy, snotty boy whose gawky legs splayed at weird angles, too-big feet flopping outward, clothes merely disheveled. "I loved him," he said.

"I know," she answered. He wanted her to think that it was a lie, but she didn't believe him.

"I would have married him."

"I know you would have," she said, although she knew he wouldn't have, or he would have out of some irrational fidelity to some inexpressible principle, hanging on with the tenacity that people reserve only for their most hopeless endeavors.

"I need a job," he said. "Jesus Christ, I'm twenty-fucking-four. I didn't even finish school."

"What do you mean? You went to Pitt."

"I didn't really graduate. I stopped going my senior year." He looked at her miserably. "Don't tell anyone."

"Who would I tell?"

"I don't know. Abbie."

"I wouldn't tell Abbie."

"Isabel," he said.

"Okay. I *won't*, though. I *won't*."

"It doesn't matter. Do you think Barry would give me a job?"

"I don't know. Probably, if you asked. Doing what, though?"

"I don't know, I don't know. I'm a good writer."

"You're a poet. We write white papers. We write studies and grants."

"God," Isaac said. "Why do people work?"

"Money," Isabel said. "Mostly."

"No one who has real money works. Everyone I know with money travels. Ask Arthur the next time you see him at a party. 'What have you been doing, Arthur?' 'Traveling.'"

Isabel laughed, but not too long. "That sounds like Arthur."

"He's not my father, you know."

"Isaac—"

"I know Barry told you. Or somebody did. Every time I say his name, you get this look. It isn't true. People are such fucks."

"Yes, they are."

He looked at her, and a hint of something other than misery teased at the corners of his mouth, the bare hint of the sun's disk behind the gray clouds that float over Western Pennsylvania all fall. He took a fortifying breath, picked himself off the floor, and then stepped carefully through the wreckage of the apartment to the little kitchen, where he found two Flintstones glasses and took a bottle of cold-thickened vodka from the freezer and poured them each a nice portion. "Maybe I should go into real estate," he said.

• • •

Just as it was getting dark, and the last house tourists were descending the walkway stairs from all the steep front yards to the equally steep sidewalks and street, as Barry and Isabel were finishing the bottle and starting to talk about where they ought to go for dinner, Barry stood up and called to an older woman walking a small dog up the street. "Veronica. Veronica!"

She looked up at his second effort and squinted toward the porch, then took a few steps in their direction. "Barry Fitzgerald? What in the world?"

She and the dog came up to the foot of the porch. "What are you doing over here, Dr. Fitzgerald? I didn't think Breezers crossed the city line unless they were on the Parkway."

"I'm a rebel. Sometimes I even go to Wilkinsburg." Barry was slightly looped from the wine. "And I could ask you the same. I thought you were living in Gateway Center. From downtown to Edgewood Towne Centre? What sort of urban pioneer are you?"

"I'm seventy-five. I moved here five years ago. Just across the street from Regent Square, so just over the border. Better taxes. I know old people are supposed to live in condos, but I read online that if you walk the stairs in your house twenty times a day, you'll live to be a hundred and twenty. Also, have you ever tried to buy groceries downtown? Besides, my little darling here"—she indicated the dog—"prefers life out here in nature."

"Veronica," Barry said, "let me introduce you to my friend Isabel. Isabel, this is Veronica Mayer!"

"Oh, hello." Isabel didn't know the protocol for meeting a woman to whom she was an utter stranger, and yet about whom she knew—at least, had heard—so much. So she descended from the porch and shook Veronica's hand. The older woman didn't look seventy-five; she certainly looked younger than Abbie did. Isabel would have thought her the younger sibling. They didn't much resemble each other physically, except that her hair was the same shocking shade of white, although it was cut into the neatly aristocratic bowl favored by a certain sort of well-heeled woman over sixty, and it shone with the frequent attention of a stylist. Otherwise, she was petite and fit. Her cheeks and jawline had begun to show the slightest sag, but her skin lacked the linen quality that Isabel associated with age, and her small eyes moved quickly and peered sharply out of deep sockets. She may have had some work done on her neck, which looked a bit too tight to Isabel. The neck was circled by an understated gold necklace that bore a Star of David. She wore a white shirt in a man's cut, a pair of blue jeans, and new running shoes. The dog's leash was leather. Louis Vuitton, Isabel noted. Given Abbie's and Isaac's descriptions of her, Isabel had imagined a rather batty old cat-lady with a distinctly dykier and certainly more penurious look. It was one point at which father's and son's otherwise divergent takes on her agreed. But here she was, and she looked like her next stop was a board meeting for the ballet. "I'm so pleased to meet you," Isabel said. "I, well, I know your nephew. And your brother."

She pursed her lips, but didn't seem especially put off by this silly thing the young lady had just blurted out. "And how do you know Dr. Fitzgerald here?"

"Ah, he's actually my boss."

"Coworker," Barry added. Like so many bosses in the non-profit and academic world, he was remarkably democratic unless he wanted something.

"Oh I see. This is your house?"

"Yes," Isabel said.

"I knew the former owners slightly. He played for the symphony."

"That's right," Isabel told her. "His wife worked for the school board. I think they were moving to Florida."

"That sounds about right. I've always thought it must be ghastly to live in a place where everyone is so old they wear coats no matter how miserably tropical it gets. Years ago, when I was about your age, actually, I worked for a law firm that had an office in Miami, and they sent me down for a few months to work on a probate thing. Some giant mess of an estate. That was in the seventies, of course. I despised it. The managing partner down there lived in this monstrously tacky Spanish Colonial mansion in Coconut Grove, and I had to stay in his guest house. Everyone did a tremendous amount of cocaine, drank heavily, and some woman always ended up naked in the pool. I'm sorry, I'm digressing. I was more incisive when I was less antiquated. In any event, I've always liked this house. I love your porch furniture."

"Isaac actually helped me pick it out. Would you like to come inside? We were just talking about going for dinner, but we could have a drink first."

"No, thank you. Perhaps lunch sometime soon? I haven't actually seen Isaac in ages. Bring him along. I trust he hasn't overly abused that apartment."

"I think," Isabel said, "that he'll be devoting more attention to it. He and Sawyer broke up recently."

"They did?" Barry seemed surprised.

"Didn't I tell you?"

"No. I tell you all the gossip, but you always hold out on me."

"Discretion is the better part of valor." Veronica smiled at Isabel. "My brother and I share an addiction to clichés, although I'm the only one who's embarrassed by it. It's probably good that they broke up. I never could imagine those two getting married."

Isabel regarded her cautiously. She said, "Sawyer said something along those lines to him, apparently. Do people have to get married to stay together?"

"Not at all. But now that the option is available, I find myself becoming very conservative in that regard. My late partner, Edith, and I would have availed ourselves of the opportunity if we'd had it, anyway."

"I'm so sorry," Isabel said. "She died?"

"Yes. Don't be too sorry. It was a long time ago, now. Unexpected, but long past. And I do have my little Bessie to keep me company. Just two old ladies, ironically, as it would have been, except that one of us is a dog."

"Well, I'm sorry anyway. Was she sick?"

"Oh, no. No. My brother had her killed." She gave a tug on the leash, and the dog turned. "Well," she said. "Goodnight. Isaac has my number. We really should have lunch, the three of us. And you too, Barry, if you like." And she walked back to the sidewalk, where the streetlights were coming on, and headed back down the hill toward her own home.

Isabel looked at Barry, and Barry, for once, only turned up his hands and shrugged. "I have *no* idea," he said.

. . .

"Tell me, how is Isaac doing?" Veronica asked Isabel. It was their second dinner together. They were eating gristly steak and *frites* at a little Belgian café not far from Barry's house in Point Breeze. It was the weekend after the clocks turned back, and it got dark at five. All but the most tenacious leaves had fallen suddenly off the trees, and even when it hadn't rained, if felt like it had rained. Isabel had gone to dinner with her for the first time just a week after they'd met. She'd mentioned to Isaac that she was meeting his aunt, and he made her swear that she wouldn't talk about him. She'd immediately betrayed the promise. Veronica was utterly charming. Like everyone else in that family, she liked to drink, and it was hard not to get swept up in her pace. Isabel was tipsy before entrees. Veronica had insisted they split a 750 mL bottle of a Trappist beer that had the viscosity of a heel of bread soaked in onion soup—that flavor as well, actually, yeasty and sweet—and some ungodly percentage of alcohol.

"He's all right," Isabel said. "I suppose. He and Sawyer are fighting over dishes."

"Poor Sawyer."

"I thought you didn't like Sawyer."

"I like Sawyer very much. I suspect he'll be much happier without my nephew."

"That's probably true. And anyway, I think that Isaac has something going on with his friend, Jake."

"Oh dear. I wonder how Abbie feels about that."

"Yeah," Isabel said. "I always got the feeling that that kid is a sort of opportunistic bisexual."

"Oh, no," Veronica waved her hand. "I meant because he's black."

"Because he's black?"

"Well, yes. You know Abbie is a terrible racist, don't you? I mean, not in the Fayette County sense. He'd never say nigger or anything like that. It's very genteel. It takes the form of condescension and silent disapproval. He's the sort of person who thinks that, oh, those studies about IQ and race are *very interesting*."

"I find that hard to believe, to be honest."

"How do you think he got along so well with those rednecks down in Fayette County? What do you think endeared him to Sherri Larimer and Donald Cavignac and that whole gang? His business acumen? Ha!"

"Well," Isabel said.

"Lord," said Veronica. "I can only imagine what else he's told you."

They finished their meals and drank more of the sweet, doughy beer. The waiter returned and asked if they'd like dessert. "We'd like another drink," Veronica said.

Isabel said she couldn't.

"Of course you can. You need a digestif."

She knew the owner, although he wasn't there that night, and she knew that he kept a bottle of Alsatian *eau-de-vie* for certain occasions. They drank a round of fiery pear liquor out of little clear thimbles. Isabel felt extraordinarily drunk.

"So," Veronica said. "Did Isaac say why it was that he and Sawyer broke up?"

"I think Sawyer broke it off with him. He said . . . I'm sorry, this is very strong. He said—Sawyer, that is—something to the effect that their relationship lacked an and-I-quote core of physical intimacy."

A strange expression chased itself across Veronica's face like the headlight of a car passing across a window at night. "He said that Sawyer said that?"

"To that effect," Isabel repeated.

"Well, that would be very odd."

"Why?"

"Because that's what Abbie told Sarah after she found out that he knocked up that poor woman."

"I'm sorry," Isabel said. Then, evenly, she hoped casually: "What poor woman?"

"Oh, back in New York. Before they moved out here. You know Abbie could never keep his dick in his pants. Cathy was her name."

"Hmm," Isabel said.

"You know, they liked to pretend that they had some kind of open marriage, which is what people do when they oughtn't have ever married in the first place. Actually, I think Isaac must be a lot like his father in that regard. Anyway, Abbie was fucking around, imagine that, and Sarah snooped and found out and threatened to end it, but you know Abbie, he can never admit defeat, not even when it's really victory. So he told her he'd 'have the thing taken care of'—I mean, honestly, is there anything quite as awful as a man speaking about an abortion, whether for or against? They're so very proprietary about it. Anyway, Sarah was giving him the whole how-could-you routine, and Abbie told her that he loved her and wanted to be with her, but that their relationship lacked a core of physical intimacy, which he must therefore seek elsewhere, and then he proposed that they make a new start of it. This was all conveniently elided in retrospect to make room for his supposed discourse with Yahweh, but the truth is that they came out here so that Abbie could save his marriage. Astonishing, isn't it, how much trouble we go through for things that are obviously doomed?"

Isabel laughed. She was drunk, and she knew she had to play that part or else give the depth of her interest away. She asked if they should get the check.

"*I'll* get the check. And don't argue. My brother may have screwed me, business-wise, of course, but I did get paid, ultimately."

"All right," Isabel said.

"Anyway, Sarah got him back when she slept with poor Arthur Imlak."

"Isaac told me that wasn't true. And I've never heard anyone describe Arthur Imlak as poor. Not even metaphorically."

"I'm sure Isaac believes that. He can be shockingly naïve, actually. And Arthur, oh, I don't really mean it, not literally. I do think he was actually in love with Sarah, though, and for all the money he made I don't think he ever got the thing he really wanted."

"He's really about to get what he wants. Did you hear? Barry is giving him the Carnegie Award."

"What on earth is that?"

"Oh, God. It's our annual—well, usually annual—award that we give at our annual gala. For contributions to sustainable urbanism."

"That seems ironic. And I didn't know you all had Carnegie money."

"We don't. Well, a little, but it's just a small operating grant. Believe it or not—I asked—it was your old business partner who had the idea. Back when he was on the board. He thought it sounded classy."

"That man." Veronica shook her head. "I sometimes wonder what ever happened to him."

"I couldn't say," Isabel said. In fact, she'd tracked him down and was hoping to find a way to meet him. She never did.

"Well, I suppose Arthur has given you enough money over the years."

"Still," Isabel said. "It's going to be terrible. People are already planning a protest. The governor—the state had just elected a Democrat who'd campaigned on a promise of a gas excise tax— was supposed to give the keynote, but we're hearing rumors he might pull out."

Veronica smiled and waved her Amex at the waiter. She sighed. "Poor Arthur," she said.

. . .

What Isabel didn't tell Veronica was that she'd argued against the whole thing. "Is it really appropriate?" she'd asked. "I mean, given his business?"

"Arthur's business *is* our business," Barry told her, and he looked at her across his desk with the slight scowl that he affected when he wanted to remind her that they were not, after all, peers. Then he told her that since she and Arthur got along so well, he thought it would be a good idea if Isabel were the one to tell him.

So there she was at another one of Imlak's absurd parties in his great glass shoebox in downtown Pittsburgh. It was a pre-Christmas Light-Up Night. A brass band was playing carols in Market Square. Philip Johnson's mad glass castle at PPG Place glowed like a giant, misshapen lightbulb. It was cold, and from far above, Isabel could see tiny skaters going around the ice rink in the plaza. She didn't know anyone else at the party. It was Arthur's peculiar genius to forever find new people to occupy the crowd scenes that his sense of social obligation occasionally required. He kept complaining about the caterers, and for a while he elbowed the bartender out from behind the bar and had a grand time mixing too-strong drinks himself. At midnight, he threw everyone out except for Isabel and a few younger and more beautiful women, whose glum dates he sent down the elevator with a gleeful and evil little wave of his fingers. He gave the ringleader of these girls a cartoonishly large satchel of coke and the iPad that controlled the house sound system. He left them with these and a bottle of booze in the grand living room, then hauled Isabel off to the kitchen to drink what he claimed to be sixty-year-old scotch. He produced a second and more realistically scaled baggie of cocaine and drew out two lines on the counter.

She bent to do one. She tossed her head back. "You gave the other ladies a volume discount." She laughed.

"I gave the youth the *stepped-on shit*," he said, relishing a phrase that someone else had taught him. "It would be silly to waste the quality on the undiscerning."

They got high.

Isabel said, "It's a terrible idea to give you the Carnegie Award, you know."

He chuckled, pleased. "Of course it's a terrible idea. It will undermine whatever credibility you have. Which isn't much, frankly."

She frowned, because even if it were true, she still didn't like the suggestion that her employer was in some way a fraud. She asked him, a little testily, why, if that were the case, would he even accept.

He did a few more lines without offering any to her. He said, "I find it entertaining to watch Barry squirm between the twinned imperatives of his organization and its principles." He rubbed his nose. "The whole notion of non-profit companies performing the good works that idiotic Americans refused to permit the true public sector to perform is an absurdity. He laughed and told her that he was in fact a good Marxist who was "heightening the contra-dictions." He seemed especially pleased by the phrase.

"Yeah, well," Isabel said, annoyed in spite of herself, "isn't it just the deranging influence of guys like you and your big piles of loose cash that prevent America from having a reasonable public sector in the first place?" She put a hand on her hip.

He told her that his piles of loose cash were ultimately the result of those same idiots ignoring their own best interest. He obscurely referred to some comment that H. L. Mencken sup-posedly made about Russia and America, but when Isabel pressed him to remember it exactly, he told her she'd have to look it up on her own. "You're the scholar," he teased. His eyes had grown narrow.

"I guess so," she said.

Imlak said, "In any event, I like superseding that moron com-mie governor that the good people of the Commonwealth have just elected. If you can't beat them, and you won't join them, undermine, undermine, undermine."

Isabel shrugged and asked him if he was ever going to attend to his other guests.

"The presence of a gauche female element," he told her, "is purely a matter of reputation management. A man must appear to be a certain thing."

Isabel still believed him when he said this, though she found it insulting, even if it wasn't directed at her, even if in saying it to her, Imlak was implicitly exempting her from his contempt. And then—it was the hour, it was the aged scotch, it was the good cocaine—she asked him flat out with the insistence that only drink and drugs and an hour past decency permit if he was really Isaac Mayer's father, his biological father. And Arthur Imlak, who not two hours before had been all loose tie and cocktail shakers and bad jokes, put his hands on the counter on either side of her; she squirmed, and he said, gravely, "Yes." His breath stank. He fixed his clouded, pinpoint eyes on hers, and he held her in his stare and said, "But you, you believe it's just a rumor." She realized that one of his hands was now gripping her wrist. It wasn't painful, but it was almost painful. Isabel couldn't think of what to say; she knew that she should shout at him, she should tell him to fuck off, but she found herself instead searching for something funny to say, as if it were up to her to make him realize that this was all hilarious, ha ha, just a joke; but humor failed her too, so she just said that yes, that was what she believed. Arthur was older than her, and she'd have doubted that he could have kept up on a three-mile run around the park, but right then he felt very big. Isabel could feel his elbows on her sides. He was much taller than she was. He was leaning forward to bring his eyes level with hers, which made their faces even closer. She didn't want to look away from him, because she was afraid it would make him angry. His whole demeanor was changed. "You are not to say anything," he said. She shook her head. Then he leaned closer. His mouth was by her ear. She could hear the sound of his tongue moving behind his teeth. She felt as if her skin was going to peel away from her own body and her throat was going to turn inside out. "Good," he said. Then, more quietly, his mouth even closer, he said, "No one would hear you." Then he was somehow on the other side of the kitchen, leaning against the counter, swirling a scotch, grinning as if none of it had happened. She made herself stop shaking. She wasn't some dumb girl. She wasn't afraid. She stopped herself from shaking and went out with him into the living room as if nothing had happened and made herself party with him and those drunken young women for another hour in some vague hope that he would not connect what had just happened with why and when she chose to leave.

. . .

Eli said that he would kill him, kill Imlak, do it himself with his own hands around the sick old man's soft neck, and Isabel thought he thought he was trying to mean it, the poor guy. "You can't kill him," she said, meaning both that it would not do to actually murder Arthur Imlak, nor did she believe Eli could actually go through with it, even if the moral question did not obtain. She'd called him after two in the morning, and he'd arrived at her apartment at four. He smelled of coffee and the cigarette he'd smoked in the car on the way.

"What are you doing here?" she asked. She hadn't asked him to come, only told him what had happened.

That was when he made the threat. That was when she said he couldn't kill Arthur.

"Arthur," he spat. "Fuck that man." He came inside, and Isabel made tea. "Isabel," he told her, "you're too old to take these drugs."

"Oh, thanks. So I'm old, and it's my fault."

"I don't mean that." He didn't mean that. They sat on the couch and drank tea. Then she lay down and put her head in his lap.

"Anyway," she said. "You can't kill Arthur. He's Isaac's father."

"No he isn't."

"He admitted it."

"They're all liars. Arthur. Abbie. Sarah. Isaac."

"You work for them."

"Well, so do you, in a way."

"Yes."

He didn't want to say any more about that. Instead, he told her that for years he'd thought of going to Canada where his sister lived, to Vancouver, out to the island, or up north on the mainland, somewhere with cheap land on a hill near the water. He would do, ironically, what Abbie had done: design and build a house, all his own, although it would be a different sort of house, and he would build most of it himself, with his own hands. It would be small. It would have thoughtful windows. It would be the sort of house that made the people who lived in it decide what they needed to keep and what they must part with. It would have a steep roof and feel like a tent beneath the tall trees. There would be a wood-burning stove in the kitchen, and he would keep a canoe at a small dock on the water, which he would take out when the weather was calm. There would be whales and eagles, and even in the winter it would be green. He dreamed of it, sometimes, the house, the water, the forest. In the dream, sometimes, a black bear came out of the trees while he stood on the porch. It shuffled across the pine needles. Its breath was visible in little puffs. When it got close to him, no more distant than the far side of a small room, it stood on two feet. The bear's sad, lovely eyes looked into Eli's, and his into the bear's. It dropped back to its feet and shook itself like a dog coming out of the water, and coughed, and wandered back into the forest. "A monster in the woods," Isabel murmured, and she thought, but later decided she'd been wrong, that she heard Eli say one of the names of God. She fell asleep around this point, and when she woke up, he was sleeping too, his head tilted back against the wall, snoring lightly, his feet on the coffee table, his legs crossed at the ankles.

II

IN RE:

ABBOT MAYER   )

dba MAYER DESIGN LAB, LLC   )

)

    and   )

)

MH PARTNERS LLP   )

ARBITRATION HEARING

THURSDAY, MARCH 21, 1991

BEFORE: SAUL MAMRY, ARBITRATOR – ATTORNEY AT LAW

APPEARANCES:

For Abbot Mayer:

    David and David, P.C.

    David Ben David, Esquire

    1001 Wood Street

    Pittsburgh, PA 15222

For MH Partners LLP

    Southman Wright & Jordan, P.C.

    A. Christopher Jordan, Esquire

    590 Grant Street, 8th Floor

    Pittsburgh, PA 15219

TRANSCRIPT OF HEARING

Witnesses

VERONICA MAYER

 Direct Examination by Mr. Jordan

 Cross-Examination by Mr. Ben David

PHILLIP HARROW

 Direct Examination by Mr. Jordan

 Cross-Examination by Mr. Ben David

ABBOT "Abbie" MAYER

 Direct Examination by Mr. Ben David

 Cross-Examination by Mr. Jordan

ARTHUR B. IMLAK

 Not Examined

PROCEEDINGS

Mr. Mamry: Thank you. We have a court reporter who is recording these proceedings, and that is by mutual consent of the parties. My name is Saul Mamry, and I will be the Arbitrator—not, as I sometimes hear it mistaken, the Arbiter—for this, well, Arbitration. The parties have agreed to binding arbitration in this matter. The results will be, as the name suggests, binding. I am neutral, and I have no prior knowledge of the facts or circumstances of the . . . circumstances. All right? We have five, I'm sorry, four witnesses who will testify today, as well as a number of joint and individual exhibits, which will be introduced into the record. Do I have that correct?

Mr. Ben David: Yes, Mr. Arbitrator.

Mr. Jordan: Yes, Mr. Arbitrator.

Mr. Mamry: Good. Excellent. Well, let's begin. I take it we have opening statements?

Mr. Jordan: Yes, Mr. Arbitrator. Mr. Arbitrator, in 1988, Mr. Abbie Mayer—

Mr. Mamry: I'm sorry to interrupt already. That's Abbot Mayer? He goes by Abbie?

Mr. Jordan: He does, Mr. Arbitrator.

Mr. Mamry: He can answer, counselor. I probably fooled you with the third person there, but as a general rule, when I address a question to a person present, the present person can answer for him- or herself. We're not adjudicating a felony here. At least, I hope not.

Mr. Jordan: Of course.

Mr. Mamry: Mr. Mayer?

Mr. Mayer: I do, Your Honor.

Mr. Mamry: Yes, thank you, Mr. Mayer. I'm not a judge. No need for your honors. Go ahead, Mr. Jordan.

Mr. Jordan: Thank you. Mr. Arbitrator, in 1988, Abbie Mayer relocated to Pittsburgh with his wife, Sarah Mayer, who is a partner in his firm, Mayer Design Lab.

Mr. Mamry: Once again, I'll interrupt. This promises to be slow going if I don't manage to keep my mouth shut. I am an inveterate kibitzer. Mrs. Mayer is not present?

Mr. Jordan: No, Mr. Arbitrator.

Mr. Mamry: Afraid she'd spill the beans?

Mr. Ben David: Mrs. Mayer is actually nine months pregnant and due any day now.

Mr. Mamry: Well, that's not precisely the sort of bean-spilling I imagined. Mazel tov, Mr. Mayer.

MR. MAYER: [unintelligible]

MR. MAMRY: I'm sorry?

MR. BEN DAVID: Nothing, Mr. Arbitrator. In addition, although Mrs. Mayer is technically a co-owner of the business, we would stipulate, and I believe Mr. Jordan will agree, that she is not an active manager. She worked principally in a support and bookkeeping capacity.

MR. JORDAN: Yes, we would so stipulate.

MR. MAMRY: I will so accept your so stipulation. May I inquire, however: wouldn't bookkeeping be relevant to the matter under dispute here? This is a financial matter, no?

MR. JORDAN: I think, Mr. Arbitrator, that I will be able to illuminate that in my opening statement. And in short, the accounting is not under dispute here. Rather, it is the question of whether or not an agreement, implicit or otherwise, was breached.

MR. MAMRY: That's right. You were giving an opening statement. We do seem to have wandered afield. Please, continue.

MR. JORDAN: Mr. Arbitrator, my client, MH Partners LLP consists of two principals, Ms. Veronica Mayer—

MR. MAMRY: Any relation?

MR. JORDAN: I'm sorry?

MR. MAMRY: To Mr. Mayer.

MR. JORDAN: Yes, I was getting to that.

MR. MAMRY: Please.

MR. JORDAN: Ms. Mayer is also the older sibling of Mr. Mayer.

MR. MAMRY: Older!

Ms. MAYER: Thank you, Mr. Arbitrator.

MR. JORDAN: Ms. Mayer is an attorney herself, but her principal business is in real estate development.

MR. MAMRY: My goodness, is anyone not a lawyer in here? I'm sorry, go on.

MR. JORDAN: Yes. Ms. Mayer's business partner is Mr. Phillip Harrow, also here. Mr. Harrow is also the proprietor and CEO of a major construction firm based in Morgantown, West Virginia, which is called Harcon. Over the last approximately nine years, beginning in 1981, Ms. Mayer and Mr. Harrow have, under the auspices of a limited partnership, MH Partners, engaged in a number of development projects together and with other companies and partners. These include residential and commercial developments, as well as a more recent series of projects involving transportation infrastructure. In 1987, Mr. Mayer, an architect by training and profession, approached Ms. Mayer about a potential relocation from his then-current residence in New York City to Western Pennsylvania and further proposed that he would join her business as an additional partner. As MH Partners was, at the time, engaged in a significant residential development project, Ms. Mayer and Mr. Harrow concluded that an architect-planner would be a strategically advantageous partner in their business. They also believed that it would significantly reduce their costs associated with design, site-planning, and environmental and wastewater remediation, etc. Mr. Mayer's specialty was in what is called sustainable design, which is to say, environmentally sound building.

Mr. Mayer did, in fact, subsequently move to Pittsburgh and did likewise join his business with MH Partners. I emphasize he joined his business, not his person. Mr. Mayer continued to operate as a private architect and designer, and his firm became, in effect, a contractor for MH Partners. Over the next approximately three years, Mayer Design Lab acted as architect and planner for

MH Partners. We have—this is Joint Exhibit 1. It is a schedule of projects over that period, along with invoices.

Mr. Mamry: I'm sorry, I'm going to interject again, here. First of all, Mr. Ben David, you have seen this exhibit and it is a joint exhibit?

Mr. Ben David: Yes, Mr. Arbitrator.

Mr. Mamry: Good. And Mr. Jordan, let me see if I understand. You are saying that although there was some, some discussion of the possibility of Mr. Mayer joining MH Partners—I suppose that would have made it MMH Partners, no? I give Mr. Harrow some credit, here. Harcon. That's rather more clever, wouldn't you all agree? So your contention is that Mr. Mayer and MH Partners discussed a formal business partnership, decided against it, and Mr. Mayer became a vendor for MH Partners?

Mr. Jordan: Partially, Mr. Arbitrator. But in fact, it is our contention that the voluminous nature of the schedule and invoices shows a de facto partnership existed between the businesses even if no formal document exists to formalize or memorialize such an understanding. As you know, a great deal of private development work is done on a quote handshake basis. That is the situation here.

Mr. Mamry: The voluminous nature of the schedule and invoices! Speak of angels and hear them flutter their wings. Mr. Ben David, would you . . . Actually, no. Strike that. Well, don't strike that. It can remain in the record. I meant it in the common usage only. I'm sure you'll address the issue of voluminousness in your opening, Mr. Ben David.

Mr. Ben David: Yes, Mr. Arbitrator.

Mr. Mamry: Then I am assured, voluminously. Go on, Mr. Jordan.

Mr. Jordan: Yes. I'm getting to the end. Mr. Arbitrator, beginning approximately two years ago, in 1989, MH Partners along with Mayer Design Lab became significantly involved in a major highway construction project, termed in local media the Mon-Fayette Expressway.

Mr. Mamry: As a point of correction, I believe it was termed by local politicians the Mon-Fayette Expressway. I believe the local media, such as they are, termed it the Highway to Nowhere.

Mr. Jordan: Well, be that as it may—

Mr. Mamry: Don't worry, Mr. Jordan. I'm only kidding. The fact that this project may or may not be a public boondoggle, white elephant, or what have you, has no probative value here and won't affect my decision or award. Contracts, implied or otherwise, are contracts regardless of the, how shall I put it, the ethical genealogy of their origin. I never begrudge another man—or woman—his successful scam.

Mr. Jordan: Thank you, Mr. Arbitrator. That's a memorable expression of a principle. To conclude, the parties to this dispute became involved in two significant and interrelated projects. First, Mr. Harrow's own company, Harcon, contracted with the Pennsylvania Department of Transportation to construct several major portions of the aforementioned highway, with MH Partners acting as Harcon's agent in the bidding and contracting phases.

Mr. Mamry: They, Harcon, I'm sorry, were literally building this Roman road?

Mr. Jordan: No, uh. They would have been the general contractor. And, let me see, second, MH Partners, in association with Mayer Design Lab, acquired significant land acreage contiguous with or congruent to the right-of-way of the highway.

The purpose of this land acquisition was for the construction of a number of housing developments—bedroom communities, Mr. Arbitrator, located in proximity to highway exits, entrances, and interchanges. Because MH Partners' explicit involvement in the bidding process for highway construction would constrain them from making these purchases directly, owing to certain rules of that bidding process, Mayer Design Lab, which created a subsidiary LLC known as MDL—

MR. MAMRY: I am sensing a naming convention. Go on.

MR. JORDAN: —and Mr. Mayer personally were engaged as agents for these purchases. Here we will submit our Exhibits 1 and 2, which are records of correspondence to this effect as well as bank records indicating transfers of funds to MDL and to Mr. Mayer for this purpose.

MR. MAMRY: All right. I am a bit idiosyncratic here. I don't like having multiple exhibits ones and twos and so forth floating around. I'll mark these MH Partners Exhibits 2 and 3. And the numbers will go up from there.

MR. JORDAN: Very good, Mr. Arbitrator.

MR. MAMRY: You said you were wrapping it up, but I admit, I find myself still in the dark middle portion of the tunnel here. Will we soon emerge into daylight?

MR. JORDAN: Yes, of course. In 1990, Ms. Mayer approached Mr. Mayer about the creation of a new business entity for the purpose of developing housing on these properties. In effect, she proposed the creation of a general contracting business that would construct homes on spec and ultimately sell them through a real estate partner to be determined. Mr. Mayer then informed Ms. Mayer that this would not be possible, because he—that is to say, his company, MDL—had sold the properties to one Arthur

B. Imlak, who is also present today; rather, actually, in fact, to a holding company controlled by Mr. Imlak.

MR. MAMRY: I shudder to think the holding company is called ABI.

MR. IMLAK: Close, but no cigar. ILH. That was originally Imlak Land Holdings.

MR. MAMRY: Yes, thank you, Mr. Imlak. That was a joke, and you'll have your turn. I'll reserve the cigar.

MR. JORDAN: It is our contention that Mr. Mayer violated a clear, historic, and mutually understood oral contract in so doing. This matter was previously adjudicated before a judge in civil court, and we would submit the records of those proceedings as Joint Exhibit . . . I'm afraid I'm not sure what number we're on.

MR. MAMRY: Joint Exhibit 4. Entered. But, I'm sorry. You've already been to trial? How in the many Names of the Lord did you manage that? That was fast! God's justice may be swift, but civil court tends to move at a more naturally geologic and less divinely Let-There-Be sort of pace.

MR. JORDAN: No, Mr. Arbitrator. We had several preliminary hearings before a judge. We'd asked for an injunction. Our intention was to overturn the illegal sale of the properties and compel their return to MH Partners for the purpose of their original intended use. Regrettably, the judge ruled the sales were legitimate—that is to say, that they were not, strictly speaking, illegal. We considered going forward seeking monetary damages in a civil forum, but at that point, both parties felt it was in their best interests, in terms of publicity and, frankly, cost, to submit to arbitration instead.

MR. MAMRY: Strictly speaking, everything is illegal. Broadly, though, nothing is. Who was the judge? Actually, never mind.

Forget it. Arbitration was probably wise, and yes, certainly cheaper than litigation. Go on.

MR. JORDAN: Very good, Mr. Arbitrator. We contend that, although the sales may technically have been legal, they violated a clearly understood oral contract, and that Mr. Mayer unfairly and unjustly profited from the sale to the sole benefit of his business and person and to the express detriment of his partners, who have suffered grievous economic harm as a result. We submit this to you, Mr. Arbitrator, and ask you to determine that such a violation did occur, and as a remedy to award the full proceeds of such sales to my clients, MH Partners LLP.

MR. MAMRY: Excellent. That all seems clear. Let's recess for five minutes. I've been drinking coffee all morning, if you know what I mean. Mr. Ben David, you may take your place in the batter's box.

[RECESS]

MR. MAMRY: We are back on the record. Thank you for indulging my brief intermission there. Mr. Ben David, if you please.

MR. BEN DAVID: Thank you. Mr. Arbitrator, the issue here is straightforward.

MR. MAMRY: That seems fairly anti-prophetic to me, Mr. Ben David. But please, go on.

MR. BEN DAVID: Yes. Our position is straightforward. In the first part—

MR. MAMRY: I'm sorry, Mr. Ben David. Again, the first part? I'm going to go out on a limb here and suggest that the first part implies a minimum of one subsequent part, possibly more, which rather mitigates against the straightforwardness of this position, does it not?

MR. BEN DAVID: I don't believe so, Mr. Arbitrator. The way is straight, if not narrow. If you would hear me out.

MR. MAMRY: Oh, yes. I am the recording angel, the man clothed in linen with the writing instrument at his side. Go on.

MR. BEN DAVID: I'll revise. Our position is twofold. First, that Mr. Mayer had every legal right to sell this property, as opposing counsel's own exhibit demonstrates, and two, that Mr. Mayer in point of fact generously offered to evenly divide the proceeds of said sales with Ms. Mayer and Mr. Harrow, an offer they refused in order to pursue the outrageous claim that Mr. Imlak should be compelled to return his legally acquired property, or, failing that, that Mr. Mayer should be required to pay the total proceeds of the sales to MH Partners and retain nothing for himself.

MR. MAMRY: Let's leave the outrageousness for the courts, counselors. We don't need any of those sorts of antics. You're both paying me to be here to arbitrate this dispute. Consider me therefore suitably pre-impressed by the heroic outrage you all feel at the terrible thing that has occurred.

MR. BEN DAVID: Of course.

MR. MAMRY: Go on.

MR. BEN DAVID: That's really it, Mr. Arbitrator. We submit, in effect, the same question as the opposing side. Did a contract exist and was it violated? If so, what should the remedy be? If not, well, not.

MR. MAMRY: I do appreciate brevity. I assume, from the phrasing, that you believe no violation occurred, and therefore no remedy is required.

MR. BEN DAVID: That's correct, Mr. Arbitrator.

Mr. Mamry: All right, then. I have a question, before we examine witnesses. You mentioned, Mr. Ben David, that Mr. Mayer offered to evenly split, I believe were your words, the proceeds of these real estate transactions with his sister and her partner over there. By evenly split you mean?

Mr. Ben David: Fifty-fifty.

Mr. Mamry: Wonder of wonders. And I am going to once again venture out onto the thinner branches here to speculate that this offer was proffered . . . excuse me, that sounds ridiculous. That he made this offer orally and no written record of it exists.

Mr. Ben David: Mr. Mayer will testify that he made that offer.

Mr. Mamry: I think we can read that as a yes, no? Good. We will swear in all the witnesses at once, I think, for the sake of efficacy, and then begin examination.

DIRECT EXAMINATION OF VERONICA MAYER

Mr. Jordan: Would you state your name for the record.

Ms. Mayer: Veronica Mayer.

Q: And your relationship to the matter at hand? Your position?

A: I am one of the two principal partners in MH Partners, LP.

Q: Veronica, how would you describe your business?

A: My background is in law, as you pointed out earlier. However, I now principally work in real estate development. Originally, that was mostly commercial real estate, but in the last five or six years, I've become more involved in residential.

Q: And what is your relationship to Mr. Harrow?

A: Mr. Harrow and I met in West Virginia about ten years ago. I was representing a commercial property developer as part of their legal team, and Mr. Harrow was hoping to broker a land purchase deal that would allow his company to serve as the general contractor for the construction of a shopping plaza. We subsequently became involved as partners in that deal, which led to the formation of MH Partners.

Q: MH Partners is?

A: A Limited Partnership that we use for a variety of joint ventures. Mr. Harrow and I both conduct business separately as well, but we frequently work on projects together. The partnership makes it easier to acquire financing and so forth, but it allows us to act as independent agents as well.

Q: So you and Mr. Harrow have been in business . . .

A: Ten years, give or take.

Q: And what about your brother, Abbie Mayer? Is he a partner?

A: No. We discussed it but ultimately decided against it.

Q: Why?

A: Firstly, because Abbie lacked the capital. We weren't a corporation. I didn't want to see my brother on the hook if, God forbid, we suffered a significant loss.

Q: And secondly?

A: Secondly, Abbie is a little . . . unusual.

Q: Unusual? What do you mean?

Mr. Ben David: Objection.

Mr. Jordan: To what?

Mr. Ben David: First of all, relevance? Second of all, speculative.

Mr. Mamry: Yes, thank you, Perry Mason. I am shocked, shocked that the lawyers are objecting. Nevertheless, I remind everyone, once again, that this is not a court of law. I think you'll just have to have faith in my ability to suss out the probative value of speculation. However, I am tempted to agree that it's a little untoward to wildly besmirch the man's character. Mr. Jordan, the relevance?

MR. JORDAN: Oral agreements, or lack thereof, are at issue, Mr. Arbitrator. We'd contend that Mr. Mayer's personality must be taken into account here.

MR. MAMRY: I eagerly await your argument that you made a deal with a wild man and subsequently suffered harm when he behaved as such. All right. Go on.

MR. JORDAN: How is Mr. Mayer unusual?

A: Well, he's temperamental, first of all. And he has a large ego. He takes stands of principle that don't always make a lot of sense. And, well . . .

Q: It's all right, Ms. Mayer. You can tell us.

A: Quite frankly, he has . . . religious convictions.

Q: Religions convictions? What's wrong with that?

A: They're unusual convictions.

MR. BEN DAVID: I really have to object again. Again, speculation, and now, hearsay as well! Is Mr. Jordan really asking Ms. Mayer to testify as to Mr. Mayer's religious beliefs?

MR. MAMRY: Hearsay is permissible in arbitration, Mr. Ben David. Again, you'll have to trust me to give it its due weight. Continue, Mr. Jordan.

MR. JORDAN: Thank you. Please describe what you mean, Veronica.

A: My brother thinks that he speaks directly to God. I don't know how else to say it. He has an idea that he is some kind of prophet.

MR. MAMRY: Well, now, that's not something you hear in a typical he-said, she-said.

Q: Indeed. But, uh. And yet, Ms. Mayer, yet you went into business with him?

A: He was my brother, and he was having financial difficulties. I wanted to help him. Plus, it never hurts to have an architect on the payroll. Anyway, I think I understood it to be metaphorical at the time.

Q: Metaphorical?

A: Yes. I mean, the beliefs. His beliefs. I didn't want to judge him on the basis of his religiosity. I suppose a lot of people pray or talk to God, in a sense. I didn't think he meant it so literally. It was something he mentioned early on, right when he was moving here—to Pittsburgh—from New York, but after that, he rarely mentioned it. I mean, for a time he rarely mentioned it.

Q: It didn't interfere with your work together?

A: Not at first.

Q: But later?

A: It became . . . an issue.

Q: How? Give us an example.

A: Well, for instance, we were working on an interchange project down in Uniontown—

Q: An interchange project?

A: Pretty common for us. Through Phil—Mr. Harrow—we'd bid on interchange construction, and we'd also work to develop commercial property, usually shopping, strip malls, plazas, that sort of thing, beside. So we discovered, well into this project, I mean, with millions already invested, the site prepared, everything, that Abbie had started speaking to some of our local business and political contacts about changing the route of the highway that was supposed to connect up to the interchange.

Q: Behind your back?

A: Yes.

Q: But why?

MR. BEN DAVID: Mr. Arbitrator—

MR. MAMRY: Yes, yes. You object. Overruled. Does that little bit of courthouse dialogue satiate your hunger to turn this into Oral Arguments? You'll have every opportunity to play Clarence Darrow on cross. Go on, Mr. Jordan.

MR. JORDAN: Why would he go behind your back?

A: He told me that the highway route was not as he'd seen it.

Q: As he'd seen it?

A: Yes. In a . . . vision. A dream.

Q: Mr. Mayer was making business decisions based on dreams?

A: Attempting to.

Q: He didn't succeed?

A: No. It was already a done deal. That project went forward, and he later apologized.

Q: For what did he apologize?

A: He said, in effect, that he'd been mistaken.

Q: You took that to mean that he'd been mistaken in his specific behavior?

A: Yes.

Q: But he meant something else.

A: I believe so, yes.

Q: What do you believe he meant?

A: I believe he meant that his . . . dream, or his vision, or whatever, was not actually about the road, but about a different piece of property.

MR. BEN DAVID: Honestly, Mr. Arbitrator, how is this relevant? Is Ms. Mayer Joseph? Is she going to tell us when to store the wheat?

MR. MAMRY: I haven't the foggiest, although you, Ms. Mayer, look nothing like a Joseph to me. But I do feel zestfully rabbinic at the moment. I promise, Mr. Ben David, that I will take the unusual nature of this testimony into account.

MR. JORDAN: But at the time, you accepted his apology and went on with business as usual.

A: Yes. Correct.

Q: Why was that necessary?

A: As you said in your opening statement, we'd bid on a significant share of the highway construction. And there were some conflict of interest provisions that, although they didn't explicitly forbid us from doing adjoining property development, convinced us that our best and cleanest bet for assembling the necessary parcels was to use a third-party buyer. Abbie was ideal. Siblings, it turns out, are treated at a much lower level of scrutiny than husbands and wives or parents and children. Perhaps the law assumes we all hate each other.

MR. MAMRY: The law assumes little other than its own relevance, Ms. Mayer.

MS. MAYER: I'm not sure I understand that comment.

MR. MAMRY: Me either. Go on.

Q: Despite your concerns? That is to say, you went through with this plan despite them?

A: Yes. And, to be honest, Abbie had developed a rapport with a number of local—that is to say, Fayette County—persons of influence that proved beneficial in acquiring much of the property that we desired.

Q: Now, I want you to be very clear about this. Did Abbie understand why you were buying this property?

A: Yes, it was clear from the beginning. We discussed it on multiple occasions. We'd seen the growth in bedroom communities north of Pittsburgh with the construction of the Parkway

North, and we envisioned a similar building boom around the Expressway. It was our intention to build on-spec housing subdivisions as well as to develop other areas for the sale of individual lots to individual buyers looking to build their own houses. To hire contractors, I mean, on their own.

Q: Yet you never memorialized this understanding in writing. Why?

A: I'm . . . a little uncomfortable in saying.

Mr. Mamry: Oh, I think I can guess, and I can assure you, Ms. Mayer, that I am not here to judge whether or not you skirted the fine line of legality in setting up straw buyers and suchlike. I'm not a judge or officer of the court, and I'm not going to rat on you. I presume that, since you're a lawyer, you complied with the strict letter, if not the broadest possible moral intent, of whatever laws we're talking about here. I have a saying, you know: we are all guilty, just not necessarily of what we're accused of. Please, speak freely.

Ms. Mayer: All right. We worried that a written agreement would become public and draw undue attention to our development plans. To use your phrase, sir, we were less concerned with strict letters than with broad moral intents. Or interpretations.

Mr. Mamry: A perfectly reasonable concern.

Mr. Jordan: How much property did you ultimately acquire?

A: All in, in excess of thirty million dollars' worth of land.

Mr. Mamry: Yikes!

Mr. Jordan: Indeed. So, Veronica, at what point did you discover that your brother had, unbeknownst to you, sold this land?

A: It would have been almost exactly a year ago. Phil and I were going to set up a meeting for the three of us to go down to Fayette County and meet with two of the county commissioners to talk about some various zoning and land use issues. But when I personally put in a call to Don Cavignac, that's one of the commissioners, he sounded confused. He said that he thought we'd unloaded that property to the gas guy. I asked what he meant, and he explained that he thought we'd sold the properties, or most of them anyway, to one Arthur Imlak.

MR. MAMRY: That would be you, Mr. Imlak?

MR. BEN DAVID: That's correct, Mr. Arbitrator.

MR. MAMRY: Mr. Ben David, I can assure you that Mr. Imlak can answer the question of whether he is or is not himself, well, himself.

MR. BEN DAVID: Apologies, Mr. Arbitrator. Go ahead, Arthur.

MR. IMLAK: C'est moi.

MR. HARROW: Say what?

MR. MAMRY: Yes, thank you. Let the record show that Mr. Imlak grinned pompously and answered in French, and that his French was in the affirmative. Mr. Imlak is the Mr. Imlak in question.

MR. JORDAN: To reiterate, neither you nor Mr. Harrow had any prior knowledge that Abbie Mayer intended to sell these properties.

A: None.

Q: Let's get to the crux of the matter.

MR. MAMRY: Yes, let's. I'd like to think that we'll eventually get to the drain we're circling.

MR. JORDAN: Of course, Mr. Arbitrator. Veronica, how much did your brother sell these properties for?

A: Roughly forty million dollars.

Q: Well, that's quite a nice profit, isn't it? And Mr. Mayer was, after all, offering to split those profits with you, was he not?

A: No, and that's exactly the problem. He was offering to split the total proceeds. So we're talking about a ten million dollar loss, in effect, borne entirely by Phil—Mr. Harrow—and myself.

Q: That's a big loss.

A: I'd probably have no choice but to seek protection in bankruptcy. And Mr. Harrow might be able to absorb the loss, but it would be very difficult.

Q: All right. Just one more item. And this goes to the real financial losses, the lost opportunity, here. What sort of opportunity losses are we talking about?

MR. BEN DAVID: I'm going to object, again. Can Ms. Mayer really be permitted to testify to some exaggerated potential economic loss based on some rosy scenario of future potential profit? At very least, it inherently prejudices any judgment against my client by suggesting that he is responsible for some detrimental effect far out of proportion to any actual and current monetary loss, if such losses even exist, I'd add.

MR. MAMRY: Your ardency is noted, your objection overruled. Please answer, Ms. Mayer.

A: We would be talking about potentially thousands of quarter-acre residential plots, to be either sold to individual home builders or developed, per our original plan, on spec. Of course, there would be many millions of dollars of expense in connecting utilities, building street plans, etc., but all told, we were looking at potential profits well in excess of one hundred million dollars.

MR. MAMRY: Double yikes.

MR. JORDAN: Thank you, Veronica. That's all I have, Mr. Arbitrator.

Mr. Mamry: All right. I can see Mr. Ben David is champing at the bit to cross.

CROSS-EXAMINATION OF VERONICA MAYER

Mr. Ben David: Ms. Mayer, you testified that you utilized my client and his business as agents for these purchases in order to skirt legal restrictions on purchasing them yourself.

Ms. Mayer: No. Contractual restrictions.

Q: I'm sorry, Ms. Mayer, I'm not sure I see the distinction.

A: Well, that may be the fault of your legal education. It's not a subtle distinction.

Q: Uh-huh. Contractual. Okay. And is it also your testimony that my client provided no funds at all toward the purchase of these properties?

A: No funds directly.

Q: I see. But indirectly?

A: Yes, Abbie paid some legal and real estate–related costs directly. But all told, we're talking maybe thirty or forty thousand dollars.

Q: And the rest of the money came from?

A: From Phil and myself.

Q: It was your money.

A: We used a number of financial vehicles. Some of it was our money. Much of it was borrowed.

Mr. Jordan: Mr. Arbitrator, all of that is contained within the exhibits already submitted.

Mr. Mamry: Yes, I'm sure those will be scintillating. Please, Mr. Ben David, continue.

Mr. Ben David: Ms. Mayer, did you give this money to Abbie Mayer?

A: I would say it was more like a loan.

Q: To be paid back?

A: Yes, in effect.

Q: Let me ask you this. Assuming your plan had gone through, as proposed, and you made these great piles of money, how was my client to be paid?

A: Paid?

Q: Yes. You say that he was acting as an agent. So I presume you were going to pay him for his services.

A: He was . . . yes. He was going to be paid.

Q: You hesitated, Ms. Mayer.

Mr. Jordan: Is that a question?

Mr. Ben David: Here's the question. How was that payment to be calculated?

A: I'm not . . . we hadn't fully worked that out.

Q: For a hundred-million dollar project? I find that hard to believe.

Mr. Mamry: Yes, Mr. Ben David. Your face betrays the towering heights of your incredulity. A veritable Babel of incredulity. I see where this is going. Ms. Mayer, I'm going to, as Mr. Ben David memorably put it, get right to the crux of it. Were you going to pay your brother over there a fee, or was he going to get a cut of profits?

A: A cut. A percentage.

Mr. Mamry: More than a few percent? More than ten?

A: Yes.

Mr. Mamry: I can tell by Mr. Jordan's frown and Mr. Ben David's triumphant grin that I have elicited the testimony that we were just about to spend many fruitless minutes nibbling at. Is there anything else, Mr. Ben David?

Mr. Ben David: Yes, Mr. Arbitrator, if you'd permit me.

MR. MAMRY: Oh, yes, indeed. Sally forth.

MR. BEN DAVID: And don't call me Sally.

MR. MAMRY: I'm sorry, what?

MR. BEN DAVID: Never mind, that was a—

MR. MAMRY: Yes I—

MR. BEN DAVID: A joke.

MR. MAMRY: Yes. I've seen the movie. Okay. Why don't you leave the obscurity to me?

MR. BEN DAVID: Yes.

MR. MAMRY: Go on.

Q: Ms. Mayer, you made a statement earlier. Do you recall what it was?

A: That's a broad net.

Q: To the effect of: it never hurts to have an architect on the payroll.

A: Yes. Okay. I did say that.

Q: Well?

A: Well?

Q: Was Mr. Mayer, my client, on the payroll?

A: Which payroll?

Q: Any payroll.

A: Any payroll? I couldn't say.

Q: Any payroll of yours, Ms. Mayer.

A: I don't recall. No.

Q: You don't recall? Or no?

A: No. I don't believe that Abby was on a payroll.

Q: Are you being lawyerly, here, Ms. Mayer?

A: Lawyerly? Perish the thought.

Q: Ms. Mayer, was Mr. Mayer receiving, from MH Partners, a regular payment or payments?

A: Regular? I wouldn't use that term.

Mr. Ben David: Mr. Arbitrator, I'm going to have to ask you to compel this witness to answer directly.

Mr. Mamry: Or what? Hold her in contempt? Throw her in the clink? You've chosen the wrong field, Mr. Ben David. I suggest you try criminal defense. Or get yourself elected DA. I think we can all, as my grandson would say, take a chill pill. Or wouldn't say. I admit, the lingo escapes me anymore. Ms. Mayer, for my benefit, did Mr. Mayer receive, let us say, so as not to prejudice the reply, periodic payments from you, Mr. Harrow, or your joint business entity?

Ms. Mayer: I would say payments. I would not say periodic.

Mr. Mamry: Okay, Ms. Mayer. You're a slippery one. I think we've reached the limits of this line of questioning. *Hak mir nisht ken tshaynik.* Have you got anything else?

Mr. Ben David: No, Mr. Arbitrator.

Mr. Mamry: Thank you. Any redirect, Mr. Jordan?

Mr. Jordan: No.

Mr. Mamry: Thank you. Ms. Mayer, you are excused, although you'll remain under oath should Mr. Jordan decide to recall you later on. Mr. Jordan, do you have any questions for Mr. Harrow?

DIRECT EXAMINATION OF PHILLIP HARROW

Mr. Jordan: Just a few, Mr. Arbitrator.

Mr. Mamry: Do go on.

Mr. Jordan: Thank you. Mr. Harrow, would you state your full name for the record?

Mr. Harrow: Phillip A. Harrow, the Construction King of Morgantown, dubba-you vee.

MR. MAMRY: Thank you, Mr. Harrow. We can do without the epithet.

MR. HARROW: No, I wasn't cussing. I just meant West Virginia.

MR. MAMRY: No, that. Forget it. Go on, Mr. Jordan.

MR. JORDAN: What is your primary business?

MR. HARROW: Construction. I am the owner of Harcon, Inc., which is a general contractor.

Q: Excellent. And your company is currently employed, among other places, in the construction of Pennsylvania Route 43, AKA the Mon-Fayette Expressway.

A: We sure are.

Q: And that's a profitable enterprise, is it not? So why get involved in all this real estate speculation?

A: Money. Look, you hear a lot of complaining about how much money goes into highways, and the public thinks that guys like me are soaking the public with cost overruns and what have you, but roads are complicated. Highways are very complicated. And very, very expensive. Unions, you know?

Q: In other words, risky. Financially speaking.

A: Yeah. For a private contractor like me. Whereas, look, houses are cheap and easy. And laying some surface roads for a subdivision is a lot easier than building an elevated, limited-access highway. And ever since I met Veronica, I've been doing real good for myself on these sorts of projects.

Q: Ms. Mayer said that the loss you could take on this sale— these sales—would be harmful to your business. Is that correct?

A: Yes. We could probably survive, but it would be close, and I'd have to take on even more debt to cover the immediate loss, plus paying back all the other creditors. No thanks.

Q: And to be clear, you, like Ms. Mayer, had no prior knowledge of Mr. Mayer's intended course of action.

A: Nope.

Q: Let me ask you further: if you had known, what would you have done?

A: Killed the sonofabitch.

Q: Phil.

A: I'm kidding. Christ. Kidding! I'd have hired you earlier and gone after a conjunction.

Q: An injunction.

A: Right. Whatever. Thrown the book at him, so to speak.

Q: In other words, Mr. Harrow, your failure to take prophylactic legal measures stands, in some way, as evidence of your lack of prior knowledge of Mr. Mayer's course of action, which, as you have already testified, you would have sought to enjoin?

A: I, uh, I'm not sure about prophylactics, but sure. I'd have tried to prevent it. If that's what you're getting at.

Q: Thank you. Yes. That's all.

MR. MAMRY: How somewhat confusing, if delightfully brief. Mr. Ben David, cross?

CROSS-EXAMINATION OF PHILLIP HARROW

MR. BEN DAVID: Mr. Harrow, did you privately suggest to Mr. Mayer that the two of you cut his sister out of this deal?

A: What? No!

Q: You never suggested to Mr. Mayer that the two of you would be better off, I quote, "without your lezzy sister, no offense."

A: I don't have a prejudiced bone in my body.

Q: Did you leave Mr. Mayer a message on his answering

machine that suggested he ought to meet you privately to talk about something just between the two of you?

A: No!

MR. BEN DAVID: Mr. Arbitrator, I submit, as our exhibit, I guess, 5, an answering machine tape to that effect.

MR. JORDAN: Mr. Arbitrator, this tape was never produced in discovery!

MR. MAMRY: This is, for the umpteenth time, not a court of law. We're in a conference room, gentlemen.

MR. JORDAN: I mean during the earlier hearings.

MR. MAMRY: I doubt very much, given your description of those hearings, that you went through discovery. And perhaps they just discovered it. In any event, I'll take it. Although I'm not sure exactly how germane it's going to be, unless Mr. Ben David has some kind of double-double-cross theory. Perhaps that will be included in the briefs.

MR. BEN DAVID: We are just demonstrating that contrary to Mr. Jordan's argument from voluminousness, which you'll note he appears to have abandoned in his examinations, that all of these players were acting independently, and that no enforceable oral contract can exist when you have these kinds of shenanigans going on behind backs.

MR. MAMRY: I do hope that's how you plan to phrase it in your brief, Mr. Ben David. I'm tempted to cut this off, as I think I get the point—

MR. HARROW: Your hon—I mean, Mr. Arbitrator, look, I'm not trying to lie, here, it's just, look, I did leave that message, but that was of a personal nature.

MR. MAMRY: A personal nature?

MR. JORDAN: Phil—

Mr. Mamry: No, Mr. Jordan. I'd like to hear. Go on, Mr. Harrow.

Mr. Harrow: Look. I was . . . I had a thing going with Sarah. With Mr. Mayer's wife.

Mr. Mayer: These are lies and deceptions, your honor!

Mr. Mamry: Mr. Mayer, please sit down. Mr. Harrow, what are you implying?

Mr. Harrow: Look, it never got physical. It was what you'd call an attraction from afar. A poetry sort of thing. Like in, do you know the opera—

Mr. Mayer: Poetry? You vile illiterate—

Mr. Mamry: Mr. Mayer, I'll ask you to leave if you interrupt again. Mr. Harrow.

Mr. Harrow: I . . . Mr. Arbitrator, I don't know how to put this. Abbie over there, he and his wife were like, some kind of swingers. You know what I mean. Like, they engaged in—

Mr. Mamry: Yes, Mr. Harrow. I too live in the twentieth century. I understand the term. I don't claim that I understand the broader contextual relevance in this particular instance, but as Maimonides said, "We are like those who, though beholding frequent flashes of lightning, still find themselves in the thickest darkness of the night." So please, Mr. Harrow, flash on.

Mr. Harrow: Well, I always just got this feeling that they were, how can I say it, swinging at me. I mean, that Sarah was. And I never had a reason to think that Abbie was anything but all for it. Hell, that was one of the first things he ever said to me. He said, "Take a chance with my wife." I'm not making that up, Your Honor. "Take a chance with my wife." But, well, I wanted to clear the air. I'm not a bad guy, and if I was going to get involved in that sort of thing, I was going to keep it, you know, classy.

MR. BEN DAVID: In other words, Mr. Harrow, you're asking us to believe that this sub rosa communication with your business partner's brother—who was himself, per your claims—a business partner as well, was because of some kind of infatuation with the man's wife?

A: I'm not sure if I understood the question, but yeah. I mean, my point is that he seemed pretty okay with it.

Q: Pretty okay with . . . ?

A: My interest. I mean, I assumed he had some on the side as well. I mean, it was no secret that he and Sarah—that's his wife—moved out here in the first place because he had some lady friend back in NYC. I always got the sense that he knocked her up. Talk about prophylactics, am I right judge? Which is what I mean when I say you've gotta keep this sort of thing classy. Cause that, well, that ain't classy.

Q: Mr. Harrow. Phillip. I want to make sure I follow you here.

MR. MAMRY: No, Mr. Ben David. I'm going to intervene here. You've insinuated that Mr. Harrow here was attempting to cut his own business partner, Ms. Mayer, out of this deal to begin with, which, obviously, would . . . obviate certain aspects of their argument regarding Mr. Mayer's responsibility to make either or both of them whole in this whole deal. Mr. Harrow contends that these backdoor communiques—the one for which you've submitted evidence, anyway—constituted an attempt, abortive or otherwise, to get permission to conduct an extramarital affair with Mr. Mayer's wife, which, however distasteful or contrary to the . . . received morality of our times, would nevertheless constitute a strong argument contra that insinuation. Have I got that essentially correct? You don't need to answer. Is there anything else?

MR. BEN DAVID: No, Mr. Arbitrator.

MR. MAMRY: Mr. Jordan, any redirect?

MR. JORDAN: No.

MR. MAMRY: All right. Is there anything else, Mr. Jordan?

MR. JORDAN: We rest.

MR. MAMRY: Good. Then let's take a quick break. Once more, I must find myself the gentleman's lounge. And we'll resume with Mr. Ben David's first witness.

[RECESS]

DIRECT EXAMINATION OF ABBOT "ABBIE" MAYER

MR. MAMRY: And we're back.

MR. BEN DAVID: Could you state your name?

MR. MAYER: Abbot Mayer. I go by Abbie.

Q: And your occupation.

A: I am an architect by training and avocation, a property developer by trade.

Q: Your relationship to MH Partners?

A: None.

Q: None?

A: Veronica is my sister, and Phil and I were friendly, and my firm did business with them.

Q: What kind of business?

A: You think a lawyer and a puffed-up backhoe driver can lay out a bedroom community or meet a modern municipal design standard?

MR. HARROW: Bedroom community? You smug motherfucker, that was my suggestion.

MR. MAMRY: Mr. Harrow, let's try to conduct this hearing as if it's entirely boring, shall we?

Mr. Ben David: Abbie, I'm just going to ask you to describe in your own words what happened.

Mr. Mayer: Very well. As has been stated, my wife and I moved to Pittsburgh a number of years ago. And yes, Mr. Mamry, I'll just go right out and say it, since my sister and her preposterous lackey over there wish to smear me with it, I came, in part, because I received a vision from God. It isn't *au courrant* to talk about God, but I have a feeling, Mr. Mamry, that you are a believer, and perhaps you'll have some understanding.

I was never an especially religious man, but one day, sitting in temple—I was only there because of an obligation to my wife's family—I was daydreaming and staring at a window when God spoke to me. Of course, God doesn't speak; it's as silly to imagine the Lord uttering actual words as it is to imagine that, because we are made in God's image, He therefore resembles in some actual, physical way, a human being. As we are, body and soul, afterimages of the totality and universality of the Divine, frozen, sub-photographic images of a vastness of being that is and moves, so too is our language less even than an echo of the primordial verb of existence. God, I learned, doesn't speak to men at all, but rather puts into their minds and hearts the knowledge of and belief in that which He would—if He did, if He even could, speak—have said.

Mr. Mamry: That's both deeply poetical and—it strikes me—wholly correct, Mr. Mayer. Also, entirely irrelevant to the matter at hand. Hashem may be the mover of all things, but yet he consigns to man alone the responsibility of conducting binding arbitration. I'm sure the Talmud has something to say about it. But for now, maybe we can continue with the narrative.

Mr. Mayer: Yes, well, as I said, I wasn't a religious person; I suppose I'm still not in the strict sense of the word. I am not, in other words, an attender of services. And I might get more mileage if I just called it a realization or a Eureka moment or some other such banal neologism. I could say I was a man who, having achieved a serious measure of professional success as an architect, secretly hated his work and hated his life and at a sudden thunderclap of personal insight decided, as Rilke said, that you must change your life.

But I cannot believe that this change came from within me. It came from without. It was implanted in me, emplaced. It is relevant to me. That is what I choose to believe. So you can all sneer if you like, or assert that because my wife and I weren't the model of *petit-bourgeois* rectitude, that therefore all this God told me to do it mumbo-jumbo is self-serving and a lie. But why would I make myself look mad unless I truly believed? I would not.

It is, however, also true that, yes, I came out here to make money. My sister was doing very well, and although the image of the architect is rather glamorous, I suppose, it is a difficult business. One depends on clients who have far too much to say about how you do your own job, and much of it is drudgery. I had managed to carve out a place as something more like an academic. In fact, I still lecture from time to time. But living one honorarium to the next is quite exhausting and precarious. It's like being an actor or musician. Unless you are very famous or are fortunate to be employed in a particularly excellent company or ensemble full time, one year's success can be the next year's poverty.

So there was an obvious attraction, and Veronica seemed happy to have me, to have a person who could speak a slightly more elevated language of aesthetics and design than Mr. Harrow, over there, with his quote "classy developments."

It also happens, unfortunately, that this business required that I involve myself with a number of unsavory elements, that is to say, that I found both my sister and Mr. Harrow willing to undertake legal and ethical shortcuts in order to serve their—and, I admit, my—personal financial ends. This often involved deliberately underbidding on properties and using political connections to nudge or coerce reluctant owners to sell. I think they just implied that I was the one who had the close personal connections with these folks, which couldn't be further from the truth, of course. I wouldn't even know where to begin.

Well, I'll admit it. I went along with this for a while, but eventually, it just got to be too much. Their greed—I don't hesitate to use the word—was overwhelming, and their methods simply abhorrent to me. Now, they'd like you to believe that I slunk around and did this all with them, threw in with these flesh-peddlers operating under the guise of darkness, but I was perfectly up front. I told them that they could buy me out, pay me for my considerable work in acquiring these properties. I say considerable work. I wasn't just, as they'd like you to believe, acting as a conduit for money not my own. I was the one who met with realtors, who examined maps, who laid out street plans, who spec'd designs for housing units. I worked my—excuse me, Mr. Mamry—my ass off. I said, here, pay me, find someone else to hold onto these, and I'll step away. Which they were obviously reluctant to do, because, as I said, the very nature of these deals required a person like myself to act as, in effect, a front man.

So, seeing that they weren't going to cooperate in all this, I just said, to hell with it. I'd known Arthur—Mr. Imlak—socially for a while, and I knew he already had some property interests down in the Uniontown area. So I approached him, and he said he'd take pretty much all of it off my hands for a not at all unreasonable sum, a sum which, moreover, he said he could deliver in cash on the barrelhead, so to speak. And I made a quite generous offer, if I do say so, to Veronica and Phil, which was to split the whole deal fifty-fifty, and then she could go her way, and I could go mine. Which they turned down. The thing they're neglecting to tell you is that in addition to the sale money, Art was offering—did offer—a cut of future royalties from gas and mineral extraction, so this whole business about taking a loss is totally bogus. They're taking a loss because they walked away from a deal that I was perfectly within my rights to make. And that, as they say, is that.

Q: Thank you. And—

A: I'm sorry, but also, one more thing: Phil Harrow never fucked my wife.

Mr. Mamry: Yes, well, and for I hope the last time, yikes. But okay. We'll try to obey the rules of decorum by covering our profanities with insincere apologies for deploying them in the first place.

Mr. Mayer: Sure. Phil Harrow never—I'm sorry, Mr. Arbitrator—fucked my wife.

Mr. Ben David: Abbie, you mentioned future royalties?

A: Yes. Arthur can probably explain it in better detail. It's a process they're developing to extract gas from underground rock formations. Very promising, apparently. So there is the potential for millions in royalties down the road.

Q: And you say they walked away from that?

A: Extraordinary though it may seem.

Q: Did you ever consider yourself under contract to hold these properties for MH Partners?

A: I considered that one possibility. A better one came along. I was within my rights to make that decision. It's not my fault that Phil and Veronica wanted to go another way. They should have bought the land themselves, then.

Q: You never signed anything? You never promised anything?

A: Not of that nature.

Q: And insofar as they contend you sprang this all on them, you say that is not, in fact, the case.

A: It's not the case.

Q: Thank you, Mr. Mayer. That's all from me.

MR. MAMRY: Cross, Mr. Jordan?

CROSS-EXAMINATION OF ABBOT "ABBIE" MAYER

MR. JORDAN: Mr. Mayer, do you own property in Fayette County?

A: Yes.

Q: And would it be fair to say that Mr. Imlak was instrumental in your acquisition of this property?

A: That's my sister's theory. She is, as usual, exaggerating.

Q: You didn't buy this property from Mr. Imlak?

A: Indirectly.

Q: To what end?

A: To what what end?

Q: Let me rephrase the question. Why did you purchase this property?

A: It seemed like a good investment. I was looking for a place to build a house.

Q: A house that you saw in one of these visions of yours?

A: You can be as snide as you like, but which one of us is an instrument of the Lord, and which is just a hack lawyer?

Q: Is that a no?

A: Yes. I perceived, in one of these visions of mine, as you so disdainfully put it, a highway rising along the face of a mountain, and off to the left beside it a clearing where I would one day reside.

Q: And it is your testimony that these, shall we say, religious convictions—

A: No.

Q: No?

A: I would not use that term.

Q: Convictions, Mr. Mayer? You have no convictions?

A: I would not use the term religious.

Mr. Mamry: Once more into the breach. I think I understand that you're trying to disestablish Mr. Mayer's credibility by painting him as a religious nut. I take the hint. For what is, I hope, the last time, I'm going to remind everyone that this isn't a court. There's no jury to try to impress. Consider your efforts to impeach Mr. Mayer noted. Is there any other reason for this line of questioning?

Mr. Jordan: There is, Mr. Arbitrator. It's to establish collusion between Mr. Mayer and Mr. Imlak.

Mr. Mamry: Oh, collusion. Oh, yes, good. A secret deal to undercut a secret deal. I have to tell you gentlemen, and lady, that this is one of the more unusual, which is not to say uninteresting, disputes I've had the professional pleasure to preside over in my days. I'm going to have a hard time splitting this baby indeed. Perhaps if I bash it, candy will fall out, like a piñata. Go ahead, Mr. Jordan.

Mr. Jordan: Thank you. Mr. Mayer, would you answer the question?

A: What was the question?

Q: Isn't it true that Mr. Imlak initially refused to sell you the property on which you later built your residence?

A: I didn't even know him at the time.

Q: So you've claimed.

MR. BEN DAVID: Oh, come on.

MR. MAMRY: Yes, I'm inclined to agree. Mr. Jordan, we understand you're calling Mr. Mayer's story into question.

MR. JORDAN: Isn't it the case, Mr. Mayer, you proposed, as a quid pro quo to Mr. Imlak, that if he were to sell you this piece of property, you would be able to assist him in purchasing parcels of land pursuant to his own business interests at below-market values?

A: No.

Q: It isn't?

A: No.

Q: Mr. Mayer, who is Sheryl Ellen Larimer?

A: She's a county commissioner in Fayette County.

Q: Currently.

A: Yes, currently. What about it?

Q: Mr. Mayer, would you call her one of these, uh, unsavory elements?

A: Well, you know what they say about politicians.

Q: Is that a yes?

A: It's a maybe.

Q: It was a yes or no question.

A: And yet here we are. Stuck in the middle with you.

Q: Mr. Mayer—

A: Look, what do you want me to say? Sherri is a . . . You do business with the people in office. Sometimes the promised land is already occupied when you arrive.

MR. IMLAK: Goddamnit.

MR. MAMRY: I'm sorry, Mr. Imlak?

MR. BEN DAVID: It's nothing, Mr. Arbitrator.

MR. JORDAN: Mr. Mayer, you said something interesting there. You said the land was already occupied. What did you mean by that?

A: Just that, that we bought . . .

Q: Mr. Mayer, you think very highly of your intellect, don't you?

A: I hold myself in a healthy regard.

Q: And yet, in fact, the man sitting beside you, Arthur Imlak, a far superior businessman, has been manipulating—

A: Oh please.

Q: —this process, and you, from the outset. Through his agent, this Sherri Larimer. Whose strong-arm tactics—

A: Veronica, what did you tell him? What did you say you, you, you woman—

Q: Don't look at her, Mr. Mayer, look at me. I'm asking the questions here. Was it you who suggested a ploy to frame a local official, or was it Sherri Larimer? Do you know, Mr. Mayer, who this Larimer woman's largest campaign contributor was? How long have the three of you—

MR. IMLAK: Goddamnit!

MR. BEN DAVID: Arthur.

MR. IMLAK: Call a caucus, Dave.

MR. BEN DAVID: Mr. Arbitrator, may I have a moment to caucus with my clients.

MR. MAMRY: Client, Mr. Ben David. You only have one. Mr. Imlak, I understand, is just a witness.

MR. BEN DAVID: Yes, of course. Client.

MR. JORDAN: Mr. Arbitrator, he can't confer with his client during cross!

MR. MAMRY: *Au contraire*, counselor. I see Mr. Ben David isn't the only aspiring DA in the room. Take five, as they say. I think we can all stand to cool down. Fan yourselves. Eat a Snickers.

[RECESS]

MR. MAMRY: During the recess, I spoke to both counselors, and it appears that we have reached an amicable agreement here. I mean amicable in the courtroom, the legal, uh, sense, since no one seems in any particular rush to fall into the other's arms. Regardless, agreement is the point of this exercise. I suppose that renders the preceding . . . proceedings a waste of time, in a sense, but all things that end justly are worth the passage. It is remarkable, isn't it, just how much truth the world can contain. Unless either party has a substantive dispute with the actual conduct of this arbitration? No? Okay, then. Obviously we can dispense with the usual post-arbitration briefs. Counselors, what I would like is for you to each submit to me a summary brief of the agreement we think we reached in sidebar. I'll make sure that we are, in fact, in harmony, and then we will all go on our merry way, thank God. Usually we'd have forty-five days from the conclusion of the arbitration, but since there are no longer issues in dispute, shall we say thirty? In time for Shavuot.

12

A month after the negotiated conclusion of this dispute with his sister and Phillip Harrow, Abbie met Sherri Larimer for a drink. His son had been born, miraculously, and he'd have preferred to write the past out of his life entirely and, once more, start in a place that was wholly new, but he felt an obligation. The settlement hadn't gone as Imlak had wanted, and now Arthur was suggesting that it might endanger their relationship, that, indeed, it might cause Imlak to try to find a means of reacquiring The Gamelands, through force or persuasion, which was unthinkable either way. The house was three-quarters complete, and they'd moved in upon Isaac's birth. It had been a long labor, and Sarah bled a lot, so the hospital kept her an extra day to be safe. When she was sleeping, Abbie drove up the mountain to fuss with the furniture before his wife and son arrived. Before he drove back to the hospital, he walked around the property. It was night and far from town and every star was out. It was April and the air smelled of new leaves. Abbie walked to the edge of the woods and there felt a huge presence, as if the ridge on which he stood were the spine of the living world and the slow air through the leaves a kind of breath. "Here we are," he said. Somewhere between the trees, something moved.

Imlak, meanwhile, was surprised at the degree of his own displeasure. A good businessman should never be unprepared for an
adverse decision; success was in the arbitrage between the least-
bad and the worse. But Abbie had assured him that there was no
way his sister or Harrow or their rat attorney would ever bring up
Sherri Larimer. "No way," he'd said. "Not with the whole thing
with Jerry Jernicki."

"Are you sure, Abbie?" Imlak had asked. "Because I do not
need that sort of thing coming back on me."

"Arthur," Ben David said. They were in his office in Pittsburgh.

"What?"

"Practice not saying that sort of thing out loud."

Imlak pouted.

In the conference room at the arbitration hearing, Imlak
raged that Abbie had proven, once again, not to know shit about
shit. And Abbie raged right back. Was it true what A. Christopher
Jordan had implied? Was Arthur the prime mover? Hadn't it been
Sherri Larimer who'd nudged them in a certain direction in the
first place? Who was really turning the wheels? Arthur slapped a
paper cup full of weak coffee off the table. It splattered against an
off-white wall. "There are no wheels, you fucking nut! Things just
move!" Then he settled down and looked at Ben David. "Give me
the verdict," he said.

Ben David said, "We're fucked."

"Goddamnit." He crossed his arms. "Abbie," he said, and his
big, rich voice was filled with a magical tone of universal owner-
ship. "Abbie, I have *plans* for that land. Those are valuable acres.
There are potential wellhead sites." He launched into the lecture
they'd heard before: "I am not haphazard in my acquisition of

property. There is an energy revolution coming. While everyone is off grubbing around for oil in the Middle East, I am going to be part of a very particular cadre of people who gets very rich. The technology is not yet mature, but it will be soon. It will allow us to extract an extraordinary volume of carbon fuel from the rock formations beneath our feet. Appalachia sits on carbon reserves that make Saudi Arabia look like a dusty filling station. It is merely a question of *getting* to it. When the technology is available, and it will be within a decade, there will be a great gold rush into this region, and there will be a few men like me who preceded these gold diggers to the claims. Will these properties you hold, or your sister and her glad-handing overgrown handyman partner, materially alter my fortunes? No. Not really. But they are still worth millions of dollars to me, in the long run. A few million against many hundreds of millions, but still. We had a deal, Abbie, and you are reneging on it."

"I'm sorry," Abbie said. He was sorry, if not for any reason Arthur Imlak might understand.

Imlak looked at Ben David. "What are we going to do? Can we buy the arbitrator?"

"Gods below, Arthur, shut the fuck up," said Ben David. "Didn't I goddamn fucking tell you never to let that sort of shit pass your goddamn lips?"

Imlak glared at him, then sighed. "Yes. You're right."

"The whole point, the whole strategy was to make this an issue of Abbie's, uh, whatever. Spiritual feelings. The arbitrator was going to conclude that Veronica and Phil never should've entrusted this wacko with whatever, but oh well, too bad for them. And you were going to look like a guy who took advantage in a perfectly legal, above-the-board, good-judge-of-character sort of way. But if they're willing to blow it all up and possibly even expose their own, shall we say, questionable dealings with certain individuals, then the best thing we can do is cut a deal. Won't be a total loss. They've got the advantage, but they're not exactly negotiating from a position of strength. Remember, that's how we ended up in arbitration to begin with. There are elements that, upon consideration, we all decided to keep out of the usual legal forums."

"Fuck," said Imlak. "Okay."

"Do you want my opinion?" Abbie asked. "As the, you know, actual client."

"No," said Ben David.

Imlak stood up and said, "Do a deal." Ben David left to find his counterpart and do just that. Arthur closed the door and turned back to Abbie. "Mayer," he said, "I'm going down to Houston for a few weeks, and then I'll be in Florida till June. And I'm going to go against the advice of my attorney, since he's not in the room to squint at me, and say the sort of thing that he doesn't like me to say. Take care of it."

"Take care of it?"

"I want the whole shebang."

What, precisely, had he meant by that? Abbie elected not to ask him. Imlak went on to make his first implication that it might even be within his power to snatch The Gamelands back. "Don't go to war with me, Abbie," he said. "You'll lose. Better keep me as a brother." So in the end, Abbie met Larimer for a drink at the far end of the dim country club bar, surrounded by men who smelled of grass and leather gloves. Since becoming county commissioner, she'd taken to wearing bright pantsuits—"like Geraldine motherfucking Ferraro!"—and she'd joined the club. Abbie had suggested a more private meeting, but she'd told him, "I don't take no private meetings. You might try to *uh-sassinate* me!" She howled. Abbie beat her to the bar and had already tossed down a large glass of vodka in order to acquire the courage for the conversation.

"Listen," he told her. "I need a favor."

"Yeah, well, I need a campaign contribution."

"Really?"

"No, ya dummy. I'm pulling your leg. But I'm not really in the favor-granting business. I'm in the business of civic responsibility and shit." She lit a smoke.

"Yes, well. It's at the, uh, request of our, uh, mutual benefactor."

"Who? Arthur? That sounds like some shit his fancy pants would say."

"Shh!" Abbie glanced around. "We're in public!"

She laughed at him. She hooted. "Public. Listen to you." She turned in her seat and spied a tall man in khaki pants. "Hey, you! Caddyshack."

"Me?" The man looked away from his conversation.

"Yeah, you. You gonna call the cops on me?"

"I'm sorry?"

"Nothing," Sherri said. "Fuck off." She waved her cigarette at him. She turned back to Abbie.

"Christ, Sherri. You're bringing up the police?"

"Fuck the police. I own them police!" She tapped the bar and grinned. "Now lay back on that couch, honey, and you tell Dr. Sherri what it is that she can do ya for."

After he told her, he drove back to The Gamelands. For no particular reason, he took the long way around, a meandering path that passed through the center of Uniontown, the empty parking lots and sooty courthouse and the high-rises from the years when it had been a prosperous place. Now it smelled like the polluted creeks that trickled through it, and its population was half what it once was, and the Walmart and Kmart plazas on the west side of town had killed the last stores on Main Street. Main Street, really, the literalization of a political theme, some of the dark storefronts still sporting dusty window displays, as if the former owners had fled in the night from a war. The mansions were all funeral homes. The handsome old mainline churches were mostly empty. Worshiping Christians had decamped to the boxy megachurches that preached a prosperity gospel to a lot of laid-off workers who imagined the mines might come back and blamed their own unions for closing them. The town had lost fifty percent of its population in twenty years. What hope was there for a place like that? Maybe Imlak's magic wells would one day employ people again, though wasn't that just a recapitulation of the lost coal economy, a brief flush time until the veins or pools or reserves or whatever they were ran dry? But maybe when the oceans all rose, and the coastal cities sank, and the vast plain of the Mississippi turned once more into a shallow sea, the people who remained would return to places like Uniontown, nine-hundred-ninety-nine feet above sea level, the dust of its twentieth-century abandonment washed away by the tropical rains.

Down Fayette Street; down the Old National Pike; past the Sweet Pea filling station; through Hopwood where cars were crowded around Roose's from whose roof the giant white illuminated rooster crowed into the night; past the big white Greek Revival house surrounded by pines on the right where the on-ramp curved into Route 40; then angling up into the mountains;

past the Watering Hole Restaurant and the Lick Hollow access road through the trees; past the scenic overlook and into the last sharp bend where the Summit Inn appeared a thousand feet ahead; over the blind peak and a sharp right onto Skyline Drive; past the Summit's golf course and into the state gamelands for which, in a fit of whimsy, he'd named his own home, then right onto his own long driveway, which he'd already, habitually, begun to take too fast. He jammed the brakes and slid on the gravel. It would become a habit.

He found Sarah sitting up with Isaac and watching an old western on TV. "You're still up," he said.

"He woke up. He's sleeping now, but I'm afraid to move. How was your meeting with Sherri?"

"Friendly, threatening, cajoling. You can imagine."

"Yes. What did she say?"

"She was cagey. She just said we'd hear from her."

"Why are you even doing this?"

"You know."

"I don't."

"Arthur must have told you."

"He didn't."

"Really?" Abbie let himself sink into a big chair in their living room. He'd started to put on weight in those days, and he frequently felt exhausted. But, he reminded himself, it was also very late.

"It isn't true, Abbie, what you think. And even if it was . . . Anyway, you told me yourself that you don't think there's any way he could take the house."

"Should we have divorced?" Abbie asked. "Instead of coming here."

"If we had," Sarah said, and she looked down at their son.

"Selfish of us," Abbie said. "Frankly, I don't know what to do. It's an unusual sensation."

"Jesus, Abbie. Try prayer."

"That's not how it works."

"I wouldn't know, clearly."

"I didn't mean it that way, Sarah."

"No, I suppose not. Still."

Abbie rubbed his face. "*Do* you ever pray?"

"You're asking me if I pray?"

"Sure. We've never really discussed it. Outside of temple, I mean. On a whim."

"I guess I do, actually. In a sense.

"What do you pray for?"

"I ask God to show me what it is that I really want."

"Hmm. What makes one desire worthier than another?"

"Christ, Abbie. I don't know. I'm going to bed. Take your son."

What did she think when she handed Isaac to him, letting his head drop a fraction of a centimeter from her hand into the bend of his arm? Isaac made a contented noise, like a giggle, in his sleep. When she was gone, Abbie stared at the boy for a long time. On the television, a lawman said, "I ain't about to leave! If there's only one honest man in this town, then it's worth stayin' and it's worth a fight." He took the boy to his room and laid him in his crib. Isaac made a sound and opened his tiny dark eyes. They watched each other for a long time.

· · ·

Over the next several years, Veronica and Phil had proceeded with their plan, modified and moderated by their settlement-reduced acreage into a more typical project, a few subdivisions—bedroom communities, ahem—to be laid out on a cluster of small hills near California, PA, just south of where the new expressway crossed I-70, the curlicuing exchanges cradled in and carried on an eruption of immense earthworks that would one day, when it was all cleared away, when the last human survivors of the nuclear wars or the viral holocaust or the end of orderly seasons were long extinct, appear to the tool-bearing badgers or the clothes-wearing crows or the dolphins in their rolling suits full of seawater or whatever animal God next saw fit, if He did see fit, to curse with self-knowledge, as the mad devotions of an incredible elder race, something worshipful and inscrutable carved into the flesh of the world and then left to be whittled down to nothing more than a hint of itself, if even that. They'd moved as quickly as they could to lay out the streets and get the building underway, perhaps believing that to delay was to invite the still-slight possibility of another reversal of legal fortune that would yank the property away from them again. Holes had been dug and cinder block foundations laid and concrete poured and the first timber frames of all those future four-bedroom colonials were now rising like the skeletons of the Behemoths and Leviathans that preceded men and women into creation.

Nothing untoward happened. If Sherri Larimer, for Abbie, or for Arthur, whichever of them she really served, or for herself, if in fact everything she did were ultimately for her benefit alone, had done anything to convince Veronica and Phil to sell the acreage that remained to them, Abbie hadn't heard of it. And he felt a vague and mounting anxiety about it, especially as their first project began to take physical form. But Sherri never said anything about it, and Arthur, oddly, never brought it up again. The

Gamelands was finished, and Arthur's money was expanding in the variety of vehicles that he himself had recommended Abbie invest it in. He dreamed less frequently, although on occasion, when he saw families of deer making their frequent crossings of the property, he wondered if his God meant something by it. But of course he lived on a mountain in Appalachia. But of course there were deer.

One night, Abbie was home with Isaac and Sarah, whose attention, he felt, had wandered even farther after the birth of the boy. He sometimes caught her regarding Isaac with a look of surprise that was something other than joy. He'd overheard her talking to him—Isaac was only a few years old—in a curiously confessional tone, in the lowered voice that she'd adopt in a restaurant or airport when she suspected that someone nearby might eavesdrop. He'd heard, or thought he'd heard, his own name in these murmured monologues, and sometimes when his son looked at him with those black eyes, pupil-less and dark as a cloudy sky over the ocean at night, he felt the terrifying presence of a competing vision, as if the boy could see what Abbie saw, or something more.

The bell rang. Sarah was watching the news. Abbie was cooking dinner. Isaac was playing an impenetrable game with his feet. Abbie wiped his hands on a towel and went to see who it was. As he passed through the living room, Sarah looked up at him. "We have a doorbell?" she said.

There were three men at the door. They had a look of savage impermanence, as if they'd been assembled by an alien sculptor with a passable but imperfect grasp of the human form. Abbie tilted his head. "Can I help you?"

"Probably," said the largest and baldest of them. He twanged slightly.

"Who is it?" Sarah called.

"Is that your wife?" the man asked.

"I'm not sure if I should answer that," Abbie said.

"Whoa," said the shorter, stockier man to his left. "That's not very hospitable."

The big man grinned. It was not reassuring. "Would you be hospitable, Boochie, if a bunch of roughnecks just showed up at your door and you wasn't expecting no one?"

"Do you guys know Sherri Larimer?" Abbie asked.

"Who don't we know?" said the third man, who was nearly as big as the first.

"Why don't you come on in?" Abbie said.

"Who is it?" Sarah called again.

"It's work," Abbie yelled back, and then he watched warily as the men came into his house and, rather improbably, unlaced and removed their large brown work boots, which they set in a neat row by the door.

What transpired between them? Abbie gave them beers, and Sarah put Isaac to bed and stood behind her husband with her arms crossed tightly, only moving from time to time to pour herself another glass of red wine. What did they propose, and how did he reply? They suggested something more than he was willing to suborn, and he countered with something so negligible that it called into question why he needed their services in the first place. "No violence," he said, when they pressed the issue. "What do we look like?" they said. Sarah snorted. "Well, okay," they said. "We know what we look like." They stayed for perhaps an hour and drank a six pack between them. Abbie asked them why they'd bothered to come, when clearly they were operating under someone else's orders and were going to do what they were going to do.

"She's your sister," they said. "We aren't gonna do anything you aren't comfortable with." Abbie said he wasn't comfortable with any of it. "Well, okay," they said. "Comfortable might not be the right word." When they left, they laced their boots and stood in the entry hall. "This is a good house," they said. "Good bones."

"Yes," Abbie said. He stood in the threshold. As they walked back to the big truck that they'd somehow arrived in silently, the smallest, who'd hardly spoken, turned back and said, "Yinz have a blessed evening. Thank you for your hospitality."

Then, once again, there was nothing, no word or indication that anything was ever going to happen, and the evening took on the retrospective fogginess of a dream. Arthur Imlak stopped by several times in the interim. No one ever said anything about anything. They gossiped about people at the club. Arthur amused them with the story of a dispute between the Chislett brothers, the one of whom had long imagined building a sort of hunting lodge and entertainment complex near Laurel Caverns, the other of whom felt gambling was an affront to the Christian God. "You know," Imlak said. "Guns and slot machines. There are rumors that Harrisburg is going to approve gaming soon. Lord knows, we need something other than the lotto to part the poor from their hard-earned disability." He smiled down at Isaac. "Don't you agree, big guy?"

Little Isaac said something that sounded very much like, "Fuck."

Imlak grinned. "Yes," he said. "Fuck."

. . .

There's a police report, and there was a brief news clip at the time, which used the word accident. Veronica and Phil and Edith were out touring the property on a drizzly Sunday. The plywood on the framed-in houses was turning dark with rain. The newly excavated foundation holes were full of mud. Veronica was in a good mood. She'd even, after the arbitration, managed a half-way reconciliation with her brother, though she thought that he regarded her oddly, uncomfortably, whenever she came to the house to see her nephew. Isaac was quite taken with her. He as yet had trouble with his Rs and called her Wanny. She'd never especially cared for children, but she loved the giggly, swishy little boy. She wondered if she should tell her brother that his kid was definitely going to turn out to be gay. She expected to visit them later that week.

Then there were three men coming over the hill. It didn't immediately occur to either woman what was happening—they might have been contractors, or local guys looking for a place to drink beer and smoke. But it was immediately clear to Phillip Harrow what was going on, as he later told the police. "I only saw it one other place," he told them. "Back when I was in college. I worked at a construction company one summer up in Cleveland, and the plumbers were on strike, so they tried to hire some non-union guys, and then a couple of guys *from the local* if you know what I mean showed up to straighten them out. It was the same look."

So Harrow puffed his chest and crossed his arms and waited until the men arrived. He noted, as Abbie had, that they appeared unfinished, cobbled together from the ugliest parts. "You're trespassing," he said.

The big one turned his head as if about to consult with one of his companions, but it was a feint. He struck Harrow once, back-handed, across the face, so impossibly hard that his feet lifted off the ground as he fell.

"Oh my God." Veronica put her hands up in front of her. She

became, as she did when she was afraid, immediately lawyerly. "Whatever it is, whatever it is, I'm sure we can work it out," she said.

Harrow groaned and lifted himself on an elbow. "Motherfucker," he said.

"Yes we can," the big one said. He took another step.

Veronica mostly thought about the cell phone. She'd left it in the car. At that time there was barely any reception in that part of the county. "What do you want?" She imagined they were about to be robbed.

Harrow had got up and lunged at the man, who stepped—for his size, daintily—aside and, as Harrow stumbled past, planted a huge, steel-toed kick into his ass, sending him skidding face down in the mud.

Edith turned and ran. Can you blame her?

"Hey!" one of the men—Boochie—yelled. "We just wanna *talk* to you!"

She ran down the grassy hill and through the wide gully beside the highway. That stretch of it had opened to regular traffic a year earlier. Veronica called after her, and those men called after her, but she was running and probably didn't hear. An irony: had the development ever been completed, the Department of Transportation would have erected a wire fence down there to prevent exactly this sort of thing from happening. She clambered up the incline to the breakdown lane beside the highway. Almost no one used the road then, or ever used it, other than a few long-haul truckers who knew that it was a quick shortcut down to I-68, that it beat the low-gear haul up over the mountain on 40. You have to assume, the police later suggested, that she intended to wave down a vehicle in some obscure and probably vain hope of getting a motorist to call for help. Veronica called after her again. Edith heard her. She stopped in mid-wave and turned back. The driver never saw her. The weather was weird, humid and rainy, and his windshield had been fogging up even with the windows open and the defroster on. He didn't even hit her head on, just clipped her. But he was doing seventy-five, and he was hauling a full tanker of gas. He weighed just under the legal max of eighty thousand pounds. You can imagine. There's nothing a human body can do but break beyond repair. He braked too hard when he realized he'd hit someone. The truck jackknifed and lifted off the road. It rolled and skidded. A few seconds passed. There was a lick of flame. It exploded. The force of it knocked those of them who were still standing to the ground.

13

"So Mayer," Adam Martens said, "how come you never told me yer joosh?"

If in his mind, Isaac said, "What the fuck are you talking about?" and walked invincibly away, then in the second-floor hallway of Laurel Highlands Junior High School he looked at the speckled linoleum and muttered, "I don't know." Elementary school had passed, for Isaac, as a largely undifferentiated blur, unmemorable and accidental, friendships determined by proximity, the coming and going of days like the cycling passage of time before the invention of history. In the evenings, he'd help his mother do the dishes while she had her extra glass of wine; in the mornings, Abbie would drive him down the mountain and drop him off at school, bellowing some aria or other and conducting with both hands as he steered with his knees.

Now everything had a brittle intentionality to it. Kids from all of the different elementary schools mixed together, and friendship was a matter of secret affinities that he didn't understand. How could you know what anyone liked until you became friends? It was as if the other kids had developed a form of telepathy over the summer and self-organized based on some Linnean principles of common interest to which he had no access. They'd all grown larger, and he felt tiny. On the first day, he'd said hello to a girl in his homeroom whom he'd known since the first grade. She looked at him as if he had worms growing through the flesh of his face and said, "*Gawd.*"

Since then he'd kept his head down and moved with a discretion bordering on invisibility. He spoke only when called on, although Mr. Krupp, his English teacher, had taken an obscure liking to him when Isaac was the only student who could name the eight parts of speech. In fact, he'd forgotten interjection, but he divided verbs into lexical and auxiliary, and this caused Krupp to actually get down on his knees in front of the class and cry, "Be still my heart, boy. My life isn't wasted after all!" Everyone looked at Isaac and laughed at him, but he felt, hazily, for the first time that year, as if he belonged to something. Krupp, meanwhile, ignored the laughter and kept going. "But you forgot," he said, and he climbed onto an unoccupied nearby chair and hollered, "INTERJECTIONS!" The chair slipped sideways and Krupp went sprawling across the floor. "No, don't help me, I'm fine," he said. He conducted the rest of the class lying on the ground.

Most of the kids thought Krupp was a weirdo, not only for his behavior, his habit of mock-weeping when students were wrong (i.e., frequently), his occasional decision simply to play audiobooks unrelated to any particular lesson plan for an entire class period, excerpts from literature and biographies that edged into the inappropriate and indecent—Isaac, particularly, remembered a segment from a history of Catherine the Great which wavered on the edge of the pornographic in its depiction of her sexual awakening—but also for the fact that they frequently arrived for second period to find the room darkened, the blinds drawn, and Mr. Krupp at his desk with his head on his arms in the dusty twilight. Alone among all the teachers Isaac ever had, Mr. Krupp kept his desk at the back of the room, and the kids would file in and sit uncomfortably at their desks until—sometimes as much as ten minutes later—their teacher would begin talking at them from behind. Once, one of the girls flipped the light switch as she walked into the room, and Krupp moaned and cried, "The light! The light!" Isaac, of course, recognized some of these symptoms from Sarah, who rarely left her bedroom before ten thirty, and who'd forced Abbie, much against his grand natural vision, to install heavy curtains on her windows.

It was in Krupp's class that he met Jake, who was seated beside him based on Krupp's obscure system of seat assignment. He based it on what he called "the small serendipities which are the numina, the true, old gods of education," to the bewildered class on the first day. Jake's last name was Isaacs, and this struck Krupp as impossibly fortuitous. Jake was one of only four black kids in the school, and while he seemed generally and effortlessly popular—he was funny; he played soccer—he was sometimes treated by kids and teachers alike with a certain anthropological curiosity that Isaac had noticed and found extraordinary and inappropriate. Jake was also in the honors track, and this was treated with open curiosity, including by most of the teaching staff. Jake took it all with a resigned humor that seemed to Isaac to be quite impossibly graceful. He quickly became Krupp's other favorite when, after a section in which they read bowdlerized excerpts from *Moby-Dick*, he'd answered Krupp's searching, "Call me *blank*? Call me *blank*?" with "Crazy!" Krupp's eyes widened and he looked as if he didn't know whether to chuckle or to die. Then Jake said, "I'm just messing with you Mr. K. It's Ishmael."

"Be still my heart," said Mr. Krupp. "Boy, I could kiss you."

"We should probably get to know each other first," Jake said.

"Mr. Isaacs," Krupp said, and he wiped a real tear from his eye, "I may reconsider my thoughts of suicide. Thank you."

Jake always made a point of greeting Isaac, but he still seemed, to Isaac, unapproachable; kind but distant; friendly only out of general disposition. But later in the school year, he helped Isaac twice in very short order. First, in health class, which was conducted by one of the appalling gym teachers whose constant hassling of the boys who avoided showering after phys ed harried Isaac almost as much as his awkward interactions with his peers. Mr. Dubinsky's boys' health class was conducted with an air of back-slapping barroom grotesquerie that Isaac found both embarrassing and terrifying, and although Dubinsky touched vaguely on the subjects of sex and hygiene, his principal interests were in the application of first aid, and his examples were all drawn from hunting accidents. Isaac, who'd already embarrassed himself by asking if the four-point deer that Adam Martens had bragged about bagging was a buck or a doe—he didn't understand what the points referred to—would never have chosen to speak, but he was called out of the pleasure of his own inattention by Dubinsky saying his name sharply and, evidently, for at least the second time. "Mayer!"

"Yes, Mr. Dubinsky?"

"I asked, what do you do if you're out hunting with your buddy and he gets bit by a snake?"

"He gets bitten by a snake?" Isaac repeated.

"Yes. A poisonous snake."

Isaac reflected briefly. With most teachers, with most adults, he was able to read the response they desired in the questions they asked and the way that they asked them; adults, really, were absurd in this way, unsubtle and indiscreet as a big TV. But Dubinsky's world was alien to Isaac, who never knew what the hell the hairy monster was getting at. So he filtered every action and adventure movie he'd ever seen, and he said, "I don't know. I guess maybe you'd suck the venom out of the wound."

And Dubinsky, without missing a beat, smirked and said, "Yeah, well, what if your buddy got bit on his penis?"

Isaac flushed and felt as if he were going to piss in his pants, and the rest of the class howled, and Dubinsky grinned as if he'd just wrapped a good set in Vegas. Then unbidden from the back, someone said, "Man, that's fucked up, Mr. Dubs."

"What did you just say to me, Jake?" Dubinsky glared toward the rear of the room. Isaac was unable to turn. He stared down at the desk.

"I said that's a fucked up thing to say."

"Young man, you better not be using that language with me, unless you want to take a trip down to administration with me. And I don't think you want that." He crossed his arms.

Jake shrugged. "I mean, you can take me down there if you want, but I don't know if Mr. Genarro wants to hear how you're talking about sucking boys' penises or whatever."

The class was quiet, and everyone but Isaac stared at Dubinsky, who'd now turned pretty red himself. Dubinsky uncrossed his arms and turned and walked back toward the blackboard, though as he went, he shook his head and muttered, ostensibly to himself but loud enough for everyone to hear, "Typical black."

Isaac wanted to thank Jake, but after class he found the thought of revisiting that moment of mortification, even in thanking someone for ending it, too awful, and he ducked out as was his habit. A few days later, it was Adam Martens. Martens closed his locker and leaned against it and said, "So, Mayer, how come you never told me yer joosh?" Martens was tall and horrible and occasionally, apropos nothing, would fix smaller boys in his stare and say, "Worthless," and then laugh to himself and walk away.

"I don't know," Isaac said.

"Like, don't you believe in Christ or nothing?"

"I don't know," Isaac said. "No."

"So then, how do you pray? If you don't believe in Christ."

"I don't know, Adam. We pray to God."

"God *is* Christ." Martens shook his head. "It's obvious."

"Not to us. We believe something else."

"Yinz probably say just a bunch of spells and shit."

"We don't say spells."

"Well," Martens shrugged and pushed himself away from the locker. "I don't stand next ta no juice."

It later occurred to Isaac that he had no idea how much or little of this Jake overheard, but there he was, suddenly, passing by, and stopping to say to Martens, "Man, leave the dude alone, Martens, you redneck motherfucker."

"Whatever, worthless," Martens said. He flipped them off. "See you queers later."

"Thanks." Isaac kept his eyes fixed on Jake's feet.

"Shit, man. No problem. He's a degenerate."

Isaac finally let himself look at Jake, and he found himself smiling, although even that seemed like something he should be wary of. "Yeah. I guess so."

"You know so. Anyway, I heard him at lunch the other day. He's just pissed that you didn't invite him to your bar mitzvah even though you invited Sandy and Aiden."

"Sandy and Aiden are Jewish. They're like the only people who I invited."

"Yeah, but Aiden and Martens play baseball together."

"Well, I don't think I can invite someone who doesn't stand next to Jews."

Jake grinned. "Shit, you ought to invite me. I mean"—his smile grew—"I'm just a *typical* black, but I *do* stand next to Jews. Plus, I could get down with some spells and shit."

"Really?"

"Shit, yeah. Sounds cool. I'll wear my Farrakhan tee-shirt."

"You have to wear a button up."

"Relax, Isaac." Jake put his hand briefly on Isaac's shoulder. Isaac blushed and felt himself start to get hard. "I'm kidding." He clapped Isaac's shoulder once more and headed to next period, and Isaac whirled and stared into his locker until it was safe to move.

• • •

For years, the Mayers nominally belonged to a Reform congregation in Pittsburgh, attending the occasional High Holy Day service, but generally giving practical Judaism a wide berth, not least because Abbie felt his own luminous experiences transcended any meaning to be found in the sing-song liturgies of ordinary secular Jews. But then Sarah decided that Isaac ought to become Bar Mitzvah, and, since it would be mad to drive in and out of Pittsburgh that frequently, she had them join Tree of Life synagogue in Uniontown, where Isaac found himself, suddenly, the sole Hebrew School student of Rabbi Patrick MacDowell, a former bank teller and Catholic who, having married a Jewish woman in his late twenties, first converted and then, at the age of thirty-one, dedicated himself to the task of becoming a rabbi. (The few other Jewish kids all went to temple in Morgantown, where there was a larger Jewish population, and this had been Sarah's intention as well, but Abbie felt Morgantown to be entirely tainted by the presence of Phil Harrow, and insisted they stay local.) Now in his forties and a widower—his wife had had a rare and undetected cardiac condition—MacDowell presided over a congregation so demographically similar to the one from Abbie's memories of his own youth that it tipped into uncanny parody. On their first Rosh Hashanah there, MacDowell had exhorted them in his dvar Torah to understand that though God's requirements may seem perplexing, a call to something impossible, they reveal themselves in due time as something other than what we may once have thought them to be, for instance, him, a nice Scotch-Catholic boy, becoming a rabbi. While he spoke, Myrna Markoupolous waddled over and, having introduced herself in a loud, wavering voice, proceeded into a story about how the rabbi had failed to come to visit her in the hospital after she'd had a stent put in the year before. Sarah had been appalled; the rest of the congregation had ignored her; Abbie smiled too broadly and suppressed his urge to laugh, and Isaac, then twelve, stared miserably at the floor.

The following Thursday, after regular school, he'd begun studying the Torah portion he'd have to read the next year for his bar mitzvah, and MacDowell, who was a man with a fondness for arcane trivia, told the mortified boy that in the olden days, a boy's bar mitzvah wasn't necessarily on or about his thirteenth calendar birthday. Rather, the men of a congregation would take him to the baths and pull down his pants and count his pubic hairs, of which the required number was thirteen. MacDowell didn't mean anything by it—he just thought it was interesting, a grace note in a symphony of unimportant but entertaining facts—but Isaac flushed and shoved his head into his arms to hide his embarrassed tears. He had the worst of it in being a slow physical but early sexual bloomer. Abbie wasn't the sort who bothered with, or understood, parental controls on the internet. Isaac had been looking at porn since he was seven or eight, and now that he was in junior high, he perceived his own diminutive physique and total hairlessness below the head as an almost existential inadequacy. The summer before, Marco Larimer, who was seventeen, had told him it was cool because he looked like a girl. It had briefly pleased and then terrified him.

He was no closer to thirteen pubic hairs when he was called before the Torah on the Saturday after his thirteenth birthday, and yet, despite this disappointment, and despite his full conviction that this Judaism business was a dusty philosophy of superstitious collectivism wholly unsuited to Man's fundamental individuality and heroic potential (Mr. Krupp, having found Isaac to be too precocious for seventh-grade honors English, had loaned him *The Fountainhead*), he felt actual pride in getting up and leading the service—it was, at least, an intellectual achievement to have learned to read Hebrew, even if only phonetically, and to have memorized all those monotonous prayers. And he felt equally pleased that he had made a friend who showed up to the permanently twilight interior of Tree of Life that Saturday morning, not out of co-religious social obligation, but because he wanted to be there.

And, Isaac reflected as he mumbled through his Torah portion, that he really should have invited Adam Martens after all, because Isaac had drawn the *Tazria-Metzora*, a long and dreaded Parsha that trolled through three chapters in Leviticus dedicated to the detailed discussion of ritual impurity, the impurity of women after childbirth (gross), and then the odd and supernatural appearance of *Tzaraat*, something between leprosy, athlete's foot, black mold, and Morgellons disease, an affliction of skin and clothing and even buildings, which, when it appeared, required the attentions of a priest and an extraordinary ritual:

> *As for the live bird, he shall take it, and then the cedar stick, the strip of crimson wool, and the hyssop, and, along with the live bird, he shall dip them into the blood of the slaughtered bird, over the spring water.*
>
> *He shall then sprinkle seven times upon the person being cleansed from tzara'ath, and he shall cleanse him. He shall then send away the live bird into the open field.*

Rabbi MacDowell had said, "You might want to play down the particulars in your dvar, Isaac," after Isaac had shown him his first draft. But Isaac had snuck them back in because he thought that Jake would be impressed.

Afterward they all went to the Uniontown Country Club to eat stuffed chicken breast and dance to DJ Don Electric, who interspersed selections of beat-less Evanescence songs with R. Kelly tracks and the Electric Slide. Adults whom Isaac barely knew gave him money, although his mother forbade him from opening the envelopes in front of anyone, and Jake told him that "that shit about the birds was cool as fuck."

"Yeah," Isaac said.

"You should tell fucking Martens that you guys, like, really do that."

"Yeah," Isaac said. He laughed. "It's like a secret ritual, you know. We don't let any non-Jews see it."

"Exactly," Jake said.

Then it was getting dark out, and the few kids' parents had picked them up, and Jake had taken off with the pleasing near-promise of a very adult handshake and a "see ya soon," and the congregants of Tree of Life had packed into their aging Buicks and gone home, and Isaac was sitting at his parents' table while his mother gazed off and occasionally patted his hand and his father laughed too loudly with some men that Isaac didn't know over by the bar. Arthur Imlak hadn't come but had sent him an envelope with a thousand dollars and a note scrawled on the back of a business card: "Not all in one place."

"Can we go?" he asked his mother.

"Ask your father," she said. She looked at him and touched his face. "Abbie, I mean."

"Yeah, Mom. God. I know who you mean."

"Your tone, honey."

"Okay."

Rather than go to Abbie, who would put his big hand on his shoulder and yank him into some loud conversation that felt like a fistfight, he slipped out the side of the banquet room and down the service stairs on the side of the building with the intention of walking around the golf course for a while before returning to the club to gather his parents and force them to drive him home. There was a pond on the sixth hole with a tall willow tree where you could hear the oddly human cadences of frog calls at night. But at the bottom of the stairs, he found his English teacher leaning against a roll door in an alcove and smoking a pungent cigarette.

"Hey, Mr. Krupp!"

"Holy Jesus shit Christ!" He caught himself before he could complete the act of tossing away the joint, like a batter checking his swing. He put his whole body into recovering from it. "You scared the hell out of me, Isaac."

"Sorry."

"You want some?"

"What? Oh, I mean, I don't smoke."

Krupp gave a chill nod of his head, acknowledgment but not agreement. "This isn't smoking, buddy. This is weed."

"Well, it's still smoking."

"That," Krupp said, "is just what they want you to believe." He extended his hand and pinched fingers.

Isaac took a tentative and then a deeper hit and felt the fog bubble up into the previously undiscovered chambers behind his eyes.

"I've got to tell you, Isaac, that that . . . would you call that a sermon?"

"Yeah. I mean, it's called a dvar Torah, technically."

"Whatever, buddy. That was a great piece of writing."

"Thanks, Mr. Krupp."

"Really." He took a long drag. "Really. I mean, I've got to tell you, the way that you linked the, the impure men who were forced by the conventions of their tribe to live apart from other people with the heroic individuality of Howard Roark. I don't know that I could have said it better. A truly impressive piece of oratory, young man."

"Thanks. Can I have some more?"

"Oh, yeah. For sure. Don't tell your dad, though."

"You know my dad?"

"Sure. I mean, I met him. Yeah. Back in the day."

"I didn't know that."

"I thought I told you. Well, anyway, you're a great kid. Or, I guess you're not a kid anymore, right? You've got a real way with words. I've had a lot of students over the years, and I've rarely, if ever, been so impressed. Did you ever think about becoming a writer?"

"I guess. I'm not sure."

"'The afflicted man who dwells outside the city until he is healed represents the man of individuality who will not submit to the second-handers all around him and therefore insists on charting his own course in the world. What his inferiors believe to be a punishment, he knows to be a blessing,'" Krupp quoted and shook his head. "Just great fucking stuff, Isaac."

"Thanks, Mr. Krupp."

"Well," Krupp said, crushing the roach beneath the collapsing toe of his old brown loafers, "I've got a gig tonight. If I were you, I'd wash my hands before I head back inside. Get the skunk off, if you know what I mean."

"Thanks, Mr. Krupp."

"I'll see you Monday, Isaac."

"See you Monday, Mr. K."

Then Isaac, stoned for the first time in his life, walked back into the club and went to the handicapped restroom and found, after washing his hands for three straight minutes, that he'd been washing his hands for three straight minutes, and he smiled at his own face in the mirror, and Isaac laughed and discovered that he couldn't stop laughing.

14

sabel was fired. Barry called her into his office and asked her to close the door. He fussed with some items on his desk. He slid a piece of letterhead on which her resignation letter had already been written across his desk. He couldn't look at her, and she took that as a small victory. "It's not that I want to," he said. But Isabel suspected—and she was right—that the question of particular desire had never entered into it for Barry. He was a man for whom life, professional and otherwise, consisted of passing like a thread through the fine demands of multiple constituencies. Stakeholders, he would have called them. He would never really please, nor not please, anyone; his project, and his paycheck, would endure.

Penny, who'd gotten her Masters of Non-Profit Management and promptly been hired as Barry's special assistant for executive projects, had warned Isabel it might be coming. The governor had personally called Barry—perhaps he'd even dialed his cell phone himself—to complain that the whole fucking thing (he said, "fucking thing") put him in an untenable position: to show up at the gala and speak about his environmental programs only to be followed onto the dais by one of the most public faces of fracking in the state, who would then be honored for nothing more or less than greenwashing his oily money through a conveniently

needy charitable organization, would be embarrassing and hypo-
critical. To cancel out of annoyance or pique would be a sign of
political weakness, showing his opponents in the statehouse that
some lousy accidental billionaire could force the chief executive
of the sixth-largest state in the Union and a critical lynchpin of
the electoral college to skip a public appearance. Etc., etc. Penny
had listened in on the conversation; the forwarding system on the
VoIP phones permitted the younger employees to do that sort of
thing with a casual ease that Isabel had been born just five or ten
years too early to inherit. Barry never had a chance. The governor
raised his voice. He reminded Barry that there was a lot of popular
displeasure with the state's system for determining and awarding
non-profit status to organizations. He had yet to really comment
on the issue. Did Barry want the Future Cities Institute to be the
public cause of his deciding to take a strong position on it?

And Barry might yet have held out, except that somehow
the *City Paper* got wind of it and ran a long expose on the links
between the biggest gasman in the Commonwealth and a number of supposed environmental non-profits, the FCI most promi-
nently. The cover featured a cartoon of Imlak as a sort of gaseous
devil rising out of Panther Hollow to drag the Institute down into
a fiery hell. An anti-fracking group organized a demonstration
and picket at the William Penn Hotel, where the dinner was to
be held, and the new state Attorney General, another Democrat
who'd promised during her own campaign to crack down on the
excesses of the industry, made several darkly imprecise comments
about "looking into" the nexus of gas money and public environmental advocacy and lobbying. "The question," she said, "is
whether these non-profits are living up to their promise as purely
public charities, advocating for the public good, or whether they

are little more than public relations arms of the fracking industry." Barry hastily announced that the 2050 Award would *not* be going to Imlak after all. Arthur only learned that Barry had hastily announced it when he read it in the *Post-Gazette* the next morning, because Barry hated confrontation and didn't bother to call him first. Imlak promptly and furiously revoked his foundation's pledge of two hundred and fifty thousand in annual general operating support over the next three years. The FCI senior staff began receiving ominous emails from their director of finance about departmental budget cuts, and then, at a staff meeting, Barry promised everyone, apropos nothing, that there wouldn't be any staff cuts, whatever anyone may have heard. No one had heard anything to that effect, and that's how they knew what was coming. Despite the modest forewarning, Isabel allowed herself briefly to believe it wouldn't be her.

It turned out that a sitting governor in the same party as the mayor and the county executive did indeed trump the twenty-second richest man in the Commonwealth. That probably should have been clear to everyone from the beginning. Imlak may have owned some state legislators and county commissioners, but the governor was a project of the national party; he was an avatar of even bigger billionaires. It was a little shocking to everyone involved, actually, Arthur included, to discover that a hundred million bucks could count, in certain circumstances, as mere loose change. And of course, although not so stratospherically wealthy as Arthur B. Imlak, the governor was a pretty rich guy himself, a millionaire many times over, and that was just how boys got when they start pulling their dicks out.

Isabel was ultimately punished for arguing against giving Arthur the ridiculous award in the first place. Barry blamed her for the whole mess; there was nothing worse for a career than being right when your boss was disastrously wrong. In the email to the staff, also pre-written, probably by a university lawyer, he thanked Isabel for her hard work and dedication and hinted vaguely at a future of *other challenges*. Penny left the office early, though not too early to be noticed or to endanger her own job, and bought Isabel a few drinks at a grotty student joint in Oakland. A group of thirty-something MBA students were eating terrible, gigantic sandwiches and drinking beer and chilled Crown Royal a little farther down the bar. One of them offered a silent toast in her direction.

"This doesn't seem like your sort of bar," she told him. A couple of them wore suits, and they had an air of easy spending.

"Double-D," he said, nodding to a companion down the bar, "likes their girly drinks."

"Double-D?" Isabel said.

"Don Danielson." The guy raised a glass full of something pinkish. Little candy worms hung off the rim.

"You still give each other nicknames?" She waved the bartender over.

"What else are we going to do, study cost accounting?" Her neighbor tipped his glass again. He had a punchable face and a fuckable body under that improperly tailored suit. She briefly considered, then decided against it.

"What about you?" he asked. "Do you like girly drinks?"

"Me?" Isabel said. "Oh, no." She ordered a cheap scotch. "Never mix, never worry."

Isabel hauled herself home with that feeling of fogged regret that came with drinking before it got dark. She fell asleep on the couch watching a Werner Herzog movie about Siberia, and she dreamed she was a fish who spoke with a German accent. The water was bracing. She woke up around nine with a headache, no blanket, and with her phone trilling on her chest.

"Eli?" she mumbled. She realized that she hadn't answered but rather had swiped him directly into voice mail. She sat up and called him back. "Eli."

"Bell, you sound terrible." He'd taken to calling her Bell because he knew it made her crazy. It was such an impossible trait of men, even the good ones, that they found this sort of minor but deliberate antagonism the funniest thing in the world. Your annoyance was the predicate for the humor of it while at the same time a demerit against your character.

"God, don't call me that."

"We kid because we love." He'd also begun using this expression when he knew Isabel was annoyed. It was his way of smuggling the word into conversations to test the waters of its more sincere use. Isabel, sinusy and hungover, was tempted to tell him right out, right there, that she loved him. Force him to either affirm it or walk it back. But what if he were to choose affirmation, and what if she really did?

There was a long pause, and then he told her that Abbie had a brain aneurysm. "My God," Isabel sat up. "Is he . . .?"

"No, no. You can't kill him. He'll live to a hundred seventy-five. But he's in the hospital."

He'd been dizzy, and he began to slur his speech. Eli had at first thought that Abbie was drunk or stoned, neither uncommon nor unlikely, but then his speech became totally nonsensical, and he vomited, and Eli called 911.

Isabel said she'd drive down, but Eli told her there was no point. Not yet. "They're doing tests, still, and he's not lucid. Come tomorrow. Call me and I'll meet you at the hospital."

So Isabel drank some water and tried to read and gave up and went to bed and lay in the dark with her mind persistently circling back to the question of when precisely it would pass from consciousness into unconsciousness, that unhealthy picking at the scabby edge of sleep. But eventually she did sleep. She dreamed of an immense, quiet forest on the other side of the continent, high pines and a steep slope down to cold water.

Abbie was hardly more lucid the next day. Sarah had been with him all night. They allowed his other visitors into his room only briefly. Abbie complained that it was too bright, even though the blinds were drawn and the lights had been dimmed. He was having trouble moving the right side of his body, and now the doctors were saying that it may not have been an aneurysm after all, but a stroke. "Of some significance," one of the in-and-out doctors added with an uncomfortable enthusiasm. Isaac and Eli took Sarah down to the cafeteria to force her to eat something, and Isabel was left momentarily alone in the room with him before two nurses come and shooed her away. Abbie's eyes had the appearance of milk pluming as it was poured into weak tea. Isabel, with nothing to say but stupid encouragement, said, "You're looking good, Abbie."

"Mmm." His throat rattled. "I fell off the truck," he said.

"What truck?"

"I tried to jump off the truck." A wide grin spread on the good side of his face; the bad side caught up a moment later, but then the whole thing turned to a grimace.

Isabel, who'd read somewhere that you should humor the lacunae of reason in stroke victims and Alzheimer's patients and the elderly in general, said, "What were you doing on the truck in the first place?"

Abbie murmured incoherently. Then his eyes focused on her, one-two, the good then the bad, just like the smile. "Excuse me, Isabellisssss . . . issima. I find myself in a state."

"You'll be fine," she said, retreating again into hospital-room banality.

He seemed to sink into the pillows. He lifted and lowered an arm weakly. "God asks it of you," he said slowly, roughly. "You think you see it. But He doesn't speak. He doesn't speak. What if your heart hears only the echo of what He meant to say? What if you hear it wrongly and still, you do as you thought He asked?"

"I don't believe in God," Isabel said.

Abbie looked past her, and then he said in a quavering voice that sounded as if it was echoing up out of a well, "Tell your mother hello, Isabel."

· · ·

Abbie, of course, had known since he'd watched her, slowly and quietly and thinking she was alone, rifle through his office on her first night at The Gamelands. She was a lousy sneak. She didn't realize that a slowly opened door creaks the loudest. She didn't think that the reading light she'd turned on to read the transcript of that awful, regrettable arbitration turned the window transparent to anyone standing outside it, invisible in the dark, catching a last smoke before toddling off to bed. She even looked like her mother. It startled him to think Cathy had been the same age as her daughter was now when they'd first met. My God.

He'd met her in eighty-four. She was an accountant for a firm that did business with his father-in-law's practice, a little hard-edged and with a square face. Northern Italian, maybe. He once told her it was alluringly masculine, and she'd surprised him by accepting it as a compliment. He hadn't necessarily meant it as a compliment, but he pretended he had. It was something about women who were good with numbers. They'd met for lunch. Why had they met for lunch? He could never remember later on. It was some pretext, something to do with a project; something to do with a public bid; something about an audit. It wasn't her idea, but he remembered it as her idea. Her firm had offices midtown, not far from Bryant Park. Unlike Sarah, she believed him to be a genius, at least for a little while. He drove her up to Connecticut to show her a house he'd designed for some absurd millionaire. It was still under construction. They spent the night there in the little trailer used by some of the workmen during the week. That was before he got fat. Before his back got bad.

Did he love her? Not especially. Did she love him? No. If Sarah's sophisticated estimation of the actual limits of Abbie's talent and intelligence were what permitted, and what sustained, her love, then Cathy Giordani's slightly overawed acquiescence to Abbie's self-made myth was what prevented her loving him. She thought too highly of him and perhaps not enough of herself. Not that she was swept away or worshipful. She was in the end a practical woman, far more practical than Sarah. She viewed Abbie, in a way, as she viewed the presidents and CEOs of the bigger companies for whom she worked as a CPA—not better than her at all, just of a different scale. Her love affair with Abbie, like her business, was more than anything mutually agreeable, companionable.

He ruined it by getting her pregnant. An accident. As much her fault as his. In fact, she was never entirely certain it *was* Abbie. He was one of only two possible candidates. But he was the more likely, and rather than turn the whole thing into a circus, he was the one she told. If the kid came out an unlikely blonde or something, she'd admit to the other guy. And when she'd told him—over a charred burger at a diner near Times Square that had the worst food but the cleanest counters and bathrooms in the neighborhood—he'd seemed, at first, almost pleased, as if in hearing it, he'd proven something to himself about himself. She'd more or less expected that and worked it into her calculated decision to tell him. She was an accountant, after all. She balanced the books. He'd told her with some regret that he and Sarah had tried and failed to get pregnant.

He insisted on paying for the doctor, although she had perfectly good insurance. He was an insupportable spendthrift. She let him because this too flattered his silly pride as a man. But he was careless, and Sarah found out. A bill or something. So there they were, back in the same diner, eating the same burgers, although her girlfriend, to whom she'd confided the pregnancy, had told her that she should lay off red meat entirely. Abbie fiddled with his napkin. His burger was half eaten. He ordered a coffee. He appeared to change his mind. "Actually, do you have any Bailey's?" he asked the waitress.

"We don't have liquor, sweetie."

"How about beer?"

"Sure."

"Bud or Bud Light?"

"Bud."

"And no coffee?"

"No, bring me that too. We'll see which way the evening goes."

The waitress rolled her eyes at Cathy in a gesture of commiseration before walking away.

He'd already told Cathy that Sarah had found out. She'd gone on eating her burger. You didn't drag your lover's fight with his wife out of him. You just had to wait.

"She said she wants me to take care of it," Abbie said at last.

"Take care of it?" Cathy put down the last bite. She sipped her water through a straw. "Like what, Don Corleone putting out a hit?"

"That's what *I* said!"

"No way, Abbie. I don't serve your wife. I'm not interested in what she wants."

"What about what I want?"

"Fuck you, Abbie. What you want? If you wanted to *take care of it*, you should've told me a month ago. It's too late. I'm committed. Sunk costs. This project is in the pipeline."

"Such a romantic."

"I'm a CPA."

"Be that as it may."

"Be that as it may nothing. This is my kid, Abbie. It's either yours or it isn't yours, but that's up to you."

"It's ours," he said. But when the waitress brought their drinks, he picked the beer.

• • •

A little later in the day, the nurses kicked Isabel out of Abbie's room, insisting that only Isaac and Sarah—family—could stay. She'd waited for Abbie to say something, to protest her exclusion from the category, but he was who he was, after all. You could only expect so much. Isaac followed her briefly out of the room and thanked her, with unlikely sincerity, for coming. She asked him if he was going to be okay. "Of course I am. Jake's staying over. Anyway, it's not like he's dead." He flashed a goofy grin. "We're not going to be rid of him that easily." And indeed, Isaac proved perhaps a more adept, if mundane, prophet than his father, who recovered, though he never lost a limp and a slight downward tug at the left side of his face, and lived for many more years.

Eli walked her down the hospital's long beige halls toward the elevators. "You should come over tonight," she told him. "I got fired. Plus all this. I'm feeling needy."

"I should stay. They might need me." He stopped in the middle of the hall.

"Not especially."

"Not especially. But it won't be much longer. We should get married, Isabel."

"Married?" She laughed, too loud. A passing doctor gave her an admonishing look.

"Yes," Eli said. "Why not?"

"How long have we even been a couple?"

"Who cares? We're going to be forty."

"Speak for yourself. I'm thirty-eight."

"You're thirty-nine. You just think I don't know when your birthday is." This, she had to admit, was true.

Several years later, when Veronica, her mobility now a little impaired by bad hips but still remarkably fit for a woman of almost ninety, had flown out to Vancouver with a group of adventurous and equally well-knit old ladies, Isabel had met her for a long lunch and told her this story, or most of this story, judiciously edited. Veronica, as ever, had insisted on a bottle of wine.

"Such a romantic," she said of Eli.

"I wasn't much better," Isabel said. "I mean, after I thought about it a little, I just said, sure."

Veronica smiled. "And he hauled you off to the far end of the continent."

"That was part of the deal. Part of the proposal. He said we had to have babies. Lots of babies. Canadian babies. Enough to survive the end of the world." She laughed. She nearly said, "He isn't entirely unlike your brother." But she caught herself.

"That's a tall order."

"Two down. But I'm not getting younger. We're thinking four."

Veronica laughed. "Enjoy the wine while you can, then."

Isabel invited her to visit them. "It's only about an hour from the city. Eli's friends with a seaplane pilot. We could get you a flight over to the island."

Veronica thanked her and said she couldn't. "Our cruise leaves tomorrow." The ladies were heading off on a National Geographic tour up along the Pacific Canadian coast and through the Inner Passage of Alaska.

"On the way back, then," Isabel offered.

"Perhaps," Veronica said. And then Isabel never heard from her again. Isabel had flown back to the island and picked up the Jeep. She drove through the long summer evening from Nanaimo over the mountains, past Cowichan Lake and down the Pacific Marine Road to Port Renfrew, then up to the wooded acres and the house that Eli had built. He'd put the kids to bed. "How was work?" she asked. He'd got a job with an organization that tried to preserve the forests on the islands, aided by his sister and some judicious exaggeration of his past employment in the field of landscape architecture. She worked for them part time as well, telecommuting with the office in Vancouver and visiting in person a few days a month. He didn't answer, but kissed her. It was almost dark.

"How was Veronica?"

"Spry," Isabel said.

It was only a month later that she received a rare email from

Isaac telling her that Veronica had been so taken with Alaska that she'd disembarked at Juneau, caught a flight up to Anchorage, and from there joined a small tour headed to Denali National Park where, hiking with a group of men half her age, she'd lost her footing on a loose section of trail, fallen fifty feet down a steep slope, and died. Isaac insisted that she was smiling when the guides recovered her body, although what evidence there was of that, or how it could be true, he never mentioned.

15

In his junior year in high school Isaac was arrested for the first time. There would be others, later, in college, for better reasons: for protesting at the Republican National Convention, then again for protesting at the Democratic National Convention; for refusing to leave the Mellon Bank Plaza after the city decided it had had enough of an Occupy protest. But there's a difference in being arrested alone than getting hauled off in a group. He'd spent the day on his bike, a long, hilly, forty-five-mile loop that took him from The Gamelands out to Dunbar along Jumonville Road and then up over the mountain to Ohiopyle and back again via some old and steep state roads. It was August, although it had been unusually cool that week, the highs barely touching seventy. In two weeks, he'd be a senior. There was already an autumnal quality in the air, and it hinted at something about his life, that it was to pass into a period of bright colors and long nights that would only ever be a glamorous disguise for a kind of chilly retrenchment. He'd hung his bike on the rack in the carport, noting that one of his father's cars was gone. One of his father's cars was always gone. Abbie, Isaac thought, was at loose ends—he had been for years—and it was making him crazier by the hour. The other day he'd wandered past the door of his office and found the old man talking to himself. He was unintelligible. Isaac banged his foot against the door when he turned to slip away. He was graceful when he rode but clumsy when he walked. Abbie turned and caught him grasping at his stubbed toe. Their eyes met. "My son," Abbie said. He'd lately got into the habit of making this weird, nominative pronouncement every time he caught sight of Isaac. It was creepy.

Isaac went into his house and peeled off his kit and took a long shower. He thought about turning on his cam, but he wasn't in the mood. He jerked off quickly and just for himself. He threw on jeans and a tee-shirt and went to get something to eat. His own kitchen was empty but for a couple of bottles of beer that he kept in the fridge. He walked to the main house and found his mother sitting at the dining room table and crying.

He was never shocked to see his parents cry. They both did frequently, his father freely weeping, often at something silly, at an opera he was listening to or at the conclusion of a sad story about children in poverty or some animal near extinction on NPR, his mother quietly, always sitting up straight, rarely at anything in particular, and if you asked her why she was crying, she always said, "I'm not."

So this time he didn't even bother to ask. He found some breakfast bars in the pantry and took two of them. He found a bottle of sparkling water in the fridge and got that as well. He stood at the island and unwrapped a bar. While he chewed, he noticed that his mother had a laptop open on the kitchen table. He saw what she was looking at.

Isaac's interest in amateur pornography would later develop into something more tongue-in-cheek, a carefully curated porn blog, sufferingintherear.tumblr.com, which featured a rather lovely collection of photos, some pornographic, others only vaguely erotic, all of them featuring boys—in various states of undress—and their bikes. Isaac didn't take them himself, of course; he would have said that he was only a curator, the site a museum of his own interest. The fact that there already existed so many images made for such impossibly singular tastes and niches of human interest was both a wonder and a shock, even for a kid like Isaac who'd grown up entirely online, always knowing that anyone could find on the internet a sheer, extraordinary volume of material for the most outrageously peculiar interests and fetishes. Suffering in the rear, by the way, was an expression from road racing—a cyclist having a terrible day, mashing on, revolution after revolution, at the back of the peloton as it rolled across some European country-side. It was the kind of silly in-joke that Isaac found funnier than it was. At that time, though, still in high school, before Tumblrs, before Twitter, when he still had, of all things, a Myspace page, Isaac's interests in the male form were less curatorially ironic and more distinctly personal. He posted jerk-off videos on a number of sites; they featured him in various states of cyclist's dress, or undress. Several had achieved more than 100,000 views.

Who knows how Sarah ever came across them? It was absurd to imagine that she spent her unoccupied days trolling through gay porn online. (Was it, though? Perhaps it was exactly what she did with her unoccupied days, at once titillated and terrified that she might encounter some image of her own son, whose activities were less secret than he imagined.) She'd snooped around just enough to formulate a vague but persistent suspicion that some-thing was going on without imagining quite what it could be. To her credit, Sarah wasn't the sort of woman, not the sort of mother, who would, in the abstract, necessarily collapse into tears at the idea of her own son masturbating for a bunch of pervs on the other end of some anonymous network. That's not to say that she would approve, only that she was a person with a broader view of human sexuality; she would have admitted some interest in the pornographic into the normal panoply of human erotic life. But abstraction makes moral tolerance easy, and seeing your only child orgasm into a pair of light blue spandex shorts would surely, regardless of any prior and deeply held beliefs in your own essential openness, trouble a mother.

Isaac, likewise, would have said that he was proud of his body, comfortable with his sexuality, unconcerned with who saw him, proud even to be seen. But seeing his mother sitting at the kitchen table watching his own dick bounce around a laptop screen, he flushed, nearly dropped his bottle of water, and hurried out of the room without saying a word. He took the keys to one of the lesser cars, a cranky Oldsmobile that his father had bought for him at the estate sale after an erstwhile colleague of Sherri Larimer's had gone to jail for check kiting and Sherri had hastily and cheaply liquidated the estate. He drove down the mountain, willing himself not to cry, because unlike his parents, he found his own tears absurd.

Club Illusion was on North Pittsburgh Street in a low, windowless building that had once been a tire shop, then a biker bar. It was owned by Bill Pattaglia's brother-in-law, who was married to Sherri Larimer's cousin, and who operated a variety of bars, nuisance and otherwise, in Uniontown, Connellsville, Masontown, and on a dark stretch of road outside of Republic. He had read an article in *USA Today* about several once-charming, then peeling, now charming again New England towns that had been revitalized, in some degree, by catering to flocks of fantastically bourgie gay tourists from New York and thereabouts. Ironically, the bar he chose to transform into a fag bar had been, in its final prior incarnation, called The Two-Stroke. The joke was lost on Bill. It had become the county's premier—and that is to say, only—gay bar. Uniontown was just then undertaking an effort to advertise itself as a tourist destination for the sort of folks who enjoyed whitewater rafting in the mountains and fall foliage and Frank Lloyd Wright (Fallingwater was nearby). In any event, business at The Two-Stroke had never been much more than a break-even affair, with half the terrifying clientele drinking for free on account of various past and future services to the Larimer family. It seemed to its owner that fags were less likely to shoot each other or run each other over with their cars. This may or may not have been true, and the regulars were finally, thoroughly local. Still, it turned out that there were plenty of gays in Fayette County who didn't really want to drive all the way to Pittsburgh to drink with their own kind. Both of the Ls in the sign were neon high heels. He'd thought of that himself.

It was a weeknight and the bar wasn't crowded. Isaac was drinking with his half-a-friend, Travis Pistella. Because of its own-ership, Illusions had few concerns with any strict construction of legality, and the Pattaglias were anyway actually related to the regional head of enforcement for the Pennsylvania Liquor Control Board. Isaac had been drinking there since he was fifteen. Tra-vis was a skinny twenty-five-year-old white boy from New Eagle who did weird drag down in Morgantown under the name Stella Travesty. As a woman, he had a style of science-fictional haute couture, as if Klaus Nomi were to have made a cameo in David Lynch's adaptation of *Dune*, but as a man, he'd never grown out of the candy-boy raver look that had marked his own teenage years: wide, torn jeans and tiny tight tee-shirts, a lot of bracelets and spiky hair badly frosted at the tips. Isaac found him slightly appalling to look at. Travis did a lot of meth and also had a desiccated look about him, but he was a sweetie. Also, although Isaac would never smoke the stuff, he didn't mind doing a toot or two of speed in the parking lot, and Travis was free with his supply.

"I can't believe your mom found your porn," Travis said. He was drinking something simultaneously effervescent and fluorescent. "I would like literally die."

"Isn't your mom dead?"

"Yes, girl. And if she wasn't, it would literally kill her."

"It's worse because I'm in it, I guess."

"Yes. Why didn't you ever tell me? I would've watched you!"

"That's why."

"Shut it down. I wouldn't have jacked off or anything! I'm not into twinks. Although you do have a fan over there." Travis dropped his voice and indicated a man at the other end of the bar, a thin guy with a tight face, in his mid-forties, sitting behind a half-drunk beer and an empty shot glass, slumping at the shoulders as if neither was his first.

"Oh my god. He looks like a washed up porn star, speaking of. Look at that mustache! I'm going to need another drink."

"Me too. I may step outside, in a minute. If you're interested."

"I'm interested. What am I going to say to her? What if she tells Abbie?"

"I thought you said they were cool."

"They're not that cool."

"He's really staring."

"God. Fuck this. Let's get high."

They went out into the lot behind the bar and sat on the hood of Travis's Cavalier and took key bumps out of a little glassine sachet. Isaac felt the bolt behind his eyes and the immediate dull ache that accompanied extreme awareness in his brain. He had no particular affection for stimulants, except insofar as they allowed him to drink more, but there really was something about meth that all the others lacked, something visceral and terrible, as if some infinitely vaster being than himself had been crammed inside of him, as if he could feel, for the flickering hours before it faded, what it must feel like to be a whole soul crammed into a tiny body during its brief, sinful, necessary transit through the living world.

"I sometimes think," Isaac said, "when I do meth, that this must be what it feels like to be a whole soul crammed into a little human body during its time as a living being."

"That's some deep shit, girl."

"Fuck you. I'm serious. Can I have a little more?"

"You can. You should smoke this shit. I don't know why you don't. I don't know about any fucking souls, but it does make you want to fuck."

A human figure reeled out of the darkness, and a slurred, nearly lisping, nasal voice snarled, "All right, who's using all the foul language?"

It was the man who'd been staring at them across the bar. He was an odd figure in the dim light of the gravel lot, more gaunt than he'd appeared inside and unsteady on his feet. He was wearing a colorful sweater, stiff jeans, and brand-less white tennis shoes. He repeated the question.

"Who the fuck are you?" Travis asked.

"What did I just tell you about the language?"

"You didn't tell us anything," Isaac said. "You asked."

"Oh, are you gonna get smart with me?" He wove as he turned his gaze on Isaac.

"I mean, I guess I am," Isaac said.

"Well, it's called your ass! Smart-ass!"

Travis and Isaac weren't able to keep themselves from laughing. The man got angrier. He got louder. "You think this is funny?"

"What the fuck, man." Isaac slid off the hood of the car. "Fuck off."

"It all starts with the bullshit."

Travis was giggling. "That's so true."

"It all starts with the bullshit."

"Look," Isaac said. "We're going to go back inside. You have a nice night."

"You boys aren't going anywhere." He straightened himself up and attempted a menacing look. It came off as constipated.

"Um, yes we are."

He raised his arm and angled his head toward his armpit. He spoke into it. "Base," he said, "Come back. This is Officer Rittenhauer requesting backup."

"Is he talking to his armpit?" Travis asked.

"I think he is," Isaac said. He grinned at the guy. "You got a mic in there, Officer?"

"Request immediate backup."

"Okay," said Isaac. "See ya." He took a step back toward the bar, but Rittenhauer interdicted him and pushed him back with one hand. "Whoa!" Isaac threw up his hands. "What the fuck, man?"

"I warned you about that language! Now you aren't going nowhere!"

"I'll go wherever the fuck I want." Maybe, Isaac reflected, he shouldn't have done that meth. He would have ordinarily found this all much funnier. He pledged, in his mind, only to smoke weed and drink from then on. But now he was angry. He stepped forward again. "What are you going to do about it, faggot?" he said.

The man gave him a level gaze. "Strike," he said quietly. "And I'll show you self-defense."

So Isaac took a swing at this wavering drunk. He'd never done that before. It was the first, and the last, time he'd ever attempt to throw a punch. In retrospect, he realized, he hadn't the slightest idea how to do it. Not that it would have mattered if he had; he'd still have found himself prostrate in the gravel, a knee in the small of his back, his hands pinned behind him. Travis, that queen, had squeaked and run off with his drugs. The gravel dug into Isaac's cheek. He squirmed but couldn't get free. And that was how Isaac stayed until Officer Rittenhauer's backup arrived.

Imlak found the despondent boy in a holding cell with three large but harmless drunks, two of them snoring on benches that seemed ill-designed to support creatures of that size, one of them leaning against a wall and emitting a sort of whale song. Isaac was sitting in the corner with his head between his legs. "Come on, son," Arthur said. "Stop crying. Let's get you home." The boy looked up. Yes, Arthur thought. He'd occasionally teased himself that Sarah was lying about the boy's provenance. But she wasn't.

He'd golfed earlier that day. He was terrible at the sport, and he should have given it up. He'd shot 105 on the not very difficult course. But the game fascinated him; it was something he felt he ought to be good at, and he tortured himself by continually going back for more. He'd still been at the club when Sarah called him. She'd been very drunk, and he'd had a few cocktails himself. It had taken several minutes of circuitous interrogation to discover that Isaac was in jail, having been picked up—that is, arrested—with a known drug dealer, although this latter character had seemingly got away, behind some kind of queer club, by Jerry Rittenhauer no less, remember him? Who knew Uniontown even had such a cosmopolitan amenity? Arthur made a note to check it out at his earliest opportunity. When he was in Florida, he got the best coke from a kid who played records in a gay club in Ybor. "Where's Abbie?" he'd asked Sarah.

"He snot ansring."

"He's not answering?"

"No. No. No."

"All right. Christ. Sarah, drink some coffee."

"He's doing pornography."

"What? Who?" For the briefest moment, Imlak imagined she meant Abbie. He pictured his erstwhile rival and almost-partner with some kind of sturdily sensualist Uniontown swinger housewife in a wood-paneled basement. There would be an old-fashioned camcorder whirring away on a tripod across the room, and Imlak nearly laughed out loud. But, of course, he knew what she was really saying. He sighed. It was the sort of thing that Abbie would take either very well or very badly, with no possible intermediate reaction and no predicting which way he'd blow. Imlak tipped out the bartender, made calls to Mayor Pattaglia and Chief Chislett, then drove down to the jail behind the courthouse and picked up his skinny, inconsolable boy.

Imlak took Isaac back to his ugly farmhouse and told the boy to take a shower and change his clothes. "I'm not as skinny as you, but I'm sure I have a pair of sweats around here somewhere. I'll leave them in the guest room. Go on. I'll call your mother and tell her I've got you."

"Don't. God."

"Don't argue, son. Hit the showers."

Imlak waited until the water was running, and then he called Sarah and said that he'd got him. No, no one was going to press any charges. It was all a big misunderstanding.

"How'd you work that out?" Sarah asked him. Icily, he thought, for the favor he'd just done.

"I implied that Chief Chislett would find no stronger financial supporter should he ever choose to run against Bill Pattaglia."

"You men and your money."

"Oh, please. How's Abbie?"

"He just came home. He's upset. I told him about the pornography."

"Was that wise, Sarah?"

"We don't lie to each other, Arthur. That's not part of the deal."

"Don't you?" Imlak thought it was extremely unlikely. "Maybe you ought to."

"No."

"Christ." Imlak glanced down the hall toward the bathroom. "Sarah, we all have our indiscretions. Abbie's no angel either, needless to say."

"Arthur, he's just a boy."

"He's not a boy. Or, he is a boy, but he's seventeen, almost eighteen. But what do the categories matter, really? Was it necessary? Your husband is a maniac."

"He's his father."

"Sarah."

"No, Arthur. We agreed. You and I. We agreed. Abbie will get over it. Isaac gets arrested at a gay bar for fighting a police officer. He's livid, and he has every right to be. We've spoiled him. But we'll all get over it."

"I'll bring him home tomorrow. It's late. He can sleep here."

"No, Abbie wants to get him."

"I'll ask him. He can decide."

"He's my son, Arthur."

"Be that as it may."

But when Isaac was out of the shower and Imlak did ask him, Isaac said he'd go home. "I may as well get it over with."

"Your mother seems to believe that you're involved in some, shall we say, sexual indiscretion, young man."

"I guess."

"She believes that Abbie is taking it rather badly."

"Fuck Abbie."

"Yes, well. I happen to know that your . . . father has a bit of a nasty streak in him, although he likes to pretend that the bad news that follows him around only ever arises from the tragic misunderstanding of other parties to the various conflicts. I think it might be wise to let him cool off."

"You think it'll be any better if I'm here? You know he thinks you're fucking my mom. Speaking of *sexual indiscretions*." Isaac looked preposterous in a gray sweatsuit three sizes too big, but he managed a very hateful look nevertheless.

Other men would have avoided the subject, changed it, talked around it, but Imlak only folded his hands in his lap and nodded and said, "Yes, your mom and I were involved."

Isaac never stopped being grateful to Arthur for that. It was all he wanted, really: for an adult to treat him as an adult, not as some precious and infinitely fragile thing, not as some beautiful miracle of creation. He said, "Did Abbie know?"

"Yes, I imagine."

"You stopped?"

"We did."

"Why?"

"For no particular reason."

"Did you love her, though?"

"I suppose I did."

"Did she love you?"

"Possibly. I never asked, and she never volunteered the information. Probably not. She loves your father."

"Ha."

"You'll find these things are more complex than you'd imagine. Also simpler."

"It's weird. God. She's so old!"

"I'm so old. And it was years ago. We weren't quite as old then. Old enough, though."

"How long ago?"

"Seventeen, eighteen years."

"Oh." He considered this. He appeared to come to a private decision.

"Are you sure you want to go back now?" Arthur asked.

"Yes. No, but I will."

"Well, my advice is you should keep it to yourself."

"Keep what?"

Imlak stood and permitted himself to kiss the boy on the top of his head. He didn't answer. Instead, he said "When you're as old as me, you'll understand that despite what you've been told all your life, the truth, in and of itself, is very rarely its own excuse."

• • •

Imlak didn't invite Abbie in, but the men shook hands at Imlak's front door and had a quiet conversation. Isaac strained to hear, but he couldn't. It felt as if he were being bargained for. He hated it. Arthur came and got him and guided him to his father, a firm hand on the small of Isaac's back. Abbie put a big hand on Isaac's shoulder, then briefly touched the boy's still-wet hair. Isaac flinched away. Abbie sighed.

They got in the car, a long old Mercedes that looked like it ought to have been hustling a foreign dignitary in from the airport. They went down the drive and turned toward Morgantown Road. There, Abbie went left, heading for the bypass.

"Shouldn't we get my car?" Isaac asked.

"*Your* car?" Abbie's hands tightened on the wheel.

"Whatever. *The* car."

"Forget the car. We'll take care of it."

"Fine."

"Right. Fine."

The big car swayed onto the bypass. Abbie gunned the engine. They wheeled around the wide curve of the highway toward the foot of the mountain. He was a reckless driver; his driving frightened Isaac in the best of times; it terrified him now. He finally put on his seatbelt. They drove in silence. No radio, only the distant sound of the tires on the road transmitted through the soft suspension and the muted sound of the big V8. The bypass reconnected with Route 40 and angled uphill. Abbie downshifted. The engine revved and whined at a higher pitch. Isaac had climbed the road on his bike and knew the ramps by heart. Twelve percent here for the first five hundred meters, then ten percent through the first curve. The last houses dropped away. The trees closed in on either side of the road. It was almost dark. Trucks coming in the other direction, lowest gear in their rightmost lane, flashed lights as they bounced out of the curve.

Abbie sighed, his prelude to saying something. Isaac almost asked him what, but thought perhaps if he didn't ask, Abbie would lose the courage to say anything or, more likely, just lose the thread of whatever he'd been thinking he ought to say.

He was unlucky. Abbie didn't forget.

"What's going on, Isaac?"

At least, Isaac thought, Abbie was going to keep it vague. He hoped that was the case. "Nothing," he said.

Abbie sighed again. He shifted again. The engine whined again and settled. They approached the first curve; the pitch diminished; the car shot forward a little. "Nothing," he repeated.

"Nothing," Isaac said again.

"You don't go to jail over nothing."

Isaac composed his most disgusted teenage face, though Abbie was watching the road and wouldn't see him. "Of course you do. That cop was drunk."

"What were you doing in a bar?"

"What do you think?" Isaac spat back.

Abbie's right arm tightened and flexed, and Isaac cringed away, fearing for a moment that Abbie would hit him. He had before. Only once, and afterward he'd entered a period of unabashed contrition that even Isaac, who was only eight at the time, had found embarrassing. He couldn't even remember why—some insistent, childish misbehavior that Abbie's yelling only encouraged until he slapped Isaac once across the face—but he remembered the weight of the hand and remembered whirling and falling to the ground. Had it even hurt? He didn't remember it hurting.

But Abbie breathed deeply. He relaxed his arm. They exited the curve. Fourteen percent now as they banked right into the next long turn. "I don't care if you're gay, Isaac. But." The *but* had no antecedent. It hung horribly.

Isaac flushed red, pale face turning sickly pink. "I'm not gay!" He didn't know why he said it. It wasn't a denial. He was; his parents knew; he knew they knew. If it remained unspoken, it was only because they all imagined themselves too advanced to ever have some dowdy conversation about teenaged sexuality. But here was Abbie, trying to do exactly that, and Isaac, seventeen, almost eighteen, was appalled. "I'm not," he repeated.

"Isaac," Abbie said.

"Fuck you."

"Isaac."

"Leave me alone."

Abbie, for his part, felt the muffled drumming of rage behind his eyes. He kept them on the road. If less articulate than he'd hoped to be when he'd planned the conversation on the way down the mountain to get his son, then nevertheless he thought he'd evinced a true, a convincing sympathy. And yet no one ever seemed to return his care in kind.

"Whatever you are," he began, then stopped abruptly again. What an awful way to phrase it. He rolled his eyes briefly heavenward.

"God," Isaac muttered, full of disgust or shame or both.

"My point," Abbie tried again. "My point is your mother and I are worried. Worried, Isaac. About school. You're not doing anything at school. About your friends. Or you don't seem to have many friends."

"Jake is my friend."

"Is that all? And that boy—"

"Fuck you."

"Careful with that mouth, Isaac."

"Oh, please."

The last curve. The road flattening to a mere five percent. The lookout on the right. The long straight. The white, crenelated Summit Inn at the peak, lit from below, a ghostly wedding cake.

"And the drugs. We know you're experimenting. And look, a little marijuana never hurt anybody, but." Again, the conjunction without a phrase to be joined to the phrase preceding it. Abbie shook his head. Isaac pursed his lips and looked away. He pressed his forehead against the cold window.

Right at the Summit. Floating through the dark over the rolling road, the headlights hardly adequate. Neither of them spoke again. Abbie drummed impatiently on the wheel. Isaac's breath fogged on the glass. Right on the driveway. The sharp curve, where he slid, as ever, on the gravel. Past the big tulip tree. Past the bright house, all its windows illuminated, flushing energy carelessly into the night. Why, Abbie thought, did Sarah insist on keeping every Goddamn light burning? They parked in the carport. Isaac leapt out of the car and almost ran for his own little enclave. Abbie yelled after him, "We expect you at dinner!"

Isaac didn't answer him but slammed the door as he went into the house. And Abbie, standing beside the car with its door still open, ground his molars and took another calming breath, only he found it didn't calm him at all, but only stoked whatever it was that burned inside him. He closed the car door so gently and slowly that it didn't fully latch. He stared at the un-flush edge of it. He kicked it as hard as he could, leaving a huge dent and sending an appalling pain shooting into his right knee.

. . .

Neither Abbie nor Sarah said anything to Isaac when he did come over to the main house for dinner. Sarah was drinking a glass of wine in the living room. Abbie was in his usual place in the kitchen, a large glass of scotch beside him, a whole fish sprawled wetly across a big cutting board. He was scaling it angrily and haphazardly with a fillet knife. Isaac got a bottle of water from the refrigerator and sat at a chair in the dining room and stared at the table. The silence—Abbie wasn't even listening to music— drew into a dark vapor that seeped into the room like a bad smell. Isaac felt he couldn't bear it anymore and pulled out his phone. It buzzed as he typed. Then Abbie pounded his fist on the counter and asked him who the fuck he was talking to, and Isaac told him it was none of his fucking business, and Abbie said he paid for the phone, he paid for it, and it was Goddamn well his business; everything that went on in that house was his business. Then Isaac said, "Fuck you, I hate you, both of you, and I wish I were dead." Then Abbie said, "Fine, kill yourself, you ungrateful, you snide little shit, you furtive little pervert, you pornographer; I can't believe you're my son." Then Isaac said, "I'm not your fucking son, I'm not, I'm not, and you know it." Then Abbie was striding across the kitchen with the knife still in his hand, maybe he'd forgotten that he had it there, maybe not, and he had grabbed Isaac by his oversized, borrowed shirt and was dragging him out of the chair. Then Sarah had run across the room and grabbed Abbie's arm, and he let go of Isaac and pushed her away. She tripped backward and fell onto the stone floor, twisting her wrist and screaming as she caught her fall. Then Isaac had bolted across the room and out one of the glass doors onto the patio and he was running across the field toward the woods. Then Abbie came running out of the house behind him, screaming incoherently, tripping down the terraces as he pounded after the boy. Isaac went into the woods. The house was the only light and it disappeared. It was cloudy and the moon was small. He held an arm in front of him, but the branches pricked him and snapped across his face. He tripped and stumbled forward, crying now, sobbing and gasping as he ran. Abbie came through the trees behind him. Had Isaac run toward the road, maybe, he'd have gotten cleanly away; he could have run for miles and miles, and the old man never would have caught him, but he was too small and lithe to go crashing through the underbrush, and Abbie was huge and angry and came through like a monster made to crush paths through the forest. Isaac tripped for real on a root or a fallen branch. His ankle turned as he fell and when he stood to run again the pain was so intense and so searing that he fell with a sad yelp to the ground in the small clearing. Abbie burst into the clearing and tripped in the same spot and flew gracelessly onto his belly. The knife he was still carrying flew out of his hand and landed in the dirt and leaves. He hauled himself onto his knees and saw the crying boy in front of him try again to stand and again cry out, again weakly, and fall back onto the ground, and then look at the crawling madman who was nevertheless in some way or other his father, his father nearly enough.

Isaac sniffed and said, "I sprained my ankle." Then Abbie was holding him, kneeling beside him, holding him and stroking his hair and crying as well. They were both of them crying in the dimly moonlit woods. Then slowly they stopped crying, and Isaac looked at Abbie and sniffed again and snorted and very nearly laughed and asked, "Did you really think you were going to kill me with a fish knife?" And Abbie sat on the ground and said, "No, no. I don't know. No." Then he stood, and he stooped and helped his son onto one foot and put the boy's other arm around his shoulder. Then they both noticed, at the edge of the clearing, huge and unafraid, silent and unmoving, a tall buck, its hard antlers like the immense branches of an ancient tree, its black eyes the night's truest version of itself, watching them. Its mouth went in lazy circles as it chewed its cud.

ACKNOWLEDGMENTS

This book wouldn't have been possible without my agent, Gail Hochman, who read the first draft and told me in the nicest possible way that it didn't make any goddamn sense. I also have to thank my erstwhile editor, Will Menaker, who saw me through a second draft not all that much better than the first, and who, to my regret, has now gone on to pursue his own weird, creative path. Thanks to the whole team at Liveright who stepped in after Will's departure to see this through with me until the end. Thank you, Trevor, for putting up with my giggling at my own jokes while I wrote them. And thanks to my cranky, rickety old beagle, whose incontinent need to get up at five-thirty every morning forced me out of bed and gave me a couple of hours to write every day before I ran to catch my bus.